I0822873

JESSICA ANN DISCIACCA

WITCHES *of* TRIORA

DARK PRINCE

DARK FLAME
PUBLISHING

JESSICA ANN DISCIACCA

WITCHES *of* TRIORA
DARK PRINCE

DARK FLAME
PUBLISHING

WITCHES OF TRIORA ~ DARK PRINCE

DARK FLAME PUBLISHING

Dark Flame Publishing books may be ordered through booksellers or by contacting Dark Flame Publishing online: JessicaAnnDisciacca.com

ISBNs: (Paperback) 979-8-9910142-6-7. (Hardcover) 979-8-9910142-7-4

NOTE TO READER

CONTENT ADVISORY: This fantasy novel contains elements that may be unsettling for some readers, particularly those who may be sensitive to themes of emotional or mental health. Within the realms of this fictional world, some depictions and discussions touch upon such challenging subjects. The intention is to weave a compelling tale while being mindful of our readers' wellbeing. If you anticipate that encounters with these themes might be triggering or discomforting, we recommend exercising caution and considering whether to continue with the story. The fantastical nature of this narrative does not diminish the potential impact of these elements, and we prioritize the comfort and mental well-being of our readers. Thank you for embarking on this fantastical journey with us, and may your reading experience be enjoyable and mindful of your emotional boundaries.

To my beautiful readers … you are worthy of love. You deserve a life, full of happiness, excitement, and fantasy. But first … you must love yourself.

Chapter One

"I'm really not sure about this hair color," I said, looking at myself in the mirror. I pulled the white strands into a ponytail, trying to see how it looked away from my face. My part line was still a deep brown, the only thing left of my original hair color.

"I don't know what you're talking about," he said, leaning forward, "I'm definitely feeling the white hair."

"Oh, shut up. You're just saying that," I replied, letting go of my long hair, allowing it to fall down the length of by back.

"How's my sister?" he asked, his gaze falling to the table in front of him.

"Still no change. I asked Orion to heal her, but his power isn't ... it isn't what we expected. Neither is mine."

"Still no sign of the goddess's powers?" Antonio asked.

I shook my head. "I don't know what went wrong. I am starting to have glimpses of the other lives from past vessels. Small moments, but nothing new as far as power goes. Maybe I'm defective."

"Hey ..." he said, leaning in towards me. "You're not defective.

You're perfect, beautiful. You always have been, you always will be."

I smiled, feeling my cheeks blush. My excitement quickly faded as our situation came smashing back into reality. "Tony ..." I whispered, "we can't keep doing this. If someone finds out—"

"No one is going to find out," he replied with a soft smile. "It's just you and me. As it should be."

I exhaled, reaching my hand up to the mirror. He did the same. "I miss you," I admitted.

"I miss you too, baby. We'll find a way to make this work. To be together. I know it."

My phone buzzed. I looked down, reading the notification that flashed across the screen. It took everything I had to hold back my tears.

"What is it?" he asked.

"A notification.... We are supposed to be leaving for New York in three days."

Pain flashed in his eyes. "I'm so sorry, Seren."

"I know. You've said that every time we've spoken."

"Because it's true. If I wouldn't have been so stupid and desperate, I would be there with you right now, planning our wedding and packing for our trip. Instead, I'm miles away from you and you're married to—" he stopped, looking as if he was going to be sick. "How's that going, by the way?"

"I don't want to talk about it," I said, uncomfortable.

"You're not feeling any ... urges, or—"

"I said I don't want to talk about it," I snapped harshly.

His eyes met mine with a heaviness I only saw when the topic of Orion came up. "Okay," he whispered.

A knock came at the door. I turned away from the mirror frantically. "Gotta go," I said.

"Okay, be careful. I love you, beautiful," Antonio whispered.

"I love you too." I waved my hand over the mirror. His handsome face faded away into the darkness just as the door opened. Frankie stepped through. Her face was wracked with worry.

"Who where you talking to?" she asked.

"Just myself," I said, standing to meet her. "What's wrong? Did something happen?"

"The team in New York... half of them are dead."

My heart fell. "What? What happened?"

"They were following up on a lead they received about an Obsidian base near Maine. There was only supposed to be a handful of dark witches and warlocks stationed there, but when they arrived, they were met with an entire squad. Outnumbered three to one. The ones who did escape were lucky. Three are in critical condition and the others are banged up pretty bad."

My attention trailed to the mirror. Antonio hadn't told me about this. Why? I reminded myself that the honesty spell was still in place between the two of us. He couldn't lie; he had to tell the truth ... right? Guilt overcame me.

"Nonna is asking for you," Frankie added, moving back towards the door.

I silently followed, not sure of what to say or do to make this situation any better. Antonio had been forthcoming with me about Obsidian's movements in the week since I had completed the rite. The ceremony that had changed everything, yet nothing at the same time.

The rite had been designed to keep our coven's powers strong and prosperous. Every three hundred years, vessels chosen by the moon goddess Aradia and her mate Cyrus would join together, unifying their power to bring forth a renaissance for our people. So, I pushed my own wants and desires aside and fulfilled my duty, yet nothing had changed. There was no surge of power or an instant revelation that Orion was my one and only.

God, it had already been a full week. I still felt like myself, but there was something deep inside of me that fought to be released. In fear of what that little seed was, I chose to keep it locked away tight, not wanting to complicate my life any further.

The dark, whispering shadows that had comforted me the night of the rite had not returned. I didn't know what to make of them, nor did I understand my encounter with Aradia. I still hadn't told anyone about that catastrophe. The goddess ... the maiden, mother, and crone. The original coven leader had handpicked me as her vessel, yet tried to kill me once I accepted the job I had never asked for. With the memories of the former vessels tormenting me day and night and the battle raging in my own heart, I had enough to worry about. Aradia and her murderous tendencies could wait.

Then there was Orion. I had made sure to keep my distance. He had tried to visit me for the first three days consistently, but I refused to see him. I couldn't. Regardless if he was my husband, my mate, my destiny: I wasn't ready for that ... for him. I was still very much in love with Antonio, and though I knew it was wrong of me to still speak with him, to hope for a future where we were together and happy, my heart wanted what it wanted. Especially after seeing the vision of our family—of what I could have had. But I chose to save Orion instead. Was it even possible to have both?

I knocked on Nonna's door before entering. She and Orion were sitting at her table in silence. I closed the door and joined them, unsure of what I was walking into. Nonna sipped her tea, looking from Orion then to me.

"The other elders are beginning to ask questions," she finally said, setting the cup down in front of her. "They are concerned about why the god's powers have not manifested inside the two of you. Why their own power is not enlightened, as it has been documented in the past. Also ..." she paused, locking her eyes onto me, "they have noticed the two of you still do not share a room."

I swallowed hard, not daring to look at Orion.

"They can think what they want," Orion finally said. "That is between Seren and I."

"No, dear boy. Your power ... your ... connection affects the entire magical community. If the enlightenment period does not occur soon, there will be a revolution. Witch will rise against witch. Panic will begin to spread throughout the covens, turning one group against another. We already have too many enemies at our gates. We do not need to be entertaining an internal riot as well." She leaned forward, taking both of our hands. "For all of our sakes, figure this shit out ... and fast."

Nonna left the room before I could say anything. I remained at the table, contemplating the warning she had just given. The pressure of this burden, this life I didn't choose for myself, was unbearable. Nor was it fair. Aradia had told me I still had a choice in the matter, but in reality, the choice was never mine to make.

I finally managed to bring my eyes to his. "The reason our abilities haven't clicked into place is because we haven't—" I stopped myself, not wanting to say it out loud.

"We don't know that for sure," he replied, not looking at me.

"What do we do?"

His knee bounced up and down quickly as he thought. "For now, if you're okay with it, we fake it."

"And what does that entail?"

"We ... act like everything is working between us. Like how the others expect the gods to be."

"You mean ... in love?"

He grimaced at the word. "Yes. The covens will be coming together for the Yule celebration. We need to act like everything is normal, so they stop looking at us and focus their attention back to Obsidian. I'm looking into other ways that we can harness the god's powers to make sure the enlightenment period occurs."

I froze, unaware he had embarked down that path. "What? Why?" I asked.

His eyes finally rose to meet mine. The softness was no longer visible. "Do you really need me to say it out loud?"

I recoiled back into my chair. More guilt. I was failing at the one thing I had been put on this earth to do. I was letting down my family, my coven, and my ... husband. "I'm trying," I whispered.

"Doesn't matter. We're running out of time. It's only been a week and they're already questioning us. This will buy us some time. Are you okay with the plan for now?"

I nodded. He rose, heading for the door without another word. A part of me wanted to reach for him: to chase after him, to take him in my arms and hold him tightly, allowing myself to be wrapped in his warmth and protection. But my heart craved another.

I returned to my room, going to the mirror and summoning Tony. He appeared within a few minutes. His bright smiling greeted me from the other side. Something inside of me fluttered to life at the sight of him.

"Hello, beautiful. How was your day?" he asked.

"Did you know?" I whispered.

His smile faded. "Know what?"

"About Maine. About our unit that was attacked." He froze, not saying a single word. "You knew, didn't you?"

"Seren, I—"

"What aren't you telling me? What do you do for my mother, exactly?" I asked, feeling his betrayal all over again.

"I don't want to lie to you."

"Then don't!" I yelled, feeling like a fool. He sat on the other side of the mirror, holding his head in one hand, silent. "You know what," I said, realizing I wasn't going to get the answers I wanted. "Forget it."

"Seren, wait—"

I waved my hand, closing the connection.

I was steaming with rage and needed an outlet. I quickly got dressed and headed outside for a run. I took off through the hills of Triora, moving my legs as fast as they would go. I pumped my arms, feeling the rush of adrenaline and endorphins. The cold winter air no longer affected me. Since the rite, it seemed that I now ran a bit colder than a normal person. Cold and frigid: what I wished my heart would become.

After a forty-five minutes sprint through town, I finally hit the outer roads. The silence was a welcoming change. The moon was waning tonight overhead. I could feel the energy of the new moon approaching. Now, with the moon goddess's essence awakened inside of me, I was more aware, more sensitive to the elements of the earth: how everything worked in tandem with one another;

how everything had life ... had a purpose.

My feet pounded against the dusting of snow. I focused on the tree line ahead. A faint cry somewhere in the woods took me off guard. I stopped, focusing my senses. Again, the sound of a young woman yelling barreled through the trees towards me. Without another thought, I took off, dodging and ducking around branches.

"Stop!" yelled the girl. "Please," she cried. She was just up ahead. Just by the tone and pitch of her voice, I could feel her pain and despair as if it were my own.

I slammed through a tangled mess of branches and dead leaves, stepping into a clearing. Instantly, I felt the magic zap, trapping me inside of a cage. Six witches and warlocks stood around me in a circle. A girl, no more than eighteen, lay in the center before me in the fetal position. She was beaten and bleeding, sobbing. She looked up at me, one eye completely swollen shut. "Please," she whimpered.

One of the warlocks walked up to the magical cage. His hands were folded behind his back and his skin appeared to glisten in the moonlight. He smiled at me, cocking his head to one side. "Hello, moon goddess," he whispered.

His dark hair was well kept. His stature was dominate and strong. The way he moved, with such grace and beauty, I almost lost my legs from underneath me. He was stunning ... angelic, in the most sinful way possible. He was dressed well, for being what he was.

"I don't believe we've had the pleasure of meeting in this lifetime," he said, seduction rolling off him with each word that parted his lips. "My name is Asmodeus Râşnov, but in previous lives, you've referred to me as Deus."

My body jolted. An electrical sensation zapped and zinged up my spin until it reached my brain. My nerves felt static as flashes—no, memories—came rushing in. Deus and I, fighting. Conversations about Obsidian's plans. Deus sharing details of the inner working of their network, then ... he was saving me ... no, the other moon goddess's vessel, wait ... plural, vessels. Flashes of his well-toned body, dripping in sweat. His smile, the feeling of his lips and teeth as they bit into my skin, not in a violent way, but a ... a sexual one. His hands, his mouth, devouring me while I screamed from the pleasure. He laughed as I cried out his name. Memory after memory came flooding in. Feelings of rage, safety, desire.

My eyelids flew open. I looked upon this demon with a sense of recognition. He smiled, and something inside of me sparked to life. I allowed my eyes to trail along his person. His beautiful crystal blue eyes, shaded by thick rows of lashes. His full, supple mouth, strong nose, and dimpled chin. His perfectly tanned skin. The small beauty mark on his right cheek. His chest was broad and strong as his black jacket hugged his frame in the most perfect way. My eye snagged on the silver ring that adorned his right hand. In the center lay a red stone.

He took a step closer, now entering the circle as he approached. He towered over me with dominance. His smile never left his lips. His eyes scanned me up and down, undressing me with each flicker.

"You've got to be kidding me," I said, coming to the realization that my past self ... selves had been romantically involved with this demon.

He laughed. Something inside of me warmed as I fought not to moan at the sound. "Did you remember something you liked? Because," he leaned his lips to my ear ever so slowly, "I remember exactly what you like. Every caress, every lick, every—"

I stepped away, not wanting to know anymore. "Alright, alright, I get it," I said, taking another step back. "Dammit," I whispered, trying to get myself together. The girl was silent, watching the interaction between the two of us. "What do you want?" I asked.

He shrugged smugly. "I heard you had been reincarnated again and I was curious what your new vessel looked like. Needless to say, I am very pleased. Aradia has a type ... my type." He winked at me, still scanning my body in the most uncomfortable, yet sexual, way I had ever experienced.

"Whatever you're thinking, stop. That is not going to happen. Not in this lifetime at least. Now, let the girl go and I will let you live."

His eyes softened. He cocked his head, still assessing me. He exhaled and rolled his eyes before he rose his hand and snapped.

The magical barrier around us lifted. He walked over to the girl. I made a move to stop him, but he held up his hand, silently ordering me to halt. He held his palm out towards her. She looked up at him, stilling trembling, then ... stopped. Her eyes turned towards me, and she smiled. She took his hand, standing as her wounds and bruises vanished. She laughed, stroking his arm with her other hand in a sexually suggestive way.

He ignored her, his eyes never leaving mine. He came towards me, assessing my silence.

"Why trap me?" I asked.

"You're not trapped, love," he answered.

I looked around me at the six other demons surrounding us. "Did my mother send you?" I asked. It wouldn't be the first time she tried to kill me. She was after my power. My own mother had no concern for my life.

He laughed. "Annalise De Salvo?" he said. "No. I don't care much for her. She's ... dramatic."

"Then what is this? What do you want?" My power welled inside of me. Small white flames began to flicker around my fingers in defense. He noticed my power, but he made no move to attack.

"As I said," he replied softly, "I only wanted to meet you. And now that I have, you are free to return to your castle, *Miss* Seren De Salvo." He took a step back, nodding in a way of a farewell. The other demons followed suit, vanishing into the thick, dark canopy of the night.

Without another thought, I took off back towards the path. I ran harder and faster than I ever had. God, how I wished I could shift. I had only done it that one time, the night of my wedding. I had tried since, but failed. My feet pounded hard against the cobble stones once I entered the town, but I didn't stop. Not until I entered the castle. I steadied myself, walking through the halls of my home. The coven members stared at me as I passed. I went straight for the briefing room where I knew Nonna would be. I entered without announcing. Aunt Thora, Nonna, and Elder Mystic sat around the table. Their eyes locked onto me with uncertainty.

"Go get the others," I huffed, still catching my breath. "We have a problem."

"What is it, bambina?" asked Nonna. "What has happened?"

I paused, gathering myself before speaking his name out loud. The very thought of the sound rolling off my tongue excited me. I pushed that feeling down, gathering myself. He was another enemy. Another threat. That was all.

"Seren," said my aunt.

I shook my head, pulling myself back from wherever I had gone. I took one more breath, parting my lips. "Asmodeus."

Chapter Two

Nonna remained standing even after I had told her and the others who I had just encountered. Frankie looked puzzled and I could feel the rage rolling off Orion.

"You mean to tell me ..." began Nonna, "that in previous lives, the moon goddess's vessel had ... relations with Asmodeus ... the demon of Lust?"

"If I am interpreting these new memories correctly," I admitted softly, "yes."

"You've got to be shitting me," said Frankie, laughing to herself.

"This isn't funny," snapped Nonna. Frankie shut her mouth.

"But why now?" asked Aunt Thora. "Seren has been with us for over six months. Why is Asmodeus just now making his presence known?"

"Who knows how these demons think?" spat Nonna. "You're sure he isn't working with your mother?"

"He said he wasn't, but I don't know," I answered. "This could be another trap."

"And he didn't try to hurt you?" asked Aunt Thora.

I shook my head.

"Frankie, you and your mother research this Asmodeus demon," Nonna ordered. "I want to know everything there is about him. From our records regarding the gods, his name is never mentioned. We have to be missing something." She snapped her eyes to me. "And you ..." I froze, feeling like I was under arrest. "If any more of your memories come back, you inform me immediately. Are we clear?"

"Of course," I replied, looking at Orion. He hadn't said a word.

"Good. Now, everyone out. I need to think," ordered Nonna.

We all funneled out of the room. Even though I hadn't personally taken part in the memories, for some reason, I still felt ashamed. I followed Orion to his room, needing to speak with him. He stopped at his door, turning his head slightly, peering back at me.

"Can I help you with something?" he asked.

"I was hoping we could speak ... in private," I replied.

He opened the door to his room and stepped inside. I followed. He went to his table, rummaging through some papers and books. I waited for him to say something, anything, but there was just silence.

"Orion," I whispered.

He exhaled, closing his eyes. "It's bad enough I have to contend with Simonelli for your heart, but now this ... the demon of Lust."

I went to him. "These aren't my memories," I tried to explain. "This was something that happened in another life. Not mine.

Please don't hold this against me. Please. I am just as shocked as the rest of you. I don't know what the other vessels were thinking to have relations with that *thing*."

"I don't understand this," he whispered, his face softening. "Why is this so hard? If we are each other's destiny, then why are we being tested time and time again?"

I shook my head. "I don't know, but ... what if there is no such thing as destiny? What if we are in charge of our own lives?"

His brow furrowed. "What do you mean?"

I hesitated, choosing my words carefully before speaking. "When I met with Aradia, I asked about the pattern of gods not being with one another. She told me that each situation varied. Some died from the separation, while others lived their lives with whomever they had chosen who weren't the god or goddess. What if it works differently then we think?"

"Cyrus did mention only his love for Aradia, not the others," Orion said. I could see his mind working to find a solution.

"I'm not saying we aren't supposed to be together. I'm just saying that I think there's more to these loopholes then we know about."

"And what are we going to do about your little lust demon problem?" he asked.

"Stay the hell away from him, as far as possible."

Orion laughed, placing his hands on either side of me, pulling me into him. Our foreheads met. I felt his breath exhale in relief.

"Regardless," he said softly, "if we end up together or not, I want you to know that you can trust me. That I will always be there for you, no matter what you need. We are connected. Always."

I wrapped my arms around him, pulling him into me. He was right. I wasn't sure what this connection meant, or where it would lead, but he was a part of me and I was a part of him.

"You are my friend, Orion. First and foremost. I am so lucky to have you."

He bent down and kissed me softly. There was no passion, no lust. Only comfort. I smiled up at him, feeling like a weight had been lifted.

I returned to my room, staring at the mirror with frustration. Even with the truth spell, I still felt like Tony was managing to hide things from me. After everything we had been through. Everything I had endured. I fell on top of my bed and yelled into the pillow with frustration. I stared up at the ceiling, thinking back to the memories of Asmodeus.

The vessel Victoria in 1716 had the clearest and most powerful memories. Josephina had come in contact with the demon, but their interactions were limited. The first memory I could recall was from the vessel Valeriana Ravenmore in the year 800. She had fallen madly in love with the demon, not knowing his true identity. When she discovered what he really was, she slammed a white blade into his chest, killing him ... so she thought. He met the next vessel, Cecilia Avalone in 1119. Cecilia remained in love with the horned god during this time, and I couldn't recall any memories of Asmodeus showing interest in her in that way.

Victoria though ... she had loved him, completely and truly, even knowing what he was. Her memories were overpowering. The recollections of them being intimate with one another ... dear God those memories were detailed. But there was a glitch after; almost as if someone had erased a part of her mind.

It didn't make any sense, but I wasn't going to ponder on it. I pulled the covers over me, willing my mind to stop. I had too much on my plate as it was. I wished in that moment that there was a way to communicate with Aradia: to ask her what this all meant, and why. What was Asmodeus after? Why did he search me out? Then again, risking contacting her would mean giving her another go at murdering me.

As I closed my eyes, determined to drift into a deep sleep, a faint tapping noise came from the mirror. My heart filled with pain, but this time, I didn't succumb to my desire.

"I like the red one," I pointed to a beautiful ballgown Frankie was holding up.

"Exactly what I was thinking," replied Frankie. "You will look like a Christmas dream in this with that white hair of yours." I turned to the mirror, still not used to my white locks.

"You think if I dye it, the color will stay?" I asked.

"Why would you want to do that? I think you look badass. Platinum blonde suits you." I rolled my eyes. "If you're wearing the red one, I'll wear the green one."

"Sounds like a plan. It will match your eyes perfectly," I replied. I was not looking forward to tomorrow. "How many formal events do we have?"

"Two or three, but the covens usually spread them out. We're having the Yule celebration here this year because of you and Orion. I believe the Fuoco Coven will be hosting the Mardi Gras party in New Orleans in a few months. They have a beautiful estate there."

"Fun," I said, frowning at the red dress.

Frankie sat next to me on the bench, taking my hand in hers. "Do you want to talk?" she asked.

"What's there to talk about? I'm failing the covens, and no matter how hard I try, or how much I want to fall in love with Orion, I—" I cut myself off before I said something I regretted.

"I get it. Believe me, I really do," she said softly.

"I feel awful. He's been so wonderful and so understanding, but I ... I don't know what's wrong with me."

"Nothing is wrong with you, cousin. You are entitled to feel the way you do. No one seems to understand the connection between the two of you, or why it hasn't clicked, but that doesn't mean the problem lies with you. Even when I was believed to be the vessel, I still didn't believe that I would instantly fall in love with Orion after the rite. He's amazing, yes, but love should come naturally. It can't be forced."

"My life is such a mess."

Frankie laughed. "Well, two days ago, I would have disagreed, but now, with the introduction of your little friendly neighborhood demon, I'm inclined to agree."

"God, don't remind me."

She leaned in close, a smile growing deviously across her face. "Tell me, what was he like? I've only ever seen demons when they've possessed someone, not in their actual form. And him being the Prince of Lust and all ... he must have been devastatingly gorgeous."

I laughed at her, pulling away. "You've got to be kidding me."

"What? A girl can be curious. Now, come on, details."

I sighed. "He was beautiful, in a haunting way. He had blue eyes and—" I froze as a memory flashed behind my eyelids. Those beautiful eyes were smiling, small lines framing them as they looked down at me. His naked body intertwined with mine. His hands, tracing the lines of my side. The cold metal of his ring grazing against my skin. A shiver went up my body. I shook my head, freeing myself from the intimate moment.

"Oh. My. God," gasped Frankie. "You just had a memory about him, didn't you?"

"I'm not having this conversation."

"The hell you aren't. Tell me ... now. I insist."

I huffed, holding my head in my hands. "We were having sex," I blurted out. "Or it was a moment just after we had been together. I don't know. They only come in flashes and they're hard to make out."

"And ... how was it?" she asked with excitement.

I looked at her, trying to hold back the smile that wanted to erupt from my lips. "It was indescribable," I whispered. She began laughing. "I mean ... out of this world. He was a demon in every sense of the word." I felt my body quiver. I stood up, beginning to pace the room, in an attempt to cool myself.

"I knew it. I mean, he's been around for thousands of years. He's the Prince of Lust ... come on! You lucky bitch."

"Frankie, it wasn't actually me. It's just memories."

"How many vessels did he sleep with?"

"Two, from what I can tell. He's had contact with most of them, but the first one to fall in love with him was Valeriana in 800. She ended up stabbing him. And then there was Victoria, in 1716. Those memories are—" I bit my lip at the thought.

"I'm so jealous."

"Jealous? Frankie, I love you, but you are morbid sometimes."

She laughed again. "Come on. If your other vessels were so

entranced with him, I am sure there are some good qualities in there somewhere."

"He's a demon. The very thing we are trying to eradicate. They are evil ... remember?"

She shrugged. "My verdict is still out."

"Nonna would kill you if she heard you right now," I said, cleaning up some of the dresses we had pulled out of my closet.

"Speaking of our dear old Nonna, she wants to meet with us in ..." she paused, checking her phone, "oh, five minutes."

"About what?"

"Obsidian."

"And you're just telling me this now?"

She shrugged. "I didn't want her doom and gloom meeting to ruin our dress day."

I headed for the door, Frankie on my tail and we made our way to the meeting room. We barged through the doors to be greeted by all the Elders and their offspring staring at us. Orion sat towards the head of the table, next to Nonna. I froze.

"Nice of you two to join us," said Nonna, arching her eyebrows. "Sit, so we can begin."

I took a seat next to Orion. He intertwined his fingers with mine, leaning in and kissing me softly. *Oh, right.* We had to put on a show. I smiled back, turning my attention to the others. Delphine Mystic, Orion's ex-girlfriend, glared at me from across the table.

"Now," Nonna started, "we have it on good authority that Obsidian will be in Paris, France, the day after Christmas. We have decided to send out a team to meet their efforts and take them down before they accomplish whatever they've set out to do."

"You mean, the team which includes Annalise's daughter, her niece, and her new son-in-law?" remarked Elder Torrian Astra.

Nonna's eyes bored into him. "Yes. Is there a problem?"

"I would say so," interjected Aris, Torrian's daughter. "Your daughter leads Obsidian's legions. She is behind the recent attacks and the source of their newfound power. How do you expect us to believe you are not working with her?"

"The daughter I loved is dead to me," Nonna spat, her voice laced with aggravation.

"Was she dead when you hesitated to kill her? Because of that hesitation, Elder Strange paid the price," said Torrian.

"The shock of my sister's existence has stunned us all," intervened Aunt Thora. "Her actions have spoken louder than any blood relation could. The Salvos stand with the covens, now and always."

"So, tell me," interrupted Delphine, "how does continuing to love our enemy benefit our covens?" She locked eyes with me in an accusing manner.

"I don't know what you mean," I replied.

Orion's hand tightened around mine.

"Oh, please," continued Delphine, "we all know about your engagement to Antonio Simonelli, your mother's right-hand spy.

If anyone should not be trusted, it is you, Seren De Salvo."

Nonna stood, slamming her hands against the table, unleashing a ripple of power. Her eyes went deadly. "That is enough!" she demanded. "My family has been through enough these past months. My daughter Thora, tortured. My granddaughter Seren, almost killed on multiple occasions. Seren willingly completed the rite. She and Orion are the gods and contain their powers. My family has given and proven enough, and if any of you believe otherwise, I will gladly accept that challenge and destroy you in the process. Do I make myself clear?"

I smiled, proud of how much of a badass my Nonna was. Frankie folded her arms across her chest, looking at the rest of the members. No one said a word. "Good," Nonna said, sitting back down in her chair. "Now, unless anyone else would like to contest the decision, the team will head out the morning after Christmas to Paris." She looked around for a response. When there was none, Nonna nodded. "Dismissed." She stretched her hands out to Aunt Thora, Frankie and I, silently signaling us to stay.

Orion leaned down next to my ear. "I'll handle Delphine," he whispered.

"Good luck with that," I replied. He kissed me on the head, following the other elders out.

Once the door was shut, Nonna relaxed. "Dear Aradia, help us," she said, holding her head in her hands.

"They're just paranoid, Mother," said Aunt Thora. "We knew

this was coming. We would have questioned the same thing if this had been another family."

"What do we need to do?" asked Frankie.

Nonna's eyes snapped to me. "No one is to know about Asmodeus," she said firmly. "We can only handle being under so much fire at a time."

"Of course," I said. "And Orion and I are working on making this marriage ... work."

"Yes, well, for all our sakes I hope you figure that out soon," added Nonna. "You two stay close to each other in Paris," she continued, gesturing between Frankie and me. "I don't want any more surprises."

"Always," said Frankie. Nonna waved her hand, releasing us to leave.

I found my way to Orion's room, wanting the latest update on Delphine. When I opened the door, I was greeted by Delphine in Orion's arms. They held each other in an intimate way that I ... I envied. Not that I envied Delphine, but I envied the fact that they got to share that. Something I now realized I had taken for granted.

Instantly, they pulled away from one another. Orion's eyes locked onto me, full of shock. Delphine bolted out of the room, holding her mouth as she passed me.

I slowly shut the door, unsure of what to say. I couldn't blame him. She was the last person he had loved and had loved him in return. To be without that intimacy for that long ... I couldn't imagine, even now having experienced it for myself.

"Little dove," he whispered, embarrassment engulfing his face.

"No, don't," I said, walking towards him. I sat on the edge of his bed, trying to make sense of it all.

"I ... it was nothing. Just a familiar comfort. I don't know what came over me," he said, running a hand through his long, curly hair.

"Longing came over you ... desire. I don't blame you Orion."

"It won't happen again," he asserted.

I reached out, taking his hand. "Don't say that." He looked at me, surprised. "Believe it or not, I do care about you, and I want you to be happy. Even if it's not with me. Delphine obviously still loves you. You deserve to be loved."

"But, what about the situation between us. I could never dishonor you like that. I wouldn't."

"We'll figure it out, Orion. If I can't ... if things don't work between us, you deserve to be happy."

"My slip up with Delphine doesn't change my feelings for you," he admitted. "I still want to try and make this work."

I looked at him, feeling completely numb inside. "Orion ... I am broken." I let the tears fall. "I am so very broken, and I don't know when or if I will ever recover. Antonio ... he destroyed me. The very thought of love, it ... it sickens me. And the thing is, I care about you. I chose you ... but I don't ... I don't love you. Not like that."

His face fell in disappointment. I didn't want to hurt him, but he needed to know. I wasn't going to stand in his way of happiness. "If Delphine makes you happy," I continued, "you have my blessing." I leaned over and kissed him gently on the cheek before heading back to my room.

Once I got there, I went to the mirror and summoned Antonio. His beautiful face appeared. His hair looked a mess, as if he hadn't slept all night. His hazel eyes were heavy and bruised underneath. A soft smile stretched across his lips.

"I didn't know if I would get the chance to speak to you again," he said hoarsely.

My tears continued, dripping from my chin. "You've destroyed me," I whispered, a tether of hope snapping inside of me. "You've completely destroyed me. Any chance I ever had at happiness is gone, thanks to you."

"No, beautiful, that isn't true. We can be happy. We can still—"

"How?" I yelled. "Tell me how, Antonio. How is my family ever going to forgive you? How will you make up for your betrayal, and prove to the covens that they can trust you again? How ... how am I ever going to trust you again? You are still keeping secrets from me. Still working with my mother on God knows what and not telling me. You are hurting innocent people and killing your own kind."

"It's more complicated than that. If you will just let me explain—"

"No! I don't want to hear any more of your lies or rationalization. We should be preparing for New York right now, but instead, I'm being shipped off to Paris and you are who-knows-where. We aren't together. We aren't preparing for our wedding, and any hope of a future we had is gone, thanks to you!"

"Beautiful, please," he whispered.

I just cried, my heart crumbling to pieces. "It hurts, Tony. It hurts so bad," I sobbed.

He reached out, touching the mirror with his hand. "I wish I could hold you right now. I wish I had a way to make all of this go away—to make it better. Please, just trust that I am working on a way for all my mistakes to be worth it."

I brought my eyes up to his, trying to read his thoughts. "What are you planning?" I asked.

"Something that will kill your mother, and Obsidian along with her."

I shook my head. "I don't believe you."

"I know, but hopefully soon, you will see. I love you, beautiful. Just hold on a little longer." With those words, he disappeared into the black fog. I looked at myself, still unsure of the person who stared back. My magic roared to life underneath my skin. The rage of his betrayal lit something inside of me that demanded release. In the mirror, my irises shifted from brown to a vibrant purple. White flames twirled around my fingers.

Tears still ran down my face as I stared at my reflection. Everything inside of me was finally coming to a head. The pressure of the title I now bore. Everyone's expectation of my relationship with Orion. The pain of realizing my mother never loved me. She was only using me to gain more power. She wanted me dead. And then … Tony.

Everything inside erupted. I screamed at the top of my lungs. Billowing clouds of white fire sprang from my fingertips, devouring everything it touched. My drapes went up in flames. I watched while the fire reached the tall ceilings, creating impenetrable walls around me. My bed snapped and crackled just before it fell in on itself, succumbing to the blaze. Though they burned and destroyed like fire, the flames were cold as ice.

My heart constricted with a single breath. I dropped to my knees, allowing the pain inside of me to escaped. In the midst of the fire, darkness consumed me. I cried and cried, until I felt like there was nothing left inside of me. I screamed and slammed my hands against the floor. Everything I had wanted to live for, the future I had dreamt about, was gone. Nothing Tony could ever do would make this right. I had to let go. I had to set myself free.

Strong arms wrapped around my shoulders, hauling me to my feet. I turned to see Orion's face peering down. He mouthed something, but I couldn't hear a single word. The fire screamed and whined, devouring everything around us.

"Seren." I finally heard his voice breaking through my panic attack. "Seren, you need to get control of yourself. You need to reel this back."

I shook my head, calming. My family stood in the doorway, watching as the room crumbling around us. "I ... I'm sorry," I whimpered.

"Focus," Orion said. "You need to consume it. If you don't, the entire castle is going up in flames."

I nodded.

He leaned his head on top of mine. "You can do this, little dove. You can control it." I closed my eyes and focused on the sounds of the fire, commanding it to obey.

With unexpected speed and force, the tunnels of flames swirled around the room, gathering into a single cylinder of blazing power. The funnel reached the ceiling, tearing through the room like a tornado. I held out my hands, Orion steadying me from behind. With a single inhale, I called the power back. The magic obeyed, reaching its arms in response before slamming inside me with more force than I had prepared for. I shook and screamed from the impact. It was like I was being torn apart from the inside. The frozen fire bit at every organ, every muscle in my body.

Orion's strong frame held me steady. I yelled, and cried, and shuddered, allowing my body to take it all back: to retract the chaos I had released. Finally, after the last cold ember was absorbed, I collapsed. Orion caught me, laying me carefully on the ground. My body was drenched in sweat. I shook from fever, which I didn't understand. How could something so cold make me so warm? Orion's touch eased some of that pain, but not enough. Nonna and Aunt Thora appeared above me.

"I got you," I heard Orion's voice. His skin was glowing, and his irises blazed a golden hue of yellow and orange. I felt a gentle tug on my magic as he siphoned some of the power out of my body into his own. "You're going to be fine."

Slowly, my skin cooled, returning to its normal temperature. The trembling stopped. I felt weak, but I was conscious. I sat up, looking at the destruction I had unleashed. Everything was charred to a crisp, except the vanity.

"If you wanted to redecorate," commented Nonna, looking around the room, "all you had to do was ask, bambina." Aunt Thora started laughing. Orion's eyes remained fixed on me.

"We can have this cleaned up and redecorated in no time," added Thora, running her fingers through my hair.

"What happened, bambina?" asked Nonna.

"I ... I lost control," I admitted. "Everything is just ... it's too much."

"Awe, sweetheart," said Thora, leaning down to kiss my sticky head. "I am so sorry this burden has fallen to you."

"You are strong, Seren," added Nonna. "A true Salvo woman, through and through." She looked around the room and smirked. "The question for now is, where will you sleep?"

"She will stay with me," insisted Orion.

I locked eyes with him, unsure of what to say.

"Perfect," Nonna said with a devious smile.

Orion helped me to my feet.

"Well," Aunt Thora said, "the good news is that your clothes are safe. All our closets act as safety vaults, just in case."

I laughed. "Of course you would make the closets fireproof."

She shrugged. "What can I say? We do love our fashion. You should get some rest. Call if you need anything."

After making our way to his room, Orion sat me on the edge of the bed, going to his dresser and pulling out one of his large black t-shirts.

"Thank you for saving me ... again," I whispered.

He smirked. "It was my turn to do the saving," he replied.

"And thank you for offering your room."

"It is my pleasure," he said, wiggling his eyebrows up and down humorously. I couldn't help but laugh. "Go take a shower. You'll feel better after."

"On it," I said, heading to his bathroom.

Once the warm water had soothed my tired muscles, I slid his oversized t-shirt onto my little frame. My white hair was still wet as I watched loose curls forming. This development was new. Before the rite, my hair was straight and now ... everything was different.

I exited the bathroom, finding Orion already in bed. He was scrolling through his phone. His eyes rose from his screen, trailing ever so slowly over my body. I fidgeted nervously, uncomfortable from his gaze.

"I like you in my shirt," he said.

I smiled, making my way over to him. “Ha, ha. Don’t get used to it.” I crawled in next to him. The bed was already warm. He shifted down under the sheets, turning off the lights before laying his head on the pillow. Our eyes met in the dark. The silence was uncomfortable. I searched to find something to say. “Your eyes glow yellow when you use your magic.”

He huffed a small laugh. “And yours glow purple. Another surprise thanks to our powers, I suppose.” I smiled, allowing my eyes to fall. “Why did you set your room on fire? What happened?” His voice was soft and understanding.

“Everything came crashing down around me. My heart finally shattered,” I said, holding myself together. I felt his warm hand caress the side of my face.

“I’m here for whatever you need,” he whispered softly.

“Thank you,” I replied, turning away from him.

I pulled the blanket up to my nose, allowing my body to relax. I closed my eyes, forcing my mind to become silent. I had exhausted the well of energy I had tapped into. The beauty of the fire still danced across my mind. Even though it acted like fire, the flames were cold to the touch. Aradia’s power fascinated me. How much more was I capable of?

Chapter Three

The sense that I was being watched stirred me from my sleep. I opened my eyes to see a man's figure sitting quietly in a chair, hidden by the shadows of the night. His legs were crossed. His hands laced together resting on his lap while he lounged causally in the chair. I sat straight up, turning behind me to see Orion still sleeping soundly. My eyes shot back to the figure. This wasn't a dream.

"You're interesting, I'll give you that," he said in a deep and seductive tone. *Lust*. I moved to wake Orion. "Nah, ah, ah. Let's leave the little horned god sleeping for now, shall we?"

"How did you get in here?" I whispered, gritting my teeth together, containing my rage.

"Doesn't matter. Now," he said, slowly uncrossing his legs and leaning over his knees, "explain this to me, Miss Salvo. How is it that you heart belongs to the Antonio boy, yet your body sleeps next to your ... *husband*? Or does this new vessel not have a sense of morals attached to it?"

Fury erupted within me at the comment. My heart began to race, that little flicker of power seeping through the small control

I had. Tendrils of white, icy power snaked through my fingers.

"Oh, calm down," he said, sitting back in the chair. The moonlight illuminated his face, revealing his beautiful features. "It was just a question. I'm just curious is all."

"Get the hell out of here," I said, now shaking.

"Fine, fine. Don't get your panties in a bunch. But I'll be back, sooner than you think." With a wink, he dissipated into the shadows without a trace.

I looked back at Orion, still unconscious. I cautiously placed my head back on the pillow, no longer able to sleep.

"You have to swear to keep this between us," I said to Frankie. We were in her room getting ready for the Yule event.

Frankie glared at me in mock distress. "Are you really doubting my loyalty, cousin?"

"If Nonna finds out, she's going to flip a shit."

"I'm fully aware of how our dear Nonna reacts. Don't worry, you have nothing to worry about from me. These lips are sealed. Though, I can't promise if dear old Mr. Lust comes knocking on my door, I won't take him for a test drive."

I began laughing. "You are terrible. You would really sleep with one of those things."

She shrugged. "From what you've described, he sounds pretty alluring to me."

"Have you or your mom learned anything about him?" I asked.

"A few things ..."

"Care to enlighten the one he's haunting?"

"He's one of the original angels who fell due to his loyalty to Lucifer. He's the demon of the sin of Lust. There's Lucifer, who is Pride. Mammon, Greed. Leviathan, Envy. Beelzebub, Gluttony. Satan, Wrath, and Belphegor, Sloth.

"Asmodeus is known for seducing kings' wives and causing havoc between marriages and lovers. He spreads lust wherever he goes. He supposedly has three heads: one of a ram, a bull, and then a man. Honestly, not a lot is written about him. He isn't really mentioned before 800 A.D. in our documents or any others."

"Great. So, we know absolutely nothing about my peeping Tom."

"I'm sure if you think hard enough, you can unlock some more of those spicy memories."

"No, thank you. I've already seen enough."

After our hair and makeup was finished, we got into our dresses, looking like two sides of a coin. She wore green, matching her beautiful eyes, and I wore red. Small pieces of my hair were pulled away from my face elegantly, but the majority of my hair trailed the length of my back.

We made our way to the ballroom. There were no formal introductions like my last ball. Everyone was already celebrating and dancing around the floor. Snow fell from the ceiling. Evergreen décor dappled with cranberry bunches littered every surface, while soft flickers of candlelight created the perfect wonderland ambience.

Orion appeared out of nowhere. He dragged his gaze over me slowly, taking in every detail. He wore a gold suit, with his curly hair pulled back into a bun. A smile stretched across his face as he bent down and kissed my hand tenderly. "You are a vision, goddess."

"And you look like a king, Horned God," I replied, bowing in front of him dramatically. He laughed, taking me into his arms. We twirled around the floor, oblivious to anyone around us. He was captivating, that was undeniable. Why couldn't I have met him first? Why couldn't I seem to love him the way he deserved? The way I needed to? He was perfect; in person and on paper.

"What are you thinking? And be honest with me," he asked, twirling me around him before bringing me back against his muscular, broad chest.

"I'm thinking ... I wished I would have met you first," I admitted honestly. "I'm thinking I don't deserve your love." The pace picked up while we glided across the dance floor, the music directing our movements. I watched Orion closely: his smile, the way his eyes flickered in the candlelight, how his face softened every time he looked at me.

He held me close and shifted us across the floor. Why couldn't this be enough? Why couldn't I be happy with him? Why couldn't I love him?

Orion leaned down as the music slowly ended. "You deserve all the love in the world, Seren De Salvo. Regardless if that love is given by me or another, you deserve to be loved. Truly, wholly, and completely." My heart fluttered at his words. Little did I know he was a poet, on top of being an amazing dancer. I let my head relax against his chest, closing my eyes. The next song was slow and graceful. A peaceful feeling washed over me: something I hadn't felt in a long while.

His fingers gently trailed down my spine. His head rested softly on top of my loose hair. I could hear his heartbeat this close. I opened my eyes, taking in the witches and warlocks around me. Everyone looked as if they were entranced by the music. Laughter, love, and happiness filled the air.

In an instant, the air in my lungs evaporated. I pulled my head away from his chest, trying to focus my eyes. Confusion hit. Across the dance floor, Orion held Delphine against his chest, gliding her gracefully to the music. Delphine looked up at him and smiled. He returned the sentiment, leaning into her ear, whispering something that made her laugh.

My Orion stopped moving. Still in his arms, I pulled away

slowly, turning my eyes to look at his chest first. Shifting darkness enveloped him, changing his golden suit to black. I followed the fog as it traveled to the man's neck. Flawless bronze skin replaced Orion's lighter complexion. A devious smile appeared next, revealing a perfect pair of white teeth with slightly elongated canines. His crystal blue eyes smiled at me as his long curly locks were replaced by the deepest black hair I had ever seen. In this light, it almost appeared blue.

I froze, not knowing what to do next. He leaned in, the side of his head grazing against mine. "Don't make a sound," he whispered, taking my hand and leading me to the balcony. Once we were alone, he faced me. I looked back at the coven members inside the ballroom. They seemed completely oblivious.

"How?" I asked, too astonished to say anything else.

Asmodeus shrugged. "Your kind do not know how to guard against mine," he replied. "To them, I appear as nothing more than a common warlock."

"Why did you appear as Orion?" I asked, holding back tears of anger.

"How else was I going to get you to dance with me?"

I clenched my jaw, stepping towards him. "What do you want from me?" I demanded.

He looked down at me and laughed softly, shaking his head. "Why do you always think someone wants something from you? Can't you just ... live in the moment?" he replied, moving around me to look at the others as they danced and laughed.

"You are a demon," I spat.

"Observant, aren't we?"

I moved in front of him, drawing his attention. "If you don't want to kill me and you aren't working with my mother, then just tell me what you want so you can leave me the hell alone."

He made a pouty face. "And miss all these temper tantrums?" He flicked the tip of my nose. "Where is the fun in that?"

"Asmodeus, please," I said, approaching my wit's end. "Stop playing games and just tell me what you want."

He tilted his head to the side, his blue eyes shimmering down at me. "Not yet, but you will know soon enough," he said, walking towards the edge of the balcony. The wind around us picked up as he turned slowly, facing me again. When his eyes casually trailed the length of my body, I could have sworn I felt his caress along with them. "I meant what I said, by the way."

"And which part are you referring to?" I asked, crossing my arms over my chest.

"You are a vision tonight. Thank you for wearing my favorite color." He gave a small bow before he dematerialized, allowing the wind to take away the black, rolling tendrils of fog.

I stormed back into the ballroom, bee-lining straight for the exit. A soft hand wrapped around my arm. I turned to see Orion with Delphine at his side. I recoiled instantly, not trusting my own instincts anymore.

"I've been looking for you all night," Orion said, looking down at me with a confused expression. "Is everything okay?"

I looked at Delphine and back to him. I wouldn't ruin this night. Not for either of them. "I'm fine," I lied. "Just not feeling much into the celebratory mood. I'm staying with Frankie tonight." Another lie. "The room is yours." I looked at Delphine, giving her my silent stamp of approval. "Have fun, you two."

Before he could say another word, I rushed from the ballroom, darting through the crowd until I entered the quiet halls of the castle. I didn't stop walking until I was behind my old bedroom door. I slammed it shut, locking myself inside.

Sheets of white and scaffolding cluttered the room. The debris had been removed and it now smelled of fresh plaster and paint. In the corner sat my unscathed vanity. I took a seat.

My mind was rushing with memories that weren't my own: feelings and desires that didn't belong to me. I didn't know where all the other women ended and I began. My body felt uneasy. My skin felt electrified. I felt like I was going to explode.

I just wanted to talk to him, one more time, for him to tell me that it was all right. For him to listen, to smile, to laugh. I wanted him ... I needed him.

I pulled at my hair, trying to make the other voices stop. The visions of the other men, the vessels, the lovers, Asmodeus, Orion, and Antonio: I just needed it all to stop. I needed quiet.

I pressed my fingers against the mirror, regretting the decision instantly. Antonio appeared, his expression full of concern and worry. I stood, pacing back and forth, smacking my hand against my head. Flashes of lovers, wars, and magic zapped behind my eyes, awakening every neuron in my body. I screamed.

"Seren," I heard Tony's voice. "What is it? What is the matter?"

"Make it stop!" I yelled, crying in pain. "I need them all to stop."

"Who? Who do you need to stop?"

"The voices. The visions. I ... I don't know who I am anymore, Tony. I don't know where I start, and they end. I don't know what my reality is and what is just a memory. I can't divide my feelings from theirs. My desires from others. I don't know what to do. Everything I do ... every choice I make is wrong. I am failing. I am failing my family, our covens, everything!" I dropped to my knees, my heart quickening. Everything around me swirled into darkness. My skin burned with pain as I cried.

"Seren, baby, listen to me," said Tony. "You are having a panic attack. Take in deep breaths slowly. In ... and out. Count to ten with each breath."

I did as he said, filling my burning lungs with the turbulent air ... *one*. The balcony doors busted open, but I continued to breath. I folded into the fetal position, counting ... *two*. A storm outside raged. Lightning flashed in the sky ... *three*. The warm tears along my cheeks seemed to sizzle against my cold flesh ... *four*. My heart felt like it was going to burst through my chest ... *five*. I was coming undone ... *six*. This burden was too heavy ... *seven*. The price, too steep ... *eight*. I was a failure ... *nine*. I was broken ... *ten*.

My body collapsed against the cold wooden floor. The tunnel vision took over. In the background, I could still hear Tony's voice. I imagined him next to me, holding me against him after we had just made love. After he had told me he loved me. I closed my eyes, allowing the tears to pool underneath my head. My body felt numb. My exhaustion pulled me under, into a sea of darkness and quiet. Yes ... finally ... quiet.

"Are you sure you're alright?" asked Frankie, sitting across from me at breakfast. I pushed the oatmeal around the bowl, without an appetite. "Your aura is all out of wack."

"I'm fine. Did you and Joe have a good time?" I asked.

She blushed. "Yes. He officially asked me to be exclusive last night. I said maybe."

"I'm happy for you," I replied, trying to muster a smile. She stared at me, trying to figure out what was going on.

Orion appeared behind her with a cup of coffee. "Did you two have a nice girl's night in last night?" he asked. Frankie narrowed her eyes on me. She opened her mouth, but I intervened first.

"We did thanks," I said, nodding for Frankie to leave. She rolled her eyes, taking her plate with her. "I'll see you two on the plane," she said before leaving.

He sat down across the table from me. "How was your night?" I asked.

He smirked, looking down at his cup of coffee. "It was nice. We spent most of the night catching up. But ... I was worried about you. I could feel that you were off."

"I'm always off these days. No reason to be alarmed." I forced a smile, pushing my food away from me.

"This ... this doesn't feel right," he said.

"What?"

"You, pushing me towards Delphine, when I have feelings for you."

I exhaled, tired of having to explain everything to everyone all the time. "We've been over this. I can't give you what you want. Not now at least. I don't want you to put your happiness on hold for me. You obviously still care about Delphine. Am I correct?"

He hesitated but nodded.

"Then explore that option. Find happiness with that hot blonde bombshell of an ex."

He smirked at that. "You're selfless, you know that? Makes me care for you even more."

"And I care for you," I replied, reaching across the table and taking his hand. "Just not in the way you deserve."

"Good morning, gods," said Adrianna, appearing at the end of the table. "Plane is ready and waiting for you to grace it."

I took a breath, wondering what to expect in Paris. This was my first official assignment. I wasn't going to mess this up.

When we arrived on the plane, the other nine team members were already waiting. Frankie was in Joe's lap. Bella and Gabby huddled together, listening to music. I took a single chair near a window. It would be a short flight.

As we took off, I lost myself in thought. The pain in my chest was still there. After waking up this morning in my room, cold and alone, everything felt numb. I could feel myself losing the desire to live. Even the thought of Tony no longer brought me the sense of happiness it once did. Was this depression? And the voices: it was as if I was trapped in a small, one-bedroom apartment with a hundred other people, yelling and talking and laughing all at once. I was going insane. It never stopped.

Somewhere between takeoff and landing, I must have fallen asleep. A hand on my shoulder gently shook me awake. I followed the group off the plane and into the hotel bus, grateful everyone seemed too tired from the flight to talk.

We settled into the hotel. I opted for my own room, needing the isolation to concentrate before the mission. We were planning to deal with only a small handful of demons tonight. We didn't know what they were after, but we were sent here to stop them regardless.

I sat down by the long, floor-to-ceiling window and looked out over the city of Paris. Hours passed as the sun fell and the moon rose. It felt like minutes. A knock came at the door, pulling me out of my trance. I opened it, allowing Frankie to enter. I said nothing. I gathered my weapons and jacket before heading for the exit. She caught my arm.

"Talk to me," she said softly. "I'm right here."

"I'm done talking, Frankie. Let's just get this over with so we can go home," I replied, pulling free of her grip and heading out of the room.

We headed down to the Musée de la Magie, the witchcraft museum on 11th Street. Our group fanned out, not wanting to attract too much attention. My guns and other weapons were concealed. It was past midnight, so the building was closed.

Tyler opened the back door with an unlocking spell. We all went in, keeping our eyes open and guards up. The museum was belowground. Archways made of what appeared to be sandstone scattered the room, dividing the space into sections. Old artifacts ranging in time periods and cultures were on display.

"What do you think they're looking for?" asked Gabby.

"Most likely, some type of relic they can conjure power from is my guess," replied Bella.

"I looked at everything they have cataloged ahead of time," added Loriana. "Nothing out of the ordinary."

"Whatever their looking for probably isn't cataloged," added

Roric.

"Good point," whispered Bella.

"Coast is clear," said Tyler as he and Orion walked from the back.

"No sign of Obsidian anywhere," reported Orion.

"Do you think the lead was bad?" asked Frankie.

"Not sure," replied Orion. "Let's head back to the hotel and make contact with the elders to see what they want us to do next." We all agreed, one-by-one funneling back into the alley behind the building.

"This doesn't make sense," I said to Orion. "Nonna's sources are always on point. Something feels off."

As if the universe heard me and laughed, a massive force of power slammed into us. We went flying back into the stone walls and street. My ears hummed from the explosion. I shook my head, trying to clear my vision, but everything spun around me.

In the distance, dozens of demon-possessed Obsidian witches and warlocks surrounded us. Their skin was detaching from their muscles and chunks of hair were missing. Puss and bile spilled from their mouths and wounds. The smell of rot and sulfur surrounded us.

Orion hauled me to my feet. "You good?" he asked.

I nodded, looking around to make sure everyone else was in one piece. Without warning, they attacked. Bullets began to fly. Obsidian demons appeared on the tops of the buildings surrounding us.

They crawled down the sides like roaches swarming. It was easily five to one at this point. One of them jumped on Orion's back as another slammed into him from the side.

I raised my gun, nailing both in the head before reloading. Now, with a gun in each hand, I took a stance and aimed. Bullet after bullet went soaring through the air, but they kept coming. For every one demon I killed, three more appeared. They were fast and moved like predators, making it hard to hit the critical spots. The team fought around me, shooting, punching, slicing, and calling on their power to defend themselves. There was no end in sight.

A scream erupted from behind me. I turned in time to see a demon jump onto Gabby's back, sinking its teeth into her neck. I flung my gun forward, praying for a clean shot as I pulled the trigger three times. The thing fell off her. She turned around, slamming two more bullets into its chest. She swayed a bit before dropping to her knees. I rushed to her side, cradling her before her head hit the ground.

"There are too many of them," she whispered. Blood was pouring from her neck. Bella and Frankie appeared, taking in the state of their friend.

"We need to pull back," I said, looking at the others. They nodded. "Fall back!" I yelled. George rushed to us, going to reload his weapon. Before he could, two demons sprang to either side of him, sinking their nails into his flesh. Their jagged, sharp teeth drove deep into his skin as they ripped him apart right in from of us. Bella let out a cry.

Roric came up beside the two demons, beheading both with a short sword, but it was too late. George's body laid in mangled pieces before us.

"Get her up," I said to the others. "We need to move now."

We took off, breaking away from the main streets, running for safety. I continued to fire off rounds behind us as the creatures ran on all fours, crawling on the walls and jumping from lamppost to lamppost. One lunged through the air. Orion turned just in time, his bullet nailing the thing in its head.

"Faster," Orion yelled. He took Gabby from Bella and Frankie, cradling her now unconscious body in his arms. Loriana and Adrianna caught up with us. Adrianna was badly wounded, holding on to Loriana for support.

"We're too slow," I said, hearing the demons growling and hissing behind us as they closed in. *Bam.* We slammed into a magical barrier which sent us all tumbling back on our asses. Static energy zapped around the air creating a dome, caging us inside. The demons circled, breathing heavily. They were demented, smacking their hands on the dome, crawling and yelling, just waiting to feed on our flesh.

A section of them parted. My mother walked confidently down the aisle as if it were her big debut. Without hesitation she stepped through the domed cage and stood before us. Her long dark brown hair framed her familiar face. If she had a demon roaming around inside of her, there were no signs. She was the perfect image of health.

"Hello again, little bean," she said, locking her eyes onto me. "Not a big fan of the white hair."

I stepped forward, no longer afraid. "Let them go and you can have me," I offered.

She laughed. "And why would I do that?"

"Because you are going to have to face two gods if you don't," I replied.

She laughed again, looking around at her demon army. "Two gods? Really? Tell me, how are those godly powers of yours developing, hm?"

My heart caught in my throat. She knew. She knew we weren't at full strength. Her eyes narrowed. "That's what I thought. If you were capable of stopping us, you would have already. Yet, here you are, running for your lives."

"How did you know we were coming?" I asked, trying to stall the inevitable.

She smiled, taking a step forward. "A little reflection told me," she answered.

"What do you mean?" asked Frankie, coming to stand by my side. My mother took in the sight of my cousin and then turned her eyes back to me.

"Why don't you ask your cousin, niece." My mother sighed with a devious smile.

Frankie looked at me. "Seren ... what is she talking about?"

I shook my head. No, no, he wouldn't. He wouldn't put me in danger. He wouldn't willingly hand me over like this. He loved me. He did. Whatever grasp I had on reality slipped away. I had nothing left to hold onto.

"Seems like she's lost her voice," said my mother. "Allow me. Seren here has been communicating with Antonio Simonelli through an enchanted mirror in her room. She told him you all would be here. That's how I found you."

"What?" Frankie said, looking at me with disappointment. "No, you wouldn't. You wouldn't do that to us."

"Frankie ... I'm sorry. I didn't know he was going to tell anyone else." Frankie just stood there. Tears welling in her eyes. "I'm so sorry."

"Well," continued my mother, "now that the cat's out of the bag, on to business. Which one of your friends would you like to watch die first?"

Without thinking, I took my gun, placing it against my temple in a last-ditch effort to make a deal. My mother froze, her eyes turning deadly. "And what do you think you're doing?" she asked.

"Let them go or I die," I replied.

"Seren," whispered Frankie.

My mother paused for a second, seeming to assess her options. Her eyes finally returned to mine as a disturbing smile crawled across her face. She brought her hands into the air, allowing the barrier to fall. It had worked.

I turned to Orion and mouthed the word 'go'. His face was wrecked, but he knew what needed to be done.

Frankie grasped my hand, taking a step towards me. "No," she said. "Like Nonna said, we're in this together. Blood ties us. We don't leave each other behind."

"Awe," said my mother, "how precious." Quicker than I could comprehend, Annalise threw out her hand, drawing Frankie toward her until her long fingers wrapped around her neck. She held her off the ground. Frankie thrashed and fought, but my mother used her siphoning power to drain her of all magic, stealing Frankie's ability to move or fight. "Toss the gun or she dies."

Without hesitation, I did as she asked.

Mother laughed, turning back to look at Frankie. "You should have run when you had a chance, niece." My mother slammed a knife into her heart multiple times, dropping her body to the ground.

A wretched scream erupted from me. I rushed to her, watching her short breaths gasping for air. She wrapped her hands around the knife, but I stopped her from removing it. If she did, she would bleed out. "No, don't," I cried, taking her hand in mine. "I'm going to get us out of this, don't worry."

"And how do you plan on doing that?" asked my mother, standing over us. "Come little bean, time to hold up your end of the bargain."

"I won't leave her!" I yelled.

"You don't have a choice."

Icy white flames licked around my fingers and slid up my arms. The rage inside of me lit my power into an inferno. I blasted tunnels of white fire into the crowds of demons. They howled and screeched. My shadows took flight, slamming into them, tearing and slicing away appendages and flesh. They rushed forward, aiming to tear me apart. Even with my powers, I was still outnumbered. There was no way I would walk out of this alive. And Frankie would die next to me, because of my mistakes.

I dropped to my knees, pulling Frankie's body into mine. I sobbed. "I am so sorry," I cried, rocking her slowly. "This is all my fault. I am so sorry. Please, don't die. Please. You can't leave me. I need you. I love you."

Suddenly, my ears began to ring. A warping noise filled the air around me. I looked up at my mother, who attempted to step towards us but slowly froze in place. The demons stopped moving. Stopped breathing. The sounds of the city quieted, until you could hear the drop of a pin. I looked around, unsure what in the hell was happening.

A dark mist crept through the crowd, coming together in front of me, taking the form of a man. Asmodeus's face was adorned by a devious grin. He looked around us, noting the demons and my mother. Then his eyes trailed to Frankie's body, withering away in my arms. I continued to cry, looking up at him. I was desperate.

"Please," I whimpered. "I'll do anything. Just save her."

He walked gracefully towards us, bending down on one knee. He gently moved a piece of Frankie's dark hair from her face. He traced his hands over her body. His brow furrowed before he removed his hand, bringing his eyes to mine. "Care to make a deal?" he asked.

"Anything," I replied without hesitation.

"Careful. One usually doesn't rush into these types of things," he said, tilting his head to one side.

"What's the deal?"

"I want access to your mind," he answered.

"What?"

"I want you to grant me access to your mind."

"What does that even mean?"

He huffed, standing to his feet. He waved his hand in the air, a roll of parchment unfolding in his hand. "Would you like me to read it word for word?" he asked. "Your dear little cousin doesn't look like she has a whole lot of time left, so she might be dead by line thirty-seven."

I looked back at Frankie. She was unconscious. Her pulse was weakening. "Fine," I whispered.

"What? Sorry, didn't quite get that."

"I'll take your stupid deal."

"Excellent now, repeat after me," he cleared his throat in a sarcastic manner. "I, Seren Lucia De Salvo." I did as he instructed.

"Give my full consent to Prince Asmodeus Râşnov, demon of Lust, to enter my mind as he so pleases." After I repeated the words he bent down next to me, flashing those white teeth.

I pulled away. "What are you doing?" I asked.

"Our deal needs to be sealed with a kiss," he instructed.

"You've got to be kidding me."

"Look," he said, pulling away, "I don't make the rules. Do you want me to save your cousin or not?"

I rolled my eyes, slamming my face into his in a quick effort to get it over with. I pulled away, looking down at Frankie, hoping to see her eyes open. "Why didn't it work?" I asked. "Why isn't she waking up?"

He chuckled softly, placing his arm underneath Frankie's leg while cradling her head against his chest. He pulled her into him, standing from the ground. "It's a bit more complicated than that, love. I'll have her mended and back to you in a flash. Now, do us all a favor and use your last ten seconds to shift yourself out of here." He evaporated, taking Frankie with him.

Time around me started to unfreeze. It began slowly, but picked up pace. Just as my mother lunged for me, I closed my eyes and shifted myself out. I landed somewhere near the Eiffel Tower, still unable to control the damn power. I took off running towards the hotel, not stopping until I hit Orion's door. I pounded over and over again until Joe opened it. They were all huddled inside, tending to Gabby and Adrianna.

"Where is Frankie?" Joe asked frantically. I didn't know what to say.

About that time, my phone rang ... it was Nonna. I picked it up hesitantly. "Hello," I said.

"You have some explaining to do, bambina," yelled Nonna. "How in the hell did Francesca magically appear in her bed just now?"

I began to sob. "She's okay? She alive?"

"Yes, she's alive," Nonna spat. "She's unconscious but alive. What in the hell happened?"

"We'll be home soon," I said, hanging up on her. "She's alive," I told Joe. "She's safe at home."

"How did she get there?" asked Joe.

"Doesn't matter. How are the others?" I asked.

Orion rushed forward, pulling me into his arms, holding me tightly. I began to sob in his embrace. "I was worried sick," he said.

"How are the others?" I asked.

"We need to leave immediately. They need a healer," explained Orion.

"Can you shift them back?" I asked.

"No. Not when they're hurt this badly. Plus, my powers haven't recovered fully from the poison. I can only shift myself short distances."

I nodded. I hadn't realized the residual impact the poison still had on Orion. I rushed to the other rooms, helping to gather everyone's belongings.

We made it to the plane in under an hour. Everyone was silent, still reeling from what had happened. As we took off, I sat away from the others, feeling the guilt of yet another mistake. Orion came and sat across from me.

"You've still been talking to Simonelli?" he asked plainly.

My face fell in shame. "I'm so sorry," I whispered. "I really thought he—" I stopped myself, feeling like a fool for even attempting to say it.

"We lost George today because—" I saw his jaw tense as he held his words back.

"Because of me ... I know." Tears fell from my face.

"How did you manage to escape?"

"I shifted to the Eiffel Tower and then went on foot from there."

"And how did Frankie get back to Castle Salvo?"

I paused, not wanting to answer that question. "She's alive. That's all that matters."

He ran his hand over his face in frustration. I could see the anger wash over him. "You're still keeping secrets," he said, with a harsher tone than I had ever heard come from him. "After everything we've been through. After everything we've sacrificed."

"I know and I'm sorry, but I can't ... I can't tell you that part."

"Unbelievable," he said, standing from his chair.

I was losing my friends. My family. The people I loved most. Maybe that wasn't such a bad thing. Maybe being alone was what

I deserved. This way ... no one else would get hurt because of me.

Chapter Four

Before the car came to a complete halt, I barreled out of the door, rushing the stairs of the castle entrance to get to Frankie. I threw open the door to her bedroom, seeing Aunt Thora at her bedside. Frankie's eyes were half opened and turned to me. I froze, unsure of how she would feel, knowing my secret about Tony.

Aunt Thora rushed forward, taking me in her arms with a warm embrace. "I am so happy you're alright," she said, kissing the top of my head.

"How is she?" I asked.

"She," said Frankie from her bed, "can speak for herself."

"Looks like all is well," added Aunt Thora. I followed her to Frankie's side, unsure of what to say.

"Mom, can you give Seren and me a moment please," asked Frankie.

"Of course." Aunt Thora said, looking between the two of us with suspicion.

I hesitantly sat in the chair next to her. There was no bandage on her chest, no blood. It was as if the whole incident never happened.

"You're really okay," I whispered.

"Surprisingly so. I look pretty good for just being stabbed in the heart and almost dying."

My breath caught. "You remember getting stabbed?"

"Of course, I do. Now, tell me what in the hell happened, and how am I still alive? And I swear to the gods, Seren Lucia De Salvo, if you lie to me again, I will rip out that tongue of yours myself. Now, start talking."

"Annalise was about to take me away, then time stopped. Asmodeus appeared out of thin air. He told me if I agreed to a deal, he could save you ... so I did."

"You made a deal with a demon? Are you out of your damn mind!?" Frankie sat straight up, looking like she was about to blow something to pieces.

"What else was I supposed to do? Let you die?"

"Yes. If it was my time, I should have crossed over."

"That wasn't an option."

"What was the deal, Seren?"

"He wanted access to my mind."

"What in the hell does that even mean?"

"Like I know."

"Do you feel ... different?" she asked.

"No, just tired." I looked over at her, feeling an overwhelming since of relief. Without another word, I threw myself on the bed, wrapping my arms around her. I held her tight as flashes of her bleeding body rattled through my mind. "I am so sorry. So, so sorry."

"I know you are, but Nonna and Mamma can't know what happened. You hear me?" she insisted.

"What? Why?"

"They're already dealing with enough. If they find out that you bargained your mind away to a prince of Hell, they might just lose their shit. I am certain Nonna would lock you in your room and through away the key."

"God, my life is a mess."

"This demon really has a hard-on for you, doesn't he?"

I laughed, laying my head next to hers. "I have the worst luck with men. Maybe I should have stayed a nun."

"That would have been the safer option for sure. Speaking of bad taste in men ... you've really been communicating with Antonio?"

I nodded.

"Why, babe? He betrayed you. He betrayed all of us."

"I missed him. I wanted to believe there was still a way to be together. I don't know. I feel so foolish for believing he would change. That he would choose me over whatever my mother is offering."

"And how do you feel now?" she asked.

"Like the last part of my heart has been ripped out and thrown into a meat grinder. I never want to fall in love again. All of this ...

it's not worth it."

"Don't say that," she said, wrapping her arms around me. "Orion is still an amazing guy."

"I gave him permission to be with Delphine," I whispered.

"You did what?" she said, pulling away from me in shock.

"I've tried to love him. I really have. Something just isn't clicking. It's not fair for him to wait for a woman who will never love him the way he deserves."

She rested her head back down against mine. "Gods, your life really is fucked up." I elbowed her as we both laughed at my shortcomings.

"I'm just going to focus on the covens. On you and the family."

The door flung open. Nonna stood on the other side of the entrance with fire blazing behind her eyes. "Seren, come," she ordered. I moved quickly, scrambling from the bed. Frankie made to follow, but Nonna held out her hand. "No, just her. You stay."

"But I—" started Frankie.

"I said stay, Francesca!" she barked.

I followed Nonna through the halls towards my room. I already knew what this was about. Someone had told her about my communication with Tony. She opened the door, allowing me to pass before shutting it behind us. I stood off to the side, unsure what she was going to do.

She nodded towards the mirror. "Go on, call him."

"What?" I replied, confused.

“Call Antonio Simonelli,” she said, slowly, as if for a child.

I took a breath, walking over to the mirror. I placed my fingers on the cold glass and thought of him. Within minutes, his face appeared. His smile fell as Nonna peered over my shoulder.

“Elder Salvo,” he said with a slight nod.

“How dare you,” Nonna said with rage and anger lacing every word. “How dare you turn against your coven, against your family. I was ready to welcome you into *my* family. To give you one of my most precious gifts ... my granddaughter! All the while, you plotted and schemed to destroy our covens, our way of life, and my granddaughter, the woman you supposedly loved, along with it.”

“You don’t know what you’re—”

“Don’t you say a damn word to me, boy,” she yelled. “And thanks to your treacherous tongue, I almost lost both of my grandbabies today. And we did lose George Vernada, your supposed friend.” The color seeped from Tony’s face. “You listen to me, you pathetic traitor, I will find you, and when I do, you will regret ever stepping foot in my house and raising a hand against my family. No one, and I mean no one, comes against a Salvo and lives!” With one quick snap of her arms, the vanity blew into a thousand little pieces. I covered my eyes, but my skin was still marred by the shards of glass and wood flying through the air.

Nonna calmed herself, unable to look at me.

“Nonna, I—”

"Enough, Seren. I don't want to hear it," she said, leaving me standing in an empty room, alone.

I began to pick up the pieces of my vanity, placing them in the large trashcan. Amid the debris, something bright shimmered in the light. I bent down and picked up the engagement ring Antonio had given me. I took it, along with the rings Orion had made for me and placed them inside a music box that I kept on the fireplace mantel. I was done with love. I was done with all of it.

The next few days, I spent alone in my room, cleaning and redecorating. I painted the walls black. I ordered a new bed with a white comforter and accent pillows. I changed all the light fixtures to gold and added a deep purple velvet couch and wingback chairs around the fireplace. I also contacted a lawyer. I drew up the annulment papers and had them delivered to Orion.

After a week of being left alone, my room was finally coming together. I added large and luscious accent rugs along with pale-stained wooden dressers. Artwork that I chose adorned my walls. Thick purple velvet curtains hung from my massive balcony windows. I placed pictures of my family and friends on the dressers, reveling in a space that felt like my own.

A heavy knock snapped me out of my zen. I wiped my brow, removing the sweat and answered it. Orion barged in, holding a large envelope. "What in the hell is this?" he said, turning quickly to face me.

"I'm pretty sure the title is at the top of the document," I answered, not wanting to have this conversation.

"What are you doing, Seren? Have you lost your mind?"

"No. Actually, I feel like myself for the first time in a long time."

"We can't get divorced. This isn't what you really want."

"Yes, we can and yes, it is. Orion, marriage isn't supposed to be like this ... to feel like this. We completed the rite. That was enough. I don't want you to feel tied to me."

"But I am," he said, stepping towards me. "I am tied to you. Forever and always."

"No. Aradia and Cyrus are tied together, because that is what they chose. We didn't choose this. This was forced on us."

"Maybe you didn't choose this, but I did." I saw the pain in his eyes.

I exhaled, placing my hands on either side of his large arms. "Orion. Think of Delphine. I am giving you an out. You two can truly be together. She loves you. That is something I will never be able to give you."

He looked at me deeply: truly looked at me, for the first time. "Why can't you just give us a chance?" he asked.

"Because ... I don't have it in me. I've tried, but I just ... I can't. I don't want to be loved, or to love in return."

"You don't know what you're even capable of, Seren!" he roared, tossing the papers across the room. "Less than a year ago, you couldn't even walk. You didn't know your family or the power you possessed and look at you now. Yes, things are ... complicated right now, but that can change. You have to allow time to heal your heart. To clear your mind."

"I've made up my mind," I whispered, not wanting to continue this conversation.

"Well guess what," he said, moving into my face. "You need my signature on that piece of paper and you're not getting it. Not until I am certain that there isn't a chance that this could work."

"Orion—"

"No! We've gone to hell and back for this opportunity, and I won't let you throw it away because you're scared. Not now ... not after everything."

I allowed a few moments of silence to go by, hoping the tension between us would ease. "I can't love you. Not in the way you want."

He ran his hands through his hair, walking slowly towards the door. "I could make you happy."

A single tear escaped my eye. "My mind knows that ... but my heart—" I whispered, choking on the words. I covered my mouth, unable to finish the sentence. With that, he left.

For the next two weeks, Nonna barely spoke to me. She was disappointed. That was to be expected. Frankie was back to her joyful self. Gabby and Adrianna were completely healed, but I made sure to keep my distance. I was responsible for their injuries, for George's death, and they all knew it.

I hid in my room under warm blankets, curled up by the fire with my head buried in books. I didn't have the desire to cook, or bake, or train. All I wanted to do was fade away into a fictional land, where a handsome and charming prince would fight my enemies for me and take me somewhere far away where we were loved by all.

A deep, rumbling laugh snapped me out of my daydream. A voice I recognized. I jolted upright, searching the room for Asmodeus, but he was nowhere to be found. I casted a protection spell, again, around my room just to be sure. I nestled down underneath my blanket and continued to read.

Weeks turned into a month. We had made it to February. The snow still dusted the ground outside. I had gotten into a routine. I would wake up, call for breakfast. Take a walk through the village. Eat lunch at a small café I had discovered on the outskirts of town. Then, I would return to the castle and visit with Frankie before barricading myself in my room, snacking on fruit and reading until early hours of the morning.

The sun peeked through the velvet curtains, illuminating my room. I sprawled out on the couch with my book still open across my chest. I stretched, rolling off the cushions, making my way to the bathroom. After a shower, I went back out into the room with a towel wrapped around me. I dried my hair, making my way to the coffee table to check my phone. I stopped dead in my tracks, searching the room, but no one was there.

Next to my phone sat a black envelope. My name was written in a flowing script of gold ink. I picked it up, still looking around me for any sign of the sender. I broke the wax seal on the back and pulled an invitation from the envelope. It was encased in an intricately cut golden paper jacket. I pulled the ribbon that held the two sides together, opening the invitation. It read:

The company of Miss. Seren Lucia De Salvo

is requested at Castle Râşnov on the 14th of February at ten in the evening for the Adoration Ball.

Please send notice of attendance or regrets by marking this paper and lighting it aflame.

~Prince Asmodeus Râşnov~

"You've got to be kidding me," I said to no one, tossing the invitation onto the table.

Another week had passed. I finally mustered up the courage to speak with Nonna. It had been almost a month since we had anything meaningful to say to one another. She was cross with me; I understood that, but not talking to her ... not being able to confide in her was killing me. I missed her. She was the person I admired the most: who I wanted to be when I grew up. She was truly my idol.

On top of that, the situation with Orion was tearing me apart. I loved him, but not as a husband. I didn't understand any of this. How was I his destiny, and he mine, yet I was missing the essential piece ... love? I didn't trust my own heart. It had betrayed me and set me on a path that cost me the trust of those I love most ... and a friend.

I walked to her office and knocked hesitantly. "Come in," I heard her voice say from the other side. I took a deep breath and entered. She looked up, saw it was me and then turned back to her paperwork.

"Is this a bad time?" I asked, approaching with caution.

"It's always a bad time," she replied, gesturing to the seat in front of her, signaling me to sit. I obeyed, not knowing where to start. Her eyes looked across at me. "What is it you need, bambina?"

"To apologize ... for everything. For everything I've messed up. I've ruined. For the people who have died because of me or gotten hurt. For our power not being renewed as it should. Everything is my fault. All of it. I don't know why I was chosen." I began to cry. Something I hadn't allowed myself to do in weeks. "I just screw everything up. I trusted the wrong person and for that, people died. I don't know how to fix this. I don't know how to fix any of it."

Nonna came around the table, pulling my head into her as she hugged me closely. "That's it. Let it out. Let it out," she said, stroking my hair with her hand.

"Can you ever find a way to forgive me?" I asked, looking up at her.

"There is nothing to forgive, Seren. You followed your heart. You fell in love, and you were vulnerable ... trusting, as you should have been. None of us could have seen what the Simonelli boy was up to. You must stop blaming yourself and let yourself heal."

"And what about our powers? How am I supposed to fix that? I've tried Nonna, truly tried to love Orion as I should, but something just doesn't fit. I care about him, but I don't love him."

Nonna shrugged. "That, I do not have the answer to. I've put in hours of research, but I've found nothing. If you don't love him, then you don't love him. I don't expect you to force yourself to be with someone you don't care for in that manner."

"So, you're not mad about the annulment?" I asked.

"I was shocked, but no, bambina, I am not mad. I know you tried. The heart is a fickle thing. Something I don't believe any of us will ever truly understand." She pulled me back into her. "Now that all of that is out of the way, are you ready to get back to work?"

I pulled away. "Wait, you mean you haven't been mad at me this entire time?"

"No, honey. I knew you needed time, so I let you be. I was confident you would come to me when you were ready. And look, here you are."

"Thank God," I said, standing to hug her fully.

She laughed. "You are my blood, my legacy. I will always be here for you and always love you."

I smiled at her, retaking my seat. "What is happening with Obsidian?" I asked.

"They're kidnapping and killing witches and warlocks. Somehow, they've figured out how to weaponize your mother's gift, siphoning the power of others. But now, they can transfer that power into their filthy demon hosts."

"Did we ever find out what they wanted in Paris?"

"Unfortunately, yes. They stole an ancient book of dark magic. I've never laid eyes on the book, so I am not sure what they plan to do with it. More questions with no answer."

"I've actually been thinking," I said, finding my voice. She looked at me intrigued. "What if my mother is working with Lucifer?"

Nonna laughed. "And why would a demon prince agree to work with a witch?"

"I'm not 100% sure, but Annalise's power is almost unmatched. She kept referring to a 'he' when she captured me. I heard her talking about 'his' plan, and then when you came to save me, she said something about the power 'he' gave her in exchange for me. Plus, the demons listen to her command. She has an angle, and I am betting he is her backer."

"We'll add it to the ever-growing list of theories." She paused, looking down at her stack of paper. "Before I forget, Giana Simonelli has been asking for you."

"What? Why?"

"She won't say. But, bambina, if he tries to use her to speak with you—"

"Don't worry, Nonna. That door is fully closed." I stood, needing to visit one more person before I spoke with Tony's sister.

I headed for Orion's room, feeling the need to explain. I knocked, waiting patiently for him to let me in but he wasn't there. I headed down to the training arena and found him sparring with Tyler and Roric. The three of them stopped as I approached. I smiled and gave an uncomfortable wave. Tyler and Roric quickly found something better to do. Orion took a water break, wiping the sweat from his neck and chest.

"Hi," I said uncomfortably.

"Little dove," he said, looking down at me from behind his thick lashes. "I thought you were going to waste away in your room if you stayed in there any longer."

"I just needed ... time."

"And did you get your time?"

"I did. Thank you."

He smiled, turning to fully face me. "What can I do for you?"

"I just ... I wanted to apologize again and ... I wanted to check in and see how you were doing."

He laughed, sitting on a bench. He patted the seat, inviting me to join. "The first few days were hard. I couldn't wrap my mind around what was happening. I've always been a rule follower, and the rules said we were meant to be together. But ... I've been happy the past few weeks. I've found my purpose again, and I feel like I can think clearly."

"Is that thanks to anyone special?" I asked, bumping him in the arm.

He smiled. "Delphine sends her thanks. She was ecstatic you asked for a divorce."

"And ... she makes you happy? Truly?"

He nodded. "I'm not going to sit here and lie to you and tell you something inside of me won't always hope that you and I will end up together. Maybe that is just Cyrus's soul calling to Aradia's, but, before the rite, before you, I loved Delphine with all my heart. She is an amazing witch, and she makes me happy."

"I'm so happy to hear that." I paused, uncomfortable to ask the question I needed. "Does that mean you've signed the divorce papers?"

He pulled his eyes from me, looking at the ceiling. He shook his head. "I ... I'm not ready. Even with Delphine in the picture, I just ... I—"

I took his hand, rubbing my thumb across the back. "It's okay. Take your time. Whenever you're ready."

"You two should get to know each other. I'm sure you would hit it off."

"I think it's still a little too soon, but yes, someday, I would love to get to know her. Maybe I could cook for the two of you sometime."

"Lemon tarts," he said, licking his lips.

I laughed. "Absolutely."

He wrapped his arm around me, pressing his lips to the top of my head. "I love you, little dove."

"And I love you, Orion."

Next on my list was Giana. I walked to the top portion of the castle where her room had been moved. She was still hooked up to machines. I had hoped once Orion and I completed the rite he could heal her, but since his powers weren't complete, that was no longer a possibility. I had brought her here in hopes of saving her, yet her condition continued to worsen. Even this I had screwed up.

I knocked, alerting her to my presence. She sat up, smiling slightly as she waved me in. I took a deep breath. Looking at her was like looking at Antonio. The resemblance was disturbing. My heart throbbed, but I pushed that feeling deep inside of me. "Elder Salvo said you wished to speak to me," I said, standing at the foot of her bed.

Her eyes fell to her hands as she fiddled with her blanket. "Your mother is an evil woman," she said softly. "Every time she would siphon the sickness out of my body, I connected with her, only for a brief moment, but ... it was enough."

"Why are you telling me this?" I asked.

Her eyes finally rose to meet mine. "I have a gift not many know about," she said. "I call it empathic sight. I can see and feel your deepest desires and inner thoughts. The past month, I've felt you."

I took a step back, unsure of how to handle this situation. "How?"

"My brother ..."

Everything inside of me began to scream, but I remained calm on the outside. “He’s found a way to communicate with you?” I asked.

“Kind of. We’ve been able to do it since we were kids. I can’t speak with him, but he can send his emotions down the line. About a month ago, I felt his pain for you. I knew he wanted me to look after you. To help if I could.”

“I’ve had enough help from the Simonellis for one lifetime, thank you very much,” I said, turning to leave.

“Please don’t go,” she called after me. I stopped, turning around towards her. “You aren’t a mistake. You were planned long ago. You are the perfect blend of what is needed to save our people.”

“What are you talking about?”

“I’ve felt your hesitation. Your anger with yourself. Your guilt. Your ... your feelings on whether or not we’d be better off without you in the picture. A leader must make sacrifices. Others must die in order to accomplish their objectives. You’ve made mistakes, but you are exactly who they always hoped you’d become. You are on the right path, Seren De Salvo. Trust those instincts, and your heart. They will lead you to your destiny. To your true calling. To your full power.”

I stared at her for a moment, before leaving without a word. I held back my emotions. This wasn’t going to set me back. I wasn’t going to let him back in. Not this time.

I rushed through the halls, trying to get back to the safety of my room. Frankie ambushed me, spinning me around with her as that bright smile lit across her face.

"What are you doing?" I asked, laughing along with her.

"I want my cousin back," she said, frowning down at me.

"I'm right here."

"I mean my fun cousin. The one who I used to have to carry up the stairs in the early hours of the morning after our all-night benders."

I laughed. "A lot has happened since those days."

"Yes, but we're alive, Seren. We are young and beautiful and powerful. And to honor us, I have planned a little date night, just you and me."

"Frankie, I—"

"Ah, ah, ah. I am not taking no for an answer. I know you've been dealing with your shit this past month, but time to get yourself back up on the horse. Tonight, we are going out, but first, I have a surprise set up in your room."

"Oh, God, what is it?"

"A massage silly. Something to loosen all those tense muscles of yours."

I looked at my cousin and smiled. "What would I do without you?"

"Hopefully you'll never have to find out. Now go," she said, smacking me on the butt. "And try to actually enjoy it."

Chapter Five

I entered my room cautiously. Candles were lit and set on every surface. Soft music played in the background and a wonderful lilac fragrance filled the air. A massage table was set up in the middle of my room with oils and lotions. A young blonde man nodded and smiled at me as I entered.

"Good afternoon," he said. "My name is Thomas. I will be your massage therapist today. I have everything ready for you. I will just step outside, and you can call for me when you are undressed and on the table."

"Thank you," I said, nodding to him nervously. I had never had a professional massage before, and I didn't know what to expect. After he left, I went to the bathroom and undressed. I laid face down on the table in nothing but my underwear. I pulled the blanket over myself, relaxing as the warmth from the table heater seeped into my skin. "I'm ready," I yelled.

I heard the door click open. I closed my eyes while he began. His hands were smooth and strong. Each stroke and movement released tension I was unaware I carried. Frankie was right ... I needed this. She always knew what I needed. Both of his hands slid down my sides, causing my skin to erupt in gooseflesh. I hadn't been touched by another in this manner in months. Even though my mind wanted nothing to do with sex, my body had other ideas.

I let out a small moan, enjoying the physical contact. His thumbs pressed down into each of my hips at the top of my panty line and then slid ever so slowly all the way up my sides, gently grazing the small portion of my breasts that were exposed. I went still, not sure if this was normal. He refocused one of his hands to my back, while the other began to massage my hamstrings. His hand slid across my skin as it traveled up, stopping right before he reached my buttcheek. I felt him lean down, his lips grazing the tip of my ear.

"How are you feeling, love?"

I sprang from the table, grabbing the sheet to cover my naked and exposed body. I threw my hand in front of me, slamming my shadows into him with force. Night enveloped my room. I moved forward, expecting to see him pinned up against the wall. Instead, my shadows funneled and swarmed around him as he consumed them.

Asmodeus stepped forward, dressed in his normal black formal suit and red tie. "That little trick doesn't work on me, darling. Sorry to disappoint."

"What in the hell are you doing in here?" I said, holding the sheet tightly against my body. "And where is the actual masseuse?"

He casually leaned back against the table, checking his nails. "I thought I was doing a rather good job back there. From all the sounds you were making, at least," he said, with a devilish grin and wink.

"Where is Thomas?"

"He's hanging off your balcony. Now, the reason I am here—"

"Oh, my God," I said, rushing towards my balcony doors. I peered over the edge. Thomas was cowering against a thin ledge of the mountain. He looked up with terror in his eyes.

"Help me!" he yelled. "Please. I don't want to die."

Asmodeus causally glanced over the side, tilting his head in surprise. "Huh. I would have expected him to fall by now," he said. "Sturdier than he looks, that one."

"Pull him up," I demanded.

"Why?"

"Because I said so. Now, pull him up."

He looked at me, trailing his eyes up and down my body as if he already knew what lay underneath the sheet. "Nah. You have your own shadows," he said plainly. "You do it." He took a step back, leaning against the wall.

I scoffed, tying the sheet around my chest. I called on my power, tendrils of darkness billowing from within me. I stretched the dark ribbons down, wrapping them securely around Thomas. He screamed, looking scared to death. I tightened my hands, pulling slowly, attempting to lift him from the surface into the air. I gritted my teeth, the weight of him draining me. I hadn't practice with my powers since Paris, and even then, I hadn't been able to lift a person.

I opened my eyes and saw him floating five feet above where he had just been. Beads of sweat trickled down my skin. I fought to hold on, to pull him up, but my physical muscles were straining from the exertion. I felt myself losing control. My grip loosened and my muscles gave, dropping Thomas from my grasp. He screamed, plummeting to the ground. I turned frantically towards Asmodeus.

"Please," I yelled. "Save him."

He rolled his eyes, pulling himself from the wall. "Fine," he said dramatically, snapping his fingers. A black mist appeared as Thomas fell onto my balcony, still screaming. Asmodeus hauled him to his feet in aggravation. "Alright, alright, enough with the screaming already," he said, pushing him towards the door.

"What about his memory?" I asked.

"Good idea," replied Asmodeus. His crystal blue eyes turned a bright shade of red. Thomas's eyes fixated on Asmodeus's, unable to look away. "You gave the goddess a subpar massage and then left. You will never return here again." His voice was deep and demanding. Thomas nodded, calming himself before casually walking out of my room. Asmodeus's eyes faded back to an icy blue. His smug smile returned. "Are you going to say thank you this time?" he asked.

I stormed past him, back into my room. "Asshole," I replied. He laughed, following behind me. "Leave, now!"

"Well, aren't you at least going to tip me? After all, you did enjoy it."

"I did not," I spat, wrapping my robe around me.

"You and I both know you did. Stop denying it."

"Why won't you just leave me alone?" I asked, spinning to confront him, arms folded. "I have enough of your kind to worry about as is."

"Oh, no, no. Don't you compare me to those things my brother creates."

I froze, looking back at him with curiosity. "Your brother?" I asked.

"Lucifer ... yes. You guessed right earlier today, during your little meeting with your *Nonna*." He said her name with such exaggeration I almost laughed. He walked towards my dresser, taking time to study each picture individually.

"You heard that?"

"I have access to your mind, remember?"

"I don't even know what that means."

He exhaled. "It means, I can look into your mind whenever I want. I can talk to you, see your memories, hear what you hear. Know what you're thinking."

"Well, that's disturbing. How do I block you out?"

He smiled. "Oh, no. I'm not giving you that little tidbit of valuable information. You'll have to figure that one out on your own, love."

"Last week, when I was reading ... did you laugh at me?"

He shrugged. "Sometimes your little daydreams amuse me."

"And what was so funny about what I was thinking?"

"*A handsome and charming prince who would fight my enemies*," he said mockingly, reciting the lines I had thought to myself. "You had that, little Salvo, and now you're trying to divorce it."

He had a point, but I wasn't going to let him know that. "Stay out of my head."

"Not the deal we made."

"Stay out of my head!" I said, stepping up to him, close enough that my crossed arms shoved into his chest.

He leaned down, ever so slowly, now only a few inches from my face. "Make me," he whispered.

Aggravation built inside of me: the frustration, and the rage. I screamed as darkness blasted from me. He just laughed, unfazed. I allowed the darkness to dissipate, still fuming.

"Are we done throwing a temper tantrum? I could rub you down again if you'd like. That seemed to calm you ... or excite you. I couldn't really tell which one towards the end."

"What do you want, demon?"

"An answer," he said shortly.

"To what?"

"My invitation. It's been over a week, and you've yet to let me know if you'll be attending my little soirée. That's bad manners, love."

"No," I spat, moving around him to gather my clothes.

He appeared out of thin air in front of me. I jumped back, startled. "And why not?" he asked.

"Because I want nothing to do with you. Haven't I made that clear?"

"You wanted something to do with me the night Francesca almost died." He cocked his head to the ceiling. "You know, come to think of it, I feel a bit used in this relationship."

"This," I said, gesturing between the two of us, "is not a relationship. And we made a deal. One I instantly regretted."

"You still haven't even said thank you. I'm a bit hurt."

I exhaled, willing to play along just to get him to leave. "Thank you, *demon*, for saving my cousin. I am sorry to inform you that I will not be attending your satanic Valentine's Day ball. Now, will you please leave, so I can get dressed?"

He walked slowly towards me. Darkness trailed behind him. His eyes glowed unnaturally. He towered above, trapping me in his icy cold gaze. He leaned down close enough that I could smell him ... lilacs. "I don't like being told no," he said, in a deep and sensual voice.

"Get used to it," I whispered.

He laughed, pulling slightly away. "You know, if I wanted to, I could have you right now. Anyway and every way I'd like."

"Using your power to force a woman to sleep with you? How

pathetic."

He chuckled. "I've never had to use my power to get another to sleep with me. I assure you of that."

"Then why threaten me with it?"

"It wasn't a threat, just a reminder of who you're dealing with." He backed away slowly, never taking his eyes from me. He still wore that smug smile I wanted to smack off his face. "And just in case you were wondering. I do not accept your declination."

"Find someone else to torture."

He arched a single brow. "Now, why would I do that?" Shadows started to mist at his feet, rising until it engulfed him. Red flickers of lightening jumped between the puffs of darkness. "See you soon, love."

He was gone.

The rest of the day, I was on guard. As night approached, I prepared myself for my date night with Frankie. Maybe, freeing my inhibitions would do me some good. No men. No drama. Just my cousin, dancing, and alcohol.

After a fabulous dinner, we hit the clubs. Drink after drink we consumed. We danced, and sang, and there was laughter. So much laughter. Nonna was right. Frankie was my other half. My soulmate. Who needed a man when I had her?

It was nearing one in the morning, but we were nowhere close to slowing down. Frankie slid into our normal reserved booth. "Awe," she said, making a pouty face. "We're out again. Where does all the vodka keep disappearing to?"

I laughed. "Down your throat," I replied.

"You have a point."

"I'll go get another. Stay put." I headed to the bar, but there was line, and I didn't feel like waiting. I said a little spell under my breath. The people in front of me suddenly decided they no longer wanted a drink and vanished, leaving the bar wide open. I smiled at the bartender as I approached.

"Another bottle?" he asked, looking me up and down with lust in his eyes.

I smiled, enjoying the attention. "Yes, please." I bit the side of my lip.

He grinned, opened the bottle, and then leaned towards me. "I get off in an hour, if you're not busy."

Without thinking, I nodded back to the booth Frankie was in. "I'll be over there."

He smiled flirtatiously, just before a couple slammed into the bar next to me. The man and woman were devouring each other. The man's hands slid up her skirt, exposing her underwear. The woman was ripping at the buttons on his shirt, not caring who saw his bare skin.

The bartender and I looked at each other, both confused and uncomfortable. I pulled my eyes from the X-rated public display, only to realize they weren't the only ones with this new revelation of sexual freedom. Men and women. Women and women. Men and men. Couples everywhere were engaged in very public displays of affection. Some were even in groups of threes and fours, tasting and exploring multiple partners freely without a care in the world.

I turned back to where I had left Frankie, bottle in hand, and then ... it all made sense. There in the booth next to my cousin was Asmodeus, his arm draped around her shoulder. Frankie was smiling from ear to ear as he leaned down, whispering something that, apparently, she found funny.

The air in the club became thick with the scent of lust. The sounds of sex bounced from wall to wall while the music thumped, setting the tone of the orgy that was taking place.

I stormed over to the two of them, slamming the bottle of vodka down on the table. I glared at him, refraining from burning the whole damn building down. Frankie's face fell.

"Seren," said Frankie, "this is Deus. He's a tourist passing through." Asmodeus was dressed more causally than I had ever seen him before. He wore a nice, tapered pair of jeans and a silk black shirt that was unbuttoned a bit too low down his chest, revealing his toned and flawless skin. A long silver chain with a ruby red pendant at the end hung from his neck, and he still had his silver ring on his finger. His hair was casually swept to the side, and his sleeves rolled up, displaying black tattoos that started in the middle of each forearm, trailing up and underneath his shirt. I couldn't make out what the tattoo was, but something inside of me couldn't help but wonder what the rest of the design looked like.

"I could show you later tonight if you ask nicely," I heard him say in my mind. My eyes flashed wide in surprise as I stumbled back. Hearing him in my head was ... disturbing and unnatural: like there was something foreign slithering through my mind.

He winked at me.

"Get up," I demanded.

"Seren," gasped Frankie. "Stop being so rude." She looked at Asmodeus with lust in her eyes.

"Frankie," I said, snapping her out of it. "This is Deus, as in Asmodeus, the demon." Her eyes sprang open, looking back at him in shock.

"Now, why did you have to go and ruin my fun?" he said, still lounging in our booth. "Come and sit. I won't bite ... unless you ask me too."

"Oh, my gods," said Frankie, scooting away from him.

He laughed. "I mean you no harm, Francesca," he said. "I am glad to see you are alive and well. The last time we met, that wasn't the case."

She swallowed, bringing her eyes back up to his. "Thank you," she said hesitantly. "For saving my life."

He bowed his head seriously. "Of course," he replied. "What a waste your death would have been. For this world to lose such a beautiful soul, far before her time."

Frankie seemed to melt at his words. She smiled at him, leaning back into his orbit.

"At least one of the Salvo women has manners," he said, turning towards me.

"Francesca," I said, snapping my fingers across the table. "Snap out of it. Demon of Lust ... remember."

"Now, now," he said, looking offended, "I haven't used my powers on her this entire time."

A couple, half naked and ravenous, slammed into my back, causing me to bump into the table, almost taking me to the floor with them while they pleasured one another with their hands and mouths. Deus laughed in amusement, two large dimples flashing on either side of his bright, sinful smile.

"Your words are beautiful," continued Frankie, leaning her chin on her fist. "Do you like poetry?"

"I love poetry," he said, smiling softly at her. "I'm an avid reader. Can't get enough literature." Frankie's smile grew as she chuckled a bit.

"What do you want, demon?" I asked, sitting across from him.

"I've come to see if you've changed your mind about my little gathering," he said.

"What gathering?" asked Frankie.

"No," I replied immediately.

"Well, looks like I'm staying then," he said, stretching out across the booth.

"What gathering?" asked Frankie, looking between us. "Is it a party?"

"The grandest party you will ever attend," he said, smiling at her. "Imagine, an exclusive party, where you may only attend via invitation. The location is a secluded castle in the wintery hills of Romania. Live entertainment and music of all kinds. Risqué attire. Gourmet food and drinks. Nothing is off limits. Your deepest fears become your darkest fantasies."

"Sounds like my kind of get together," she said.

He snapped his fingers, making an invitation appear instantly in his hand. He slid it to Frankie, locking eyes with me ... smirking. "All you have to do is write the word 'yes' and then light it on fire, and you're in," he instructed her.

Frankie pulled a tube of lipstick from her purse, scribbling on the invitation. "Frankie no—" before I could snatch it from her hands, Asmodeus snapped his fingers again and the piece of paper went up in flames. Frankie clapped with excitement.

"You're in, sweetheart," he said, leaning across the table towards me. "How about you ... change your mind yet?"

"You're evil," I said, barely restraining my power from unleashing.

"So I've been told."

The cute bartender from early approached the table, seeming to assess the situation. "Hi, uh, I'm Adam, from early," he said, looking at me with a kind smile. "The bar got really slow all the sudden." He paused, looking around at the sexual mayhem. "I guess the guests had enough to drink, so they cut my shift early. Do you want to grab a drink somewhere more ... boring?" he laughed.

Asmodeus sat back, crossing his arms over his chest, appraising Adam. I contemplated it, but didn't want poor Adam to end up dead after our drink thanks to my new friendly neighborhood demon.

He smirked. "*Now, I am still behind on cultural references, so excuse me if I am mistaken but, did you just compare me to a ... Spider-Man?*" he asked in my head.

"*Stop listening to my thoughts,*" I fired back.

"*No.*"

I growled, turning back to Adam. "Thank you for the offer, but I'm feeling a bit sick from all the alcohol. Maybe another time," I said, as politely as I could.

"*That's never going to happen,*" Deus said silently to me.

"*Maybe after I get rid of you, I'll change my mind.*"

"*No, you won't.*"

"Okay," Adam said, looking uncomfortable. "Well, have a good night."

Asmodeus stood from the table, extending his hand towards Frankie. "May I have the honor of escorting you back to your castle?"

She smiled, taking his hand as he pulled her from the booth. "Absolutely," she replied. I rolled my eyes, following them down the streets of Triora.

Frankie was very intoxicated, falling all over him and herself the entire way. He was a gentleman, helping her stay upright and not pointing out her drunkenness. I didn't say a word the entire time. I just watched, trying to keep my mind free of any thoughts he might steal.

Once we got to the entrance of the castle, he bid Frankie good night, kissing the top of her hand before helping her up the stairs. He turned back towards me, casually placing his hands behind his back. He stepped in front of me, too close for comfort.

"Your cousin is sweet," he said, his eyes examining my face. "Unlike you."

"You're a demon. Why do you care if I am sweet?"

"Just an observation. Now that we've gotten your dear cousin off to bed, would you like to see the rest of my tattoo?" I pushed past him and ascended the front stairs. He laughed behind me. "Good night, love."

"Fuck off, Deus," I said, before shutting the castle doors.

When I got to my room, I showered and then crawled into bed. I reached to turn the light on my nightstand off when I saw a new black envelope, addressed to *Smartass*. I couldn't stop the smile that stretched across my face. I picked it up, wrote the words *fuck you ... yes* and then lit the damn thing on fire. I felt a silky, dark laugh slither down my spine as soon as the invitation dissipated in thin air. I shut the light, closing my eyes, allowing the alcohol to swiftly drift me to sleep.

"Oh, my gods, I am beyond excited," exclaimed Frankie. "What are you going to wear? I have absolutely nothing in my closet."

"Frankie, you own more clothes than any clothing shop in town. How is that possible?" I asked, lounging lazily on her bed.

"But nothing for a ball hosted by the Prince of Lust. Ah, the very sound of it excites me."

"Are you forgetting he is a demon?" I asked.

"I mean ... he's a very polite demon," she said, matter-of-fact.

"You've got to be kidding me. You're taken with him, aren't you?"

She flailed her hands in the air. "Okay, yes, so what if I am? He is polite, poetic, and sexy as hell."

"He's after something. He has to be. All demons want something," I said, trying to work out different scenarios in my head. "Maybe he wants to steal my power, like my mother is trying to do."

"Or maybe, he's just looking to have some fun."

"Stop being so foolish."

She shrugged. "He saved me. I'm giving him the benefit of the doubt here."

"Yeah, at the cost of him popping into my head for a quick conference call anytime he feels like it."

"How's that whole ... arrangement going, by the way?" she asked, plopping down next to me.

"Annoying as hell. I never know when I'm alone or when he's snooping. My own head isn't even safe anymore."

"There has to be a way to keep him out," Frankie said, tapping her finger against her lip. "I think I read something about this when I was researching him. Let me review some documents and I will get back to you. But for now," she stood, holding up two very revealing lacy garments that seemed more like lingerie than dresses, "black or green?"

"Always green. Matches your eyes," I said.

"Perfect! Now your turn."

I stood, heading for the door. "I'm showing up in sweatpants. He insisted I attend; he gets what he gets."

"You're no fun. Less than twenty-four hours away!"

I laughed, leaving her to her clothes.

It was night and the castle was winding down for the day. I stopped at one of the large arched windows in front of the main hall. The wind was cold, but I enjoyed the breeze. I slid my hand in the pocket of my jacket, my fingers rolling across the beads of my rosary.

Since the rite, I had felt unworthy when it came to my Christian faith. I hadn't studied the Bible in months. I no longer knew where I belonged. I didn't feel worthy of God's love, of Aradia's power—any of it. I kept the rosary with me for comfort. It was the one thing that remained consistent through all the changes I had experienced this past year.

"Seren," I heard a weak voice call. I turned to see Giana, bracing herself against the wall. Tears fell down her face as she fought to stay up right.

I rushed forward, catching her before she fell. She flung her arms around me, sobbing. Her body was frail from the sickness. "What are you doing out of bed?" I asked, helping her back to her room.

"I needed to find you," she whimpered. "Please, Seren. Please save him."

"What happened? What is going on?" I asked.

"Tony ... he's hurt, bad. He hasn't felt like himself in weeks. This morning, the pain began, and it hasn't stopped. And now ... now I can't feel him. I'm worried he's ... he's dead." Pain tore through my chest.

"Do you know where he is?" I asked, setting her on the edge of the bed.

"He's close ... I think Rome."

"I'll see what I can do," I replied, helping her to settle in before pulling the covers over her fragile body.

Her hand reached out, gripping my wrist weakly. "Please don't let him die because he loved me. Please," she begged.

I nodded, forcing a small smile of reassurance.

I headed for Nonna's room, not wanting to go behind her back again. She was with Aunt Thora, sipping on wine and laughing in front of the fire. They both turned, faces twisting with concern. "What is it? What's wrong?" asked Nonna.

"I'm going somewhere, but I wanted you to know before I took off," I replied.

"Go on," Nonna said.

"Antonio. He's in Rome and he's hurt."

"And that's our problem how?" asked Aunt Thora.

"I want to bring him in. To keep him here ... as our prisoner," I replied.

Nonna made a ticking noise with her tongue.

"Do you really think that is wise?" asked Thora. "Bringing him back here? You two living under the same roof again? Sweetheart, I'm just concerned. You've made so much progress. I don't want to see you regress."

"I know what he is," I replied. "My eyes are wide open, and I won't be fooled again, but ... but I can't let him die. Not like this."

Aunt Thora looked at Nonna, her face softening. Thora turned back to me and nodded. "Do what you need to do. We trust you," said Thora.

"Thank you," I said, rushing to Orion's room.

I knocked hastily. He opened the door, smiling back at Delphine. He froze, seeing my face in front of him. "Hi," I said, waving at Delphine. "Sorry to interrupt, but I need to ask you a huge favor."

"I'm listening," he said.

Chapter Six

If what Giana said was true, Antonio was out in the open on his own, no longer protected by Obsidian's protection spell. I scried for him and within seconds, nailed his location down. Giana was right, Antonio was badly hurt.

Orion shifted us to an alleyway in Rome where Tony was hiding behind a dumpster. He was beaten and bleeding out. He was also unconscious, which made things easier for me. We brought him back to the castle where Nonna and Aunt Thora had already made up a cell for him. His family was waiting, along with a healer. We placed him on the bed, and I left, not wanting to look at him a moment longer.

I thanked Orion for his help and then returned to my bedroom. I couldn't sleep. My mind was spinning. After all this time, Tony was here, back under the same roof. Maybe Aunt Thora was right ... this wasn't a good idea.

No, I was strong. I could handle this. I distracted myself with a book and a bottle of wine that night. Not thinking about my soon to be ex-husband down the hall with another woman, nor my ex-fiancé in a cell fighting for his life. Tonight, it was just me and a character named Zane.

I woke up on the couch. My book had fallen to the ground along with the bottle of wine I had finished off by myself. I ran my hands over my face, feeling fuzzy and heavy. I hauled my ass off the cushion, shuffling to the bathroom. My attention caught on a black box that was sitting on my bed. I looked around, confused how it got in here. I went over, pulling the card from the ribbon.

Better than sweatpants

~A

I rolled my eyes, undoing the box. I pulled back the tissue paper and lifted a red lacy outfit from the package. It was some hybrid between a very skimpy dress and a stripper costume. It was sheer and strapless, the front lacing like a corset. The sweetheart neckline plunged low. Below the waist, the dress flared into silk fabric. The front was open to bare my legs all the way up to my hips, but the back was long and flowy like a formal dress. A matching mask sat at the bottom of the box.

I shook my head, throwing the dress on the bed. "I'm still wearing sweatpants!" I yelled, looking around the room, expecting him to appear. I laughed at myself.

Knock, knock. came at the door. I turned in surprise. Was Deus now using the door, instead of just popping in randomly whenever he felt like it? My heart fell. Oh, God ... if someone saw him, it would cause Nonna so many new problems. I ran to the door, swinging it open with haste. Orion stood in front of me, his face wracked with guilt. Without a word, I stepped aside.

"What's wrong?" I asked. "What's going on?"

"How are you, after everything last night?" he asked.

"Besides a little hung over, I'm fine. Why?"

He exhaled, moving to the edge of my bed, and sat. He leaned over his knees, placing his elbows along his legs, breathing deeply. I sat next to him, placing a hand on his back. "What's going on, Orion?" I asked softly.

He took his time. "I have to tell you something." He paused, obviously uncomfortable. He took a deep breath and without looking at me said, "Delphine and I ... we slept together last night."

Something inside of me stung. It wasn't hurt or pain but ... jealousy. Not that he had been with Delphine, but the fact that he got to share that with another, and I was destined to be alone. "I ... I know we aren't together ... but our bond. I just ... I can't help but feel like I've betrayed you in some way."

"Orion, you haven't betrayed me in the least. You are free to be with who you chose."

"But the bond—"

"Will always be there," I interrupted, taking his hand in mine. "No matter who we love or where we go, we will always be connected in some way ... and I am so thankful for that. You are my best friend, Orion, and you get to be happy. That's what matters. That's what I've always wanted."

He finally looked at me. Something like guilt or longing flashed across his face. "You're okay with this? You're sure?"

"Absolutely," I forced myself to say. "Now, get back to your woman before she wakes up. I insist," I said, pushing him off the bed.

He walked over to the door, looking back at me one last time. "You're my best friend too, little dove. I will always love you. Thank you ... truly."

I nodded, holding back tears.

After he left, I forced myself to shower. I got ready and headed to Nonna's room, but she wasn't there. Something in me already knew where I would find her ... Tony's cell. I forced myself to go down into the dungeon. Better to rip off the band aid early than to torture myself with what-ifs.

Nonna, Frankie, and Aunt Thora were standing outside his cell. The healers were inside. Tony screamed in pain. A part of me wanted to run into the room and comfort him, but I refrained. Frankie reached down and held my hand. He thrashed and strained. The healers were pulling the same black poison from his blood as they had from me, once upon a time. I remembered that pain and wouldn't wish it on anyone ... not even him.

"Three broken ribs," Aunt Thora said, "a broken arm and leg. He was missing almost two liters of blood. His magic is also drained."

"Will he recover?" I asked.

"Physically, yes," continued Thora, "but we're unsure about his magic. The fact that he's still alive leads me to believe they didn't take it all, or he would be dead." The healers finished. His mother, Rosemary, rushed to his side, rubbing his head with a cool rag.

Nonna turned towards me before leaving. "I love you, bambina, but don't you dare try anything stupid."

"I won't," I replied. Aunt Thora followed her out.

"Do you want me to stay?" asked Frankie.

"I got this," I replied.

"Okay. Call if you need anything."

I turned back to the door and knocked before unlocking the cell. Anthony, Tony's father, was in the corner. His mother's attention turned towards me, as did Tony's.

"Can we have the room please?" I said softly.

Rosemary kissed her son, before heading out.

I stood at the foot of the bed. His eyes were barely open. "What did the healers say?" I asked.

"I should be healed physically in a few days, but they're unsure about my magic," he said with a raspy voice.

"Why were you dumped in alleyway?"

"I escaped."

I laughed. "You expect me to believe that? After all this time, you just now managed to escape?"

"It's true. I still can't lie to you … the spell, remember?"

"Doesn't mean you can't spin the truth. You're a master at that." I stared at him, looking at the man I once loved. The man I almost sacrificed everything for.

"I'm happy to see you, beautiful."

"Don't call me that," I snapped, feeling a pain in my heart.

"Thank you … for coming for me."

"Tony, just … just stop, alright," I said. "Things aren't going to be the same between us. They never will be again. I saved you to honor the memory of what we once had … of what we could have been, but that is never going to happen."

"I don't believe that."

"I don't care what you believe. I've made up my mind and I'm not turning back." I turned, leaving the cell and him in it.

I met up with Frankie, Bella, and Gabby for lunch. I filled them in about Orion and about Tony. Frankie informed us that she and Joe were taking a break. He wanted something serious, and she was not ready for that again.

I returned to my room, needing some time to myself before tonight's festivities. I went to my dresser, pulling out a pair of my baggiest sweatpants and an old t-shirt that had paint stains on it. I laughed, placing it on the bed. I went to the restroom and when I returned, my sweats were burned to ash and the red dress Asmodeus sent hung on the bed post.

Aggravation overtook me. I went to my dresser, pulling another pair of ugly sweats from the drawer and threw them on the bed. I stood back and watched. A moment later they erupted into flames, not leaving a single burn mark on my bedspread.

"*Are we going to have to burn your entire wardrobe, or are you going to give me what I want?*" Asmodeus said in my head.

"Never," I yelled out loud.

I tore through my dresser pulling every pajama, sweat outfit, and workout attire I had. As soon as they hit the floor or another surface they erupted into flames. I screamed at the top of my lungs while he laughed in my head, amused by my lack of control. Finally, after burning through all my comfortable attire, I plopped down on the couch, pulling my book onto my lap, desperate for a distraction.

"Does that mean I win?" I heard him say in my head.

"*No, it means you owe me new clothes,*" I thought.

"*Those were all hideous anyways. I'll take you shopping. What do you say?*"

"*Cash will do just fine, asshole.*"

He laughed. "*I don't get to see what my money buys?*"

"*No. Now bug off.*"

I read the first line of my book about five times, unable to comprehend what I was reading. I grunted, tossing the book onto the table. I laid down on the couch, watching the fire devour the wood. My eyes glazed over as the flames gracefully formed into dancing ballerinas, twirling, and leaping across the logs. A soft melody of music filled the air around me. I smiled, taking comfort in the beauty of it all.

"Are you doing that?" I asked out loud.

"*Maybe*," came a reply in my head.

"Thank you," I whispered, allowing the song to drift me away.

In the last moments before I fell into a deep and warm sleep, I heard him whisper, *"Wear the dress."*

CHAPTER SEVEN

I was shaken violently awake. "Get up," yelled Frankie. "How can you be sleeping right now? We only have an hour to get you ready, and you haven't even started." I looked into the fire. The ballerinas were gone and so was the music.

Frankie's hair was already done up into beautiful spiraling ringlets. Her makeup was loud and dramatic, just like her personality. There was something different about her nose. I focused my eyes, making sure I was actually seeing correctly.

"What is that?" I asked.

"What's what?"

"In your nose ... is that ... is that a ring?" She turned her head to me fully. A small silver ring now adorned her septum.

"So, what if it is?"

"When in the hell did you have time to get that done?"

"I've wanted it for a while now, and I thought this occasion was the perfect time. It goes with my outfit, don't you think?"

I started laughing. "Oh, your mother is going to kill you."

"I am a grown ass woman. I can do whatever I want to my face. Ah," she gasped, running to my bed. "Where in all of heavens did you get this dress?"

"Asmodeus," I said, making my way over to her.

"He's sending you clothes now? You lucky bitch."

I chuckled. "Well, he torched all my sweatpants and pajamas and threatened to light my closet on fire if I didn't agree, so I have no choice."

"Why wouldn't you want to wear this? It's exquisite."

"Hmm, maybe because a demon sent it to me, who just happens to be one of the princes of Hell?"

"Oh, semantics. Come on, let's start on that white rat's nest of yours."

I sat in front of the vanity for an hour, Frankie painting my face like a whore's. My hair was pinned up high, fully displaying my neck and shoulders. The dress was exquisite, but I felt completely naked. My breasts were pushed up to my chin and the lace of the bodice was transparent. My legs were fully exposed. I wore open-toed high heels with strings that wrapped up my calf and tied at the top. Gold dusted my shoulders, arms, neck, and chest. The only jewelry I wore was a gold pair of dangling earrings. I placed the red lace mask over my eyes, completing the look.

Frankie snapped a few selfies after we finished. She stated that she wanted to remember her first demon ball—as if there'd be more to follow.

Precisely at ten o'clock, a cloud of dark smoke appeared in front of the fireplace. As it faded, a small troll-like creature stepped out.

He had long pointed ears, wrinkled skin, and a pair of sharp teeth. He wore a tailored suit and a pair of gold-rimmed glasses. Frankie and I staggered back. I called on my white flame and she readied her starlight.

"Salvos, yes," the creature said in a screeching voice. Frankie and I looked at each other, unsure if we should answer. "Master sent me to retrieve you for the ball. Come, come, we will be late." He waved his hands, signaling for us to join him. We hesitantly made our way over.

"I don't mean to be rude," Frankie asked, "but what are you?"

"A goldaburg. We serve at the master's request. My name is Gallo. I am master's trusted goldaburg." He held out his hands. Gallo had three fingers, a thumb, and long talons for nails. We took his hands. He smiled at us, with his large mouth full of flesh-ripping teeth. Darkness surrounded us. The wind twirled and ripped through the air until we were greeted by the sound of a beautiful symphony echoing throughout the most extravagant ballroom I could have ever imagined.

The walls towered above us at least sixty feet high. Golden décor and accents adorned every wall, fixture and detail, along with mirrors and crystal chandeliers. The floor was made of the most luxurious white marble that reflected the shimmering crystals. Floor-to-ceiling glass windows lined two of the four walls. The landscape outside was the most beautiful of all. Mountains covered in snow stretched for miles: not a light or a house in sight.

The moon stretched high into the sky and called to me. My power felt alive in this place.

Acrobats, wearing almost nothing, were suspended from the ceiling, hanging from metal hoops and long ribbons of fabric. Their faces were painted dramatically. Fire-breathers danced and lit the air around us, on platforms positioned throughout the room. Diamonds seemed to hang in the air, along with red rubies. Rows and rows of food lined the outer walls. People, witches, and I presumed demons surrounded us, dancing and laughing as they enjoyed one another.

A platform displaying a throne was perched against the main wall. Large, elegant candelabras swayed around the oversized chair. The cushion was red and lined with beautiful gold embroidery. The chair felt familiar in some way. Before I knew what I was doing, I moved towards it, needing to touch it or—

A flash of a memory erupted throughout my senses. I was sitting on Asmodeus's lap in this chair ... his throne. He was laughing while I ran my fingers through his hair. He bit the tip of my finger. I pulled back, taking his face in my hands and pressing my lips firmly against his. I felt him harden underneath me. His hands began to slide up my thigh, under my dress, needing to feel me, needing to please me. Warmth spread through my body as did the warm liquid that seeped from between my legs, just from a single touch. I pushed him back into the chair, straddling my legs on either side.

He tore at my dress, devouring my breasts aggressively, more satisfying than I had ever experienced. I gripped the sides of the throne, feeling the metal crack underneath my fingers. I arched my neck back, begging him to kiss me, to consume me. He ripped my dress apart, pushing his own pants down. His fingertips dug into my hips as he placed me right above him, right where I needed him. I felt his grip tighten just before he slammed—

"Seren," said a deep and sultry voice. I felt his hand on my elbow, steadying me as I stumbled backwards, finding it hard to regain my balance. I looked up to see the man—or rather, —demon I had just been fantasizing about. He was dressed in a long black suit jacket with silk embroidered designs. A simple, yet beautiful golden crown sat on top of his dark hair with a red ruby in the center.

I looked back at the throne, noting the two hand marks on either side where I ... where one of the vessels had physically indented it during her hot and heavy sex session with the Prince of Lust.

Asmodeus followed my line of sight and smiled. "Did you like that memory?" he asked.

I pulled out of his touch. "It wasn't my memory."

He shrugged. "Whatever you say."

I scanned the room for Frankie. She was already entertaining a young and very handsome suiter. He had beautiful long golden blonde hair, a tapered waist and broad shoulders. "Who is Frankie talking to?"

Asmodeus laughed. "One of my brothers."

"Which one?" I asked.

"Leviathan, but he prefers Levi."

Envy. "You've got to be kidding me," I said, moving to go and stop her before she sold her soul to a prince of Hell. Asmodeus's hand gripped my arm.

"Leave her be," he said placidly. "She is safe, I assure you." The image of Frankie's body, unresponsive and full of blood, lingered behind my eyes.

"And why should I trust you?"

His eyes narrowed. "Love, if I wanted you or your little cousin dead, you wouldn't be in my home. I don't mix work with pleasure."

I exhaled, still feeling uneasy. I focused on my lovely cousin. I would do anything to keep her safe ... anything. I would never risk losing her again. "Make a deal," I whispered.

"What?" he asked.

"Strike another deal with me. Anything, in exchange for Frankie remaining safe at all times when under your roof."

"Are you really that eager to get your hands on me again, love?"

"I would do anything to keep her safe; thus, my involvement with you."

He arched a brow. "You've never asked what happens to you if you break a deal with one of us."

"Whatever it is, I'm sure it's not good. You all being demons and whatnot."

He chuckled, taking a step towards me. "Ask me what happens to you if you break a deal."

I looked at him with suspicion, realizing I was dealing with a demon prince who liked to play games. Fine, I'd play along ... for now. "What happens to me if I break your little deal, Prince of Hell?"

His smiled, reaching out, taking a curl that framed my face between his fingers, studying the loose strand. "Oh, nothing too bad. Just that your soul becomes mine."

I took a step back, realizing I had screwed myself. "What? Why did you not tell me this before I agreed the first time?"

"It was in the contract, love. It isn't my fault if you didn't stop to read the fine print."

"My cousin was dying, you inconsiderate asshole!"

He shrugged. "Not my problem. Now, would you still like to make a deal?"

I chewed on the corner of my mouth, glancing back to Frankie, who was laughing hysterically with Envy. I exhaled deeply. "Make the deal."

I seemed to have taken him off guard. He waited for a moment before nodding. "Repeat: I, Seren Lucia De Salvo, promise to attend a dinner with Prince Asmodeus Râşnov at the time of his choosing, in exchange for the safe keeping of Francesca Rose De Salvo when on his property."

I repeated the words, leaning in quickly to get the kiss over with, but he grabbed onto my arms, preventing me from moving forward.

"What?" I asked. "No kiss this time."

"No," he smiled. "A kiss is still required, but last time you about busted my lip with how hard you came at me. Can you try and be a little softer this time? I am fragile after all."

I rolled my eyes. "Big demon baby." I leaned in slower until I felt his soft, warm lips press against mine. Something chilling and exciting zapped through me at the contact. I exhaled, relaxing, feeling ... safe. He stepped into the kiss, seeming hesitant before wrapping his hand around my waist, the other gently holding my face. His thumb trailed the length of my jaw, until he finally pulled away.

I opened my eyes, greeted by a thick fog of darkness. His magic and my own, intertwining together. Shooting stars and rolling clouds of gray and blue tumbled around us. Streams of red danced and swirled throughout the darkness. It was quiet here. Quiet and peaceful. I smiled, still standing close enough to smell his lilac fragrance. His crystal eyes shimmered down at me. He slowly released my waist, taking a step back from me. The darkness faded, the sounds and sights of the other guests coming back into focus.

"Would you like to dance?" he asked, offering his hand with a slight bow. I took it, following him to the dance floor.

The crowd parted and cleared a path, their eyes locked on us. They whispered and smiled to one another. I felt myself heat with embarrassment and nervousness, looking around the floor at the strangers that were now judging every inch of my being.

"Eyes up here," he said, smiling down at me.

The music began and off we went. The melody was slow, yet transcending, as if the musicians themselves were enchanted. He held me close, placing his right hand on my lower back and his left cradling my right palm. He was elegant and graceful, as you'd expect a royal to be. His eyes never left my face. The rest of the guests joined the dance shortly after. I remained transfixed in his eyes.

"What are you thinking? And be honest," he said.

I huffed with amusement. The last time he had asked me that question, he had been wearing Orion's face. "I'm thinking I have a poor track record with men. I'm wondering what you hope to gain from seducing me. I'm wondering how I can ever trust my judgment, after all the mistakes I've made that have hurt the ones I love."

"Hmm," he said, pulling his eyes away from mine. "And I think you're too hard on yourself."

"I'm a vessel for half a dozen other women to share. What do you expect?"

He laughed. "No, love, you're just you. You have their memories, and you all share a power. That is all."

"You know how this whole thing works?" I asked, a bit surprised.

"A little. Each of the vessels have been different. You all share some of the same traits, but you all are your own individual selves."

"And you've fallen in love with each one?" I asked. His face became stern. The music faded as the guests slowed their dance.

"Walk with me," he insisted, turning away and heading for the doors. I trailed after him, desperate for the answers I knew he possessed. We exited the ballroom into a long and extravagant hall. More goldaburgs scurried around, attending to the needs of the castle.

"I'm sorry," I said. "I didn't mean to push too far."

"You have every right to ask questions. You're stuck with the memories as much as I am. What do you want to know? And before you ask, yes, I will be honest with you."

I hesitated, but if he was willing to share some insight with me, I was going to jump at the opportunity. "Were you in love with them all?"

"No. The first was Val ...Valeriana. She was the first vessel. I met her in a time of great darkness. She was the first thing I truly ever loved. But I destroyed that love with my obsession. She stabbed me in the heart when she found out what I was. Sent me back to Hell. I had to fight my way out. Not an easy thing, I will admit."

"And ... Victoria."

I watched his jaw clinch. "Victoria ... loved me completely, as I did her. But the god and goddess curse has quite a few hidden turns woven into the link between the moon goddess and the horned god. Because of that, it destroyed our love."

"What do you mean?"

He stopped, turning to face me. "I'd rather not go deeper into that memory vault." I nodded and followed him as we continued to walk.

"Your home is ... magnificent," I said, taking in all the large open windows. "Where are we?"

"You sound surprised."

"I am. I mean ... you're a prince of hell. I was expecting more, black and ... death."

"Glad I could surprise you."

"Where are we?"

"Brașov, Romania, far up in the mountains. There is a small town at the base of my lands. Generations of families have resided there for centuries, but it is a small and remote place."

"Sounds perfect."

I felt his eyes on me while I stared out the window. "Next question," he said, continuing our tour.

"Have you killed people?"

"Yes."

"Have you tortured people?"

"Yes."

"Have you ... eaten people?"

He stopped; brows furrowed as he looked down at me. "Define *eaten*." I laughed, unable to control myself. He laughed as well, sending a shocking chill through me. "No, I do not *eat* people."

"How many people have you slept with?"

"I'm the demon of Lust. Do you really think I keep count?" My cheeks blushed. "How many have you slept with?"

I bit the side of my lip. "One," I replied. I looked at his face, but there was no expression of disappointment. In fact, there was no expression at all. "Do you work for Lucifer?"

"Father, no. I can't stand that arrogant son of a bitch, or anything he is involved in. Most of our brothers feel that way. Though, over the millennia, certain brothers have changed allegiances from time to time, to serve their own needs."

"And Levi?"

"He is my favorite. The only one out of the six I truly trust."

We entered a beautiful gallery full of art and sculptures from differing eras and cultures. I twirled around, in awe of the grandeur. This place ... this was heaven. I felt the smile stretch across my face. I was happy. This place made me happy, and I didn't want to fight it. I just wanted to ... be.

I turned my eyes back to Asmodeus. His smile was soft while he watched me take in his home, as if he was enjoying my happiness. Feeding off it somehow. "Prince," I said softly.

"Yes, love."

I took a step closer to him, now able to feel his breath on my face. "What do you really want with me?" His eyes held secrets. So many secrets.

"To stop my brother from attaining your power. He is already the most powerful out of the seven of us. If he gets his hands on the power of a god, we're all fucked."

There it was. The truth. "Thank you for being honest."

He nodded. "Come. Time to return to the ball. I have my duties to uphold." He extended his arm to me.

I looped mine around his. "And what are those duties?"

"Lust, of course," he said, winking at me.

As we entered the ballroom, the party was in full swing. Everyone was laughing and gliding across the dance floor. Asmodeus pulled two glasses of wine from a passing server, handing me one. "Blood wine," he said, bringing it to his lips. I hesitated. "Don't worry. It's not actually blood. It's a wine that contains a little bit of magic. Stronger than most, but without the hangover."

Two women approached him, more scandalously dressed than even I. They drew their hands down his chest, making small moaning noises. One of them turned his face towards her and kissed him gently. I brought the wine to my lips and took a big gulp. The two women looked at me and laughed. "She's adorable," one said in a sensual tone.

"Can she join us?" the other asked.

"I don't think she's into that form of entertainment," replied Asmodeus.

One of them drew a hand down my arms, pulling me into her. "Have you ever tried?" she asked. Her entrancing, blue eyes captivated me. She had long, wavy red hair. Her skin was sun kissed and her body was sinful.

"Tried ... what?" I asked, completely naive.

She smiled, stepping in closer. Her hands trailed the sides of my body, grasping at my hips and pulling them into hers. "Multiples, of course," she said, looking back at Asmodeus and the other woman. "The prince, Tia, me," she paused, turning her eyes back to mine, "and you." I froze, not knowing how to respond.

Asmodeus laughed, pulling the woman back to him. "Come, Zion. I don't believe our guest has that kind of appetite for such delights."

"And what does our guest crave?" came a deep male voice behind me.

I turned to see the beautiful blonde male Frankie had been speaking with early. He wore a deep forest green suit. His hair was long, reaching past his shoulders. His eyes were the same shade of green as Frankie's and seemed illuminated, just like Asmodeus's. Frankie's arm was wrapped around his tightly. She was beaming.

"Hello, Envy," I said, nodding to him.

He smiled. "I prefer Levi, but hello to you too, Miss, Salvo. Nice to make your acquaintance."

Princes and their manners, I thought.

"Did you really expect us to be savages?" Asmodeus asked in my mind. I turned to him, but he just stared at his fingernails, appearing more interested in his cuticles than his brother.

I turned back to Levi and smiled. “Nice to meet you as well, prince.” He was magnificent. He reminded me of a Renaissance statue: perfectly sculpted out of marble. He had a slightly smaller frame than Asmodeus, but every inch of him was pure muscle. His nose was elegant and long. His lips were thin, but I was certain his brilliant smile made women go weak in the knees. I could have stared at it for eternity.

“*I can arrange a room for the two of you if you'd like,*” Asmodeus thought.

“*What? I can't admire your brother's looks?*” I sent back.

“*You're a free woman. Do as you please. Though, I'm sure he'd love to hear your thoughts out loud.*”

“*So sensitive, demon.*”

“*I am not.*”

“*By the looks of it, you'll be busy yourself tonight with Tweedledee and Tweedledum.*”

“*Now, that's not very nice. They were polite and offered for you to join.*”

I scoffed. “*Like I would ever.*”

He shrugged. “*Don't look your nose down at something you've never tried.*”

“What is going on here?” asked Levi, gesturing between the two of us. My eyes snapped back to his.

Frankie leaned into Levi. “They talk to each other … silently. Creepy, right?” she whispered.

Levi looked at his brother in astonishment, cocking an eyebrow. “And how did you manage to gain access to her mind, my clever brother?”

“A bargain he struck with her, for saving my life,” answered Frankie.

Levi laughed. “Wicked, wicked, prince.”

“Jealous?” asked Asmodeus, winking at his brother.

Levi looked down at Frankie and smiled. “Not tonight,” he said. She beamed up at him with ... admiration.

“Oh, for fucks sake,” I said, shaking my head. Asmodeus laughed.

“When do you plan to unleash?” Levi asked his brother.

“In a moment,” Asmodeus answered. Zion and Tia jumped up and down with joy.

“Unleash?” I asked.

“His power,” answered Levi. “Things are about to get very ... sensual.” He looked at Frankie, biting his lip.

“Excuse us,” I said, pulling her away from him and finding a quiet corner. “What are you doing?” I asked.

“I’m having fun,” she replied. “What? You’re the only one that gets a handsome prince of hell to dote after you?”

“Exactly. Prince. Of. Hell. Frankie, Stop and think.”

She ran her hands down my arms in a soothing manner. “Seren,” she spoke softly. “I am my own woman, and I am making my own choices. You only get to live once. And if I choose to sleep with a prince of hell, that is my choice. You need to let go a little, cousin. Live. We were born into this magical world the majority of the human race doesn't even know exists. Let go and just ... be."

I took a breath, trying to combat my hesitation and worry. "Okay," I replied, knowing it was impossible to try and control Frankie. "Just ... stay inside the castle. Don't go anywhere with him."

"Why?" she asked.

"I ... I made another deal with Asmodeus that you would remain safe as long as you were in his presence."

"In exchange for ...?"

"Having dinner with him ... once."

She laughed, shaking her head. "How painful for you."

We returned to the others. Frankie resumed her flirtation with Levi. I stood back and watched, trying not to kill him. Asmodeus walked to my side, looking at the two of them, huddled together, laughing.

"Having a hard time understanding her decision?" he asked.

"Very," I replied coldly.

"The bargain stands. She will remain safe while here. You have my word. Now, home you go," he said, offering his hand to me.

I turned around stunned. "What? I am not leaving her. Where she goes, I go."

"Not an option tonight, I am afraid. She may stay, but you cannot."

"Are you seriously kicking me out?"

"Only this once," he said." It's for your own good. My ... power needs to be unleashed. It's a custom of this celebration. I don't think you'll find it very comfortable."

"What happens when you unleash your power?"

"People lose the ability to control themselves. Their animalist instincts take over. Morality, reservation, hesitation no longer exists. Desire spikes. Sexual inhibitions rise. The feeling in general is heightened. Everything about the experience is ... enlightened."

"And how often do you need to release your power?" I asked, trying to make sense of it all.

"Often enough."

"And if you don't?"

"I become ... aggressive." He held out his hand again. "Off to home you go."

"But—" Before I could protest, he twirled in front of me, pulling my body into his. His arms wrapped around my torso, holding tightly. Dark mist surrounded us. He held my head against his chest firmly. I kept my eyes open, watching the static storm appear. The wind whipped up around us. Streaks of red, shot through the dark cloud. We began to spin. I closed my eyes, trying to refrain from being sick. In a flash, we were standing in my room. I remained in his embrace until the room stopped moving.

I pulled away, allowing my legs to adjust. He gently released me, stepping back. "Frankie," I whispered.

"She will be back in her room by tomorrow morning. You have my word," he said. The dark clouds began to swirl around him.

"Wait," I said, before he could leave. The fog faded. "Thank you ... for the invitation."

"You're welcome, love. Rest easy," he said, fading away into the shadows.

I undressed, wiping the paint from my face, and allowing my hair to fall loosely around my shoulders. Frankie would be safe. He gave me his word and despite my hesitation, I believed him. I went to my sweats drawer and opened it, forgetting he had burned them all to ash. Laughing to myself, I put on a pair of leggings and a long sweater before headed to the one place I shouldn't be.

I peeked inside the small window of Tony's cell. He was asleep. His face looked less bruised, and he appeared to be on the mend. I slid down the wall in front of his door and cried.

Chapter Eight

I fell asleep somewhere around six in the morning. Two hours later, I bolted down the hall to Frankie's room, desperate to lay eyes on her. I barreled through the door without knocking. She was sprawled out across the bed, still in her revealing dress. Her hair was matted to her face. I slid onto the bed, touching her to confirm she was breathing. She moaned, rolling to her back. I exhaled a sigh of relief.

"You're alive," I said, falling back against the pillow next to her.

"Am I ever," she said, laughing to herself.

I propped myself on my elbow. "Tell me everything," I insisted.

She smiled widely. "My advice, you need to take Deus for a test drive immediately. If he is anything like Levi, your mind is going to be blown."

I laughed. "You slut."

"And I'm proud of it. But seriously, I don't know how I'm ever going to have sex with anyone else every again. Nothing is going to compare."

"That good?"

"Beyond amazing," she said, sitting up. "Mind blowing. Transcending. Explosive. There aren't enough adjectives to describe what he did and how he did it. He didn't even take me until I had come from his mouth about a half dozen times."

"When did you get home?"

"Around five in the morning. The party was insane! After Deus released his power, it was like everyone lost their minds. The dancing, the alcohol, the sex. Gods, there was so much sex. People were just doing it out in the open. No one held back."

"Did you and Levi do it in the ballroom?"

"No. He said he would have been too jealous if anyone laid eyes on me, so he took me in one of the spare bedrooms."

"And did Deus ... just take whoever he wanted?"

Frankie narrowed her eyes. "Is someone jealous?"

"No. I was just asking. Never mind. I don't care."

She laughed. "He had women all over him, but I didn't stick around long enough to watch him have sex with anyone. Levi was very impatient."

I laughed to myself. "My God, if Nonna and Aunt Thora knew what we were up to, they—"

She straightened in front of me, pointing her finger in my face. "And you are not going to say a damn word ... to anyone. I've kept your secrets and you're going to keep this one for me. You're not going to ruin this. I'm not done having my fun."

I put my hands up surrender. "Aye, aye, captain. As long as you remain safe." She fell back onto the bed. I laid down next to her, finally allowing myself the much-needed sleep my body demanded.

I dreamt, for the first time in a long while. I danced among my kind. I laughed and felt light as a feather. There was no worry, no stress. I was happy. The weight I had carried for months was gone.

I woke up before Frankie. We had slept most of the day away. It was around three in the afternoon by the time I finished showering. I came out of the bathroom and was surrounded by bags of clothing: matching sweat outfits, name-brand workout attire, and piles and piles of little lacy bits for sleepwear. Everything was fashionable and picked with taste.

"Hello," I said, looking around the room, but no one was there. "I'm not wearing this," I yelled, holding up a black lace negligée.

"*A shame,*" I heard in my mind. "*Did you find your present?*"

"*Present? Aren't all these presents?*"

"*No, they're replacements. A mercy, really. You should be thanking me for burning most of your clothes.*"

I laughed, looking around the pile of bags.

"*On your nightstand,*" he whispered.

I moved to the side of my bed. A small black box with a gold bow waited for me. I opened it. Inside was a delicate, intricately cut key. A red ruby sat in the center. It hung from a long silver chain.

"*One dance, and you're already giving me a key to your place?*" I asked.

"*That was our second dance, technically. The key is so you can use my castle as an escape whenever you'd like. Hold it and just shift."*

"*But I can't shift,*" I admitted. "*Not controlled, at least.*"

"*Figure it out. I'll be your reward.*"

I smiled, shaking my head. "*Asshole.*"

"*So, you've said.*"

"*Plus, I don't like sharing,*" I admitted, thinking back to the two beautiful women draped across his body.

"*Oh?*"

"*Never mind,*" I whispered, placing the key back in the box.

"*You're supposed to wear it.*"

"*Yes, I know what a necklace is, thank you.*"

"*Now, about our dinner date ...*"

"*It's not a date ... just dinner.*"

"*Whatever you say. Are you free this evening?*"

"*No,*" *I said flatly.*

"*Tomorrow?*"

"*Nope,*" *I replied.*

"*Fine, suit yourself. I'll just take you whenever I want.*"

"*The hell you will.*"

"*You have no choice. A bargain is a bargain. Ta-ta,*" he said. I could feel him let go of the connection this time. He had been in my mind enough times that I was beginning to recognize when he was listening and when I was alone—something I would use to my advantage.

I left the room, unsure where I was going, but I knew one thing

… I was weak. I needed to begin training again. As if Aradia was listening, Orion appeared next to me with a smile on his face. He handed me a single rose. "What is this for?" I asked.

He shrugged. "I came to your room last night to give it to you, but you were gone," he replied.

"Why?" I asked, a bit taken back.

"Regardless of what is or isn't between us, I still love you, little dove. I just wanted you to have something on Valentine's Day."

"And what did you get Delphine?"

"Chocolates. A bracelet. A few records she likes. And a few other things."

"Oh?"

He laughed. "We're not ready for that part of share and tell yet. Where are you headed?"

"I was actually heading to train. I haven't really done much since Paris and I'm feeling a bit out of shape."

"Well, I'm free now if you want to work on anything."

I stopped, knowing exactly what I wanted his help with. "Shifting," I blurted. "I need help with shifting."

The next two weeks were painful. My body seemed to revolt against everything I tried to accomplish. My muscles were in constant pain from the training. Shifting was no better. I could trigger it, but I couldn't control it. There were multiple times that I ended up somewhere I didn't recognize. I had to send Orion my location so he could come and retrieve me. I fell out of the sky once, slamming into a busy crossroad. My face was scratched to hell, along with my forearms.

I fell into a pond another day. I ended up back at the castle. In a random field. High up in a tree. I was hopeless. The amount of power it took to shift was immense. I was constantly drained. Sleeping was no longer a problem.

Deus had gone silent, which I was thankful for. Though, his presence was a bit missed, if I was being honest. It was nice knowing I wasn't alone. And I did miss the gifts. After staring at the key for a solid week straight, I finally gave in and wore it. I hide the key underneath my clothes so no one would ask questions.

Orion was off today with Delphine, which meant I had time to recover, thank God. My muscles were killing me, and my power was drained. I made my way to Frankie's room to see if she wanted to do dinner. She was in the middle of reading something that looked very old.

"What's that?" I asked.

"A solution to your little mind invasion problem ... I think."

"Really? You found a way to keep him out?"

"Maybe ... If I'm reading this right. Latin and all. It's a warding technique, but you'll have to practice it."

"I'll do anything. Tell me how."

"It says here you need to push your magic up and into your mind, creating a safeguard or a wall. Depending on how strong the intruder is, your wall will need to be reinforced, by allowing parts of yourself to be woven within the wall."

"What in the hell does that mean?" I asked.

"Like I know. I'm just translating here."

"Well, thanks anyways," I said. A green puff of smoke appeared in the corner of her room. "Uh, Frankie," I said, pointing to it.

She turned and looked. A smile exploded on her mouth as she sprung up with a squeal. Before the figure fully materialized, she barreled towards the smoke, arms wide. Levi formed, just in time to catch her as she jumped into his arms. He took her mouth instantly, without a care in the world, slamming her into the nearest wall.

"Uh, still here," I said, feeling out of place.

Frankie giggled. Levi pulled away, landing his eyes on me. "Sorry, Seren," he said, his voice heavy. "Didn't see you there."

"Yeah, got that," I replied. "This is still going on?" I asked, motioning between the two of them.

"This as in ...?" Frankie said, walking back over towards me.

"Whatever *this* is," I said, aggravated.

"I can't seem to stay away," he replied, wrapping his arms around her from behind. He nuzzled his nose into her neck. She laughed again.

"I'm ... I'm gonna go," I said, pushing off the bed.

"I'll call you later," she yelled, right before he slammed her into the mattress. I closed the door, hearing echoes of their laughter sounding from her room. I couldn't believe she was still carrying on with him. She was going to get hurt. That's all there was to it, but what did I know?

I headed for the dining hall when Nonna approached me with a solemn face. "What's wrong?" I asked.

She stopped me, taking my hands in hers, her eyes heavy. "Bambina, I need to ask something of you, but if you do not feel comfortable, you absolutely do not have to do it."

"I'll do whatever you need," I replied. "What is it?"

"The Simonelli boy. I've tried to get information out of him, but he will only speak with you."

My heart dropped. I had done my damnedest to avoid his cell for weeks, ever since my breakdown on Valentine's night. I took a moment, gathering my strength before saying, "I'll do it." For Nonna.

"You are sure? It won't be too much?" she asked.

"I'm fine, Nonna ... really." A lie.

Nonna rattled off the list of questions and information she wanted me to obtain from Antonio. She had been trying to get the intel for weeks, but he was playing hard to get.

She led me to his cell and left before I entered. I took a deep breath, preparing myself to be in the same room with him. The guard unlocked the door, and I stepped in. A normal bed was now pushed up against the wall. A small table with four chairs flanked the other side. A desk, along with bookshelves, filled the space. He appeared to be making himself at home.

Tony stood slowly as I entered from behind the desk. His eyes locked onto me, as if he were seeing me for the first time. He allowed himself to smile, walking hesitantly towards me. I laced my hands together, fighting the desire to hug him, to hold him, to kiss him. "Nonna said you were playing hard to get," I said. I could hear the trembling in my own voice.

"I just wanted a reason to talk to you," he replied, stopping in front of me. "That is all. I'll give her whatever she wants. I'll tell you everything."

I finally brought my eyes to his. Pain struck me in that moment. The months of crying and mourning him. It was all too much. "I can't do this," I said, turning back towards the door. Before I could leave, he grabbed my hand, pulling me back to him. He whipped me around, now standing face to face.

"Please stay. Stay with me. Just for a little while," he begged.

Tears silently fell. "I hate you," I whispered. Pain filled his eyes. "I hate you for what you've done to me. I hate you for all of it. For lying to me, for using me, for working with my psychotic mother. I hate you for choosing them over me. For even allowing me to fall in love with you in the first place. I hate our memories. I hate the fact that I gave myself to you and that I still think about you when I'm alone. When I can't sleep, because I can't help but wonder why I wasn't enough for you. Why I couldn't be enough."

"Beautiful, I am sorry," he said, tears spilling down his cheek.

I stepped forward, backing him up. "I hate that I can't seem to move past you. That I can never have the life I wanted with you. I hate that I ever loved and still can't seem to move on. You have ruined me. I hate love and everything that comes with it, because of you. You have robbed me of the most beautiful connection two people could ever have!"

He continued to cry.

"I wish you never would have come to the abbey that day," I continued. "I wish you would have let those demon hounds tear me apart, because it would have been better than this. Better than living every day with the memories of a happiness I'm unsure was even real."

"Everything was real. I swear it," he sobbed.

"Nothing was true. You had an agenda the entire time. You knew what my mother wanted from me, and you allowed her to believe you could deliver me to her on a silver platter. I hate everything about us ... everything about you ... everything I am because of you!" The rage inside of me grew. I was coming undone. If I didn't leave now, I was going to set this room on fire and him along with it.

I felt trapped like a bird in a cage.

I need to escape.

I needed quiet.

I needed to be freed.

In a hazy fog, a zapping sensation ran through my body. My limbs felt like they were being ripped apart. Black mist surrounded me. My white fire fought to escape. Ice began to form along my fingers as I shifted between time and space, unsure of my destination.

Bam. My feet slammed into something hard. A floor or a surface, I was unsure. My power billowed inside of me. The white, icy fire licked around, fighting to be freed. Before the darkness faded, I unleashed, giving into my baser need.

I screamed with rage, allowing everything I had bottled up to explode from within. My fire burned so bright and hot I watched as it began to form into ice. Something was containing me and my flame, but I didn't care. I let the power escape. My body was trembling, and my mind felt frantic, but I kept pushing. Ice encased me reaching high into the air, forming a large oval.

My power finally let go, sending me to my knees. I cried, feeling empty and numb. I was trembling from the excessive use of power. Beads of sweat trailed along my skin. My heart felt like it was going to explode out of my chest. My throat felt dry and constricted. My eyes, still filled with tears, blinked slowly, trying to clear away the hazy film that obstructed my vision.

A shadow of a figure was on the other side of my ice cocoon. The ice began to disappear: not melt, but disappear entirely. Unable to keep my eyes open a moment longer, I fell into a deep sleep.

Chapter Nine

My hands flexed as I came to. My fingers slid over a smooth, silky fabric. I smiled, nuzzling my face into the pillow. I rolled on my back and stretched, feeling like I had been sleeping on a cloud. I opened my eyes, greeted by an oval-domed ceiling. The top was made entirely of glass, sunlight softly peeping through. I sat up, looking around me, unsure where I had shifted.

I was in an oversized bed, the largest I had ever seen, made of deep mahogany. The headboard was tall and masculine. Red silk sheets draped across my body. The room was tall, stretching at least fifty feet in the air. The large, open space held a desk, table, seating area, and a few dressers scattered throughout. Circular stairs led to a second and third landing. Intricate wood carvings made up the spindles of the banister.

The walls were the same deep mahogany wood as the bed, but filled with books all the way to the ceiling. The lighting was soft and subtle. Artwork, statues, and instruments filled the open space. This was truly the grandest room I had every laid eyes on. Still, the question remained ... where was I?

The large carved wooden door opened, revealing a goldaburg

...Gallo. He carried a steaming tray and made little grunting noises as he waddled over to me. He was barely taller than the nightstand where he placed the tray and removed the plate cover, pouring me a cup of coffee. Two poached eggs sat in fancy little stemmed cups. Two slices of toast. A beautiful array of fruit, and two pieces of bacon.

Gallo nodded. "Master says eat," he said in his scratchy voice. "He will be with you shortly." He waddled off, back through the doorway. Master? Gallo?

I slammed my hands over my face. I was in Deus's house ... in his room ... in his— I paused, taking another look at the bed. Oh, my God. I didn't sleep with him ... did I?"

I heard a laugh in the back of my mind. "*Calm yourself,*" he whispered in my mind. "*I was a complete gentleman. We didn't even snuggle.*"

"*You slept with me?*" I yelled down the line.

"*It's my bed. Where else would I sleep? You snore, by the way.*"

"*You could have put me in a guest room.*"

"*Now, why would I do that?*" I rolled my eyes. "*I felt that. Eat up. I'll see you soon.*"

I looked at the plate, feeling the hunger twist in my stomach. I picked up the coffee first, adding some cream and a sugar cube. The aroma was heavenly. And the taste ... oh, my God, the taste was even better. I had never had something so smooth and flavorful. The rest of the food was just as delightful. I cleaned my plate, laying back on the bed with a full belly. The food pulled me under, sending me back into a soft sleep.

I felt a tickling sensation along my wrist. My skin rose into goose-flesh in response. I moaned, extending the rest of my arm out to the source of pleasure. I nuzzled my cold nose further into the pillow, not wanting to wake from my peaceful slumber. The tickling sensation continued, traveling up my arm to my shoulder. I arched my neck back, enjoying the feeling. The pleasure continued to my chest, tracing along my collar bone before trailing back up to my neck and then my face.

I parted my lips. My breathing became heavy. I felt the light touches along my jaw before it traced the outside of my lips. The sensation was electric. I felt myself smiling as I bit my lip in response. I heard a soft low laugh coming from nearby.

"Stay out of my dreams," I thought, sending it to Deus, before returning my attention to the pleasurable sensation.

"But I'd make all your dreams come true," he replied.

"Doubtful." The feeling returned to my lips. I moaned again.

"Do you like this?" he asked.

"*You're ruining it. Stay out of my dreams.*" I demanded.

I felt a warm breath along my earlobe. "This isn't a dream, love," he whispered.

My eyes flew open. I sat straight up. He pulled away, laughing. He rested with his back against the headboard, arms folded across his chest. I pulled the sheets up to my neck, feeling exposed. I quickly scanned his body, trying not to stare too long. He wore a black t-shirt with black silk pants.

"You're cute when you sleep," he said, winking at me.

"How long have you been here?"

He shrugged. "Thirty minutes or so."

I scoffed. "Creeper."

"My bed, my rules."

"Why am I here?" I asked, trying to make sense of it all.

"I was hoping you could tell me." He turned his body towards me, resting his head on his propped elbow. "I was at my desk last night, reading, and then all the sudden you slammed into my room, attempting to burn the whole castle to the ground. Do you know how old this place is? You would have incinerated a piece of history."

It all started to flood back. "But I ... I can't control my shifting, and I don't even know where this place is. I've never even seen the outside."

"But you know what I look like. And you were wearing the key I gave you. It must have acted as an anchor. Regardless, you came in hot. I was able to contain your flame before you torched my room. Our powers mixing created a little ice igloo. Once I knew you were done being dramatic, I let you out, but you were unconscious. So, I carried you to bed and let you sleep."

I ran my hands through my hair. "I'm ... I'm so sorry," I said. "I didn't mean to bring you into all my ... issues." I thought of Tony and what happened before I lost my mind. All the things I had said. His face and how he had cried. God, I felt awful and relieved and free, all at the same time. I looked up at Deus. He studied me silently.

"Aren't you going to ask me what happened?" I asked.

"If you want to tell me, you can. I'm not going to push."

"You could just look in my head and see anyways."

"I could, but believe it or not, I don't sift through your personal memories. I have better things to do."

"Like plan dances and read books?" I asked.

"Exactly. But I do ask that you try and refrain from burning anything in this specific room, if you could."

"I can do that."

He smiled, standing from the bed. "The washroom is that way," he said, pointing to two stained-glass doors. "I've placed a change of clothes in there for you. When you're ready, I'll take you home."

I froze. Home. Orion and Delphine. Antonio. The war. Obsidian. That was all at home. Here ... here there was nothing. There was quiet. I needed quiet right now. My mind was spinning, but the sheer thought of home sent me spiraling into a panic attack.

I shouldn't. I couldn't. No, this wasn't right. He was a demon. A very polite demon, as Frankie liked to point out, but I couldn't trust him.

I just needed a few days, that was all. Just to gather my thoughts and emotions. I was no good to anyone this messed up. If I could just work to center myself, maybe I could actually be useful for a change, instead of always screwing everything up.

"Deus," I said softly.

"Yes?"

"Would you mind if I ... if I stay here for a while? I just ... I need a break. I'll take one of the other rooms. You won't even know I'm here."

He paused, a small, devious smile stretching across his face. "You are welcome to stay as long as you would like, Seren De Salvo. But unfortunately, we do not have any spare rooms prepared, so you will stay here ... with me."

"I can sleep on the couch."

"And ruin my Italian leather? I think not. The bed is big enough for five people." He turned and headed for the door. "Shower," he called back without turning. "I will send someone to fetch you when you are finished." The door shut, leaving me alone, in the Prince of Lust's private bedroom.

I showered, feeling like I had just cleaned the weight of the year from my skin. After dressing into a pair of leather leggings and a red sweater that fell off my shoulders, I sat in front of the fireplace. I needed to tell my family I was okay. I didn't want them to worry. Realizing I didn't have my cellphone on me, I held a hand mirror I had taken with me from the bathroom. I wrote on a piece of parchment, instructing Frankie to find the nearest reflective surface and repeat this spell. I was taking a page from Antonio's book. I set the paper on fire and sent it to her.

Within ten minutes, I felt the mirror pulse in my hand. I took a breath, holding it up in front of me. I repeated the spell and Frankie's beautiful face appeared. "Oh, thank Aradia," she exclaimed. "What in the hell happened? I was about to light Tony's balls on fire."

"I ... I shifted accidently," I admitted.

"Where are you? We'll send Orion to come get you," she said.

"No," I said too quickly. "No, I'm fine. I'm ... I'm where I need to be for now."

"What are you talking about, Seren? You belong here, with us."

"It's not forever. I'm just ... I'm out of control. I can't contain my powers. My mind is in shambles half the time with all the other vessel's memories floating around. My emotions are up and down. I just need some time to get myself together. Once I am, I will return home, and we'll destroy Obsidian once and for all. But right now, I'm no good to anyone the way I am."

"Why haven't you told me any of this? I would have helped you. I feel awful," she said. I could hear the guilt in her voice.

"There's nothing you could have done for me. I need to do this on my own. And I'm only a reflection away. I'll write you every day, and we can talk through here until I come home."

"But you are coming home ... right?" she asked.

"Yes."

"You promise?"

"I promise."

"Will you at least tell me where you are?"

"I can't. But I'm safe ... I think."

"You think? You're not making me feel any better," she said.

"I'll be fine, Frankie. Just tell Nonna I'm sorry, and I love her. Tell your mom the same. Tell them I'm okay. I love you, Frankie."

"I love you too, Seren." She blew a kiss before fading into the darkness.

My reflection stared back at me. A moment later, a knock came at the door. I slid on the knee-high black leather boots and went to answer it. A stunning woman with bright red hair and deep chocolate eyes stood on the other side. She was tall and lean, with a full chest, thin waist, and a sinful pair of lips.

"Lady Salvo?"

"Please, call me Seren," I said.

"Seren," she said with a bow. "It is a pleasure to meet you. I am Malphasia, but you may call me Mal for short. Prince Râșnov requested I share more of the grounds with you. Shall we?" she said, gesturing to hall.

I followed her, closing the door behind me. "Do you live here?" I asked, trying to be polite.

"Most of the time, yes," she answered.

"Are you one of De- Prince Râşnov's ... female companions?" I asked, unsure of what to call them.

She laughed. Something like a chill ran through me at the sound. Every nerve ending in my body yelled danger at the sound. "No. I work for him. I am his assassin."

"So, you kill people?" I asked to clarify.

"Among other things, yes."

For a moment, I almost forgot where I was and what he was. "Are you a demon as well?" I asked.

"I am." I looked at her. Like, really looked at her. She was perfect and alluring and sensual. Everything the nuns used to tell me sin was. If I could paint sin, it would be her ... or Deus, for that matter. "Is that a problem?" she asked.

"No, no. I'm sorry for staring. I just ... I'm used to the types of demons that are hideous and repulsive. Not the kind of demons you want to crawl into bed with."

She huffed another laugh. "Yes, I've seen Lucifer's demons. Not nearly as appealing. And thank you for the compliment. I wouldn't mind crawling in bed with you either." She continued forward. I opened my mouth to respond, but could think of nothing to say.

She gave me a tour of the castle. Room after room held hidden treasures and beauty. The kitchen was massive, updated with the newest appliances and cookware. There was a training facility that made the one back home look like a joke, with shelves of weapons ranging across time periods, and firearms and bullets: as many as you could ever possibly need. She showed me the residential quarters, where any, including herself, whom Deus allowed to live under his roof stayed. He didn't have a spare room available for me, my culo.

We passed a few libraries and a sewing room. Another area of the castle was meant for more political matters. She then brought me out to the grounds. Magnificent horses of every breed and size were kept inside an enormous stable. "Prince Râşnov has given the order that you may ride anytime you'd like," she said.

"Oh, that's okay. I've never ridden a horse," I admitted.

His garage was next, which contained a sickening collection of cars. Collector cars, limited editions, trucks, convertibles, luxury vehicles: you name it, he had it. "Where does all the money come from?" I asked Mal.

"The prince has made profitable deals over the centuries. He invests, owns businesses, and pursues ... other means of financial stability. He is very knowledgeable when it comes to politics as well."

"So, it's a lot like the covens and how they conduct business."

"You could say that," she said, leading me back into the castle.

"Are there others like you that works for him?"

Her eyes turned towards me as we stopped in front of a beautiful window overlooking the grounds. "Topside, yes. Bottomside, yes, but they aren't so pretty."

"What do you mean?" I asked.

"He has an army of loyal demons, daki, which are upper ranking demons like myself, along with a large amount of lower ranked demons, enmu, ready to serve him here, on earth. But in hell ... he commands legions. His castle there is not like this one. There, you will face the horrors I am sure you have heard of."

"So ... he's a monster?" I asked.

"He's a prince of hell. He does what he must. But he is honorable to those he chooses. I chose to serve Asmodeus of my own free will. So did the others loyal to him. He is a monster in the most glorious of ways." I smiled at her, unsure of what else to say. "Here is where I leave you. You are free to roam as you please, but the prince has asked that you not go into the dungeons below the castle."

"Why?"

"He has captured and is interrogating some of Lucifer's demons. The prince does not want your presence here to be discovered by the Morning Star. It is for your safety."

I nodded. "Thank you for the tour," I said.

"Of course." She turned and left.

I found the kitchen, filling a cup with more coffee and continued to explore. I walked down each hall twice, trying to remember the layout of this maze. I found my way to the ballroom, where the throne still perched on its platform. I stood before it, looking at the handprints I now knew Victoria had left in the metal. I reached out, against my better judgment, and touched them.

A memory flooded to the surface. I was crying. Deus was in front of me, his face wracked with guilt.

"You can't do this," I cried. "You can't sell yourself for me. I won't let you."

"This is my fault, love," he said, reaching for her. "I should have never interfered. I should have stayed away. After Val, I should have known better ... but I ... I couldn't."

I wrapped my arms around him, crying profusely. "I don't care what happens. I won't leave you. I won't let him take you."

"The deal is already sealed. Tomorrow, I am his until you awake again."

"No!" I screamed. I could feel the panic and rage ripping through me. "I won't let you! I won't let you! He will torture you. He will kill everything good inside of you. He hates you the most."

"I know, baby, but it's done. You and Samual will live. Your families will be safe," he said, running his hand down my face.

"This is my fault," I cried. "If I just would have slept with Samual. If I would have completed the rite. I should have listened to myself."

"It's okay," he said softly. "You did what you thought was right. Now, kiss me." He took my face, and pressed his lips against mine in the most passionate and all-consuming kiss I could have ever

imagined. He pulled away slowly, tears rolling down his face. "Now, close your eyes, my love."

"No," I cried, my body now shaking. "Please, Deus. Please don't leave me."

"I will always be with you. Forever and eternity." He pressed his lips against mine one last time. The world began to spin. My mind blurred as I held onto him with desperation. Bright lights flooded my mind in strobing flashes of color, like flashes of shooting stars. Every memory of him and me: every touch, every laugh, every kiss. Then ... a blinding white light, fading away slowly as I opened my eyes.

In front of me stood a man I had never seen before. He was handsome, yet something dark roamed underneath is skin. His face was wet from tears, and he was holding me against him. I pushed away, uncertain of who he was.

"Where am I? What's going on?" I asked.

The dark-haired man wiped his face, placing his hands in his pockets and smiled. "Let's get you home," he whispered.

He held out his hand and I took it. In a dark haze, I was standing in front of my house. Samual was there with a panicked look on his face. As soon as the dark fog faded, I let go of the man, taking off towards the one my heart loved. I jumped into his arms as he kissed me profusely.

"Thank the gods," Samual said, searching my face for any signs of injury. "We've been worried sick. Where have you been?"

"I ... I don't know," I answered. Samual pulled me into him,

holding me closely. I looked back at the mysterious man. He stood in the fog, his hands still in his pockets, just staring. I could still make out the tears on his face. He dropped his head, evaporating into the night.

I snapped back into reality, pulling my hand from the throne immediately. I dropped to my knees, still feeling Victoria's pain and anger. I cried for a woman I didn't know; for a love that wasn't mine. Something inside of me lit to life. The need to be near him. The need to hold him and wipe away his tears. To make him happy, to make him whole.

I took off down the hall, in search of him. In search of Deus. I looked in every room I passed, but I couldn't find him. I threw open the doors to his bedroom. There he was, sitting on the other side of his desk, hunched over a book. His head rose, making eye contact with me. Without thinking I ran towards him. He stood up with a confused look on his face. I rushed forward, throwing my arms around him and pulling his lips down to mine.

He inhaled sharply, wrapping his arms around my waist, pulling me close, succumbing to the desire I felt. I moved my lips, running my hands through his hair and down his smooth skin. It was like muscle memory. He picked me up, slamming me onto the desk. He pushed everything from the surface, making room for me as he leaned over, pressing his body fully into mine. His lips traced from my mouth down to my neck. I moaned with pleasure as he nipped and licked every inch.

His hands slid up my thighs and under my sweater. The moment they made contact with my bare skin, I wanted to erupt. Darkness flooded the room. Constellations and stars filled the air above us while small streaks of red swirls danced within my magic. He licked the surface of my stomach, tracing his tongue along my pant line. I needed him. I needed his mouth on mine. Now.

I sat up, pulling his face back into me. Frantically, our hands couldn't cover enough of each other. He gripped the back of my head, fisting my hair with his fingers and pulling with force. I let out a cry as he sunk his teeth into my neck. Heat pooled between my legs. He moved his lips back to mine. His tongue plunged deep inside my mouth while his free hand fought to unbutton my pants.

He suddenly pulled away, taking a breath. I instantly mourned the taste of him. His eyes met mine. They were the color of a red sapphire. Brilliantly sparkling and shining as the stars around us stretched across the darkness.

He let go of me, stumbling backwards. "Get out," he said in a deep and haunting tone.

I shook my head. "What?" I asked.

"Get out!" he yelled. The room rumbled as he unleashed his power. He turned to me, and I no longer recognized the Deus I knew. Something dark and demonic had taken over. His handsome face shifted, revealing the demon I feared him to be. Something frightening and unnatural. The bedroom doors blew open, slamming against the wall. Without another word, I took off in fear. I ran down the halls, not know where to go or where I was headed. All I knew was that I was afraid.

I ran until I was outside. I needed to find somewhere safe, somewhere to hide. I headed into the snow, not thinking my plan through. I ran and ran, until the cold wind burned my lungs, and my body begged me to stop. I had entered the woods near the castle. I stumbled across a cave and prayed nothing was hiding inside before I entered. I pressed my back along the sharp wall of the rocks and huddled down inside.

I was already freezing. My body trembled. Even with the goddess's power and my cooler-than-normal body temperature, I could feel the frostbite beginning to set in. I still couldn't make sense of what had just happened. What I had allowed to happen. Why had he acted that way? What did I do wrong? I watched the opening of the cave as the sun set. I lit a fire with my magic, desperate for any type of warmth.

"*I'm sorry,*" I heard him say in my mind. "*I didn't mean to frighten you. There is just so much that you still don't know. Please come back. It's getting late.*" I ignored him, laying down next to the fire. I pushed my magic outward, protecting myself from the demon. I built a wall full of my pain and fear, imagining myself weaving it by hand. Every painful thing I had endured. Everything I had lost was now a part of what would protect me. I closed my eyes, still shivering.

A few hours must have passed, for when I opened my eyes all the daylight was gone, and the temperature was unbearable. I tried to push myself up, but I was too cold. My limbs felt numb. I crawled closer to the fire, trying to stay warm. I curled up as close as I could manage. My eyes were heavy, and all my body seemed to want to do was sleep.

My skin was warm, but my body still shivered from the cold. I opened my eyes, taking in the familiar glass-domed ceiling and mahogany wood of Deus's bedroom. I tried to sit up, but I was too weak.

"Here," his sensual voice said. "Drink this."

I turned as much I could manage and saw Deus's face, back to its normal state. He was holding a teacup. I nodded, allowing him to bring the sustenance to my lips. I sipped slowly, the warmth of the amber liquid defrosting my insides. He pulled the cup away, placing it on the nightstand next to me.

I stared at him for a long while, not sure what to say. He had scared the living shit out of me. I also felt embarrassment. In the most passionate moment, possibly of my entire life, he had denied me. Rejected me. Yelled at me to get out.

He held his head. "I didn't mean to embarrass you," he whispered.

My eyes widened. "Get out of my head," I tried to yell, but my voice was hoarse.

"Will you please allow me to explain?"

"Do I have a choice?"

"You always have a choice with me. Always." I stared at him, then finally nodded my consent. "What ... what caused you to react in that manner when you found me yesterday?"

I paused, thinking back to the feelings that got me into this mess. "I relived one of Victoria's memories. The memory where—" I froze, finally piecing it all together. "Where you took hers away. Where you erased yourself from her mind." He reeled back. "What happened?"

He stood from the chair. "I'm not ready to talk about that part of my life with you. I'm sorry, but I can't," he said. His face was cold and more unfeeling than I had ever seen. "But I can tell you this: what you want ... what you desire, I can't give you."

"And what is it you think I want?"

He looked back at me with heavy eyes. "Someone who is devoted ... who loves you. Seren, that part of myself died along with Victoria all those years ago. I had that with her, and I am certain I never want that again. When you kissed me, I won't deny there was something there. It would have been easy for me to take you on that very desk," he paused, looking over at the wooden surface. "But that wouldn't have been fair ... for either of us."

I nodded, knowing what he said was true. "For what it's worth: whatever happened between you and Victoria, I felt her pain ... and I'm sorry for the suffering you both endured," I said.

"Thank you. Get some rest. Call if you need anything," he said before leaving the room.

That night I drifted in and out of sleep, hoping he would return, but he never did. Above me, the moon and stars traveled across the sky. My feelings were a mess. I felt ashamed—like I had looked in on a private moment between two people who loved each other more passionately, more intimately, than I could understand. Their love made what Tony and I had shared look like child's play. But at the same time, their memories were stuck in my head.

Early the next morning before the sun rose, I got out of bed, sliding on a pair of slippers. I climbed the stairs to the third-floor balcony where two stained-glass doors stood. I pushed them open and stepped onto the terrace. It was snowing softly as the sun rose just across the horizon. Rows of snowcapped mountains and pine trees littered the landscape. The clouds were full of yellows and reds, reaching as far as the eye could see. It was the most beautiful thing I had ever seen.

I closed my eyes, feeling the small flakes of winter landing on my skin. I stretched my hands up to the sky and twirled around in circles, over and over again until the world began to tilt. I focused on my feelings. Tried to feel something ... anything, but everything inside of me had gone numb ... utterly silent. I opened my eyes to a figure leaning against the doorframe. My breath caught in my chest. Deus.

I stopped spinning, feeling foolish. I didn't know what to say or do, so I just stood there, doe-eyed. He was smiling softly with a blanket draped over his arm. He stepped onto the terrace, slowly closing the distance in between us. Once he was in front of me, he wrapped the warm fabric around my shoulders.

"And here I thought you would have had enough of the cold," he said, looking down at me with those entrancing blue eyes.

"It was just so beautiful, I couldn't resist," I said, forcing myself to turn away towards the rising sun.

"It is, isn't it?" he said, standing next to me.

I was so nervous with him there, I couldn't stop fidgeting. Finally, unable to take the awkwardness anymore, I turned to him. "I am so sorry," I said frantically. "I didn't ask for these memories. And I feel so invasive even having them or repeating them out loud. Especially, because you've been nothing but kind and generous towards me. I never wanted to make you feel uncomfortable. And about yesterday. I am sorry for kissing you like that, but I—" I stopped myself before I admitted the truth.

He watched me carefully, taking a step closer. "You what, Seren?"

I swallowed, dropping my eyes from his. "Nothing," I whispered.

Once the sun was high in the sky, I followed him back into the room, descending the rows of stairs until we reached the main level. He looked at me, half frozen with my hair damp from the snow. "I've filled the closet with clothes in your size," he said. "Feel free to come and go as you please."

"Are you working today?" I asked.

"Always," he said, with a half-smile. "Call if you need anything." I nodded and then he left the room.

Something in my heart tightened. He was mad at me or had lost interest. Whichever it was, I desperately missed the flirtatious Deus from before I had overstepped the boundaries of our arrangement. Leave it to me to screw up another friendship. Maybe I was destined to be alone. That way, I couldn't hurt anyone else.

My emotions were a mess. And my mind ... God, my mind was a war zone. I held my head, willing them to shut up. To be silent just for a damn moment so I could think on my own. So I could hear my own thoughts, my own voice for once, but the silence never came. I was going mad. I couldn't do this anymore, nor did I want to. Aradia had made a mistaken when choosing me to be her vessel. Maybe letting her kill me during the rite would have been the right thing to do.

I dressed in a pair of black pants and a black sweater and headed into town, desperate for a distraction. The people were jovial and full of life. I wondered if they knew their town sat at the base of castle occupied by a prince of hell. If they did, they didn't seem to care. I exited the wall that encased the small village and headed back into the wilderness. After almost freezing to death, the cold didn't affect me as it once did. I didn't understand it, but something inside of me craved its stillness. I found an open clearing near a steep cliff and laid down in the snow.

I looked up at the sky, losing track of time. The sun traveled across the sphere, beginning to set in the distance. Everything was so quiet here. My mind began to turn. I closed my eyes, allowing my emotions to escape. I thought about the 'what ifs' in my life. What if I was still in Montecassino? Would I be dead by now? What if my mother had succeeded and Orion had never come for me? What if I had chosen the life with Antonio that Aradia had presented?

What if ... what if I never went home? Would my family be safer for it? My mother would never stop hunting me. But if I ended it ... Tears fell down my cheeks. Maybe that was the answer to all of this. Every other vessel had died in some horrible or tragic way. Maybe that was my destiny. I was a liability alive. If my mother or Lucifer got their hands on my power, it would be the end of our covens. But if I died, it would all be over. Aradia was right ... I needed to die.

I sat up, looking at the edge of the cliff. The wind licked at my face, freezing the tears as they fell. God, I wanted this to be over. I wanted this to end. I didn't want to disappoint another person or watch someone else die or be in pain because of me. I stood, removing my gloves, hat, and coat. I placed them neatly in a pile. The cold burned my skin, but I no longer cared. It would all be over soon.

I thought of Frankie, wishing I could speak to her one last time as I stepped closer to the edge. I thought of Nonna and how grateful I was to have spent time with her. I thought of Aunt Thora, admiring the mother she was. My toes now hovered over the edge of the cliff. I looked down, unable to see the bottom. That was good. The impact would be powerful enough that I wouldn't feel a thing.

I held out my arms, taking in a deep breath as I looked up to the sky. "God," I cried, "If you are real ... if you are really up there. Please forgive me. Please understand. I didn't ask for any of this. And I hope ... I hope by ending this, that you will take mercy on me and see my sacrifice as something good. I'm ridding your world of an evil that should have never been born." I took in a deep breath, closing my eyes. "Please forgive me," I whispered, allowing the weight of my body to pull me forward.

My stomach dropped as I went tumbling off the edge. I sucked in air to scream, but my voice was mute. I kept my eyes closed, hurtling to the ground, waiting for the impact that would end it all. Suddenly, a warm, hard form slammed into me. His arms wrapped around me as the black tendrils around us swarmed, pulling us through space before slamming me to the ground of

Deus's bedroom.

I scurried back, taking in a deep breath. My heart pounded in my chest in panic and my body still felt like it was falling. I began coughing, trying to regain my balance. Deus stood and began pacing back and forth in front of me. He ran his hands through his hair. His face was stricken with stress. His chest rose and fell. He was trying to calm himself.

"What was that?" he asked harshly. "Why would you throw yourself off a cliff, Seren? How reckless and cowardly are you?"

I sat against the foot of his bed on the floor, trying to contain my emotions, but I couldn't. I began crying, feeling like the failure I was. I covered my face, trying to hide my pathetic weakness from him, but my body trembled. Lost in my own darkness, I barely felt him take me into his arms, lifting me from the ground and into his lap. He held me closely against his chest as I sobbed. He stroked my hair, curling my body against his.

I didn't know how long I was wrapped in his arms. At some point, I drifted off to sleep, drowning in my own depression. When I woke, we were in his bed. His arms were still tightly secured around me. There was nothing sexual; he was like my lifeline: something stable and tangible I could hold onto as I fought for a reason to live.

I unwound myself from his embrace, careful not to wake him. I took a warm shower and then stared at myself in the mirror. Who was I? Everyone told me that after the rite I would still be me, but I didn't feel like myself. I didn't know who I was anymore. How did they all get through this? How did the ones before me survive?

I dressed and returned to the bedroom, my hair still wet and dripping. Deus was up, sitting at the table that was now filled with breakfast foods. He stood as I approached and smiled softly.

"Morning," I whispered.

"Good morning. Would you like some breakfast?" he asked.

"Coffee would be nice," I said, moving to the chair across from him. He filled my plate and sat it in front of me, but I didn't have an appetite. I sipped on the coffee, staring at the design of his large, decorative carpet. I wondered how old it was and where it came from. I heard him put his fork down. He scooted his chair towards me, leaning over his knees, bringing his face closer to mine.

"Why, Seren?" he said softly.

"Why not?" I whispered. "Give me one good reason why I should remain alive. I'm doing no one any good by breathing. If I were dead, at least Obsidian would stop and the people I love would be safe."

"That isn't true."

"Isn't it? All I've done is make a mess of everything. I've failed at the one single job I was born to do: to fall in love with Orion. To complete the rite and usher in the enlightenment for our covens. Instead, I gave my heart to a traitor. I was born to a woman who wants me dead. I've gotten my friends killed. I've disappointed my Nonna, and I can't control these fucking powers. I am a walking liability. If I am dead, it all stops. Orion can marry Delphine. Frankie can take her rightful place by her mother's side, and Obsidian fails. If I am dead, they can't harvest my power. Everyone wins."

He took my hand, brushing his thumb along the back. "If you die, Frankie loses her soulmate. Your Nonna would die of a broken heart. Your aunt would lose control of her family and her coven along with it. Your mother would exploit their time of grief and destroy the covens when they would be at their weakest. Obsidian wins if you die. Your mother wins."

I looked at him, my eyes becoming heavy. "I just need it all to stop," I explained. "I need it all to just go away. I don't know why I was picked for this. I'm not strong like the others. I've tried, but I am weak."

"You're not weak. You've already overcome so much in such a short time. Believe it or not, all the vessels have gone through something similar: learning how to divide memories from reality. You aren't alone in this. I'm not going to say it won't be hard, but it is possible. Seren, if you give up ... if you stop fighting, everything your family has fought for—fought to protect—dies along with you."

"You don't know that," I said.

"I do. Plus, if you die, who would I flirt with?"

A small smile tugged at the corner of my lips, but I fought it. "You're the demon of Lust. I'm sure you'd figure something out."

"Don't hold it back ... the urge to smile," he said. "You're beautiful when you smile."

"Snoop," I whispered.

"Always," he replied, pulling me from my chair as he stood. He snapped his fingers, and a song began to play from the record player. He took me in his arms softly, moving us across the room. He brushed his knuckles down the side of my cheek tenderly. My eyes locked onto his, holding on to the spark of life he represented.

"I'm sorry for the way I spoke to you," he said. "I was wrong. I've been wrong a lot the past few days."

"No, I was wrong. The way I threw myself at you was embarrassing."

He shrugged. "What can I say, demon of Lust and all." I smiled, enjoying the silence as we danced.

When the song ended, he pulled away and returned to the table. He picked up a black leather-bound book and handed it to me.

"What is this?" I asked.

"Open it." I did as he instructed. There was a schedule inside. It read:

- *5:00 A.M.: Wake up.*
- *5:30 A.M.: Eat breakfast and journal.*
- *6:00 A.M.: Mind weaving with Hashen*
- *9:00 A.M.: Meditation*
- *10:00 A.M.: Power training with Deus*

- *1:00 P.M.: Lunch*
- *2:00 P.M.: Meditation and journaling*
- *3:00 P.M.: Physical training with Mal*
- *6:00 P.M.: Dinner*
- *7:00 P.M.: Educational reading*
- *9:00 P.M.: Bed*

"Is this a bootcamp schedule?" I asked.

"No, it's to help you heal," he said, kneeling before me as I sat on the edge of the bed. "I want you to be happy, Seren. I want you to find your happiness."

"I don't think I'm meant to be happy."

"And why do you say that?"

"I was created for a purpose. My future has never been my own. My path was never mine to choose. I'm a vessel. A place to store power. An object." I looked back at him, feeling the weight of my honesty leaving my body in a wave of relief. "Objects don't get happy-ever-afters. Once their purpose is fulfilled, they get put on a shelf as a reminder, or thrown away. I'm a thing, Asmodeus. Not a person. Just ... a thing."

Cautiously, he placed a lose curl behind my ear that had fallen. "I've known your kind over many millennia and lifetimes. Each life has been different. They each have chosen differently. I've watched as the vessels have experienced happiness, sadness, hatred, sorrow: all while fulfilling their purpose as the moon goddess and as their individual selves. You are not an object, Seren De Salvo. You are a being, who possesses a soul. Who can think for herself. And who can choose her own path in life."

I began laughing. I covered my mouth, trying not to be rude.

"And what is so funny?" he asked.

I looked up at him, noting the smile that had reached his eyes. "My life must be pretty messed up if I'm taking life advice from a demon."

"Well, this demon has been around quite a long time. I'd like to think myself knowledgeable on a plethora of subjects," he replied.

I nodded, holding the journal against my chest. "You make it very hard not to like you," I admitted.

"Good," he said, rising to his feet and pulling me along with him. "Now, Mal informed me you were interested in the horses and didn't know how to ride. Why don't we spend the day teaching you. What do you say?"

"You have time?"

"For you ... always," he said, pulling me into him as we faded into the darkness, reappearing at the stables. He handed me a jacket and gloves. A stable boy brought out a beautiful white horse. I couldn't help but smile at the magnificent beast.

"She's beautiful," I said, running my hand along her neck.

"She reminded me of you," he replied, helping me into my saddle. As he mounted his black steed, the doors to the stable opened, and before me appeared an endless world of possibilities.

Chapter Ten

I stuck to the plan. For the next seven weeks, I did nothing but heal. Hashen was a daki demon who was a master at mind weaving. He could enter the mind of anyone who he made physical contact with and rearrange, replace, or destroy any memory he chose. He also had the ability to completely shatter a person's psyche. He was frightening and possibly the largest individual I had ever laid eyes on. He had rich brown skin, with dreads that came to the middle of his back. His eyes were a golden yellow. And his muscles ... This guy looked like he could toss a truck.

He was calm and patient, but didn't take any crap. He taught me how to divide the different memories of the other vessels. I was able to compartmentalize each one, sorting through every memory that I had access to. In my mind, I created rows of filing cabinets for each woman. When a memory surfaced, I would observe and listen. Then, when I was certain I knew who the memory belonged to, I would file it away in their color-coordinated cabinet. I spent hours with Hashen, traveling through each memory. Because he was a weaver, he was able to enter my mind and stand beside me, offering guidance during the process.

He explained his gift to me, and the risks it could pose. A mind weaver could slip into another's mind, walking beside them in a memory. If left there too long or if the visitor went too deep, they could potentially go mad or even die. The gift also took an incredible amount of power and life force. If pushed too far, the weaver could kill themselves.

I meditated and journaled twice a day, sometimes more. This helped center me. It was a way of releasing all my anxiety and the things I worried about. I started to regain control of myself. By writing my inner fears down, I noticed patterns of thoughts and trigger points that had taken away my peace or caused me undue stress. It helped me begin to sort through my own issues and discover new connections and explanations for why I felt or reacted in certain ways.

Mal was a badass from hell ... literally. I had never seen someone move and strike like she did. She began to teach me different fighting styles like krav maga, sambo, and judo. She also taught me how to work through pain. How to channel it and control it, instead of allowing it to control me. I began to teach my body to no longer respond when pain was present, entering state of calm and focus instead of allowing the physical pain to overcome me. I was fascinated by this technique.

Deus and I worked on my power. Slowly but surely, I began to control where I shifted, starting with short distances. He told me it could take years for me to travel across countries, but as long as I practice, the ability would come. He made me shift all throughout the house, timing me on how fast I could dematerialize and rematerialize at my intending location.

We also worked on my shadow magic. It was like lifting weights. He instructed me to use my power to lift objects varying in size and shape. The smaller objects I could move easily, but the heavier ones posed a challenge. Practice left me drenched in my own sweat. The progress came slowly, but was evident. We moved on to my white flame. To prevent premature burnout, I had to control the amount of energy I forced into it. If I only had a larger power source, I could do so much more.

At night, I would study. Book after book about the demon princes, Hell, the rebellion, and the first coven of witches. His collection of historical volumes and scrolls was impressive, to say the least. I even began to read the Bible again, no longer feeling unworthy. God was real. That was evident.

Instead of looking at the scripture as a manuscript on how to live my life, I studied the stories, placing them with recalled memories and facts that I found while cross-referencing cultures and dates. Looking at these people—these ... saints—in a different light provided me with a new sense of understanding and clarity.

Deus told me about the rebellion. When Lucifer rebelled against God, he, Deus, and their five other brothers were the first to fall from heaven's grace, becoming the seven princes of hell. Their wings were torn from their bodies and their souls ripped from their persons. That was Deus's tattoo: a permanent burn marking of his wings done in ink, as a constant reminder of what he had lost. Each of the sins had one, though different in pattern and size.

For many centuries, the demon princes roamed the earth, eating, devouring, and destroying all they came in contact with. Lucifer was the first to somehow acquire his soul back. Asmodeus recovered his when he met Valeriana in 800. Their lineage and lives were fascinating. Even as demented as some of the stories were, I craved more.

Deus was ever the gentleman. He shared stories from his past about encounters he had with his brothers, the previous vessels, and historical figures. He never brought up Victoria, and neither did I. That seemed like a topic that was off the table, though I was desperate to understand their story.

At night, we shared a bed. He slept on his side, and I slept on mine. Slowly but surely, we developed a mutual respect for one another. Before I knew it, I felt myself beginning to heal.

I wrote Frankie every day and spoke to her through the mirror at least twice a week. To my surprise, she was still seeing Levi. She would tell me all the places he would take her and the romantic dates he would prepare along, with all the gifts he showered her with. No one knew about her fling, but she seemed happy. She told me how much Nonna and Aunt Thora missed me and wished I would come home. Nonna's birthday was next week, and the thought of a visit had crossed my mind.

Since my disappearance, Tony had become forthcoming with his information regarding Obsidian and their whereabouts. All coven members were informed about their activities for the past three years. Everyone was training and readying for war. Nonna and the elders had successfully destroyed five Obsidian bases. They still didn't know the exact details of my mother's plan, but witches and warlocks continued to go missing, showing up dead, their power drained. Frankie said she was researching the book of spells my mother had acquired from the museum in Paris, but wasn't having much luck.

Orion and Delphine were happily out in the open. Orion still checked in with Frankie twice a week for updates on me, but he seemed to be moving on. Everyone was happy ... even better ... without me.

The sunrise here was my favorite part of each day. I had been away from my family and coven now for ten weeks. Winter was coming to an end as the flowers and trees were beginning to bloom to life. I leaned over the balcony in Deus's bedroom with a cup of warm coffee in my hands. My white hair was loose and fluttering through the wind. The air smelled of rain and pollen. I wore a thin robe over my nightgown, the crisp air kissing my skin.

Deus strolled across the balcony and leaned next to me with a mug in his hand. He was in his normal black silk pajama pants and black robe. Even sleeping next to him every night, he kept himself covered modestly. I still had yet to see the rest of that tattoo.

"Good morning," he said, taking a sip.

"Morning. Did you sleep well?" I asked.

"Like the dead." I laughed, bringing my coffee to my lips, watching the sun rise. "What's so funny?"

"Like the dead," I repeated. "You're a demon, you can't really die."

"I'll let you in on a little secret ... we *can* truly die."

I turned my eyes to him with shock. "What? I didn't think that possible. Nothing I have read mentions anything related to that subject."

"Well, of course not. We aren't going to allow our most protected secret to be published now, are we? Don't worry, only the seven of us know how to kill one another."

"Way to ruin my morning," I said, pushing away from the balcony and heading back inside. He followed after me.

"What? The thought of me dead no longer excites you?" he asked sarcastically.

I turned swiftly towards him. He halted only a few inches away. "No, in fact, I've grown quite fond of you. You're like a cat I fed once and can't seem to get rid of." I turned and continued walking, smiling as I heard him laughing behind me.

"I'm your pet now, am I?"

"More like my bitch," I said, returning to the main floor.

In an instance I felt him wrap his arms around me, shifting us from one side of the room to the other, landing us on the bed.

He had me pinned by the wrists, underneath his body. I started laughing, fighting to get free.

"Oh, I'm your bitch now, am I?" he asked, smiling down at me.

"Has a nice ring to it, don't you think?"

A sensual laugh rattled deep inside of him. His eyes slowly scanned my face, lingering longer than normal on my lips. His irises flashed red, only for a moment.

"You know what I think?" he said. He leaned down next to my ear and whispered. "I think you secretly wish I was your bitch. Then, you'd have me do all those dirty little things that you dream about at night."

My eyes widened. "How dare you enter my dreams," I said, smiling.

"Push me out," he replied.

"I can when I'm awake, but come on, I'm asleep for heaven's sake."

He shrugged. "I can't help it. Your dreams are very ... delicious."

I laughed, feeling his body stiffen against mine. I froze. I didn't know what was going on, but something was different about him this morning. He slowly brought his fingers to my face, tracing the outlines of my jaw and then my lips. His eyes glowed again as his head snapped to the side in a predatory fashion.

His breathing became heavy. He licked his lips, while his hand continued to travel from my face down to my neck. I fought to control myself. It had been so long since I had been touched like this. Since I had wanted ... someone. "Deus," I whispered, watching his eyes become fixated on my chest. His irises remained red, swirling and blazing different shades.

He slowly began to pull the edge of my robe away from my chest, revealing the thin, strap of my nightgown. With a single finger, he slid the piece of string down my shoulder to my arm. I could feel the warmth beginning to spread throughout my body. My insides were throbbing, and the heat began to pool between my legs. I arched back, wanting more, but his hands froze.

His breathing was heavy, and I could tell he was trying to control himself. He shook his head, sitting up, leaning over his knees at the edge of the bed. I pulled myself from the mattress, closing my robe around me. I didn't know what had just happened, but I could tell he was off. I placed a hand on his shoulder. He flinched.

"Hey," I said softly. "What just happened?" He ignored me, not say a word or looking in my direction. I wasn't going to play this game. We had come too far. I slid off the bed and knelt in front of him, forcing his eyes to look at me. "Deus, talk to me. What is it?"

Finally, his icy blue irises found mine. "I'm sorry," he said. "I shouldn't have done that. I lost control."

I laughed uncomfortably. "Do you hear me complaining?" I asked.

His face remained stern and serious. "This can't happen, Seren. Nothing is ever going to happen between you and me. Not like that." Something inside of me cringe at those words. I felt embarrassed and self-conscious, even though I wasn't the one who had initiated it this time. I sat back.

"I didn't realize," I finally said. "I'm sorry."

"No, it was my fault." He paused, looking at his red sapphire ring. "Remember at the ball, when you were asking me about unleashing my power? Well, I haven't in a while, and when I don't, I get ... I get sexually aggressive. I think that's what is happening."

The insecurities just kept piling on. Great. "How do you release your power?" I asked. He looked at me and cocked his head. It all clicked into place. "Ah, you need to have sex. I see."

"I haven't released it in a few weeks. I can feel it building."

I stood from the floor, not wanting to continue this conversation any further. "I understand. Well, don't let me stop you. You have a castle full of willing participants who would be more than happy to help you *release* your power multiple times over. Have fun," I said, shutting the doors to the bathroom before he could say another word.

I turned on the shower and jumped in. The water was ice cold.

Chapter Eleven

When I got out of the shower, he was gone. I sat down and opened my journal, flipping to a blank page and wrote the date. May 18. I stopped ... Nonna's birthday. All my other worries seemed to dissipate. God, did I miss her. I missed all of them. The bedroom door opened. I turned to see Deus walking towards me. He was in a casual pair of blue jeans and a formfitting black shirt. The black markings of his winged tattoo on either of his arms peeked from underneath the sleeves of his shirt. His face looked wrecked.

"Have a nice fuck?" I asked.

"Do you really want to know the details?" he replied.

"Absolutely not," I said, feeling sick to my stomach. "I need a favor, if you don't mind."

"Needy much?" he said, appearing relieved I had changed the subject.

"I need you to shift me home." He froze. Confusion and panic rushed to his face.

"Seren, if this is about this morning, please—" he said desperately. I couldn't deny I enjoyed it a little, but today wasn't about him. It was about Nonna, and I needed to get to her.

"It's not ... it's Nonna's birthday today, and I want to spend it with her."

His posture relaxed a little, but I could still tell he was worried. "Will you be staying?" he asked.

"Maybe. Do you even care?"

He paused for a moment. "This is your life. If you wish to return home, that is always your choice."

I walked over to him, smiling softly. He was a confusing demon; I'd give him that. "For now, I just want to see my family. I'm not making any decisions just yet."

He nodded, looking into my eyes with hesitation. "When would you like to leave?"

"As soon as possible, please." He wrapped his arms around my waist, pulling my body into him, never taking his eyes off me. He held me tighter than normal. The black tendrils swirls around us as the shift began. I closed my eyes and when I opened them again, we were standing in my room.

Nothing had been touched. Everything was just as I had left it. I smiled, taking it all in. Something inside of my fluttered to life. I pulled away from Deus and went to my dresser of pictures. I picked up the one of the four of us, Nonna, Frankie, Aunt Thora, and me at my first ball. I looked back at him and smiled. "Thank you," I said.

"Of course."

I rushed to the door, eager to get to them.

"Seren," he said, stopping me in my tracks. He stood in the middle of the room, struggling to find his words. "If ... if you choose to stay, I ... " he paused. He gathered himself and then brought his eyes up to mine and smiled. "I wish you all the happiness in the world."

I rushed to him, wrapping my arms around his broad frame in an embrace. He hugged me back, holding me tightly to him. "This isn't goodbye, you stupid demon," I said, pulling away, looking up at him.

He smirked. "It'd be better for you if it was," he replied.

"Well, as you so often remind me, this is my life, and I have a choice. And I choose to keep you in it ... for now."

"In that case, I am honored."

"Better be, asshole." He laughed, running the back of his knuckles down my face. They continued to my neck, stopping at the chain I wore.

"Keep this on you ... just in case," he said.

"Will I still be able to talk to you through the bond?"

"As long as you don't block me out, I'll be a dirty thought away," he said with a wink. I laughed. "Have fun with your family, love. I'll see you in your dreams." He vanished right in front of me. Something like loss struck me in that moment. I had grown used to his presence, and now without him I felt ... incomplete.

I gathered myself before I rushed towards Frankie's room. As soon as I arrived, I pounded on the door frantically, not wanting to wait a moment longer.

"Oh, my gods," I heard her yell from the other side. "Okay, okay, I'm coming." She flung the door open with attitude and stopped dead in her tracks. She screamed at the top of her lungs as she lunged for me. "Oh, my gods, Oh, my gods, Oh, my gods! You're here. It's really you."

I laughed. "I hope so," I said, looking at her. "God, how I've missed you."

"And I you. Does this mean your home ... for good?" she asked.

"I ... I don't know," I said honestly. Her face fell into a frown. "I'm here for Nonna's birthday."

"Oh, my gods, she is going to be so ecstatic. I can't wait," she squealed, closing her door, and pulling me through the halls. The coven members looked shocked at my presence, but I focused on my family: the reason I was here.

Frankie pushed open Nonna's door without even knocking. Nonna was sipping tea by the fireplace. She turned her head towards us. Her mouth fell open as the teacup fell to the floor and shattered. She covered her face, beginning to cry. "Oh," she gasped. Without another thought, I ran to her. She wrapped me in her arms as we both held each other, crying with joy. "Bambina, it's really you. You're here."

"I'm here, Nonna," I said, pulling away from her. "I'm here for your birthday."

"The best gift I could ever receive."

Aunt Thora came rushing in. She stopped and looked at me with a smile. "I came as soon as Frankie texted," she huffed. I laughed, pulling her into my embrace. Frankie joined our little circle.

Nonna looked at all of us and smiled with happiness. "The Salvo women. My blood," she said. "Together. Again"

"Now, we can celebrate," said Frankie.

We spent the next three hours locked in Nonna's room together. Without telling where I had been or who I had been with, I explained why I left, and how I had worked to heal during my time away. They all seemed supportive and happy that I had found a way to process the darkest time of my life.

After four bottles of wine, we were all rolling on the floor, sharing memories with one another as if I had never left. Nonna was very toasted, and Aunt Thora wasn't too far behind. A knock came at the door.

"Come in," laughed Nonna, crying from a story she had just told us about her and her sister Rose setting a cathedral on fire in their youth.

The door opened, revealing Orion standing on the other side. His face was somber. I stopped laughing, feeling like the wind had just been torn out of the room.

"Orion," I said softly.

"I heard you were home," he said. "You weren't going to come say hello?" I leapt to my feet, rushing towards him, not stopping until I was wrapped in his familiar embrace. The warmth and scent of summer overtook me. I laughed with happiness, pulling away from him. I took his face in my hands.

"I've missed you," I whispered.

He kissed me tenderly on the head. "Gods, how I've missed you." I looked back at my family, noting they were watching us with great attention.

"Do you mind if I step out for a second?" I asked.

"Go on, bambina. But promise you'll be back," demanded Nonna.

"I promise." I turned to leave.

"Oh, and Seren," said Frankie. "There is something we need to talk about after you and Orion are done. Before you go anywhere, call me first, okay?" I nodded, following him to my room.

Once we were alone, he pulled me into him again. We sat in my room, sharing what we had been up to the past two and a half months. I shared the journey I had ventured on along with my new knowledge and abilities. He told me how his powers had grown in leaps and bounds and how the politics had been since I left. We laughed and smiled, picking up where we left of.

Even though I knew he and I would never be romantically involved, I now believed a person could have more than one soulmate. Parts of themselves scattered throughout the world. Frankie was one and Orion was another. Yet, a part of myself still felt incomplete.

We laid across my bed, enjoying each other's presence. Even though we weren't together, in some weird way, he was a part of me. He sat up, propping his head on his hand. His eyes went serious. "What is it?" I asked.

"I need to speak with you about something," he said softly.

"Of course."

He pulled a large, rolled envelope from his back pocket, handing it to me. I opened the small prongs and pulled out the document ... our divorce papers. He had signed them. I looked back at him, allowing a small, caring smile to spread across my lips. "Thank you," I whispered, holding back tears.

"I know you care for me, and I know I can't force you to feel the way I want you to. You were right, it isn't fair ... to either of us."

I reached out, taking his hand. "Whoever you choose is going to be the luckiest girl in the world."

He paused, taking a deep breath. "Actually, there's something else I'd like to discuss with you."

I looked at him eagerly. "I'm listening."

"I'm planning on asking Delphine to marry me, and I would like your blessing."

I smiled, looking at my friend. "Orion ... that is wonderful. I am so happy for you," I said, pulling him into a hug.

"So, you're okay with it? Really?" he asked.

"Of course, I am. I am beyond elated for you and Delphine. She is going to be so happy."

He smiled, looking down at the comforter. "I have to say … I'm nervous."

I laughed, hitting him in the arm. "She is going to say yes, a thousand times over. She's been in love with you for the better part of a decade. You have nothing to worry about."

"You think?" he asked.

"I know."

My door flew open without warning, banging into the wall. Antonio Simonelli stood on the other side, looking like he had just ran a marathon. His eyes were wide, staring at me as if he had seen a ghost. He took a step into my room and without thinking I threw my hand out towards him. My tendrils of black shadows wrapped around his body, slamming him into the wall, pinning him there.

Frankie came rushing into the room, along with Nonna, and Thora. I stood from my bed, holding him with more calm and control than I had ever displayed. With my other hand, I allowed my white flame to ignite, ready to set his culo on fire. Orion slowly rose from the bed, looking to my family. Tony fought my restraints, but there was no use. I was now too strong.

"Seren, put him down," demanded Frankie. She looked at Tony. "I told you, you idiot, let us talk with her before you saw her."

I looked at her in shock. "Excuse me?" I exclaimed.

Nonna stepped forward. "Bambina, we released him from his cell a month ago. He is restricted to the castle grounds, but he has been an asset, to say the least."

I shook my head. "After all he did, you released him?"

"Sweetheart," said Aunt Thora. "Let us explain."

I looked to Orion. His face was cold. "I voted against it," he said, looking at my ex-fiancé with disgust. I dropped Tony to the floor, taking in deep and calming breaths while I thought.

"Seren," said Frankie, taking a step towards me.

"Everyone out," I demanded. They all froze, looking at one another. "I said, out!" One by one they left, leaving me alone with the man who had shattered me.

He stood to his feet, rubbing his neck in discomfort. "You've gotten stronger," he said.

"You have no idea," I replied.

"How have you been?" he asked. I didn't answer. I just stood there, looking at the man I once dreamt of a life with. "The silent treatment ... really?"

"I have nothing to say to you, Antonio." He made to take a step forward, but I held out my hand.

"I've been working to redeem myself," he explained. I could hear the desperation in his voice. "I've told the elders all I know. I've helped save lives."

"And what about the lives we lost because of you? A few good deeds don't undo all you've tarnished."

"Of course not. You're right, but I am working to atone for my sins. To be a better man for you."

"You're wasting your time. There is nothing you could say or do that would ever make me trust you again. Whatever angle your working or game you're playing, stop."

"Beautiful, please—"

"Enough." I walked over to him, allowing myself to get close. His scent brought back memories that now made me sick. I looked at him ... really looked at him for the first time in months. In that moment, I let it all go. I let the pain, the anger, the rage, the disappointment ... all of it go. This man had hurt me. He had betrayed me and yet, I was still standing. Stronger than before.

"I forgive you, Antonio," I whispered, allowing myself to smile. Tears of relief fell down my cheeks.

"What?" he asked, seeming confused.

"I forgive you, for everything. I'm letting it all go. I'm moving on." I took a deep breath, taking a step back. "Please leave."

"But—"

"Antonio, please." Still looking confused, he headed for the door. A moment later Frankie came in to check on me, but there was no need. I was okay. For the first time in a long time, I was okay.

That night, we celebrated the great Lucia Rosetta De Salvo. We drank entirely too much and ate more than our fill. We danced and sang until Nonna passed out, drunk off wine and happiness. After we got her to bed, I returned to my room and crawled underneath the sheets. I looked over at the other side of the bed ... empty.

"Deus ... you there?" I asked in my head.

"I'm here, love," he responded a moment later.

"What are you doing?"

"Reading in bed. How's your family?"

"Drunk and tucked in for the night." I heard his laugh and I smiled.

"Happy to hear that the night went well for all of you."

"It did. I've missed them." There was a long pause.

"The bed is lonely without you here," he commented.

I smiled. *"You don't have a trove of women entertaining you at this very moment?"*

"They would all pale in comparison to my usual bedmate."

My heart fluttered and I blushed. *"You're a confusing demon. And quite frankly, you tend to piss me off."*

I felt his laugh shimmer down the bond. *"I miss seeing your little brow furrow when I piss you off. It is the highlight of my day."*

"Evil, wicked demon."

"You have no idea, love." My toes curled and I smiled into my pillow. *"Get some rest. I'll talk to you tomorrow."*

"Good night, Deus."

"Night, love."

CHAPTER TWELVE

The next morning, I awoke in my own bed, in my own room. I looked around and somehow, it felt empty. I fought the feeling that was creeping underneath my skin ... I missed him. I got up and began my day journaling. I meditated before heading down to the training arena. I was still determined to maintain my normal routine as much as possible. Loriana, Adrianna, Roric, and Tyler were sparring with one another. I hadn't spoken to them since Paris. I still felt guilt for George. I always would.

"Well, well ... what do we have here?" said Loriana, strolling forward.

"Good morning," I said to all of them. They surrounded me. "I ... I wanted to apologize to each of you about Paris. It was my fault we were ambushed and my fault we lost George." I looked at Adrianna. "And it was my fault you got hurt. I'm sorry ... truly." They stared at me for a few moments. Finally, Roric, with his large frame and light brown hair, approached me.

He placed his hands on either side of my shoulders. "You were willing to sacrifice yourself so we all could go free," he said softly. "That is the sign of a true leader." He pulled me in for a hug. The rest of them gathered around, waiting their turn. My heart felt light and relieved. Another puzzle piece clicked into place in my healing journey.

"Now," said Loriana, "I'd like to kick your ass." They all started laughing.

"Let's see how soft you've gotten on your little three-month vacation," added Tyler. I smiled, knowing damn well they were in for a surprise.

Loriana approached the mat first while the others stood around us. She bent down in her stance, getting her bearings. I calmed myself, watching her closely. She charged, aiming to take me to the floor. I used her momentum, grabbing her by the waist and swinging her into the air, landing her back to the mat. The others started laughing, looking at each other with surprise.

"I've learned a few things," I said, offering her my hand to stand. She jumped to her feet, reared back her fist and aimed for my face. I dodged, swung, and landed a blow to her stomach. I went low to the mat, swinging my leg around, taking hers out from underneath, sending her to her back ... again.

The others looked at each other and then nodded to one another. They all attacked. I swung, jabbed, and dodged, taking a few blows, but I remained standing as they worked in tandem, trying to take me down. I remained calm, not allowing the pain in my body to distract me. I moved with grace and each attack was intentional and planned.

I slammed Tyler back hard enough he went flying into the benches. Roric was next. He was large, but slow. I moved around him, staying low until he revealed his weak spots. I took advantage, slamming my fist into all of them. I smashed my fist into his face, hearing the crack of his cartilage. Blood poured from his nose, causing him to stumble back in a dazed state. I ran towards him, jumping in the air as I sent my fist flying straight for his face. As soon as I made contact, he went down.

Adrianna was quick, but sloppy. She extended her arm too far, allowing me to use it as leverage, flipping her over my back to the mat. I stood, looking at the four of them. I breathed deeply and smiled.

"What in the hell is going on here?" I heard Orion's deep voice behind me.

Tyler pulled himself from the broken pieces of the wooden benches and stood, rubbing the back of his neck. "Apparently," Tyler said, "Seren here sent herself to some type of boot camp these past months. She just handed us our asses."

Roric stood, still hold his face. "Fuck," he said, looking down at the blood. "She broke my nose."

"I'm seeing double," added Adrianna as Loriana helped her to her feet. They all started laughing.

Orion's eyes turned towards me. "Who's been training you?" he asked.

"I can't say," I replied.

"Really .... Well, then show me what you've learned," he insisted, moving into the ring. The others backed away, lining the edges, readying for a show. I took a deep breath, centering myself again. Orion was a talented fighter, but he wasn't Mal, or Deus, for that matter. I was unsure if I could beat him at this stage in my training, but I was at least going to give him a run for his money.

I relaxed my muscles, watching for his customary ticks. He circled me, yet I remained still, watching ... waiting. From behind, he chose to attack. I moved instantly, anticipating the move. He reared back, attempting to elbow me in the face. I pivoted, crouching low and sent my elbow up into his chin, followed by two right jabs to the face. He attempted to grab me, but I dropped to my back and used my legs to drop him to floor.

I flipped up, landing on my feet. He swung his legs, trying to take mine out, but I darted aside. With a powerful push, he returned to his feet, landing a blow to my stomach and my side. I pushed the pain away, turning out of his reach just in time to miss his third punch. I focused myself, my power awakening inside of me. With a final push, I sent my palm directly into Orion's sternum and with it, my power. He went flying back, slamming into the wall.

I instantly panicked, rushing to him as he fell to the floor. He shook his head, seeming shocked. "I am so sorry. I didn't mean to hurt you," I said, helping him to his feet.

He looked at me with question. "Where in the hell did you learn to do that?" he asked.

"I told you ... I can't say," I replied.

"Did you just get your ass handed to you by a little 120-pound girl?" asked Loriana, laughing to herself.

"I really regret not recording this now," added Adrianna.

"Note to self," said Tyler, "avoiding pissing Seren off from now on."

They all laughed but Orion's eyes remained on me. Finally, he smiled, pulling me into him. "I am so proud of you," he said. "Maybe I need to start taking lessons from you."

"It was a lucky punch," I said.

"You and I both know that had nothing to do with luck. Whoever is training you, ask them if they're taking new student."

I laughed, imagining Mal's face. "I don't think they are, but if a spot opens up, I'll give them your number," I replied.

"What in the hell happened to you all?" I heard Tony's voice from across the ring. I froze, still holding onto Orion. His grip tightening around me. The others didn't say a word. They gathered their stuff, ignoring him, walking towards the exit. Orion remained by my side.

Tyler stopped next to Tony, looking back at me. "Word of advice," Tyler said to him. "I wouldn't try fucking her over again. Something tells me she won't hesitate to kill you this time. Not that I'd be sad about that."

"You did that to all of them?" asked Tony. "Even Orion."

"Yes," I replied shortly.

"Full of surprises, aren't you?" he said. I smiled, thinking about Deus. Tony looked at Orion. "Your mother just arrived. She's asking for you."

Orion smirked at me. "I would ask if you were good," he said, "but after that little display, I'm confident you can handle yourself just fine."

"I'm good, thanks," I said. Orion kissed me on the head before taking his leave.

Tony and I were now alone. "How's your sister?" I asked, filling the silence.

"Not good. She's regressing."

"Well, hopefully Orion's powers kick in so he can heal her fully."

"That would be nice." He paused, looking at me in a way that made me uncomfortable. "Would you like to get something to eat? I'd like to talk to you."

"I don't think that's a good idea."

"It's about your mother. There are things ... there are things I haven't told the coven, because they are personal—regarding you."

I froze, wondering if he was baiting me. "Fine," I said. "Lead the way."

We headed to my room and ordered lunch from the dining hall. Until the food arrived, we sat in uncomfortable silence. I changed and then rearranged items in my room as a distraction. He just watched. Once the food arrived, we took it on my balcony.

"Alright, Tony. Stop playing games," I said, flipping open the container. "Out with it."

He placed his fork down and smiled at me. "It's about where your mother has been getting her power," he said. I waited for him to continue, but he just chewed his food.

"Okay, so?" I finally gave in.

He licked his lips and leaned forward. "She's been working with the demon prince Lucifer. They've struck a bargain. I'm not sure what that bargain is, but in exchange for whatever she gave him, he has granted her access to his power and to his army of demons."

I sat back, keeping a calm demeanor. "A little late to the game, aren't you?"

Tony's face went slack. "You knew about Lucifer?" he asked.

I nodded. "Yes."

He scooted closer. "I don't know the details, but I think the bargain has something to do with you. I know your mother has found a way to take your power, but I'm not sure how."

"Figures," I said. My mother's attempts to kill me no longer affected my emotions.

He studied me for a moment. "Aren't you going to ask me what a prince of hell is?" he asked.

I smirked. "Oh, you mean, Lucifer, Satan, Mammon, Beelzebub, Belphegor, Leviathan, and Asmodeus? The original seven that fell, led by Lucifer himself? I'm aware, thank you."

His face looked shocked. "How?"

"I read. Now, is there anything else?" I asked. He just looked at me blankly. I nodded, now understanding. "Ah, you thought that by bringing me this information about Lucifer and my mother, I would lean on you for more details. Well, doesn't look like that's going to happen," I said, standing to my feet. "Now, please leave."

"Seren, please," he begged, looking defeated.

I took a breath, gathering myself. "Tony, if you still care about me; if you ever cared about me, you need to let me go. I can't keep doing this with you and I won't."

"I can't," he whispered. "I still ... I still love you."

I walked towards the door, stopping by his side. I placed my hand on his shoulder. "You need to let me go. Please, Tony. Let me go." And with that, I left.

I headed to Frankie's room to tell her about my lunch. I could hear laughter coming from her room. I rolled my eyes, pulling out my phone and calling her. It rang twice before she answered.

"Hello," she giggled.

"I'm outside of your room. Is it safe to enter?" I asked.

"Oh, uh—"

"Tell Levi put his pants on and let me in," I said, hanging up on her. A moment later, she opened the door with a wide grin on her face.

"Well, hello, sweet cousin," she said. I walked inside and was greeted by a shirtless Levi, draped across her bed. He had pants on, thank God. His blonde hair flowed down his shoulders. Markings on his chest, similar to the ones I had seen on Deus's forearms, wrapped around his arms and shoulders. The points of the wings were visible on his chest, as if he were cocooning himself with them before they were ripped from his body.

"Hi there, goddess," he said, winking at me.

"Hi Levi. How are you?" I said formally.

"I would be a lot better if you would have waited another thirty minutes before interrupting," he replied, grinning at Frankie.

I made a puking face. Frankie laughed. "Oh, stop being so jealous," she said to him. "Seren is welcome here anytime."

He shrugged. "Envy and all. I don't like sharing what is mine," he said.

"I have some news you both might want to hear," I said. Levi sat up, still disinterested.

"What is it?" asked Frankie.

"Tony just informed me that my mother is indeed working with Lucifer. The night of the ball, Deus mentioned something about him wanting my power, so I already figured as much," I explained. "That is how she has become so powerful. He has handed over his armies to her. She made some type of bargain with him. Tony wasn't sure what it was, but he thinks it has something to do with me."

"Shit," Frankie said, looking worried. "We need to tell Mamma and Nonna."

"We will. I just wanted to talk to you first since—" I gestured to Levi.

He put his hands up in a defensive manner. "I have nothing to do with anything Lucifer schemes or plots," he said. "I assure you. I can't stand that fucking prick." I believed him, because Deus trusted him. Levi stood, finally putting his shirt on. The door knocked.

"My gods, what is this? Grand Central Station?" said Frankie, swinging the door open. Joseph stood at the door, looking inside at the three of us.

"Can I come in?" he grunted.

"Is everything okay?" asked Frankie.

"We've been called out," Joe said. "Demons have attacked the Vatican and are possessing people around the area."

"Normal humans?" I asked.

"People of the cloth," he clarified.

"Shit," whispered Frankie, her eyes filling with worry.

Joe stepped towards her. "Hey," he said tenderly, taking her hand. Levi's eyes snapped to their contact. "It's going to be okay. We've been training for this. Hopefully, it will be a quick job and we'll be back before morning."

Frankie smiled at him.

Levi appeared next to them, assessing the situation. Finally, he grabbed Joe's wrists and pulled it away from Frankie's hand. Joe pulled out of his restraint. "Don't touch her again," Levi ordered.

"And who the hell are you?" asked Joe.

"Someone you don't want to piss off," Levi growled, stepping in front of Frankie.

Joe took a step towards him. "I will touch her," he said matter-of-fact, "whenever I please."

Levi's eyes flashed green. His jaw tightened and his stare went deadly. Frankie placed a hand on Levi, pulling his attention away from Joe.

"Thank you," Frankie said. "We'll be down shortly." Levi wasn't breathing. His eyes now blazed a radiant chartreuse color. I took Joe's arm, ushering him to the door. I slammed it shut behind him, locking it. Frankie was in front of Levi, running her hands down his face, trying to soothe him. "I'm right here, baby," she said softly. "No one's going to take me away."

I felt uncomfortable watching. She was so ... intimate and caring with him. It made me question if their time together had become more than just sex. He took a few breaths, closing his eyes and calming himself. He pulled her into him, burying his nose in the crook of her neck. She held him, stroking his head with light touches. Finally, he pulled away, returning to the regal prince I knew.

"I'm sorry," he said. "To the both of you. Sometimes I ... I can't control the envy."

"You didn't kill him, so we're good," I said, smiling at him.

Frankie kissed him on the lips. "You have nothing to be envious about," she said. "I'm all yours. Only yours." I watched his demeanor soften. His eyes reflected—

"Hold on," I said. I looked between the two of them. "What in the hell is going on here?"

Frankie looked at me and then at him and smiled.

"I'm in love with your cousin," Levi admitted, smiling down at her.

I shook my head in shock. "Wait a second ... I mean ... how ... when?" I asked.

"I wasn't planning on falling in love with the Prince of Envy," Frankie said, still smiling, "but it just happened. And ... he makes me happy. Really happy." He drew his fingers through her hair. She turned back towards me. Her face fell. "Are you angry with me?"

I walked over to her, taking her hands in mine. "I'm happy for you," I said, pulling her into a hug. She laughed, squeezing me tightly. "Nonna is going to flip."

"I haven't really thought that far ahead," she said.

"Regardless," I replied, looking at Levi. "As long as he keeps you safe and gives you everything you've always wanted, you have my support." She smiled.

Levi nodded. "You have my word."

I looked at her and laughed. "Who would have thought demons were so well mannered."

"You'd be surprised what they're capable of," she said playfully. My mind flashed to a yesterday morning. Deus's strong body on top of mine: his mouth, and his hands—those eyes. My entire body trembled at the memory. I could feel the needing welling between my legs. I pushed the thought away, trying to focus.

"We should probably meet the others," I said, needing a distraction.

"Right," she replied, pushing up on her toes to kiss Levi before going into her bathroom to retrieve something.

Levi casually walked over to me with a smile on his face. He leaned his lips down to my ear, close enough that I could feel his warm breath. "Tell my brother I said hello," he whispered.

My eyes widened. He pulled away. "You know?" I asked in shock.

He shrugged. "I figured you probably have something to do with why he has continued to refuse my request for a visit."

"Why haven't you told Frankie?"

"That is between you and her. When you are ready to tell her where you've been ... sleeping," he said, winking at me, "is completely up to you."

"We aren't ... that," I said uncomfortably.

"Hmm," he said, furrowing his brow. "He must be in a pleasant mood then. Sleeping next to a female he can't fu—"

"He just did yesterday with another," I said without thinking. Something in my stomach felt sick at the admission.

Levi's face looked surprised. "Really? Who has he been taking?"

I shrugged. "Whoever he wants in the castle. I don't know." I gritted my teeth together, trying to suppress the image of his perfectly sculpted body against another woman. His lips, kissing someone else's. His hands, touching— I closed my eyes tightly.

No. No. Absolutely not. This was not happening. I was not getting jea— I froze, bringing my eyes back to Levi. His grin dripped with sin. "You," I gasped.

"Me?"

"Are you making me feel this way?" I asked.

"Not entirely. I am only amplifying what is already there. Sorry … I'll try to control myself next time. It was just too easy, and your jealousy tastes divine. You know, goddess and all."

"Stay out of my emotions, Levi."

"Maybe you need to read into those emotions a little more," he said. "Take a closer look."

"Take a closer look at what?" Frankie said, returning to the main room.

"Nothing. Your … boyfriend is being a pest," I said.

"But a very handsome pest," he said, pulling her into his side.

"I'm leaving," I said, not waiting for Frankie. I needed a moment to myself.

I headed downstairs, trying to clear my mind. Frankie was in love with a prince of hell. And he was obviously infatuated with her. I couldn't wrap my mind around it. Though, I could understand the appeal. Both brothers were well educated, polite, caring, and possibly the most beautiful men I had ever seen. I was sure the other five would appear to be the same.

And then, there was Deus. Levi had said he only amplified what was already there. Was I jealous of the other women he was sleeping with? I pushed those thoughts out of my mind every time they came up, not letting myself go down that rabbit hole. But if I was jealous, that meant something was there: that I felt something for him.

I had promised myself I would never love again. After everything I had been through, I had deemed it not worth the risk. Then, there was the fact that he was still obviously in love with Victoria. He still refused to talk about her. Every time I even got close to the subject, he'd shut down.

Frankie caught up to me. "Why are we running?" she asked.

"What?"

"You're basically running. Slow the hell down," she said.

"Oh, sorry," I replied.

She laughed. "Eager to kill some demons?"

"Actually, sounds like a perfect Friday morning."

She smiled, looking down at the floor. "You're really okay with Levi and me?"

"I really am," I said, taking her hand in mine. "I do have a favor to ask though. And I need you to keep it between the two of us."

"Of course. Anything."

"I need you to use your research skills to dig up everything you can on Victoria Prather."

"The vessel? Why?"

"And I need you not to ask question. At least not right now. I am still trying to sort through some things. But when I am ready, you will be the first to know. Always."

"Consider it done."

Chapter Thirteen

The ten of us flew to Rome before night fell. The city seemed unaware that demons had taken over its most beloved institution. We met with our contact within the Vatican who led us to St. Peters Square where the demons had been contained. Witches who lived close to the city had responded first to the threat and were able to contain them until we could arrive.

Twelve men, archbishops and cardinals, were in the square along, with three nuns. My eyes focused on the nuns. Images of Sister Odette and Sister Francis flashed through my memory. A sense of loss and betrayal raked over me. I hadn't seen a nun since I had left the abbey. It was evident they were possessed. Their bodies moved and ticked in unnatural ways. Drool and bile dripped from their mouths. Some of their clothes were torn, revealing wounds underneath the cloth.

The six witches and warlocks that were keeping the cage locked into place around the square looked exhausted. Orion signaled for Adrianna, Bella, Gabby, Tyler, Joe, and Loriana to relieve them. Their magic must have been tapped. One of the warlocks walked over to us, breathing heavily.

"Everett," said Orion to the warlock. "Nice to see you again."

"You as well," Everett replied.

"Have they said anything?" asked Orion.

"No, not a damn thing. They've just been standing there, like they're waiting for something."

"I don't like this," added Frankie.

"Me either," I said, walking around the wall towards them. As if synced together, their heads all snapped in my directions as soon as I stepped into sight. "Found what they were waiting for," I called back to the others. Frankie came to my side. All fifteen of them creeped to the edge of the cage closest to me.

"Hello, little goddess," said one of them.

"What do you want?" I asked.

"Just your powers," it said.

My vision began to blur. My mind scrambled, revealing another memory from one of the vessels. I stepped back, holding my head as the details came through. I calmly focused, allowing the memory to surface so I could understand it and file it away correctly.

I was somewhere in a desert. Sand was all around me, and the heat was unbearable. I looked down at my sandaled feet and the thin, white fabric draped over my body. This had to be a memory from either Valeriana or Cecilia. A man stood in front of me by a camel. His tanned skin was blistered. His thick black beard was covered in blood. Around us lay the seven dead innocents. He had killed them and begun to eat their remains.

The thing charged me. I threw up my hand, a wooden beaded bracelet swinging around my wrist. Cecilia. The demon froze in place, unable to break free of my shadows. I calmy walked over to it, placing my hand on its chest. I concentrated, connecting myself to the creature. Flashes of pain and anger consumed me. A raging heat exploded. The demon began to shake and scream. Steam rose from its skin. I was in pain, but didn't release the monster. I saw the monster's memories, of him killing and destroying everything around it. I was in his head, able to see what he could see.

I snapped to the present, taking a step back, trying to regain my balance. Frankie and Orion were at my side, helping stabilize me. She had weaved herself into his memory ... like Hashen could, in a way. But how?

"Are you okay?" asked Frankie.

"Yea, I'm fine. Just give me a moment," I replied.

I moved back around the wall, sliding myself to the ground. I focused, allowing the calm to take over. I revisited the memory, collecting its sounds, smells, and visuals. I compressed it, folding it into a file before opening the blue cabinet labeled Cecilia and storing it away. After I closed it, the heaviness fell away. My mind was my own once again.

I returned to the rest of the group. The demons stood in a line, breathing heavily as they stared at me. "Pull one out," I said.

"What?" asked Orion.

"I need one of them," I explained. "Pull out a nun."

"What is going on?" asked Frankie.

"I need you all to just trust me," I said.

I had never been in someone's mind, let alone a demon's, but if Cecilia could do it, so could I. There was a reason that memory resurfaced in this moment. They were trying to tell me something. I wondered if Deus had known about this power. Maybe that was why he had me working with Hashen: to understand how to navigate my mind along with another's.

Orion stuck his hand through the shield, grabbing one of the nuns by her neck. She thrashed and flailed, scratching at his forearms. Wherever she slashed his skin with her nails, he would instantly heal, leaving no remains of the wounds. His power was growing. I smiled to myself with pride.

I sent out my black tendrils, wrapping them around the nun. Orion let her go as I drew her in towards me. I focused on my power, holding her tightly. She spat and shook, trying to get free.

"What do you want?" I asked.

"Ah, Ah!" it screamed. "You will see soon enough."

"Actually, I'd like to see now," I said, placing my hand on its chest. I focused on the heat I remembered from Cecilia's memory. A white glow appeared where I touched it. I closed my eyes and focused closer. In my mind, I saw a small thread of my white light, traveling through the nun. It ran up her spine, following the flashing lights of her nervous system. Finally, I could see her brain. It was consumed by darkness. It feasted on it, tearing the tissue apart little by little.

I snaked my white thread around the black fog, clamping down. It fought me, but it was no match. Flashes, of a man, dominate and beautiful appeared. I couldn't make out details, but I could feel his power. It called out to me. It felt ... familiar and comforting. The demons bowed before him. "Draw her out," he said, in an elegant voice I had never heard before, "and then call for me." I pulled my thread out of the blackness as fast as possible, trying to get back to the group. I allowed the light to retrace its path until it threaded back into me.

I gasped, stumbling away from the demon. With one powerful motion of my hand, I tightened my shadows around the nuns neck, severing her head from her body. The corpse dropped, the head bouncing across the cobblestone floor.

"What the hell was that?" asked Frankie.

"I can weave," I said, surprised.

"You can what?" asked Orion.

"I'll tell you later. We need to get out of here now." I demanded. "Kill them and let's go."

"Why? What is going on?" asked Orion.

"Lucifer is on his way," I said. Orion's eyes widened.

"Drop the shield and fire," ordered Frankie. The others did as instructed, littering the square with bullet shells. The demons didn't stand a chance.

"Move," yelled Orion. We took off, back through the Vatican.

Inside a large, vaulted hallway, white fog began to descend. Demon-possessed witches appeared out of thin air along the walls and ceiling of the room, surrounding us. There were sixteen of us with our Rome associates, and dozens of them. We readied ourselves, preparing to fight our way out.

I loaded my guns, one in either hand. "We escape or we die," Orion yelled. "No one gets taken." The group all yelled in agreement.

Without waiting, the fighting began. The demons descended, slamming into the ground around us. I swung the barrels of my guns towards anything that moved, nailing each of my targets where I intended. This wasn't like Paris. I was prepared.

They were everywhere, but so was I: sending out my shadows, slicing and dismembering them one by one. After reloading, I continued to drop the creatures. They began to fall from the domed ceiling like roaches. I had no clue where they were coming from, but I wasn't going to wait to find out.

"Orion!" I yelled, pointing to the ceiling. He nodded, coming to my side. I dropped my guns, and we threw our hands up, lighting the ceiling on fire. White and yellow flames mixed and melded together as it rained demon ash. Starlight blasted from Frankie, sending all the demons near her to the floor.

My mother appeared out of a white fog, sauntering towards me. One of the other witches pointed a gun at her, releasing the trigger. My mother slowed the bullet, dropping it to the floor before it could harm her. She threw out her hand towards her attacker.

The witch's body flung itself into my mother's grip like a magnet. Annalise held her by the neck, slamming her other hand into her chest, ripping out her heart and tossing it to the ground.

Orion stepping in front of me, but I gently pulled him back. "This is my fight," I said to him softly, with a nod.

"This is our fight," I heard Frankie say, next to me. She took my hand in hers and smiled. "Blood ties us, remember?" I nodded, feeling her love through our bond.

Orion appeared on my other side, taking my hand in his.

"Awe," said my mother. "Now, isn't that just the sweetest thing I've ever seen." She stopped a few feet away as thc battle raged around us. "Where have you been hiding, little bean?"

"I'm not giving over my power," I said confidently. "I'll die first."

She laughed. "Oh, I will be taking your power, and unfortunately for you, it will kill you."

"You're sick," spat Frankie.

My mother's eyes slid to my cousin. "Dear niece, how did you manage to survive?"

"Wouldn't you like to know," Frankie bit back.

My mother laughed. "Oh, I think I have a few ideas," she said, winking at me.

My mind raced, forming a plan. I thought back to my training, my power. Faster and faster, my head sifted through idea after idea until I found what I needed. I squeezed both of their hands. They turned towards me. "When I give the signal," I said, "burn this place to the ground."

"What?" Orion asked.

"Trust me," I whispered. "I love you both." I went to walk away, but Frankie held on tight. I look back at her and smiled. "Trust me," I said with a nod. Her face was twisted with fear, but she let go. I walked towards my mother with my head held high. She smiled at me, almost endearingly.

"Giving up so easily?" she asked.

"I just want this over," I replied honestly.

"None of them will survive. You know this."

"Let's just get this over with," I said, waiting for her to make the next move.

She smiled, stepping towards me. "As you wish, little bean." She reached out her hands and placed either one on my arms. As soon as I felt her magic begin to tug on mine, I wrapped my arms around her waist, pulling her into an embrace.

"Now!" I yelled back at Orion and Frankie.

Without hesitation, beams of sunlight and starlight blasted through the air. My mother fought to get free of my grip, but I held on tighter, sending my small white threads into her mind. They wove and weaved through her system until I located her brain. There was no darkness there. It was just my mother. The evil she had become was all her own. I wrapped the threads around her, pulling at her memories, but she threw her guard up, preventing me from seeing anything.

I felt her power pulling on mine as she absorbed my magic, just as I had anticipated. Still connected to her, I pulled away and looked up at her face. She smiled, feeling the immense power I contained. I relaxed, preparing myself for what came next. Her eyes flickered with confusion. She went to pull away, but I held firm.

“Siphon this, bitch,” I said, sending every ounce of my power down the bridge that she had built between us with her gift. I overloaded her body, filling it with darkness. My white flames blasted through her veins, winding and snaking up each stream until it reached her vital organs.

She began to scream, fighting to pull away, but I held firm. I gritted my teeth, battling to ignore my own pain. My mother began to convulse. Her skin glowed white. My fingers dug into her back, holding on until I gave her everything she wanted. My power, my heat, my strengths.

Bam!

An explosive light ripped us apart, blasting us across the room from one another. I heard the crack of my skull as it made contact with the stone wall. I fell to the floor, unable to move. By overloading Annalise, I was now walking a very thin line between consciousness and burn out.

My power gave out. I could feel the barriers around my mind falling away in large chunks. My body was freezing, and my limbs began to shake. I tried to focus, opening my eyes to see where the others were, but everything was a blur.

Black fog appeared in front of me as I laid my face against the cold marble, unable to move on my own. Arms wrapped themselves around my body, swirling me into a gust of darkness and wind. The next thing I knew, I was being placed on my bed back at Castle Salvo. My dark savior stood above me. Even though I couldn't make out the details of his face, I knew who it was.

"Deus," I said softly.

"Shh, shh, I'm here. Everything will be fine," he said, placing his hands over my body.

"The others," I rasped.

"Levi has it taken care of. Now, lay back and relax, this is going to sting a little."

I did as I was told. I felt a warm, creeping essence roll across my entire body, hovering there for a moment, before it began to burrow against my skin. I gritted my teeth, clinching my fists, allowing Deus's power to heal me. My vision began to clear. There was a dark essence laced with strings of red, vein-like structures absorbing into my skin. This continued for another minute, until I felt my lifeforce return. My body stilled and my mind cleared.

Deus allowed his hands to fall, taking a deep breath in. He studied my face as he ran his hand through my hair. "How do you feel?" he asked.

"Tired, but better. What did you do?" I asked.

"I transferred my lifeforce into you."

"You can do that?" I gasped. "Can you teach me?"

He smiled. "Unfortunately, that is a talent only the seven of us originals have."

"Thank you ... for coming for me."

He sat on the edge of my bed, his hands in his lap. "I would have come sooner if you didn't have a wall around your mind. Why don't you leave a door open for me from now on?"

I laughed. "I'll think about it."

"What happened?" he asked.

I smiled at his beautiful face. The way his eyes were full of concern and tenderness. Who would have thought a demon was capable of such compassion and emotion? "Let me show you," I replied, opening my mind fully to him. I felt his presence slip into the door I had carved. The smell of lilacs filled my nostrils. I relived every moment in the Vatican, including my decision to sacrifice myself to save the ones I loved. I felt him slip away back through the door slowly.

"Lucifer," Deus said softly. "He is behind your mother's power."

"Apparently. Antonio also confirmed it to me early."

"Antonio? Your ex-fiancé?" he asked.

I felt a heaviness in my heart at the sound of the word fiancé. "Correct."

"When did you speak with him?"

"I'm too tired to talk," I replied. "Get back in my head." He nodded, focusing as he slithered his way back through the door. I shared what had happened and what I had learned since I returned home. This time, I felt him pull away quicker as if he was running for the exit. My eyes flashed to his. "What's wrong?" I asked.

"Nothing." He looked away from me, straightening his posture a bit. He looked to my bedroom door and without a single goodbye, he dissipated into thin air.

The door to my room flew open without warning. Frankie, Orion, and the others flew in. "Oh, thank Aradia," said Frankie, jumping on top of me.

I hugged her back, feeling relief. "Is everyone okay?" I asked.

Orion nodded. "Everyone from our group yes," he said. "The other witches lost two of their own."

"And Annalise?" I asked.

Frankie pulled away. "We saw her passed out on the floor one moment," she said, "and then she was gone before we could capture her."

"Then it got really weird," added Loriana, stepping to the side of my bed.

"Yea," agreed Adrianna. "Dark green smoke seeped into the room and caused the rest of the demons to melt into some type of green, acid-y substance. Then the next thing we knew, we were at the front steps of Castle Salvo."

I looked at Frankie. She smiled, dropping her eyes to the bed. Levi.

"We looked for you," said Orion, "but you were gone."

"I must have shifted unknowingly," I said.

"But we watched you burn yourself out," Orion replied. "How did you have any power left to shift?"

I felt Frankie's eyes assessing me, searching for the truth. I shrugged. "I don't know. I don't remember much after I overloaded my mother with my power."

"That was brilliant, by the way," said Roric. "How did you know you'd survive it?"

I didn't answer him. Frankie's hand tightened around mine.

"You did what?" I heard Antonio's voice coming from the door. Everyone turned to look at him. He entered the room slowly. I exhaled, feeling the exhaustion of it all hit me.

"It's none of your concern," intervened Orion.

"*She* is my concern," Tony said, getting into Orion's face. "And where in the hell were you? Allowing her to sacrifice herself like that? It should have never been an option."

"Don't you dare question me, traitor," snapped Orion. "You weren't there. You don't know what we were up against." I saw fire twirling around Orion's hands. His temper was getting the best of him.

"Orion," I whispered. His eyes flashed to mine. "Can you all please give us the room." I nodded at Frankie, her eyes full of worry. "I'm okay."

One by one, they left, leaving Tony and I alone. His face was guilty. "I should have been there," he said, coming to the side of my bed.

"And which side would you have been on?" I asked.

His eyes found mine, filling with sadness. "Yours ... always."

"I don't want your help or protection, Antonio. I can make my own choices."

"I know you're more than capable of thinking for yourself. That's one of the things I love most about you." He sat on the edge of the bed. "I just ... I just wish you weren't in this position. Where you feel you must sacrifice yourself to save others." He allowed his eyes to fall to his hands. "If you die, I ... I'd have no reason for living."

I sat myself up against the headboard; my limbs, still feeling heavy. "Don't say that," I whispered. "You need to find something else to live for, because it can't be me ... not anymore."

"Why can't it? I'm doing everything I can to show you how sorry I am. To show you that you can trust me and that I am still the man you fell in love with. Still the man you agreed to marry and begin a life with. What do you want me to do, beautiful? I will do anything if you'll give me another chance." He reached out his hand, cupping the side of my face gently.

I felt a tear run down my cheek. "I need you to let me go," I whispered.

"Never," he said, leaning in to kiss me. Before I could stop him, he was thrown into the wall next to my bed, held there by small black swirls of fog laced with hints of red.

"The lady asked you to leave her alone," came Deus's voice, calm and collected. "Not to kiss her." He strolled from the corner of my room, now standing in between Tony and me. I wondered if he had been there lurking the entire time.

Tony gritted his teeth, trying to break free of Deus's magic, but my demon was too strong. "Stay away from her," Tony yelled, looking fearful for me. "Seren, run," he instructed.

Deus laughed. Without taking his eyes off Tony, he extended his hand out to me, and I took it, rising to stand next to him. Tony looked between the two of us, trying to connect the dots. "She has nothing to fear from me, warlock," Deus said. "Now, if I let you down, do you promise to scurry away like the good little rat you are?"

"I'm not leaving her with you," Tony said, his voice laced with venom.

"That," Deus replied, "is not up to you." Deus looked to me, question in his face.

I turned to Tony. "I want you to leave," I said firmly.

"What?" Tony replied with confusion.

"I want you to leave," I repeated. I turned to Deus. "Let him go, please." Deus rolled his eyes and snapped his fingers. Tony fell to the ground. He stood instantly, looking between the two of us.

"Who is this?" Tony asked.

Dues laughed softly. "You don't want to know," he said under his breath.

"Seren, please," Tony pleaded again.

"I'm staying here. Now get out." I threw my arm towards the door, and it blew open, slamming against the wall. Tony looked shocked. He backed away from us, his eyes still wracked with worry and confusion. Once he had crossed the threshold, I slammed the door in his face with my power and locked it.

Deus turned his head towards me with his devilish smile spreading across his face. "Were you really going to allow that snake to kiss you?" he asked.

I shrugged. "Why do you care?" I said, crawling back into my bed.

"And here I thought you had higher standards for yourself."

I laughed. "I've been shacking up with a demon prince for the past three months."

"Point taken," he replied, sitting next to me. I smiled at him, holding back another laugh. "What is on your mind?"

I bit the bottom of my lip. "You were jealous, weren't you?" I asked.

He smiled slowly, allowing it to reach his eyes. "I'm the demon of Lust. I don't get jealous. That's Levi's thing."

I rolled my eyes, scooting over in the bed. "I have a favor to ask," I whispered, looking up into his icy blue irises.

"Anything."

"Stay with me. Just for tonight," I said. "I don't want to be alone."

He looked at the place next to me hesitantly. "Is that the only reason you want me to stay?"

I shrugged. "For tonight ... yes."

He nodded, laying down on the pillow next to mine. His presence calmed something inside of me. I moved towards him, placing my head in the crook of his arm. I curled my body against his, craving the comforting smell of lilacs. He wrapped his arms around me, turning his body into mine.

"Good night, love."

"Good night, demon."

Chapter Fourteen

"I fucking knew it!" A voice yelled, pulling me out of the most peaceful slumber I had ever known. I snapped my eyes open, sitting up. Frankie stood next to my bed, looking down at me and ... Deus. He stretched, opening his eyes slowly, a smile already plastered across his bronze cheeks.

"Well, good morning, Francesca," greeted Deus, folding his hands behind his head. "Will my brother be joining us, or will this just be a threesome?"

Green and black smoked appeared behind Frankie. Levi appearing instantly. "You will not be laying a hand on her!" growled Levi, his chest puffed and temper rising.

Deus laughed. "Calm down, little brother. I've got my own Salvo," he said, nodding his head towards me.

I jabbed him in the stomach. He grunted with a laugh. "I'm not yours," I said. "Frankie, it's not what it looks like."

"Then what in the hell is this, huh?" she asked. "Deus in your bed? You disappearing for months on end? You come back more powerful and trained than before?"

"Yes," I said, "I was staying at Deus's castle, but we're not ...

whatever you're thinking."

"So, you're just snuggle buddies then?" she asked.

"We do share a bed back home," added Deus.

I ran my hand over my face. "You're not helping," I grunted. He smiled at me and winked.

"You're fucking him?" asked Frankie.

"No, no," I said, crawling over Deus to get to her. "We aren't sleeping together. He's just ... he helped me with my lack of control, and he's been training me to understand and hone my goddess powers."

Frankie crossed her arms, eyebrow raised as she looked from me to Deus and then back to me again. "But you all share a bed every night, and you don't have sex?"

"Yes," I answered.

"Then when does he release his power?" she asked.

"You know about that?" I asked, surprised.

"Yea, yea, Deus releases his power through sex. If he doesn't, he becomes weak and eventually reverts to his demonic tendencies. Levi told me about all the brothers and their powers," she explained.

My eyes snapped to Deus. He hadn't told me about reverting back to demonic part. "So not having sex weakens you," I asked.

He sat against the headboard, looking at his nails. He shrugged. "Minute detail," he replied.

"He's fine," I said to Frankie. "He just slept with someone three days ago, or maybe even this morning. I don't know. I don't keep track."

Levi snorted. Deus's eyes went deadly with rage as a black tendril of his magic laced around Levi's neck, strangling him. Levi reached for his throat, straining.

"Alright, alright," gargled Levi. Deus let go. At the same time, Levi and Deus looked at the door.

"Your Nonna is coming," Deus said.

Levi laughed. "I feel like we're teenagers, hiding from their parents."

"Would you like to deal with two pissed off coven elders?" Deus asked. Levi remained silent. "I didn't think so." Deus vanished from my bed. Levi leaned over, kissing Frankie on the head before vanishing into a greenish-black puff of smoke.

A moment later, a knock came at the door. "Come in," I answered. Nonna and Aunt Thora walked in, looking between the two of us.

"How are we feeling?" Aunt Thora asked, making her way to Frankie's side.

"Fine," Frankie answered.

"Much better," I said. Nonna came to my side and patted my cheek.

"Glad to hear it," Nonna said. "Now, let's talk about how you all survived."

Frankie and I looked at each other.

"Ladies," said Aunt Thora. "We aren't idiots. We know you two have been keeping things from us."

"Out with it," snapped Nonna.

"I don't know what you two are talking about," answered Frankie.

Nonna's eyes narrowed on her. "*A mysterious green smoked filled the room,*" Nonna recited, "*causing all of the demons to boil, as if being consumed by neon green acid.*" Frankie looked at me again. "Yes, the others were very detailed in their accounts of what occurred in the Vatican. And you," she said, turning to me. "You overpowered your mother, using the last bit of life force you could muster to save the others, yet somehow, you miraculously shifted home. A gift that takes an enormous amount of power to control. Especially that far of a distance."

I shrugged, sitting on the edge of my bed. "A miracle indeed," I replied.

Nonna let out a wave of power, knocking over my belongings on my dressers and rattling the ceiling lights. "That is enough!" she screamed in aggravation. "You two are going to tell us what the hell has been going on, or I swear to Aradia, I will strap you both down and steal the memories from you."

Frankie's eyes caught mine. She gave me a small smile and shrugged. I shook my head slightly, begging her not to with my eyes, but I already knew there was no way around this. I sent up a little prayer in that moment.

"Two princes of hell saved us," Frankie said bluntly.

Aunt Thora and Nonna went rigid. "Excuse me?" asked Nonna.

Frankie made an uncomfortable face. "Surprise," she said, followed by an uncomfortable laugh.

"What did they gain from saving you?" asked Thora, seeming confused. "What did you offer?" Frankie went silent. Aunt Thora turned her attention to me. "What did you give them? What did you barter with?"

"Nothing," replied Frankie.

"Then what?" Aunt Thora raised her voice, which I had never seen before. "Stop playing games with me, Francesca Rose, and tell us what in the hell is going on!"

I stood, making my way over to Aunt Thora and Frankie. "It's nothing bad, Aunt Thora. They're ... they're our friends," I admitted.

"They're demons," Aunt Thora yelled. "You can't be friends with a demon. They aren't capable of caring for anything or anyone else but themselves."

"That's not true," said Frankie. Her voice trembled a bit.

Nonna's eyes went wide. Her mouth fell open. "Oh ... oh, no," Nonna said in a low voice. She approached Frankie, standing face to face with her. "Please, bambina," she said, shaking her head. "Please tell me you're not ... *in love* with it."

I took Frankie's hand. She looked at me with tears in her eyes.

She inhaled deeply, calming herself before she returned her gaze to Nonna. "Yes. I'm in love with him." Aunt Thora's mouth fell. She backed away, covering her face in shock.

Nonna looked at the both of us. "How could the two of you be so foolish?" asked Nonna. "Francesca ... allowing yourself to be fooled by a prince of hell. To actually believe that he could care for you. How much of an idiot are you?" She turned her eyes to me. "And you ... letting your cousin be so stupid, and keeping something this grave from your family. Have you not learned anything?"

"It's not like that," I said. "Please, just hear us out."

"What is there to say?" she continued. "You are sleeping with the enemy, Francesca. In what reality have you convinced yourself there could ever be a future with that thing?" Frankie was sobbing. "He will use you, until he has taken every ounce of your humanity and power. Then, he will toss you aside like the whores he has taken in the past." Frankie buried herself in my arms, continuing to cry.

A dark green cloud of smoke appeared next to Nonna. "Shit," I grumbled, knowing what came next.

Nonna stepped back, Aunt Thora by her side as they prepared to attack. Levi materialized, took one look at Frankie, and his stance went feral. He turned his focus towards Aunt Thora and Nonna. His eyes blazed green.

"How did you get in here?" demanded Nonna.

Levi reached for Frankie. She turned into him, continuing to cry. He wrapped his arms around her, running his hand through her hair, kissing the top of her head. Something in my heart softened at the sight of them together. He took her face in his palms, bringing her eyes to his. He smiled at her. I watched as her pain seemed to evaporate at the sight of him.

"Let her go you, foul demon!" yelled Aunt Thora.

Levi kissed Frankie on the head and then turned towards my aunt and Nonna. He gave a bow. I could tell he was resisting the urge to kill them. In that moment, I opened the small door I had made for Deus, securing a backup plan to make sure everyone would survive.

"Deus," I said inside my mind.

A moment later. *"Yes, love?"* he replied.

"I need you on standby. I might need some assistance to make sure your brother doesn't kill my aunt or Nonna."

"Oh, what did I miss?"

"Just be prepared to help."

"And what do I get out of this? Care to make a bargain?"

"Deus!"

His sultry laugh glazed across my mind.

"Salvo Elders," greeted Levi, "my name is Leviathan Whitelore."

Nonna's eyes flashed to Frankie. "Envy?" she spat.

"That is correct," answered Levi. "I am the Prince of Envy. I don't mean you nor your children any harm."

"Impossible," said Thora, moving to stand in front of him without fear. "Whatever bargain you have struck with my daughter, I demand you release her from the deal and free her immediately. If payment is owed, I will pay whatever the cost."

"No bargain has been made, Elder Salvo," answered Levi.

"Then what do you want?" asked Thora with a hint of desperation. "Please, just free my daughter."

Levi looked behind him to Frankie. He smiled, extending his hand to her. She took it, joining him at his side. "I'm afraid I have no power over Francesca," he said, looking at her longingly. "In fact, she is the one who holds the power over me."

Aunt Thora watched them. "This can't be happening," she whispered.

"Mamma," said Frankie desperately, "he's not what you think, and I'm not as naive as you both presume. If you can't accept my choice, then there is nothing left to be said."

Nonna looked between the three of us. Her eyes burrowing into me longer than I liked. "Where is yours?" she asked.

"My what?" I asked.

"Your dark prince," she replied. A dark fog appeared behind her, laced with hints of red. I dropped my head into my hands.

"You called," Deus whispered in Nonna's ear. Without hesitation, Nonna swung her arms around, blasting him into the wall. Electricity zapped, pinning him to the surface.

I rushed to her side. "Let him go!" I demanded. She ignored me, focusing her rage and anger, taking it out on Deus. My white flame began to roll around my arms. "I said, let him go!" I shouted.

Nonna dropped her hands, sending Deus to the ground. I rushed to his side. He was slow to get up. I allowed him to lean on me until he got his bearings.

"You Salvo women are feisty," Deus said, "I'll give you that."

"Which one are you?" Nonna asked, her face stone cold.

"Lust, Elder Salvo," he replied with a nod. "At your service." He winked. I elbowed him in the side. He laughed.

Nonna's eyes slid back to me. "And you're sleeping with this one?" she asked.

"No," I said quickly.

"Not yet," Deus added.

"You're making it worse," I growled at him under my breath.

"I don't think this could get any worse, love," he whispered back.

"This is who you've been with the past three months?" Nonna asked. I nodded, unable to speak. Nonna walked forward, judging him, assessing every feature with distaste. She stopped, only coming to his lower chest. "I do not like you," she said. "I do not trust you." She paused, looking at me and then back at Deus. "But whatever you did to heal my granddaughter ... you have my gratitude," she said, then left the room without another word. Aunt Thora looked at the four of us, shaking her head in disbelief and disappointment before following Nonna out.

"Family reunions must be a blast," commented Deus.

"I think theirs would rival ours," added Levi. The brothers

laughed. Deus made a painful hiss, leaning against the nightstand, grabbing at his side. I reached for him instantly. Levi and Frankie rushed over.

"What's wrong?" I asked.

"Your Nonna throws quite a punch," Deus replied. "Nothing to worry about."

"Asmodeus," Levi said firmly.

Deus's eyes snapped to Levi. "I said, there is nothing to worry about," Deus growled.

I looked between the two brothers before grabbing the end of Deus's shirt and pulling it up. A large purple bruise had formed along his left ribcage.

"Why aren't you healing?" I asked.

"Your Nonna is an elder," he said. "She is powerful. It will just take time."

"How much time?" I demanded.

"It will be gone by tomorrow," he said. "No need to worry about me."

"You need to—" Levi started to say.

"I swear to Father—" Deus growled at Levi, matching his brother's stance.

"What?" I asked. "What does he need?" The brothers still stared each other down. I stepped in the middle of them, looking at Levi. "Tell me," I demanded. "Tell me now."

Levi broke his stare from Deus, looking between the two of us hesitantly. "He needs to fuck someone," Levi finally answered.

Bam. A fist came flying over my shoulder, landing in the center of Levi's face. He stumbled back, planting his feet before he fell. Levi's face raged, his eyes turning a bright green. He went to charge Deus, but Frankie stepped in front of him before he unleashed.

"Levi," she whispered. "Take me away. I don't want to stay here tonight," she said. He snapped out of his anger, wrapping her in his arms before shifting them away.

I turned back to Deus. "Was that really necessary?" I asked.

He shrugged. "I warned him. Little twat," he replied.

"Get in the bed," I said. "I'll find you someone so you can heal." I took a single step before he caught me by the arm.

"That won't be necessary. I told you I will be fine."

"That bruise doesn't look fine to me."

"Seren, enough." His jaw tensed while his eyes slightly vibrated. I could tell his temper was beginning to flare.

"I just ... I just want you to be okay. I know how your power works. What's the big deal?"

"In your bed?" he asked, pointing to the mattress. "You want me to fuck another woman in your bed?"

"Well ... it's not ideal, but I don't want you to die either."

He took a step towards me, towering above. He pulled me into him, pressing my body against his. My breath snagged. He wrapped one hand around my hip and the other against the back of my neck. He yanked hard, forcing my face up to his. "Then say it," he said, his voice laced with seduction. "Tell me you're okay, imagining my lips on another woman. Picture me buried deep inside of her, my hands roving over her body ... her breasts. Tell me that you're okay with another woman's mouth wrapped around my cock and my head between her legs." He paused, searching my eyes. "Say it and I will take the first person you find in that hallway."

I swallowed, no longer able to speak. What was he doing? He needed this. It was what kept him powerful. Strong. But why was he fighting me? Everything he had just described, I wanted done to me. Not to another woman. God, even the thought of another woman touching him made me murderous. No. I couldn't go there. I couldn't feel this way. Not about him. I promised myself, I would never feel these things about another man again ... especially the demon of Lust.

I stepped back, out of his grip. He looked at me with heavy eyes, still searching for his answer. "I need you to leave," I whispered.

His face looked confused. "What?" he asked.

"I can't do this. Not with you. I ... I need you to leave. Please Deus."

I could see the hurt and confusion in his eyes. Even only if it was for a moment. "I see," he said, fading into the darkness.

I failed to sleep. My mind was a whirlwind of thoughts and emotions. I kept the door for Deus securely locked that night as I sifted through my own feelings, trying to make sense of what was happening. To be physically attracted to him was one thing. He was beautiful in every sense of the word, but to love him? I couldn't. Especially because I would never know if he loved me for me, or because I carried a part of Victoria: the woman he truly longed for.

I called Frankie that morning to make sure she was okay. Levi had whisked her away to somewhere in Scotland. She seemed in better spirits, but not ready to face our elders yet. She told me she had found the information I asked about and it was waiting for me in her room. As soon as I hung up the phone, I shifted to her room, not wanting to waste another minute.

There, on the desk, were journals and books that told the story of the woman Deus truly loved ... Victoria Prather. I picked up a small canvas. A stunning woman with thick dark brown hair and chocolate eyes stared back at me. Her face was long and elegant. Her lips, full and sensual. Everything about her was perfect. She was captivating. My heart fell.

I sat in Frankie's chair and began to read. Page after page of her journal, there was never mention of Deus. She only talked about Samual. As I sifted through her accounts, I noticed there was a jump in dates. An entire year was erased from her life. There was a journal missing. I closed the leather case, sliding my hand down the front.

I closed my eyes, focusing on Victoria. On Deus. What I felt when her memories surfaced. The need. Passion. Desire. I waited. "Come on, come on," I said, trying to trigger a memory. Finally—

Flash. *An address read, 176 N Elborn St, England. Inside, there was an old fireplace in one of the bedrooms. Feminine fingers dug into the mortar, pulling a brick free from its place. A black leather-bound journal hid deep inside. Through her eyes, I looked back at a servant who stood behind me. "The covens can't know about him ... not yet. I must find a way to free myself from this burden. For now, my heart will remain here ... hidden."*

I pulled myself out of the memory, frantic to get into that room. I knew the address and what the room looked like. I could do this. I could shift there.

I logged into Frankie's laptop, pulling up the most recent photo and map of the location. After memorizing the details, I closed my eyes and willed my shadows to form around me, pulling me through space. With my well of power full, thanks to Deus, I had the strength I needed to make this work. With one powerful pull, I slammed into an ally wall, stumbling to stay up right. I looked around, smiling at myself. I had done it. I shifted to another country, all on my own. I took a deep breath, rushing to the front of176 N Elborn St.

I pounded on the door until a little old lady appeared. "Hello, may I help you?" she said in a British accent.

"Good day," I replied, looking around me to make sure we weren't drawing any attention. "Is anyone else home by chance?"

"No dearie, just me," she replied.

I smiled, waving my hand around her face, "*Somnum*," I whispered. The little old lady collapsed into my arms, sound asleep. I ushered her to the ground softly before shutting the door and running upstairs. I checked each bedroom until I recognized the fireplace. *Bingo.* Frantically, I rushed to the stones, running my fingers over the brick I recognized. It had been mortared over. I grabbed the fireplace fork and chipped away at the grit until it became loose.

I wrapped my fingers around the stone and pulled it free, tossing the brick to the ground. I reached inside, pulling out the black journal just as I had seen. I smiled, held it against my chest, and shifted myself back to Frankie's room. I was completely exhausted by the two large jumps, but I was too riled up to care. I sat back at the desk, staring at the journal I hoped would contain the answers I desperately craved. I opened the cover slowly.

21st of August, 1717.

I met the most enticing gentleman today. He could have been, quite possibly, the most beautiful being I have ever laid eyes on. His elegant stature and entrancing blue eyes caught hold of me in a way I never knew possible. The sound of his voice, and that smile, I can't seem to get out of my mind. I feel guilty. I love my Samual. But this man. This dark angel has drawn me in, and I don't want him to let me go.

30th of September 1717.

I've lost all sense of control. Deus has awakened something inside of me I cannot quench. The sight of him sends me into a heated frenzy. He has consumed my thoughts, my dreams. I cannot seem to focus on anything but him. The way he looks at me makes me want to run away with him. No matter that he is a demon. I have lost my mind, and I never want to find it again. Not if it means being without him.

7th of December 1717.

I've done it. I've left home and I've run away with Deus. I cannot be without him. He is where I belong. Where my heart calls home. My coven is outraged. They have vowed to tear the goddess from me. They say I am unworthy, but I don't care. Let them try. With Deus by my side, there is nothing we cannot accomplish. Gods, I have never felt this passion and love for another. I only believed it existed in literature. The way he consumes me in every way: mind, body, and soul. Though the bond hasn't clicked into place, I believe in time it will. This love is too all-consuming for it to be anything other than destined. I love him more than life itself. Without him, I'd be nothing. I cannot be apart from him, nor he I. He is the love of my life. My destiny. My mate.

I closed the book, not wanting to read another word. Mate ... they were ...mates. Tears ran down my face. I had to sever whatever was between us. This complicated web of past and present needed to end, for everyone's sake. I held the journal tightly, clenching the key around my neck. I closed my eyes and thought of Deus. In a smooth and quick shift, I appeared in his room.

I opened my eyes to see him sitting at his desk with his head buried in a book. Victoria was right. He was the most beautiful being ever created. It was amazing how similar she and I were, even born three hundred years apart from one another. Is that why he attached himself to me? To hold onto the memory of her? His mate. My heart felt heavy. I forced my emotions down, trying to remain calm and collected. His eyes rose to meet me. A small smile stretched across his face as he straightened in the chair.

"Well, hello," he said. "Miss me already?"

I took a deep breath. "Deus, we need to talk."

"Sure. Are you hungry? I was just about to call down for lunch."

"No. I won't be staying long."

His brow furrowed with confusion. "What's wrong? Did something happen?"

"No. I—" I walked to the front of his desk, still clutching the journal in my hand. I collected myself, bringing my eyes up to his. "I want to thank you for everything you've done for me. You quite literally saved my life, multiple times. If there was any way I could repay you, I would, but I feel our time together has come to an end."

He laughed, sitting back in his chair. "What is this all about, love?"

"Deus, please," I said in a serious tone. "I've decided it's best if I return home. Permanently."

He paused, looking down at his book. "As I have always told you, this is your life, you get to make your own decisions as to how you live it."

I huffed a laugh. "If only that were true."

He stood from his chair, making his way around the desk. He reached for me, but I stepped back. "What is this really about?" Reluctantly, I held out the journal towards him. He looked down at the black leather-bound book. "What is this?"

"Victoria's journal, filled with memories and stories about how much the two of you loved each other."

"Where did you find this?" he asked sternly.

"Why does it matter?"

He refused to take it. I placed it on his desk. His eyes were locked on the little black book, his jaw tense.

"You still love her?" I asked, knowing the answer would break my heart.

"I will always love her. She was my reason for existing." His reason for existing. His mate. With that admission, I let go of whatever fairytale hope I had of being with him. This was for the best.

"Can I ask you something?" I whispered, fighting to get the words to leave my lips. He remained still, not saying a word. "The first night we met ... did you seek me out because you hoped to find her? That through me, you would have another chance at the love you two shared? The life you had been robbed of?"

He swallowed, raising his head high. He looked down at me with his beautiful eyes. "You are nothing like Victoria," he said, his tone firm, nearly harsh.

I smiled, keeping the pain I felt inside from overtaking me. "I see," I whispered, taking a step back. I met his eyes one last time. "Thank you again, Asmodeus. For everything." With that I shifted.

Chapter Fifteen

One week became two, then two became four. Summer had arrived and I spent every moment possible in the sun. Orion proposed to Delphine. I was happy for my friend, but something inside of me was envious. Frankie tried to get me to open up about Deus, but I remained sealed. I journaled about him often, but I never shared my pain with anyone.

Frankie spent more time away from home. She continued her relationship with Levi and didn't care what anyone thought. Nonna and Aunt Thora ignored Frankie's involvement with the demon prince, unable to process her choice in partner.

I buried myself in books and training while Nonna and I resumed our magic lessons. I dove deeper into the elements of the earth and what our ancestors relied on centuries before our time. When I wasn't studying or training, I would bask in the sun, drawing in its energy in order to recenter myself. Tony began to join me, finding any excuse to be nearby. He was relentless, I'd give him that.

Little by little, I began speaking to him again. I didn't fully trust him, and I didn't know if I ever would, but being with him like this reminded me of why I fell in love with him in the first place. He was smart, charming, and handsome, but he wasn't Deus.

Against my better judgement, I had come to admire the Prince of Lust. He had helped me discover a side of myself I never knew I possessed. He gave me the tools to regain my sense of purpose and to create a strength I only ever admired in others. Deus had helped me hone my powers and focus my emotions into something I could harness. He had awakened a version of myself I now was proud of ... a version I loved.

At night, I'd lay in bed, creating constellations in my room, trying to force myself to stay awake. When I closed my eyes, I relived Victoria's memories: her intimate moments with Deus, how they fell in love, all they shared. Experiences I would never have with him.

I filed them away in her red cabinet, but it didn't stop the pain. I didn't know how it was possible to be jealous of a dead woman, but I was. So instead of sleeping, I would head down to the kitchen in the early hours of the morning. I began baking and cooking again, focusing on anything I could that wouldn't remind me of Deus. By the time it was breakfast, the castle had a banquet table full of homemade baked goods and entrees.

During my lesson with Nonna one morning, she was unusually quiet. Something was bothering her, but I didn't want to pry. I mixed the ingredients as the recipe called for, creating the perfect appearance potion, allowing you to take the form of another.

"Very good, bambina," Nonna said, looking over her balcony.

"Anything else for today?" I asked.

"No, that will be all." I got up to leave, kissing her on the cheek before turning towards the door. "Bambina," Nonna called after me.

"Yes?"

She paused for a moment. "I worry about Francesca."

I returned to my chair next to her. "I really don't think you have anything to worry about. Honestly, she's probably the safest she could be when she's with Levi. You saw how protective he was of her."'

Nonna huffed. "Yes, jealous, one could say."

I laughed. "Envy will do that to a person."

"But he's not a person. He's a ... a demon."

"Yes. And we're witches. The people out there are humans. There is a whole world full of beings, each species and race capable of doing horrible things. But each is capable of creating beauty ... creating good."

She turned her eyes towards me. "You have come so far, Seren. I am proud of the woman you have grown into."

"Thank you."

She looked back out over the balcony. "And how is your prince?"

My heart banged against my chest painfully at the thought of him. "He's not my prince, and I don't know. We no longer speak."

"And why is that?"

"It's complicated."

"I enjoy complicated matters," she said with a small smile.

I sat back, fiddling with my fingers. "He and Victoria Prather were in love. I think mated even. I don't know the complete story, but he was forced to take away her memories of him to save her. He is still very much in love with her. I think ... I think a part of him found me in hope of reconnecting with the piece of Victoria I carry. To relive the love they once shared. And that love ... God, Nonna. I've felt it ... seen it. It was powerful beyond words."

"Are those his words, or yours?" she asked.

"It doesn't matter. This is for the best. As you like to remind me, he is a demon after all. They can't be trusted."

She laughed. "Well, I might be eating my words here in a moment."

"What are you talking about?"

She turned to me. "How are the relations between Levi, Deus, and their other brothers?"

"Complicated. Unpredictable. Volatile," I answered, recalling the stories Deus told.

"And how do they feel about Lucifer?"

"They hate him the most."

She smiled. "Perfect."

"What are you planning, Nonna?"

"Something that has made me question my own sanity. Something that is a risk, but the payoff it might possess is priceless." She paused. "Do you think Deus and Levi would agree to meet in front of the council?"

"To what gain?"

"If Deus is afraid of Lucifer acquiring your powers, his brothers must be as well. I propose that we proposition his brothers to join us in the fight against Lucifer and Obsidian."

The wind was knocked out of me. "You've got to be kidding me," I said in shock.

"Oh, I very much wish I was, bambina, but I don't see any other choice. Your mother and those demonic witches have already acquired a concerning amount of power by killing our members. The possibility of them getting ahold of you, or an elder ... It will never stop. We need a larger weapon in our arsenal, and those brothers might be the answers to our prayers."

"Deus and Levi are one thing, but I have no clue how the others are, or what they will demand as payment."

"Well, that's where I am hoping Deus and Levi will assist. They know their family and hopefully, how to control them."

I hung my head, thinking through the possibilities. "I don't know about Deus, but I will ask Frankie to talk to Levi," I replied.

"Thank you, bambina." We sat for a long while, looking over the vast landscape of our home ... of Triora.

“I’m nervous,” admitted Frankie, fidgeting in front of the briefing room doors.

“You and me both,” I replied.

“Yeah, well, you’re not the one they’re all going to sneer at for sleeping with a demon.”

“I thought you didn’t care what anyone thought?”

She shrugged. “I don’t ... I mean, not really. It’s just ... they’re all going stare and judge. Gods, I can’t believe Nonna came up with this plan. Of all people.”

“I know, right?” I chewed on the side of my mouth anxiously. “Levi said Deus would come?” I asked.

She nodded. “You still haven’t spoken to him?”

“No. Not since the journal incident.”

She grabbed my hand. “I wish things would have turned out differently for you,” she whispered.

“It’s for the best.”

“What’s for the best?” asked Levi, strolling towards us. He pulled Frankie into his arms, devouring her mouth.

I refrained from throwing up. “I’m never going to get use to that,” I admitted, looking away.

"Give it a couple decades," said a familiar voice. Deus stepped out from behind Levi, looking as dapper as ever. He stood in front of me with his hands casually in his pockets. His hair was brushed to the side; his eyes, entrancing as ever. "Hello, love."

I looked at the man I had slept in the same bed with for three months. The man who had helped me find a reason to live: who had seen me at my worst ... yet I couldn't speak. "Hi," I managed to get out. I turned back to the door, waiting for the games to begin.

I saw him step next to me in my peripheral vision. I focused on breathing. "A month without speaking to me, and all I get is a simple 'hi'?" he said, staring at me.

I refrained from meeting his gaze. "I'm just trying to focus right now," I replied. Not completely a lie.

"Ah, yes. Your Nonna's plan to get all of us demons to work together. Homicidal, but brilliant," he said sarcastically.

"If you don't think it's going to work, then why are you here?"

"I'm here for the drama. Between your family, your coven, and my brothers. This should be good."

I finally turned to him, feeling my temper flare. "If you're not going to take this seriously then you can leave."

He gave me a half-cocked smile. "I missed that pissy little face of yours."

I rolled my eyes, returning my attention to the door. "Please just stop," I said, already exhausted from the exchange. I couldn't do this banter with him. Not now. Not when a day hadn't gone by where I hadn't thought of him, or missed sleeping and waking up beside him, or wondered if he was thinking about me. I took a deep breath, gathering myself.

The doors finally opened and the four of us walked in. I took my seat next to Nonna. Deus sat beside me. Frankie sat by Aunt Thora, with Levi at her side. Antonio, Orion, and the rest of our squad was in the room with the elders. They stared; curiosity peaked. Antonio's eyes blazed at the sight of Deus. I focused on Nonna.

"And who do we have the honor of meeting?" asked Elder Torrian.

Nonna smiled softly, flicking her eyes between Frankie and I. "Covens," she said. "I would like to introduce Leviathan Whitelore and Asmodeus Râşnov, two princes of hell."

The covens erupted in outrage. Elders stood, yelling, and screaming. Some readied their magic, preparing to attack. A few pushed their offspring behind them protectively. Deus and Levi just sat, covering their mouths as they looked at one another and chuckled in amusement.

"Enough!" yelled Nonna, standing to her feet. "Sit down and shut up. All of you," she demanded.

"I like her," Deus whispered in my ear.

"Which ones are they?" asked Elder Mystic.

"Envy," answered Levi.

"And you?" asked Elder Cavelleer from the Fuoco Coven.

Deus's eyes turned to hers slowly. His smiled stretched across his face. "Lust," he answered, the words rolling off his tongue sensuously.

"For fucks sake," Antonio muttered, placing his elbows on the table.

Deus laughed. "What's wrong little warlock?" he asked. "Feeling inadequate?" Antonio stood from his chair, pulling a spear off the wall with his magic, hurtling it through the air towards Deus. Deus held his hand out, creating a red barrier around us. As soon as the spear made contact with the shield, it disintegrated into small shards of red ash. "You're going to have to do better than that."

"Enough," roared Nonna. "Both of you, put your cocks back in your pants so we can get down to business." Nonna sat back down. "Now, about why you are here today."

Aunt Thora took over. "Obsidian has been working directly with Lucifer to obtain more power by siphoning the witches they have been kidnapping. Their strength grows by the minute. They have their eyes set on Seren, and if Lucifer gets his hands on the power of the goddess, the tables will turn, and not in our favor."

"If Lucifer is our enemy," said Elder Torrian Astra, "then why are we currently sharing a table with two of his brothers?"

"Lucy and the rest of us don't see eye-to-eye," answered Deus. "We're here to offer you an alliance."

Elder Angela Ferrara scoffed. "Please. A demon prince offering an alliance. What is the price?"

"No demands have been made," added Levi, smiling at Frankie. "We only wish to stop our brother."

Elder Astra looked from Levi to Frankie for a long moment. "You're sleeping with a demon prince?" he asked in astonishment. "The Salvo heirs are in bed with the princes of hell."

"That has no bearing on the issue at hand," intervened Nonna. The elders began to chatter amongst themselves.

"The hell it doesn't," yelled Elder Astra.

"This goes against everything we believe in," said another.

"This is a disgrace to our kind!"

"This can't be right," said Elder Ketra Strange. "My father sacrificed his life to save Seren. And for what? To have her soul sold to a demon prince of hell?"

"Goddess or not, she should be put down for her disgraceful behavior. She and her whore of a cousin," demanded Torrian Astra.

The room was instantly blasted with black and red fog. The lights flickered as the walls shook. A powerful force erupted through the conference room. Sounds of static and lightening thundered all around. One minute, Deus was beside me, and the next, his hand was around Torrian's throat, slamming him into the table. The wood cracked. Deus stood over him, his demeanor perfectly controlled.

"Here we are," said Deus, "offering our assistance to the less fortunate, and you have the audacity to spit in our faces. We, the only things that might actually stand a chance against your enemy. Threatening the only people standing in the way of your extinction? Not a smart move, if I do say so." The other elders stood, readying to defend Torrian.

Levi stood gracefully, throwing his arms out to his sides. Everyone in the room except for Nonna, Frankie, Aunt Thora, and I went flying back against the wall, unable to move. Red lightening flashed above us. Torrian's face turned shades of purple.

I opened the crack in my shield. *"Deus, let him go ... please,"* I thought. *"You've made your point."*

"As you wish," Deus said out loud. He released Torrian. Levi lowered his hands, sending the other coven members to the floor. The black haze dissipated while the members stood to their feet.

I looked around at them, feeling a sense of betrayal. "We have come to you with a plan that could actually work," I said to all of them. "Are you so closed-minded that you would ignore a way to save our families? Our way of life?"

"You are our goddess, and you share a bed with a demon!" yelled Torrian. "You are destined to mate with Orion."

"This isn't how it's done," said Elder Bloodborn. "You and Orion are destined."

"Nowhere does it say that we are destined," I replied. "The only mates ever mentioned are Cyrus and Aradia. I am not Aradia, and Orion is not Cyrus. We have the memories of the others, but we are not them. We have remained ourselves. And who are you to question destiny?" I paused. "And just to be clear, I do not share a bed with any demon."

"This needs to stop," Orion said, coming to my side. Delphine joined him, taking his hand with hers. "We are not our former vessels. We have our own minds, our own hearts. None of you can truly understand what Seren and I have been through. We are free to choose who we love, and we are free to build our own lives as we see fit. Our lives are not yours to control." Orion stopped, turning his attention to Deus. Their eyes locked. "If Seren and the other Salvo women trust the princes, then so do I."

Deus nodded his thanks.

"As do I," said Loriana, coming to my side. She smiled at me.

"And I." Roric

"I," Tyler.

"We do," said Gabby and Bella in unison.

"I," said Aunt Thora, coming to my side. She smiled down at me. Frankie ran to her mother, embracing her.

"And I," said Nonna firmly. She looked back at the coven as they watched. One by one, they filed out of the room without a word. Tony stopped, looking back at Orion and me. He shook his head before taking his leave.

Orion turned back to me and smiled. Delphine appeared at his side. "My mother wishes to speak with us," she said to Orion.

He exhaled. "I'm sure she does." "Talk later?" he asked me.

"Of course," I replied. He leaned over and kissed me on my head.

Once they left, Nonna sat back in her chair. She rubbed her temples.

"That went as expected," said Aunt Thora.

"We haven't heard the last from them, that's for sure," said Nonna. She poured herself a glass of wine and downed it.

"What can we do to help?" asked Frankie.

Nonna looked at the two of us and then at the princes. "I am assuming you both have residences?" she asked.

They nodded.

"How fortified are your lands against your brother?"

"He doesn't know where we reside," explained Levi.

"We have shielded our lands from our other brothers for millennia," added Deus. "No one finds our palaces unless we allow it."

"Have you both discussed how to sway your brothers to our cause?" asked Aunt Thora.

Levi's face seemed deep in thought. "The Consort," Levi said softly.

"What's the Consort?" asked Frankie.

"A gathering that happens every one hundred years, during the summer solstice," explained Levi. "All our brothers meet for a dinner party and a display of power. We renegotiate land, businesses, political movements, all of it."

"Lucifer will be there?" asked Thora.

"Yes," said Levi.

"Why not kill him then?" asked Frankie.

"We can't," Deus said. "Once we step across the threshold of the chosen location, we are unable to harm one another, or anyone on the premises. It's to make sure we all behave."

"And which brothers do you predict will join us?" asked Aunt Thora.

Levi looked at Deus. "Belz and Mammon, possibly," said Levi. "Belphegor will depend on his mood and laziness this decade. Satan, most likely not. He's always tended to side with Lucifer."

"If there's a chance, shouldn't we try?" asked Frankie.

"We all will attend," Nonna said adamantly. "I'm not sending my bloodline into a den of vipers alone."

"Our brothers aren't going to like this," added Levi.

"I don't give a fuck what your brothers like," spat Nonna. "This is my family, and I am in charge of protecting it. When and where is this thing happening?

"June twentieth," said Levi, "six days from now."

I turned to Deus. "And you weren't going to tell me?" I asked.

He laughed. "I'm not the one who has refused to speak to the other for a month."

The doors to the room flew open. On the other side stood the coven elders. Neither Elder Mystic nor Orion was with them. Elder Torrian Astra stepped to the front with authority. "Elder Lucia De Salvo and Elder Thora De Salvo," he addressed. "The elders have found you unfit to serve as the heads of your coven. You have been removed from your stations, effective immediately. Seren and

Francesca De Salvo. You are henceforth banned from any and all coven properties. Your clearance has been revoked and you will be escorted off the property immediately."

"How dare you threaten to remove a Salvo from her own home?" yelled Nonna. "The ignorance of the lot of you."

"The vote has been called," added Torrian. "Your time as elder is done, Lucia. Unit, take them." Warlock and witches entered the room.

"Grab onto one another," Deus said, turning towards us. Magic erupted from the others, attempting to stop us before we escaped. Deus shielded me with his body, folding me into his arms. Once we had all locked hands, he shifted us to his castle. We landed in the ballroom.

"The nerve of that son of a bitch," yelled Nonna, pulling away from the group.

Aunt Thora straightened, taking in the grandeur of the room. She circled around herself, her eyes blazing with awe. "Medieval architecture," said Thora quietly. "Constructed in the thirteenth century, but obvious improvements and additions have been made." She looked out the window. "Snow-peaked mountains. Not a city in sight. Romania?"

Deus smiled. "Very good," Deus said. "You Salvo women never disappoint."

Nonna walked away, talking to herself, cussing and yelling under her breath in frustration.

"What do we do now?" asked Frankie.

"We will think of something," said Thora, pulling Frankie into her side. "We always do."

"You are all welcome to stay here as long as you'd like," offered Deus.

"Thank you, prince," replied Thora.

"Deus is just fine." His eyes trailed to me. I didn't say a word. This was the last place I wanted to be.

Nonna stormed back over to our group. "I'm going to castrate that incompetent, power hungry fucker," she said. Magic rippled off her in heat waves. "I will contact our allies and try to smooth things over with them. In the meantime, we focus on the Consort."

Deus turned to Levi. "Will you be staying or returning to Scotland?" he asked.

"I need to check in on a few things back home, but for now, I think it's safer if we stay together," answered Levi.

Deus nodded. "Gallo," he called.

The little goldaburg appeared in a flash. Nonna and Aunt Thora took a step back, staring at the little demon. "Yes, your majesty," he said in his scratchy voice.

"Please prepare Prince Whitelore's usual room. Also, prepare two adjoining rooms for the elders."

"Three," I corrected.

Deus looked at me and glared. "They will be staying for the

foreseeable future," he continued. "Please inform the household."

Gallo's eyes trailed along each of us. "Four witches now, your majesty," he said. "Is that wise?"

"Did I ask your opinion, emnu?" said Deus casually.

"What's an emnu?" asked Thora.

"Lower-level demon," Frankie replied.

"No," Gallo spat.

"Then go," demanded Deus. The little demon flashed out of sight. Then, in a breath, three more goldaburgs appeared. They looked the same: long pointed ears, wide almond eyes, elongated mouths taking up much of their face, adorned with sharp little teeth.

"Rooms are ready," one said.

"Your majesty," finished another.

"They will take you to your quarters," explained Deus. "I will send someone before dinner to give you all a tour of the grounds. Hot meals should also be waiting for you when you arrive."

"Thank you again," said Aunt Thora, following one of the goldaburgs. Nonna passed him without a word. She had lost her position, her coven, and her home all in the same day; it would take some time to process. Levi took Frankie into his arms and vanished. His goldaburg spat, snapping out of sight.

I turned back to Deus. "Thank you," I said with a small nod.

"I'm offended you don't wish to resume our previous sleeping arrangements," he admitted.

"I figured you would need your strength in preparation for the Consort. I didn't want to occupy the bed," I replied, turning and following the goldaburg to my new room.

Chapter Sixteen

The next morning, I found Mal and continued my training. She beat the shit out of me, but I didn't care. It was a welcomed distraction. I needed to feel something, anything, besides what I was feeling about Deus. Hashen returned that evening. I rushed to his chambers, eager to discuss what I had done with the demon.

"So, you mean to tell me, I am like you?" I asked, astonished.

"I don't believe a demon and god's power is exactly the same," he answered in his deep voice, "but it would appear there are similarities. I suggest we begin training with other beings to push the possibilities of your power."

I smiled widely. "I am so excited."

"Have you begun to explore your ability to shift realms?" he asked, pouring himself a cup of tea.

I froze. "What?"

"Your ability to talk with the dead. To cross over."

"I don't know what you're talking about," I admitted. "I thought the horned god had the power over life."

"No, Seren. He has the power to heal and mend. You have the

power over death."

My mind was swimming. "This just keeps getting better," I whispered. I looked at Hashen. "I don't even know where to begin with that power."

He laughed, sipping his tea. A monster of a man, with a tiny teacup. It was a sight. "One power at a time, I say. Let's focus on the mind weaving for now. That is what I can help you with. Talking to the dead ... not my expertise."

A goldaburg appeared in the doorway. It nodded. "Lady Seren, your presence has been requested in Prince Râșnov's chambers," it said.

"Tell him I'm busy," I replied.

"He insists," it snapped, waddling away.

I exhaled. "Is he always this demanding?"

"Yes," Hashen said flatly. "He's a spoiled prince, what do you expect?"

I laughed, heading for his room. I was the first to arrive. The room was unchanged from the last time I had visited. His bed was neatly made. The round table to the side of the room was filled with food. I walked through the open area that had once brought me so much peace. I stopped at his desk, spotting Victoria's journal. My heart ached.

"Is your new bedroom to your liking?" His voice came from behind me.

I turned towards him. He was dressed casually, with a black

cotton shirt that hugged all his muscles perfectly, and a pair of jeans. "I slept well, thank you. Will the others be joining us?"

"Shortly," he said. "I wanted to speak with you first."

"In regard to ..."

He took another step towards me, pinning me against the desk. He smiled, laughing softly. "Seren ... what is this awkwardness between us? Have I done something to offend you?"

"No. We're all just dealing with a lot right now. I'm trying to stay focused."

"And do I distract you? Is that it?"

How perfectly constructed he was: down to the smallest details. The way his hair was perfectly arranged, not a piece out of place. His handsome face, perfectly shaven. His lips ... so smooth and lush. "No."

"Then what?"

I gathered the strength to push myself off the desk, sliding out from under his body. "Listen, we're fine, okay? I just want to focus on killing your prick of a brother and getting my coven back." I took a seat at the table and poured myself a cup of coffee.

The door opened. In came the others ... thank God.

"Good morning, brother," Levi said, smacking Deus on the shoulder. "You're looking ... stronger. How many did you fuck last night?" I felt an uncomfortable twisting in my gut. I needed to get the hell out of here ... and fast.

"Don't make me kick your ass this early in the morning,

Leviathan," replied Deus.

"I'd love to see you try," taunted Levi.

"Alright, alright, either fight or kiss, but I'm famished and ready to eat," said Frankie, taking a seat next to me.

Nonna stepped next to us, looking around Deus's room. "Well, this is ... excessive," she said.

"Oh, stop it, Mother," Thora said, taking a seat at the table. "You're just jealous."

"This isn't the only library," I added. "He has two others, bigger than this even."

Nonna huffed. "Maybe I'd like a tour after all," she said, taking a seat across from Aunt Thora. Levi and Deus took their seats, filling plates of food for us as they passed them around the table.

"Did you sleep well?" I asked Nonna.

"Not at all," she answered. "I was up all night, reaching out to those I believe loyal to this family. I've had plenty of replies, but a handful of rejections. Have you tried to make contact with Orion?"

"Yes. My messages aren't getting through. What have your contacts said?"

"They will stand by our claim as the rightful elders of the Étoile coven," Nonna said. "Many of our coven members agree. They plan to push the elders out of our castle. I don't know how long that is going to take, but that's their plan thus far."

"But what does that mean about the agreements made between

us and the other six covens?" asked Frankie.

"If it comes down to it," Aunt Thora said, "our coven has decided. We will break away from the six until the issues at hand are resolved. They are loyal to our family and only our family."

"This is all my fault," Frankie said, guilt washing over her.

"No, bambina," said Nonna. "This is the fault of those ignorant and power-hungry pissants who strive to overthrow our influence. This is a power move on their part. Nothing more. Let's see how they fair against Obsidian without us. They'll come crawling back. I have no doubt."

"But until then," Aunt Thora added, "we need to reach out to every member who you believe will be loyal to us. Building our connections and keeping them alive will ensure we have a home to return to."

We both nodded. "In the meantime," said Nonna, looking across the table at Levi and Deus, "why don't you tell us about your family, boys?"

"What would you like to know?" asked Deus.

"Everything," replied Nonna.

"Well," Deus began, "we, the original seven, are a reflection of our sins. They make up much of our personalities and bear weight on the decisions we make."

"So, because you represent lust," Nonna said, "does that mean you are unable to remain faithful?"

I choked on the strawberry in my mouth.

Deus gave a little laugh. “No, Elder Salvo,” he said, looking at me tenderly. “I am very capable of being faithful, if I choose. Though I don’t see the benefit.”

I felt Nonna’s eyes shift to me, assessing my reaction, but I remained calm. “And Lucifer?” said Nonna. “Tell us about our enemy.”

“I am not going to lie to you,” answered Deus. “He is the most powerful of us all. He was an archangel. Though he no longer has his grace, remnants of his power have remained. He was the first to fall. Father cast him out of heaven. Then, after discovering that we helped plan to overthrow him, Father banned us from the heavens, forcing us to live on Earth, amongst his most cherished creations. Our souls were ripped from us, causing us to become demonic in nature and action.

“One-by-one, we redeemed our souls, finding our grace again throughout the ages. This allowed us to control our power and our sins. Each sin is detrimental to humans, if they overindulge, yet needed. Lust, for example, can be the gateway to the most incredible and passionate connection a being can ever experience with another.”

“Envy,” interrupted Levi, “motivates you to push yourself harder, to be better, and achieve higher success. The same goes for the other five. Each, in moderation, has led to revelations and times of renaissance throughout the existence of this world.”

“But Lucifer,” continued Deus, “rejected his soul after finding it. And because of that, he is the most ruthless of us all."

"What is his plan?" asked Thora.

Levi shrugged. "Ultimate power," he answered. "To be worshipped by the creations Father chose to love over him. To mock the creator, in every way he can possibly imagine."

"And can he be killed?" Nonna asked.

Deus kept his attention on his food. Levi looked at him and then back to Nonna. "He can," he answered.

"How?" Thora.

"We cannot reveal that," Deus said plainly. "The seven of us made deal long ago that if one of us reveled our cherished secret, we would cease being."

"Isn't that convenient?" Nonna said, cutting into her quiche.

"But what does he want with Seren?" asked Thora. "He has never shown interested in any of the vessels before. Not like this."

"Well," said Nonna, leaning on her elbows, "we know he is working with Annalise. She believes Seren's power can be transferred to her, but how do they plan to do that?"

A dizziness overcame me as a memory from Aradia, for the first time, blazed through my mind.

She was writing in a book. Her book of spells. The cover looked familiar. She handed it to someone. "Just in case the plan goes wrong," she whispered. "Hide this until it is needed."

I swayed, snapping back into reality. My eyes widened. Finally, the connection. It all made sense now. "Aradia's spell book. That was what they stole in Paris," I whispered.

Deus's jaw clenched. "Your mother is in possession of the grimoire?" asked Deus.

"What are you to talking about?" asked Nonna.

I turned to her. "The book Obsidian was after in Paris, all those months ago. It wasn't just any spell book. It was written by the first witches: by Aradia herself. It contains a spell in it to separate the goddess entity from the vessel, killing the original host."

Nonna dropped her head. "Annalise," she whispered bitterly.

"We need to destroy it, then," suggested Frankie.

"We can't," said Levi. "I've tried. Three hundred years ago, when—" he stopped, looking at Deus.

Deus was deathly still.

"What do you know?" asked Nonna. "Please, prince ... we need all the information we can get."

If Deus clenched his jaw any tighter, I feared his teeth might shatter. This had something to do with Victoria. I turned to my family. "Leave it, Nonna," I insisted.

"Leave what?" she asked again. "Bambina, if there is something we don't know... something that could endanger your life, we need to know. We need to be prepared."

"You're right," said Deus, still not looking up from the table. He took a deep breath. "Three hundred years ago, Victoria Prather's coven tried to use Aradia's grimoire on her. Lucifer gave them the book."

"But why?" asked Aunt Thora. "Why would a coven turn on their goddess?"

"Because she was in love," said Frankie, staring at Deus. "With you," she whispered.

He closed his eyes and nodded. He was in pain. "I made a deal with Lucifer and took away Victoria's memories of our ... relationship. In exchange, her coven agreed not to strip the goddess entity from her, which would have killed the host." My heart was bleeding for him. I wanted so badly to reach out and take his hand, but I refrained.

"So, Annalise plans to use the book on Seren," Nonna whispered. She looked distraught. "Prince," she said, looking up from her plate. "Do you, by chance, have anything stronger than coffee?"

Deus gave a small smile and nodded, flicking his wrist as a bottle of whisky and glass appeared. Nonna poured and then slammed it back before refilling it.

Frankie took my hand. "We won't let her use it on you," she whispered. I smiled, but something inside of me went quiet.

I stood from the table, still forcing a smile. "If you'll excuse me for a moment," I said, leaving the room.

As soon as the door shut behind me, I walked down the hall, not knowing where I was heading. I just needed to go; to move. Soon, my walk turned into a jog, and then my jog into a sprint.

As I turned the corner, I ran. I ran as fast as I could, feeling the burning in my lungs and in my muscles. I slammed through the front doors, down the driveway, and into town. Panic and fear threaded through me. My magic welled in response to my emotions. I could feel the need for it to be released.

Desperate for any relief, I gave in. *Flash*. I stumbled as my feet hit the ground. Tokyo. I had shifted to Tokyo. But I didn't care. I didn't stop running. I had to get away. I had to get farther away. *Flash*. Africa. Run. *Flash*. Paris. Run. *Flash*. The ocean. Run. *Flash*. A mountain peak, full of soft snow.

I fell into it, trying to gather myself and my emotions. The freezing chill felt like a soothing, familiar embrace. I sat there, allowing the bitter cold to clear my mind, helping me focus and think about what came next. Obsidian removing the goddess entity from me was no longer a theory, but an actual possibility; and they had the means to do it. A book, written by the god who started this whole shit show and a power-hungry fallen angel. God, I was screwed.

I lost track of time, just sitting in the snow. Finally, I pulled out my phone, figuring it would probably be a good idea to figure out where in the hell I had landed myself. Rocky Mountains, Colorado. "Shit," I said out loud. I reached for my power, but it was tapped. I was able to shift my way down to a little shop in Estes Park. I ordered a cup of coffee to warm myself and then let the walls around my mind fall.

Deus strolled through the door of the coffee shop five minutes later. He seemed unfazed, as always. He sat in the chair across from me. The woman at the counter smiled brightly, bringing him a cup of coffee without being asked. He nodded and thanked her. She was swooning.

I laughed. "Does that always happen?" I asked.

"You already know the answer to that," he replied.

"I know you don't like to talk about it, but I'm ... I'm sorry about how things ended with Victoria. That wasn't fair to either of you. For what it's worth, I know how much she loved you." He dropped his eyes from me and didn't respond. God, when was I going to learn? The feeling of stupidity and embarrassment enveloped me. I pulled back, regretting that I had allowed him to know my location. "Can we go, please," I finally said, not wanting to be alone with him a moment longer.

"How did you get yourself across the world?" he asked.

"Shifting," I said, confused.

"Obviously, smartass, but it takes years to harness enough power to go this great of a distance. Yet, here you are."

I shrugged. "I don't know. I just felt panicked and wanted to run. So, I did. Went through about half a dozen countries before ending up on top of that mountain, actually."

He laughed, swirling his finger on the mug's rim. "You're amazing," he said.

Yeah well, I'm not Victoria, so ... I thought. His eyes snapped to mine in complete shock. *Shit.* I forgot to shut the door between us. He stared at me. Not knowing what to do and feeling more uncomfortable than ever, I stood and bolted for the door. I couldn't shift, but I could walk.

"Seren," I heard him following me, but I kept moving. I crunched through the snow, completely underdressed for this climate, but I didn't care. I had to try and put as much space between him and I as possible. His grip latch around my arm, swinging me back to face him. "What did you mean by that?" he asked.

"Just forget you ever heard that," I said, trying to leave, but he held me in place.

"What did you mean?" he asked again, more aggressively.

"What do you mean, what did I mean?" I yelled, flailing my arms on either side of me. "I'm repeating what you told me a month ago, remember? Right after I brought Victoria's journal to you." I stepped towards him, feeling like I was going to explode. "You want to know why I didn't contact you after I left that day? Why I've been acting so off? It's because I feel like you are constantly comparing me to her, or expecting me to be her. Well, I'm not Deus, okay? I'm just plain old Seren. Nothing special here. Just a stupid, naïve girl, who can't seem to figure out her life or make the right choices. Who is tired of having to fight for everything she has. Who is exhausted from having to run for her life. Who is done with being compared to a woman who died three hundred years ago."

I took a breath, relieved to finally speak my truth. His gaze was on the floor. "I am sorry for what you've been through," I said in a softer tone. "For what you've lost. But sometimes, the way you act, the way you are with me ... it isn't fair. I feel like I am living in her shadow, when all I want," I paused, gathering my courage. "When all I want is for you to just look at me, for me, and not for the part ... for the part of her I carry."

His eyes finally met mine. His face was blank. "I am sorry if that is how I've made you feel. That wasn't my intent."

I chuckled. "Of course it wasn't." All of that, and that's the only response he could come up with? *Dumbass*, I thought to myself this time, with my walls securely in place. "Can you please take me back to my family? I'm tired and I need rest."

He nodded. I stepped into him, feeling the pain of being this close. He held me loosely, shifting us back into his room. The others were gone, and the table had been cleared. I stepped away, turning for the door.

"Seren," he called. I turned around, heaviness in my heart. His face had softened. His posture seemed vulnerable. "For what it's worth, I've always seen you for who you are ... not her," he said, his voice slightly trembling. "It's just ... she was the love of my life. A very long life and ... I was desperate for any piece of her I was able to hold onto. That was the initial reason I sought you out that first day in the woods. I was hoping to reclaim something of her ... anything." Tears fell from his eyes.

I fought the urge, but lost. In an instant I was wrapping my arms around his neck and holding him close to my body as he broke. His arms gripped my waist while he buried his head in my neck. I held on, allowing him to grieve for the love he had been robbed of. It was amazing how human he appeared in that moment. He wasn't a prince, or a demon. He was just Deus. Someone who could experience loss, grief, and love.

He finally pulled away, looking down at me. His face was calm and his eyes no longer full of tears. As I stood in front of him, with my arms still wrapped around his neck, something inside of my heart slammed forward. It wasn't desire or lust, but something deeper. It slammed again, rattling me to the core. His eyes widened. I let go, taking a step back, unsure of what had just happened.

"I should ... I should go," I said.

He grabbed my hand. "No," he whispered. "I want you to stay."

"Deus ... I ... I can't."

"Why?" He asked, pulling me into him. His fingers traced the side of my face. "I won't try anything. I promise," he said, with a devious smile. His moment of vulnerability was gone, now replaced with the charming prince I'd come to know.

"I'm not worried about that," I said, dropping my eyes to the floor. "I just think its best if we don't blur that line right now."

His eyes filled with disappointment, but he nodded. "I understand."

"Thank you," I whispered, pulling away from him.

"Oh, and Seren," he said as I reached his door. I turned back, looking at my beautiful dark prince. "I'm calling in our bargain."

"What?" I asked, confused.

"You owe me a dinner, remember?"

"I've had dinner with you plenty of times."

"Not one that I've called in for the bargain. Loopholes and all," he said matter-of-fact.

I rolled my eyes. "Fine, asshole. I'll have dinner with you."

"Tomorrow it is," he said, standing at the foot of his bed with his hands behind his back.

"See you then, demon." I shut the door and headed to my bedroom. Alone.

Chapter Seventeen

"I just want to get to the Consort so we can get this show on the road," I said, standing in front of the mirror.

"So, this little dinner date means nothing to you?" asked Frankie, fluffing my hair around my shoulders.

"It's not a date," I said flatly. "Thus, my reluctance to let you help pick out this outfit."

Her head popped around my shoulder. "You and I both know you didn't get the fashion gene in the family."

"You can be so rude sometimes," I said, laughing at her.

She shrugged. "Honesty hurts, what can I say. At least now you look presentable." Frankie had picked out a white flowing summer dress that was knitted around the bodice. It hugged my waist and fell loosely to the ground. My hair was in tight curls around my face. I stared at myself with an uneasy feeling.

"What is it?" she asked, apparently noticing my change in mood.

"Do you think I look like her?" I whispered.

"Who?"

"My mother. It's ... the curls, right?"

Frankie rubbed the sides of my arms. "You are nothing like her. We'll just say you look like my mom." We both laughed. "Now, get a move on."

I slouched. "I really don't want to," I whined.

"You and I both know that's a lie. But regardless, will you finally tell me what in the hell happened between you and him?"

I bit the bottom of my lip. "I've been fighting feelings for him. And he's still in love with Victoria."

"Ah, figured," she said. "Have you told him about your feelings?"

I shook my head. "I don't see the point. He flat out told me I was nothing like Victoria. He mourns her ... still."

"You know you can love more than one person in a lifetime, right?"

"Yes, but ... the connection I have with her. I would never know if he loved me for me or some piece of her. He told me she was the love of his life. I don't think he is open exploring that with another."

"Well, my vote is you tell him. The fact that he has thawed the ice around your heart after everything with Antonio and Orion speaks volumes."

"I don't think I can," I admitted.

"Then that is your choice. But you're always going to wonder what if. Can you live with that?"

I laughed. "Depends how long I get to live, I guess."

She smacked me in the arm. "Don't talk like that. We're all walking out of this thing alive. Now, get your culo to his room before I haul you there myself. And I pray, for the love of Aradia, I don't see you till morning."

I leaned over and kissed her cheek. "I'll check in tonight. Thanks for everything."

"Always."

I made my way to his room, not sure what to expect. When I turned the corner, he was waiting for me. He wore a black form fitting pair of slacks and black button-up shirt. He was casually elegant, as always. I dropped my head, trying to hide my smile and settle my nerves as I approached.

"Good evening," I whispered.

"Hello, love," he said, with a soft grin. "You look lovely."

"Yea, well, Frankie insisted I couldn't go to dinner in my usual attire, so she forced me into this thing," I said, reaching for the sides of my dress.

"I'll thank her later. Are you ready for an adventure?"

"Just dinner ... right?"

He shrugged. "I have a few things planned in between."

"The bargain was dinner, Deus," I said firmly.

"Oh, stop your whining," he said, pulling me into him. Before I could protest, he shifted us out of the castle. We landed in the back of a brick building. Music and celebration sounded from the streets ahead.

"Where are we?" I asked.

"Salzburg, Austria. The city of music," he said, offering me his arm. I took it as we walked into the busy streets.

The buildings were immaculate. Beautiful shops displayed pastries and finer goods. The lights hanging above brought the city to life, stretching up the sides of the structures. People and children danced and laughed, passing us by without a care in the world.

The city was built into a hill with a river at the base and a large castle at the top. Beautifully constructed bridges hung over the river, draped with soft lighting. Streamers and ribbons decorated the streets while the music sang all around us. It was magical.

"Did you know that Mozart was born here?" Deus asked, leaning into me.

"I didn't."

He nodded. "This was also where they shot *The Sound of Music*, so I was told."

"Well, aren't you full of surprises."

He laughed. "Wouldn't you like to know?" I rolled my eyes. "I felt that."

We continued to stroll through the paved streets until we came to a massive, elaborate cathedral. A large rose window was placed high above the door. The stained glass reflected familiar biblical stories. We approached the steps to the front doors, and I stilled.

Deus looked back at me. "What's wrong?"

"I just ... I haven't been inside a church since the abbey. I mean, the Vatican, yes, but that was more like a museum than a church. What are we doing here anyway?"

"There's a musical performance here this evening. We can go somewhere else if you'd like."

"No, I'll be fine. It just took me off guard. You're not going to burst into flames once we step inside, are you?"

He laughed, walking us up the front stairs. "Doesn't quite work like that," he explained.

We crossed through the threshold and were greeted by thousands of candles scattering the floor, surfaces, and walls. A grand piano along with an array of string instruments sat on a platform at the front of the church. Deus led us into a pew, and we sat, surrounded by other audience members.

A few moments later the performance began. It started soft, filling the air with tender melodies and phrases. Then, as the violins strung together in the most alluring and captivating melody, my heart leapt from my chest. The power of the musical composition overcame me. I felt like my entire body was transcending. My skin rose in response, gooseflesh spreading as zaps of excitement shot down my spine and radiated underneath my skin. Transfixed on the beautiful music, I felt tears fall from my eyes, silently.

Deus's hand found mine. I looked back. He was smiling at me, as if he had been watching my response the entire time. I returned the gesture before focusing back on the music. After the performance concluded, the audience members silently shuffled out of the cathedral. My heart felt heavy yet inspired.

"What did you think?" asked Deus.

"It was the most beautiful thing I've ever experienced."

"I didn't know you were such a fan of classical music."

"I was raised in a church. We were only allowed to listen to hymns and classical music." He smiled, walking next to me with his hands in his pockets. "Thank you for taking me."

"It was my pleasure. Now, on to the dining portion of the evening."

We sat along the Salzach river, privately. We were served a large variety of food and wine. Talking wasn't necessary. The view of this city was more than I could handle. As they served the final course, Deus sipped on an espresso.

"I'd like to share something with you," he said hesitantly.

"And what might that be?" I asked.

"Victoria."

A large knot formed in my throat. There went my perfect evening. "You don't have to ... really."

"I'd like to. It is important you understand the full story." He placed his cup on the saucer. "I met Victoria right after she had discovered she was the vessel. She had already begun to explore a future with Samual, the horned god of her time, but I didn't care. Back then I was selfish and reckless. I found her captivating and enjoyed the challenge of tearing her from another.

"As time continued, I found that my feelings for her had taken root. I couldn't stay away. She felt the same. That was when she agreed to go away with me ... to Râşnov Castle. We lived there for quite some time together in peace. Her coven knew she had refused Samual, but when they found out that she had chosen a demon prince over their horned god, they made a deal with Lucifer. In exchange for Lucifer providing a way to transfer the goddess entity into another vessel, Lucifer would choose the witch it transferred to: resulting in Victoria's death.

"When I discovered the plan, I did the only thing I knew I could. I told the covens I would erase Victoria's memories of our time together, replacing some of them with Samual in my stead. To get them out of the deal with Lucifer, I begged him to release the covens. He agreed. In exchange, I would become his prisoner for the next three hundred years, until the next goddess awakened.

"Lucifer kept me in a cell far beneath the earth, in Hell. He would use my sin as entertainment, forcing me to cause others to stray away from their partners or to perform acts they would normally refuse, leaving their lives in shambles after the magic wore off. He'd torture me during his perverse parties. Cut me up like a butcher, then allow me to heal before doing it all over again.

"When my power began to diminish, he found it amusing to send creatures in to—" he tilted his head and strained. I reached for his hand, holding it firmly. "The worst torment came when Lucifer allowed me to watch Victoria's life from the cell he had me trapped in. I didn't know if it was a mercy or some demented mindfuck. But I watched nonetheless. She was happy, for a few months, but then she began to fall out of love with Samual. She rejected his advances and turned him away.

"He eventually moved on, finding another woman who he grew old with. Victoria, on the other hand—" he froze, holding back tears. "She knew she was missing something. That a part of her was not whole. She searched for answers, but she found none. I knew where she kept her journal. I made sure to erase that part of her mind as well. Which is why I was surprised to learn you had found it.

"After a few years, she fell into depression ... She ended up hanging herself from a tree deep in the woods. No one ever found her body. I watched for days, months, as her body just hung there, being torn apart by animals and insects. Her coven had no regard for her. Her family abandoned her. She died alone ... because of me." He paused, dropping his eyes. "I can't go through that again, Seren. Loving someone that deeply, only to watch them suffer and die, because of what I am ... because of me."

I didn't know what to say. He had just shared the most torturous part of his life with me. I didn't understand why, but I was honored that he trusted me. I wiped away the tears that had escaped my eyes. "Thank you for sharing that with me," I said softly.

He pulled his hand away from mine. "You deserve to know the truth of the matter. Especially since you'll be face to face with my brothers in a few days. I didn't want them to use the situation against you."

"I appreciate that. I'm going to find a way to kill Lucifer," I said plainly. "I don't care that you're keeping that secret. I will find the answer, and I will destroy him."

He smiled. "If anyone could, it would be you, Seren De Salvo."

"Any hints you can give me, by chance?"

"Unfortunately, not."

I scoffed. "Demons."

I thought over his story. I couldn't imagine being Lucifer's prisoner for a single day, let alone three hundred years. The pain and suffering he must have endured. At least it was now over. The bargain ended when—

I froze, drawing my eyes up to his in shock. "The rite ... " I whispered.

He placed his cup down on the saucer. "What?" he asked.

"The rite. When Aradia blessed me with her power ... you were unleashed. Freed of the bargain. Free to return to Earth, correct?"

"Yes." His brow was furrowed, trying to follow where I was going.

I swallowed, trying to make sense of it all. "There's ... there's something I've never told anyone." I took another breath, unable to look at him. "During the rite, when I was in the presence of Aradia ... when I passed her final test, and she announced I was officially the vessel ... she tried to kill me."

Deus shook his head, straightening his posture. "Why would

she do that? It doesn't make sense. You were her chosen vessel, handpicked by the goddess herself."

"I still don't know, but ... during that time, her heavenly realm became a storm of shadows and static red light. She was terrified, and angry. She kept yelling at me that she wouldn't let it happen again. Then she asked me what I was. I was so confused. I didn't know what she wanted, or how to answer.

"She reached inside of my soul and gripped something dark and ... foreign. When she touched it, she reeled back in pain, like it had burned her. Right after that, she attempted to kill me, but ... but shadowed tendrils pulled me from her realm just in time."

I took a breath, bringing my eyes to his face. He was looking at the table, trying to make sense of it all. "Was it you?" I asked. His eyes rose to mine. "Did you save me all those months ago?"

He hesitated for a moment, still seeming overwhelmed by my admission. "I'm sorry, but I honestly don't know." My body slouched in disappointment. "But ... when I was released from the bargain, my magic exploded from within me. It had been contained for so many centuries. Once I was freed, it unleashed across the realm. I remember feeling a pull when I returned to Earth, but I didn't know what it meant."

My hearth fluttered. Maybe his power found me. Maybe it knew me because ... because, just maybe, we were meant to be together. Subconsciously, his power sought me out and saved me.

He took a breath, running a hand through his hair. "Maybe my power connected with the part of Victoria you activated during the rite," he said, rubbing his face. That small ember of hope faded at his rationalization. "I honestly don't know."

"Or maybe it was just an odd coincidence," I said, trying to lessen the severity. "Maybe I'm just grasping at straws, trying to make sense of it all." I laughed uncomfortably.

He reached across the table, taking my hand. "I am sorry you had to go through that with Aradia. I can only imagine the fear you must have felt."

I shrugged. "I'm used to it by now. Demons want me dead. Princes of hell. My mother," I said, making a dramatic face. "Why not add a god to that list?"

"Seren," he said, not sidetracked by my pathetic attempt at humor.

I pulled my hand away, finishing off my espresso. "I'm sure it's nothing. Just forget I ever told you about it."

Deus waited a moment, looking at me with pity in his eyes. He then stood from his chair, extending his hand toward me. "Dance with me," he whispered. I looked at his hand, fearing the closeness he offered.

Against my better judgment, I placed the espresso cup down and slid into his arms. I laid the side of my face against his warm chest, his lilac smell engulfing me. He swayed us softly. I was aware of every place his hands touched me. Now knowing what he had been through ... I was wrecked for him. Because of him. If the goal was not to fall in love with him, I was failing miserably.

Maybe Frankie was right. Maybe I just needed to bite the bullet and tell him how I felt. I pulled away, looking into his icy blue eyes. His face was soft and relaxed. I opened my mouth, but I froze. His brow furrowed. "Seren," he said. "Is everything okay?"

I dropped my head, losing the courage. He had just told me about how he lost the love of his life. And I had tried to justify my feelings for him with some random, unexplainable magical occurrence. This was not the time. I brought my eyes back up to him, forcing a smile. "Victoria was lucky to have you," I whispered.

He smirked. "I was the lucky one."

I pulled away slightly. "I think I'm ready to return home," I said.

He looked surprised, but didn't refuse. "Of course."

I held onto him, shifting back inside his room. I pulled away tenderly. "Thank you for a lovely evening," I said.

"It was, wasn't it?"

I smiled. "And Deus," I paused, choosing my words wisely. "For what it's worth, you deserve to be happy, and I hope you find that again. Demon or not, you are the kindest man I've ever known."

He smirked. "You don't know me very well then."

I tried to think of something smart or witty to say, but all I could think about was a quote I had read, by the poet Sade Andria Zabala. "Tell me every terrible thing you ever did and let me love you anyways," I said with a soft smile.

His smile fell and his eyes softened before he replied, "And I would ask you to show me your flaws, but I fear it would make me love you more than I already do."

"Good night, demon."

"Good night, love."

Chapter Eighteen

The next few days after our dinner, I had avoided Deus. Our night was special and meant something to me, and I didn't want to ruin that. I needed to keep a firm grasp on my emotions and my head. Instead, I researched my new ability: realm shifting. I scoured his libraries, pulling any resource I found about what I now knew as 'a whispering traveler'. From the other vessel's memories, Cecilia was the only one who had successful crossed into the afterlife and returned. Victoria was afraid of what awaited her. Josephina had no interested, and Valeriana didn't know the gift existed.

Out of all the vessels, Cecilia had most dedicated her life to her magic. She was a scholar in her time. She traveled across the world, studying from different teachers and in different cultures. She had helped many lost souls cross over. I didn't have access to what she saw or how she did it, but I prayed those memories would surface.

The night of the Consort finally arrived. We had spent the week studying up on the different sins and their pasts, but I still didn't feel prepared. They were all highly intelligent and masters of manipulations and lies. No matter how much research I did, it would never be enough. How was a twenty-one year old, newly turned witch going to persuade them to join Deus and Levi in an alliance against their brother ... the king of hell?

"Aradia, I am nervous," said Frankie.

"You and me both," I replied.

"Make that three," added Aunt Thora, coming to our sides.

"Enough, you babies," interrupted Nonna. "We're going in there tonight with our heads held high. We're going to let them all know exactly who they've decided to fuck with." We all laughed.

"I love it when she gets like this," said Aunt Thora.

"Don't we all," I replied.

Nonna wore a black diamond dress, her hair pinned in an elegant updo. She was a vision of royalty. Aunt Thora wore gold. Her long dark brown curls ran wild around her face. She appeared fierce and regal. Frankie chose green, Levi's signature color. Her strapless silk dress ran to the floor, with one long slit running up her leg. With her hair swept to one side, she was a vision of envy.

I, on the other hand, chose red. Delicate lace straps crossed my shoulders and plunged low to my navel. The short dress exposed my entire back, stopping right at the curve of my butt and barely covering my hips. An elegant silk train draped from my left side. I chose strappy, golden stiletto heels and my neck, wrists, and ears dripped with gold and diamonds. My hair was pinned on top of my head, only a few loose curls framing my face.

We headed to the ballroom. Inside waited Levi and Deus. They appeared to be in the middle of a serious conversation when we entered. Deus turned toward me, and my breath caught. He was the very sight of lust incarnate. His black hair was slicked to one side, shining from the light. A black fitted suit hugged every inch of his muscular body. His eyes blazed red as they landed on me. I smiled, feeling the heat and need rolling off him. They quickly faded as he shook his head.

Levi's voice rose while Frankie stood in front of him, dramatically waving her hands in the air. Nonna and Aunt Thora stood off to the side, hiding their laughter.

"You are not wearing that!" yelled Levi.

"And what would you have me wear?" Frankie replied. "A paper sack?"

"They will want what is mine," he growled, his eyes flashing to a bright green.

"Oh, stop it. Seren looks like a damn whore. They won't even notice me," she spat.

Deus approached me slowly.

"Uh, excuse me," I said to Frankie.

"No offense," she said quickly.

"Well, some taken," I replied.

Deus leaned down towards me. "But a very expensive whore," he whispered.

"Takes one to know one," I replied.

He shrugged. "Touché."

"Oh, my Aradia," yelled Frankie. "You look just as handsome as Deus. Stop being such a jealous baby."

"Then stop looking at him," Levi said, stepping into her face. His eyes were blazing with envy and ... desire.

"I can look at whoever the hell I want, you demon baby," she spat. In the next moment, he had her swept up in his arms, kissing her passionately. She pulled him in, viciously taking his mouth with hers.

"Alright, alright," said Deus. "Save it until after the party. We need to be leaving." We all gathered in a circle, looking at one another for strength.

Nonna looked at the three of us and smiled. "Remember," she said softly. "Salvo women stick together. Blood ties us ... always and forever."

"Always and forever," the three of us said as one. We clasped hands.

"Everyone ready to visit the city of gluttony?" asked Deus.

"Los Angeles, here we come," answered Levi.

In a mixture of green and red smoke, we shifted to the front gates of an enormous estate on top of a hill. The mansion made Castle Salvo look like a hovel. Beautiful people surrounded us, walking through the gates towards the entrance. The women were dressed scantily, showing off their best assets. The looked like they had been airbrushed or plucked straight out of a magazine.

We ascended the long driveway. In the front yard, circus acrobats performed stunts. Wild animals were leashed, taunted by their audiences. Music fluttered through the air, and torches lined the driveway created an old-world ambience. People danced all around us, some clothed, some naked. Alcohol and food littered every surface.

We made our way to the large double doors of the mansion. Two men dressed in leather pants and masks opened them for us. Inside, the party continued. Nonna gasped behind me. People were fucking on the stairs and on any surface they could find. Acrobats hung from ribbons on the ceiling, flipping and twirling effortlessly. In the next room was a gambling den. Tables upon tables were filled with people betting their money, property, and souls in a game they were all destined to lose.

Another area held every tasty indulgence one could image. A large chocolate fountain sat in the center of the room. A naked woman lay covered in chocolate as three men licked it off her. I felt my body heat at the sight. I must have stopped moving because a moment later, I felt a hand on my lower back.

"Keep moving, love," whispered Deus in my ear.

I took a deep breath, turning into his touch. I felt an overwhelming need to ... feel him. To have his hands on me. Our group continued forward while we stood, locked in a stare. His eyes blazed red. His lips turned up into that devilish smile I had come to love. I focused on his lips. God, how I wished I could taste him again. To feel those lips trailing down the column of my neck, followed by that tongue I was sure he—

"Put your wall back up," he growled, holding me against him. "You're making it very hard for me to focus."

"I am?" I asked, running my hands up his chest and then to the back of his head. My God, his hair was so soft and thick. I flattened my body against his, before I allowed my fingertips to trail down his smooth face. He closed his eyes, leaning into my touch. I boldly stroked my thumb along his bottom lip. He was so warm. He groaned.

"Seren," he whispered. His voice dripped with sex. "If you don't stop ..."

"What?" I asked eagerly. "What will you do? Tell me ... please."

His eyes opened, his face leaning into mine. "Tell me your deepest fears and I'll turn them into your darkest fantasies." He nuzzled his nose against mine. "Tell me what you want, love."

"You," I said honestly. I had lost control of everything. I didn't know if it was one of their powers or if I was finally done lying to myself. "I want you, Deus."

His blazing eyes grew hotter, his fingers digging into my waist. He moved his head, ever so slowly, towards me, focused on my lips. I closed my eyes, anticipating the feeling of him. Before my prayers could be answer, I felt a hand on my chest, pushing us apart.

"Asmodeus," came Levi's voice sternly. He looked to me and then back to his brother. Deus shook his head, his eyes fading back to blue. "You need to stay focused."

"Right," Deus said, running a hand over his face. I wrapped my arms around myself, feeling exposed. The pressure and warmth inside of me still yearned for him. I turned around without another look in his direction and headed toward my family.

"What in the hell was that?" Frankie asked, grinning from ear to ear.

"He must have lost control of his power, and I was in the wrong place at the wrong time," I answered.

"Or the right place at the right time. It looked to me like you were the one that held all the power just now," she said, winking at me.

Nonna watched me closely but didn't say a word. Deus and Levi made their way back towards us. I could feel his eyes on me, but I refused to meet them. I needed to get myself together. We headed towards two large golden doors at the back of the mansion away, from the rest of the entertainment.

"Are they actually made of pure gold?" asked Aunt Thora.

"He's Gluttony," replied Levi. "Would you expect anything less?"

"My gods," whispered Nonna under her breath.

"Everyone ready to make a mess of things?" Deus asked.

I stepped to the other side of Frankie. She grasped my hand firmly. "Everything is going to be okay," she whispered.

"One can hope," I replied.

The doors opened. The room was lit only by candlelight. Sensual music filled the air. A long black table sat in the center of the room with a massive fireplace built into the wall on the other side. Deus led the way.

The first brother I saw was a tall, broad man. His long white hair contrasted his mahogany skin in the most captivating way. His eyes glowed slightly, changing from hazel to green. He stepped forward, smiling at Deus, extending his hand towards him. Deus grinned, taken it, and pulled him into an embrace. "Brother," the man said, deep and masculine.

"Mammon," replied Deus smiling. *Greed*. "It's been too long."

"It has," he replied, pulling away from my demon. "Glad to see you've finally freed yourself from our brother's bargain."

"Believe me," Deus said, "as am I."

Mammon's attention turned to Levi and then Frankie at his side. Mammon smiled deviously. "What have you brought me, little brother?" Mammon asked, approaching Frankie.

Levi put his arm out, stopping him from getting any closer. "Don't you fucking think about it," Levi growled.

Mammon began laughing. "I'm just teasing, Leviathan. Get over here," he said, pulling him into a hug. Levi was still raging with jealousy. "But in all seriousness, who have you brought with you this evening? I didn't realize we were allowed escorts."

Deus stepped forward. "Meet the Salvo witches, head of the Étoile Coven," he said. "Elder Lucia De Salvo." Nonna nodded. "Her daughter, Elder Thora De Salvo. And her granddaughters,

Francesca and Seren."

Mammon stepped in front of me, taking his gaze up and down my body. I smiled, pretending to be flattered. "This one," Mammon said. "She is different."

"Excellent eye, brother," Deus said. "Seren is this cycle's moon goddess vessel."

Mammon's eyes went wide. "Fascinating," he replied. "I haven't met one of you in over six hundred years."

"The pleasure is mine, your majesty," I said, bowing my head slightly.

"Why are we all standing in the doorway?" asked a smooth and sophisticated voice. A man with light brown hair neatly shaped to his head strolled over to us. He had the same shade of blue eyes as Deus. He wasn't as tall, but his body was toned and tapered. He was cleanly shaven and dressed in the most elegant of fashions. All the brothers seemed to have that in common. He had a dimple in his chin and dominate eyebrows. He was a vision, just like the rest.

"Belz," said, Deus, hugging his brother. *Gluttony.*

Levi smiled and went for a hug next. Another brother came up behind him. He looked the most different. His body was built for war; it reminded me of Orion. His hair was longer than Belz, but well-kept and crimson. He had chocolate brown eyes and facial hair that was neatly trimmed and edged. His thin lips didn't smile.

Deus nodded. "Satan," he said, extending his hand out towards him. *Wrath.*

"I am so happy you came," said Belz. "I was worried you'd might reject the invitation, due to your little spat with Lucifer a few years back."

"You mean three hundred years," answered Satan in a mocking tone. His voice was deep and monotone.

"I'm a big boy," answered Deus.

"Yes, you are," said a sultry female voice. I turned behind me to see a gorgeous woman. She was petite with long straight black hair. She appeared of Asian descent, with flawless pale skin, green eyes, and lips full and sinful. She wore a dress that revealed her small torso and full chest. If Deus was Lust, she was his counterpart.

"Akira," said Deus, "it's been a while."

"Too long," she replied. "This one over here keeps me busy," Akira gestured to Belz. "I'm thinking about changing my allegiance. Care for a new court member?" she asked, trailing her eyes down his body. Jealousy began to well inside of me with a rage. Levi huffed next to me and smiled.

"I'd be honored," Deus replied with a small bow.

"Now, now," intervened Belz. "No poaching my court members during Consort. It's bad manners brother." Belz wrapped his arm around Deus's shoulder, pulling him against his side. The brothers laughed playfully.

Akira turned to Belz. "We are waiting on Lucifer and Belphegor, your grace ... per usual," she said, appearing bored.

"Of course we are," Belz said, looking at the rest of us. "And who do we have here?"

Levi stepped forward. "The Salvo witches from the Étoile Coven," he introduced. "Elders Lucia and Thora De Salvo. And granddaughters Francesca and Seren. Seren is the vessel of Aradia."

Akira's eyes blazed brightly as she seemed to study me slowly. She didn't say a word.

"And I assume you've claimed one Leviathan, you selfish bastard," said Belz.

"Francesca is mine," Levi said, pulling her into him.

Belz laughed. "Perfect," he said, smiling at Aunt Thora.

"Are we going to stand around and stare at one another, or can we begin?" asked Satan.

"Fine, fine," said Belz. "Everyone sit."

We made our way around the table and took our seats. I sat between Nonna and Frankie. Belz placed Aunt Thora next to him and Deus was on the other side of the table, in between Mammon and Akira.

In the middle of the first course, the doors opened. In strolled a tall, thin man with dark black hair and deep brown eyes that could have been mistaken for black. He was pale, and his face was charming and alluring. His hair seemed disheveled: long on the top and shorter on the sides. He wore a long black dress coat and black pants. He took a seat without a word towards the end of the table.

"Nice of you to show up, Belphagor," greeted Mammon, taking a sip of his wine. *Sloth.*

"You're lucky I'm here at all, fuck twat," he replied, pouring his own glass. Belz, Levi, and Mammon laughed.

Deus leaned down the table. "How have you been, Gor?" he asked.

"Busy," he replied shortly.

"Doing what exactly?" asked Belz.

"Whatever the fuck I please," he said, making a dramatic facial expression.

Belz leaned towards us. "You'll have to excuse Belphagor," he said. "He's our *little* brother. He still hasn't mastered the transition between puberty and adulthood."

I heard the wine glass slam against the table as Gor poured himself another. "You're lucky the treaty is in place right now," threatened Gor.

"Or what?" asked Belz. "You going to bore us to death with your poetry and history lessons? Maybe if you'd spend even a quarter of your time out in the real world, you'd actually find something worth living for. Instead, you're hold up in that ancient piece of shit in the middle of the desert."

I looked at the rage that consumed Gor. Features I ... recognized. A memory came to the light: Cecilia's memory, based on the attire and her bracelet.

She was smiling with Gor, sitting around a large pool of water. They were digging through book after book, looking for something ... studying something. He laughed, and a beautiful smile spread across his face, revealing two dimples. The book they were looking through was titled—

"Daut," I said out loud, staring at Gor. I snapped out of the memory, shaking my head to focus.

His gaze whipped to me. "What did you just say?" Gor asked, his face firm.

I licked my lips, taking a sip of wine. "I'm sorry," I said, looking at the beautiful demon. "I had a memory of you and Cecilia, studying a book titled Daut."

His eyes enlarged. He looked around the table. "Who brought the vessel?" he asked.

"She's Levi's new girlfriend's cousin," answered Mammon.

Gor straightened and returned his attention to the wine in front of him, not saying another word.

A moment later, the doors opened again. In strolled Lucifer and at his side ... my mother. He was exactly what you envisioned when you heard the word angel. He had beautiful blonde, almost white, hair. His eyes were icy blue, like Deus's. His skin was the color of bronze and had an unearthly glow. He was tall and lean like Levi. He was absolutely stunning. So was my mother.

Belz looked from my mother to Aunt Thora. "You're a twin," he said with delight. "This night just got better."

I remained calm, even as my mother's eyes locked onto me. I wanted to look at Deus, but I held back.

"Now, whose daughter is whose?" asked Mammon.

"The green-eyed one is my sister's," answered my mother, moving to the back of my chair. "And this one," she said, running her hand down my face, "is all mine." I refrained from biting one of her fingers off.

"Annalise," I said through my teeth.

"Now, now, little bean," she replied, "calling your mommy by her first name is rude." She turned her eyes to Nonna. "Mother," she said shortly, then moved to the other side of the table. Nonna ignored her. Once she settled next to Mammon and Lucifer, her eyes drilled into Frankie, then moved to Aunt Thora.

"I feel I owe you an apology," Annalise said to Thora. I exhaled; this wasn't going anywhere good.

"I don't want anything from you," replied Thora.

Annalise laughed. "Glad to see she survived a knife to the heart," she said, taking a sip of wine.

Thora went deathly still. Frankie grabbed my hand underneath the table. We had never told Thora or Nonna that Frankie almost died.

"What are you playing at, Annalise?" spat Nonna.

My mother looked between Frankie and me. "Keeping secrets, are we?" she said. Her eyes trailed back to Thora's. "I stabbed your daughter in the heart. Multiple times, if I recall correctly. She almost died, but obviously didn't. Must have something to do with her princely lover."

Every glass, plate, and object on the table blew into pieces with a single bang. Thora stood to her feet, her chair flying back against the wall. Her hand shot out towards Annalise. My mother grabbed at her neck, fighting to breath as she slowly hovered out of her chair.

"You stabbed my daughter in the heart? Your niece!" Aunt Thora screamed. Veins popped out of her neck and face. Some of the princes began to snicker, sitting back in their chairs, enjoying the entertainment.

Aunt Thora was shaking with rage. In one swift motion, she threw Annalise into the wall. She stormed towards her, picking her up by the neck and slamming her fist into her face, knocking her back to the floor.

"You crazy bitch. Stay the hell away from my daughter," Thora said, returning to her spot next to Belz.

Annalise laughed, wiping the blood from her mouth. She stood to her feet as if unfazed, strolling back to her chair. Thora's eyes were still blazing with hate. Nonna, remained still, not intervening.

Satan's eyes glowed a deep shade of red and blue, mixing into purple. A smile appeared on his face: the first I had seen all night. "I like this family," he commented.

Lucifer finally took a seat directly across from me. His blue eyes were fixed on mine. I felt something inside of me reach towards him. I couldn't place it, but I was uncomfortable with any connection. This demon had been plotting with my mother to kill me and steal my power.

"Salvo witches," Lucifer said with a nod. His voice was smooth and entrancing.

I instantly wanted to believe every word he said. Something inside of me wanted to make him proud. To ... please him. My power stirred in his presence, dancing with delight. I tried to push it down, but there was something between us, I just didn't know what. He smiled at me, sending a rush of excitement through my entire body. I felt Deus's eyes on me.

"Are you alright," he asked in my mind.

"Yes," I lied. *"Just uncomfortable.*

"It will all be over soon, love."

Lucifer's attention shifted down the table to Deus. "Brother," he said to him. "Nice to see you. I've missed having you as my little house pet."

"Can't say I feel the same, Lucy," Deus replied, seeming collected.

"Your party is extravagant as always, Belz," said Levi, cutting off conversation between Deus and Lucifer.

"I do love to show off," Belz replied. "Are you envious brother? The last time you held the Consort at your little humble abode, I don't remember it holding a candle to this." Levi's eyes grew green with envy. Belz laughed.

"Father, help me," whispered Mammon under his breath.

Lucifer chewed his food, laughing at the others. The rest of the meal was tense. My family didn't say a word. My mother took her time assessing each of us. Nonna kept her eyes down and Thora looked like she was about to gouge Annalise's eyes out at any moment. Levi kept a firm hand on Frankie, and I refrained from looking at Deus ... or Lucifer for that matter.

Akira took any opportunity to touch Deus. She played with his hair, fixed his jacket, or found reasons to run her hand down his arm.

At the end of dinner, Belz clapped his hands. From the side door, a dozen beautiful women entered the room wearing belly dancing attire. They danced for us, though all of them seemed to have their eyes on Deus. His eyes blazed red during the dance. Once their little show concluded, I excused myself, claiming to need some fresh air.

I gripped the stone railing, cracking it slightly underneath the strength of my fingers. I took deep breaths, trying to focus. I looked back, seeing them all surrounding him. He allowed them to touch him, sit on his lap, and press their lips against his skin. I was coming unhinged.

"Levi's power getting the best of you?" came Lucifer's voice from the doorway. I was so fixated on Deus, I didn't even notice him creep onto the terrace.

"Why would I be jealous?" I replied.

He shrugged. "You tell me." He walked over casually, placing his hands next to mine, looking up at the setting sun. "The sun is beautiful tonight, is it not?"

"Longest day of the year and all," I replied snippily, my mind drifting back to last year at this time. Our solstice ball, where Tony and I shared our first kiss. I pushed the memory down, fighting to stay focused.

"Where is your horned god?" he asked.

"Safe somewhere else."

He laughed. "Not your cup of tea?"

"Orion is perfect. We just ... don't fit."

"Interesting. I've always found the whole vessel thing fascinating. Sometimes the two gods fall in love, while other times they choose others. Are you and Antonio Simonelli still a thing?"

"Nope. You know, working with my psychotic mother to kill me kind of ruins the mood and all."

He laughed. "I like you." He leaned in close to my face. "By the way, I've convinced your mother to lay off. She's very obsessive, that one."

I turned to face him. "What are you talking about?"

"I've convinced her not to kill you. I've taken the little book of spells and hidden it from her. You are safe ... for now."

"At what cost?"

He paused, smiling softly. Something corrupt slithered behind his eyes.

"I know how your kind works," I added. "Everything has a cost."

"No debt is to be paid, Seren De Salvo. Though, I would love to know exactly where my brother Asmodeus likes to hide away. I've been searching for ages. His magic is strong; not as strong as mine, but still, he's able to hide from me."

"And why would you think I know the location of his ... hide-away?"

His eyes dramatically shifted down. "Come now, little witch. Surely you haven't forgotten who you're speaking with."

"How could I? Now, back to the point. Why are you here with my mother if you're not helping her?"

"To get to you, of course."

"I am sure you know where I live. What has stopped you from coming for me?"

He grinned, turning his eyes to the open sky. "The timing hasn't been right. I needed you to ... marinate a bit longer. You need time to come into you own."

"To what end?"

He smiled and held out his hand, tilting his head slightly. "Dance with me."

"You came all this way to dance with me?"

He shrugged. "Maybe."

In that moment, an orchestra began to play *Once Upon a December*. The air felt light, and the smell of jasmine flooded my senses. My body relaxed and the urge to step into him, to take his hand was overwhelming. I reached my fingers out, so slowly it felt like time had stopped. Once I made contact, he took me into his arms, floating us high into the air. We danced through the sky, over the ocean, as the melody carried us into a dream. A magical reality where there was nothing else ... only him and I.

He held me close, calling to my magic as if we were one. We continued higher until we waltzed over the top of the mansion. I didn't look down. I couldn't. I was fixated in his eyes. His face. Everything about this demon was alluring. Once the music began to fade, he drifted me safely back to the balcony. I stepped away from him, unsure of what had just occurred.

He bowed. "Thank you for the dance, Seren. It is a pleasure to finally meet you." He stepped back into the room with the others. I took a moment before returning.

Deus sat in a chair, his hair tousled, and his shirt ripped open. Three of the women were on him, kissing him, touching him, tasting him. His hands and lips devoured each of their bodies. I slowly entered, trying my best not to focus on him, but it took all my restraint. Gor appeared, dragging my attention from the lustful demon.

"Hello, Seren," he said in a deep and haunting voice.

"Belphegor," I said shortly.

"Gor ... please. Now, about that little memory slip at dinner."

I smirked. "For being the demon of Sloth, you get straight to the point, don't you?"

"When it's something I actually give a fuck about, yes. You mentioned The Daut. Any other memory surface about me, by chance?"

I paused, opening Cecilia's filing cabinet, sifting through. "No," I finally said. "That was the first."

His face seemed disappointed. "Ah, I see. Never mind then." He went to walk away, but I reached out, stopping him. His body was cold, not warm like Deus's. I retracked my hand quickly.

"Did you know Cecilia well?" I asked.

"That is for another time and another place, goddess," he said softly. My eyes trailed back to Deus. Akira now sat in his lap, kissing and fondling him.

I made my way over to Mammon and Belz. "Ah, moon goddess," said Mammon with a smile on his face. "How are the powers coming along?"

"I learn a little more about my abilities each and every day," I replied, trying to appear naïve.

"Are you actively training?" asked Belz.

"I am," I replied.

"Good. Glad to see a goddess who is interested in her powers," said Belz. "I knew Josephina well. She was not as assertive as you appear to be. Though, she was assertive in other ways, I suppose," he and Mammon laughed.

I scoffed. "Was every vessel involved with one of you at some point or another?" I asked.

They both shrugged. "It seems that power calls to power in a way," answered Belz.

"We are also very talented in bed," add Mammon. "Care to explore your options?" He took a step towards me, brushing the back of his knuckles down the side of my arm. His eyes glowed as he smiled. "I may be the demon of Greed," he whispered, "but I will assure your satisfaction long before taking mine." Belz found his way to my aunt as Mammon pushed me back into a hallway against the wall.

He gently trailed his fingers down my jaw and then my neck, not stopping until he traced the seam at the top of my dress. His other hand caressed the inside of my thigh, moving slowly upward. He watched me closely, taking in my reaction. I was nervous more than anything, but my body didn't feel the same as it did when Deus touch me. He leaned into me, pressing his lips to my throat. I closed my eyes, allowing it to happen.

"Mm, goddess," he whispered against my skin. "I want to be so very greedy with you." My hands remained against the wall. I didn't reach for him like I did Deus. The desire just wasn't there. He slowly pulled my dress up around my hips, pressing his body against mine. He kissed down my neck and before he could reach my chest, he was flung against the wall next to me, held there by black and red shadows.

I snapped myself out of it. I moved away, pulling my dress back over my legs. "Brother," said Mammon, struggling to breath.

Deus dropped Mammon, with a short smile. "Sorry about that," Deus said. "Thought you were the help."

Mammon rubbed his neck. "Is that so?" he said, looking from Deus to me. "I'm sorry, I didn't know you had claimed her." Deus looked back at me. His jaw clinched he rolled his shoulders, fighting to contain his rage.

"Not at all," Deus said. "If I was interrupting something, please continue."

My own rage sprang to life. "I'm sorry," I said, stepping into him. "Weren't you just swapping spit with Akira? Where is she, by the way? Did you really finish that fast already?" I huffed mockingly. "Your ability to last is disappointing, for being the demon of Lust and all."

"Sounds like jealousy to me," Deus replied, towering above. "Should I get Levi or are you able to contain your little emotions?"

Mammon laughed, putting his hands up. "I think I'm going to find somewhere else to be," he said. "I'd rather not get on your bad side, Deus."

"Oh, by all means," Deus said, gesturing to me, "take her off my hands. Father, would that be a blessing."

"Oh, really," I replied, now yelling. "You are the one that sought me out, not the other way around." Mammon snuck past us. "Don't act like I've encouraged you in anyway. Actually, I've done the complete opposite."

"Ha, right. Is that what you were doing when you showed up in my room, with the intent of burning everything to the ground?"

I felt like I was going to explode. White tendrils of fire lit around my fingers. "Funny, since you were the one who insisted I sleep in your bed."

"Did you really think I was going to trust you alone in my home?" he roared.

"Frankly, I don't care if you trust me or not. I could care less about you. You're a means to an end," I said, trying to calm myself.

"Is that why you allow me to touch you the way I do? Especially that day in my bedroom? Is that why you told me you wanted me out in the hall a few hours ago? The reason why you've become obsessed with Victoria?!" His face was now in mine.

Hearing him speak to me in this way broke the little piece of hope I was harboring deep inside. Maybe I was the one with the problem: pining over a man who didn't want me in that way.

Without another word, I stepped around him, reentering the party. I found Nonna and told her I was heading home. She insisted she come with me, but I refused. I just needed to be alone. I shifted back to his castle. I headed to the stables and mounted the white horse I had trained on. I road hard and fast. Something was freeing about being able to ride. The wind in my hair. The warm air on my skin. Everything about this was freeing.

I rode to the spot by the cliff where I had completed shattered that day. I looked over, thinking back to the woman who had thrown herself off the ledge. I wasn't that person anymore. I wasn't going to allow him to derail who I was becoming. I loved this version of myself. I felt powerful and strong. Something I had never been.

When I returned to the castle, I bumped into Nonna in the hall. I followed her back to her room. She poured me a class of wine as we sat by the window. "What is it, bambina?" she asked. "What has you so unhinged?"

I laughed. "Is that a trick question?"

"I think I know, but I want you to say it."

I paused, biting the side of my mouth. "There's nothing to say, Nonna."

"Stop lying to yourself and admit it. You've fallen in love with him. You've allowed yourself to fall in love with Asmodeus."

I laughed. "Nonna, you are mistaken. I do not love *that* demon."

"No, maybe not the demon, but you love the angel he has been to you." I froze. "I don't know the details of your relationship, but I do know that before you left in February, you were a shell of yourself. You were depressed, unhinged, fighting to find your purpose. When you returned to us, you had become stronger, focused, confident, and fearless. You mastered your demons and found light in this life." She paused, leaning in towards me, taking my hand. "And it is because of him. Because your heart found where it belonged."

My eyes filled with tears. I shook my head. "No. I can't. He loves another."

"As you did months ago. But Antonio was never your soulmate, nor Orion. Your heart desired more, and I believe you've found it, bambina. Don't let this chance at a life worth cherishing pass you by." My heart fluttered to life, but as soon as that ember sparked, I killed it.

"He is a means to an end," I said coldly. "We need him to kill Lucifer. Once that is done ... we are done," I said, standing. I kissed Nonna goodnight before returning to my room.

Chapter Nineteen

Knock, knock, knock came from my door the next morning. I answered it, finding Gallo on the other side. "Master requests to speak with you in his chambers," he screeched.

"Well," I replied, "you can tell *master* he can go fuck right off." I went to shut the door, but he stopped it with his hand. He was strong for such a little creature.

"He said you would say that," Gallo replied. "Master says—"

"Fuck your master," I yelled, pushing the door shut. Before I could turn around, Gallo shifted inside of my room, grabbing onto my leg and shifting us out. I fought on the journey there, but he held on, against my best efforts. We landed in the middle of Deus's room. I slammed into the ground on my ass as Gallo finally let go and backed away. Deus stepped into view.

Gallo was breathing heavy. "I brought her as you commanded, master," he huffed. "This one ... not easy."

Deus smirked. "You're telling me," he replied. "Thank you, Gallo. That will be all." The little demon disappeared. Deus extended his hand to help me up, but I refused, standing on my own.

"What in the hell do you think you're doing?" I spat. "Forcing me here."

"I told you once before, I don't take no for an answer."

"I thought we said all we needed to last night."

"Right, about that," he said, pausing for a moment. "I am sorry I acted in such a way. I was high off my power, and I felt Mammon's lust. When I discovered it was you he had targeted I ..." he paused again.

"You?"

"It doesn't matter. I spoke out of turn with you and for that, I apologize."

"Is that all?" I asked.

"Do you accept?"

"No."

He laughed, taking a step towards me. "Seren, I was not myself last night. Truly, I am sorry."

I looked at him for a few moments, admiring how beautiful he was. "You know, I do care about you," I admitted. "I meant it a few nights ago, when I said I hoped you would find happiness again. And for you to speak to me the way you did—"

He placed a hand on either of my arms, stepping in closer. "If I'm being honest," he said, softly, "I was jealous last night." My eyes snapped to his.

"What? Why?"

He hesitated. "I've never seen you like that with anyone else—even the Simonelli boy, and well ... Levi got the best of me."

"Deus, you've made it extremely clear you have no interest in me like that. Why would you care who I choose to fuck?"

"So, you admit it then," he said, pacing in front of me, "you wanted to fuck Mammon?"

"I didn't say that."

"Then why were you letting him touch you like that? Put his lips on you? If I hadn't found the two of you—"

"I would have stopped it," I said, exhausted from this banter. "I didn't want him like that. I don't want anyone like that." I took a deep breath, sitting on the edge of his bed.

He sat next to me, calming himself. "I'm sorry I overreacted," he said softly. "It wasn't my place."

"Can we just forget about it? We have other things to focus on at the moment."

"Like your dance with Lucifer?"

"How in the hell were you keeping tabs on me that closely with all those women you were entertaining last night?"

He shrugged. "It's a gift."

"He told me he hid the grimoire from my mother. I don't know what game he's playing at."

"Oh, he's playing a game alright. He always is. Don't trust a word that comes out of his mouth, Seren. If you choose to listen to one thing, I've ever told you, listen to that."

"I know, Deus. I'm not a complete idiot." I paused, thinking back to his brothers. One in particular. "On that note ..."

He looked at me with suspension in his eyes. "What are you planning?"

"I need a favor."

"I'm not going to like this favor, am I?"

"Depends on if you're still feeling jealous." I smiled at him.

He returned the gesture, pinching my chin in between his fingers. "What is it you need?"

"Take me to Gor."

He went rigid. "Why?"

"Cecilia was involved with him at some point. I think he has the answer to figuring out how to shift realms."

His jaw tightened. "And do you plan on staying with him?"

"If he offers, yes."

There was a long pause before Deus finally said, "No." He stood, putting distance between us.

"If you won't take me, I'll just ask Levi."

"He won't go against what I say, but nice try."

"Well, I guess I'm going backpacking through Egypt," I said, standing from the bed, moving towards the door. He shifted in front of me. "Are we really going to do this?"

"You don't even know him," he said. I could tell he was working to hold that temper of his back.

"I didn't know you very well when I agreed to stay here. Plus, Cecilia trusted him. Why shouldn't I?"

"Don't be stupid. You aren't Cecilia."

"Not Cecilia, not Aradia, not Victoria. Yeah, I'm aware ... now move," I demanded, reaching around him to the doorknob. He caught my wrist, pinning me to the door. His eyes blazed crimson, his jaw tight with aggravation.

"You drive me insane. Do you know that?" he growled. "In my entire life, I have never met someone who infuriated me the way you do."

"Well, lucky for you I'll be staying at your brother's for the foreseeable future. Now, let me go!"

"Make a deal," he demanded.

"No more deal."

"Make. A. Deal. Then, I'll take you," he said.

I looked into his furious eyes, trying to read him. "What's the deal?"

"That you'll keep your mind open to me."

"Not a chance," I said instantly.

He yelled and pulled back, freeing me from the door he had me pinned to. "Fine. You will check in with me once a day through the bond."

"Why?" I asked, curiously.

He exhaled in frustration. "Will you for once just do something I ask?"

"Fine," I replied, rolling my eyes. "I, Seren De Salvo, promise to check in through my mind once a day with Prince Asmodeus Râşnov, blah, blah, bl—" before I could finish, I was back up against the door, his lips on mine. He held my face in between his hands while his mouth grazed against mine with more passion and desire than I had ever experienced. Without thinking, I wrapped my arms around his neck, pulling him into me.

He gripped the back of my hair while his other hand moved to my waist, holding me against him. I was unable to breath, but I didn't care. This ... he was more than I could have ever imagined. The feeling of him. The taste. I opened my mouth, allowing his tongue to slide across mine. My entire body came to life. I felt my power erupt from within, but I didn't open my eyes. I didn't let go. I never wanted this to end.

He slowed, pressing his lips against mine, stealing on more kiss softly before pulling away. I felt the smile stretch across my face, unable to contain the joy I felt. I opened my eyes and was greeted by the heat of the desert. We stood on top of the sand as the wind whipped small grains up around us. My face fell, realizing he had held up his end of the deal. A part of me was disappointed.

I looked up at him, not sure of what to say. His eyes faded back to blue. His face was blank. My heart clenched. I stepped out of his arms, bringing my hands to my lips. They were swollen in the most delightful way. I swallowed, gathering myself. "Thank you," I said softly. He slid the key around my neck, which granted me access to his lands.

He placed his hands into his pockets. "Wear this at all times. And remember the deal," he replied.

I nodded, stepping around him towards the ancient building that I presumed was Gor's home. Deus grabbed my arm, and I looked up at him, hoping he would tell me not to go. Praying that he would take me back home and finish what we had started. I just needed something—anything. But instead, he stared at me blankly.

"I hope you find the answers you're looking for," he said.

I forced a smile across my face. "Me too."

In my next breath, he was gone. I took a moment to gather myself. I was in over my head when it came to him. If that kiss had almost undone me, God only knew what would happen if ... no, I couldn't go there. I couldn't let myself. But ... the way he kissed me. It felt different than the other bargains. It felt raw, and all-consuming.

"I was wondering when you would show up," I heard a voice from behind me.

I twirled instantly. Gor smiled, dressed in loose pants and a white linen button up shirt. He stepped in front of me, looking down with those deep black holes he had for eyes. He appeared more relaxed than when I saw him last night at the Consort. "Come," he said, moving past me. "I've already had a room prepared."

"How did you know?" I asked, chasing after him.

He laughed. "If you are anything like Cecilia, I knew your curiosity would get the best of you eventually." We entered his palace of history and artifacts. Everything that surrounded us was priceless. Carvings, statues, and pottery, all ancient and worth more than I could imagine. As we traveled through the rooms, I noticed there were no servants, no guests ... it was just him.

"Do you live alone?" I asked.

"The help comes when needed, but for the most part, I prefer it that way," he replied. "I enjoy the solitude and silence. This world today is overstimulating, with their televisions, phones, and need for excess. I enjoy the simpler parts of life."

"I see," I said, following him to a wooden door. He pushed it open, revealing a room with a large window, a massive four-post bed with white sheets, a few furnishings and a bathroom at the back. "Thank you," I said.

He nodded. "Of course," he replied. "I will let you get settled and then I will see you for dinner, say around eight?"

"Sounds perfect."

He closed the door, leaving me in silence. I went over and sat on the edge of the bed, still thinking about that kiss. I focused, closing my eyes, allowing the small door in my mind I had created just for him to crack. I slid my power along the border, searching. His shadows intertwined with mine instantly. I jumped.

"Already regretting your decision to stay with my brother?" he asked playfully in my mind.

"No. He's very polite. He's a lot like you actually," I replied.

"How so?"

"He insisted I stay in his bed." A small flourish of anger ripple

down the bond. I smiled. *"Deus?"*

"Yes?"

I debated on asking him about the kiss, but I knew he wouldn't give me the answer I wanted. *"Thanks again,"* I replied, pulling the door between us shut.

I was left with my thoughts for the remaining part of the day. I gathered the questions I would ask and made list after list of potential ways to kill a prince of hell, but nothing tracked. They were celestial beings. How did one go about killing something truly immortal?

I managed to get an hour of sleep before it was time to attend dinner. I traveled through the magnificent halls, stretching high into the sky. Candles and torches lit the way. Beautiful open courtyards with pools in the center were spread throughout the palace. I finally found the dining room. Gor stood as I approached. He pulled out my chair and I took a seat next to him. He filled my plate with chicken, naan, and vegetables.

"This looks amazing," I commented.

"Thank you," he replied.

"Did you have a cook come in?"

He smiled. "No. I'm more than capable of working a stove."

"You cooked all of this?" I asked, astonished.

"I did. I usually cook most of my food."

"Very impressive, demon prince," I said with a smile.

"I know." He took a seat, pouring us a glass of white wine.

"Now, why exactly have you come?"

"I randomly recall moments of the other vessel's lives. I can't control when I see them or what I see, but most of the time, it's for a purpose. When I saw you at the Consort, Cecilia's memories began to resurface. I was told that my goddess power allows me to travel between the living and the dead: to speak to them. Then, I recalled a memory of you and Cecilia researching the underworld. I know out of all the vessels, she was the most versed in our magic. If anyone would know how to get there, she would have."

He smiled. "You are right about that. She was brilliant," he said softly, rolling the wine in his glass. Something like longing appeared on his face. I tried to refrain, but I couldn't resist.

"Did you and Cecilia—" I paused, feeling like I was approaching a topic too personal with a stranger I had just met.

His eyes met mine. "I would have moved the ocean and stars for her, but she did not return my affections," he said. "She was in love with the horned vessel at the time, Amon. Though we had our time of romance, after some time here, she returned to her ... mate."

"I'm sorry," I whispered.

"No need to be sorry. The world is a cruel and unpredictable place."

"What was she like?" I asked.

"Brilliant beyond her time. She was a scholar. She asked the right questions, educated herself, and could solve any problem.

She couldn't absorb enough information. When her powers manifested after the rite, she went searching. She wanted to know everything she could about how her gifts worked and what her limitations were. Valeriana, before her, was unaware of the power she contained; she didn't relay a lot of information to Cecilia.

"A few years after she had come into her gifts, Cecilia came here, during her conquest for knowledge. She had begun to see spirits. She wanted to know what her powers could do. That was when we stumbled upon each other." He paused, taking a deep drink of wine. "She stayed for two years before returning home."

"Did she find what she was looking for?" I asked.

He smiled softly. "She did. She was able to travel in between Hell and this plane. She did many great things with her gift, including piss off Lucifer royally."

"How so?" I asked, my interest heightened.

"Lucifer is the only one that has complete control over Hell. My other brothers and I can travel in between the realms, and we have our own territories in Hell, but Lucifer controls the vast majority. We're unable to step foot on his territory without him knowing. Cecilia, on the other hand, could pop in whenever she liked. She wasn't bound to the same restrictions and rules as the rest of us. As you can imagine, Lucy didn't like that very much, and Cecilia was a bit of a ... snoop."

"Did she have any contact with your other brothers?" I asked.

"Not a personal one, if that's what you're asking. I know she met

Deus, but that didn't result in anything."

I finished the food on my plate and sat back in the chair. "Will you teach me?"

He laughed, shaking his head. "To enter the underworld?"

"That's the place."

"And why would you want to go there? I can assure you, it is a horrific realm. One I loathe with my entire being."

"Power ... I want power."

"Careful, little goddess. You're starting to sound like your enemy."

"Not because I want to conquer or rule. I just ... I want to be prepared. I want to know my full capability. If I am to face your brother, I need to have every weapon accessible."

He thought for a moment. "I suppose it would be handy to have a back entrance in and out of Hell at a moment's notice. Does this have anything to do with Deus working on your behalf to turn everyone against Lucifer?" I froze. He leaned towards me. "You and my brother—"

"No," I said quickly. Too quickly.

He leaned back, folding his hands over his chest. "I want to know why Deus has taken up your torch. It will help me make my decision, And Seren, just in case you've forgotten, I'm Sloth. I have all the time in the world."

I huffed, placing my fork on the plate. "We believe Lucifer wants my power for himself," I answered. "He has found a way to separate me from the goddess entity, but if he does, I'll die in the process."

"And Lucy gets an immense power boost, which would completely throw the balance off for the rest of us."

I nodded.

"Are you aware of the power struggle between Deus and Lucifer?

"Not beyond the fact that he imprisoned Deus for the past three hundred years. And they hate each other."

He laughed. "It's a little more complicated than that. See, back home in heaven, Lucifer and Deus were the closest. Their bond was unbreakable, but as Lucy's struggle with his pride grew, their interests began to change. As far as power is concerned, the order goes Lucifer, Deus, Satan, Belz and then Mammon, Levi, and I are pretty equal.

"After we got booted out of the pearly gates, Lucifer continued his obsession to overthrowing Father. Satan, of course, being wrath, was all for it, but Deus was the one that diverted first. He was devastated that he had fallen from grace, and lost faith in Lucifer and his plan.

"When my brothers and I saw him walk away, it gave us the strength to do the same. Lucifer's pride was destroyed. He still blames Deus for breaking up our merry band to this day. Without all seven of us united, Lucifer doesn't stand a chance of completing his plan. That's why I assume he wants your power. It would get him one step closer."

I sat quietly, processing the new information. "Why did you all agree to follow Lucifer in the rebellion?" I asked.

He played with the flame of the candle that sat in front of me. "We each had our own reasons. Our sins had always been there, creeping beneath the surface. I wanted more time to myself, to do as I pleased, when I pleased. Satan was tired of training legions for a war that never seemed to come. Levi was jealous of Father's affection towards the humans. Belz wanted more out of life. He was never satisfied with what he had. Mammon hoarded his grace and power, not wanting to share it with Father's creations. Deus was obsessed with the creation of sex. He even snuck down to earth a couple of times and had a tryst with humans. And Lucy ... he was envious of Father. He and Michael were what you would call heirs to the throne. But the day of ascension for Lucy would never come, because Father would never die."

"And you like being alone?" I asked.

He paused for a moment, lifting his eyes slowly to mine. "Most of the time ... yes, but there is still a piece of me that craves to share this life with another. I thought I had found that, with Cecilia, but I was wrong."

I thought of Deus in that moment. For the first time, I thought of what life might look like with him: however short that would be for me.

I stood from my seat. "Thank you for the lovely meal. I'm feeling a bit tired so I'm going to head back to my room. I will see you in the morning."

He nodded with a small smile.

When I got to my room, I noticed a floral arrangement on the small round table by the window. Besides it sat an envelope. I picked it up, opening the paper carefully.

Dearest Seren,

I am happy to see you have finally left the confines of wherever you've been hiding, and I am now able to send you this letter. I must say, I am a bit hurt to discover you've chosen that particular brother to reside with for the time being. I thought after our meeting at the Consort, I would be the obvious choice. My pride has been struck. If you wanted to see the pyramids, I would have been more than happy to escort you myself. Especially since I was the one that helped the Egyptians construct them. Whose idea do you think it was to use Father's chosen people as slaves?

I am writing to extend an invitation to my humble abode in New York City. I have a flat I feel you would appreciate. I hope this letter finds you well and that you consider my proposal.

Yours truly,

Lucifer Morningstar

I crumbled up the letter, throwing it into the waste basket. *Shit,* I thought. He knew where I was. I needed to work Gor fast so I could gain what I came for and get the hell out of here.

That night, I slept with one eye open.

The next morning, there was a knock on the door. A small Egyptian woman with yellow eyes was on the other side. She bowed to me and then nodded down the hall. I followed her silently. She led me to two golden doors with hieroglyphics carved into the surface, along with artwork of pharaohs and gods. She gestured towards the door and then left. I knocked.

"Come in," came Gor's voice.

I pushed the doors open to reveal a massive room with piles and piles of books stacked twice my height. There was a wooden table by the window, covered with papers and more books. His bed was off to the side, unmade. His entire room was a wreck.

"Good morning," he said.

"Morning."

"How did you sleep?"

"Fine, thank you." I strolled over to him at the table. "I received a letter last night," I admitted.

His eyes met mine. "From whom?"

"Lucifer. He is not happy I chose to stay with you over him."

"Did he indicate he knew the reason for you visit?"

"No, but I think he might be aware of my connection with Deus. From the tone of his letter, I believe he thinks I'm brother hopping."

Gor laughed. "Well then, we best get a move on."

"You're going to help me?"

He looked at me, standing tall. He was still in his white robe and linen pants, not bothering to dress for the day. "On one condition." He paused. "You promise complete honesty."

"I can do that," I replied.

He nodded. "Good, now let's begin."

I sat at his table as he began to educate me on the realms of Hell. He showed me maps of how the territories were divided and where the access points where. There were three ways to enter. The first path was at the very northern passage of Hell. These were the gates most people passed through after they died. He told me that there would be a lot of eyes on that particular entrance, since it was literally the highway to hell.

The next was straight into Lucifer's castle. The doorway was warded and spelled. As soon as I stepped foot through the gate, he would be informed. The last was through a cave system, high up above Satan's border. This entrance would be challenging due to harsh climates and demons of all shapes and sizes I'd have to fight through until I found my way to my destination.

"Now," he said, taking a seat and running his hand through his hair. "Onto the fun part."

It had been hours of looking over maps and reading documents about the realms. There was still so much to learn, but first, I needed to get myself there. "This hasn't been the fun part?" I said sarcastically.

He grinned. "Are you trying to say I'm a boring teacher, Miss Salvo?"

"Not at all. Now, you were saying?"

"Right. Let's move onto how you're going to be getting yourself there in the first place."

"Now I'm intrigued."

"Thought you'd be. There are two ways you enter with your particular gifts. The first is called gate melding. This is going to take time, but once you've got it, you'll have access whenever you need. Unless the gate is destroyed, that is."

"And how do I gate meld?"

"Over the next few weeks, you are going to bestow parts of your power into a doorway of your own making. It takes time, but once you've created the gate, you can access it whenever you need. It's exhausting work, I must warn you."

"And the second way?" I asked.

"You essentially die."

"Oh, is that it?"

He laughed. "Your goddess power will tie you to this plane longer than any normal soul. In Hell, time moves a lot slower. So, you can die here, visit our little hellhole below, and as long as you pull yourself out in time, you should be able to return."

"Sounds risky."

"It is. That's why we're going with the gate melding first."

I paused, looking over the maps on the table. "Can I ask you something?"

"Isn't that why you're here?"

I smirked. "What happens to one of the original seven, if you actually were to die?"

He tapped his fingers on the table for a moment before answering. "The world cannot go on without one of our sins. Thus, if we were to truly die, we would be restrained in hell for eternity, never able to reach the surface again. We would still be able to rule our kingdoms below and have some control over what happened topside, but our souls would be torn from our bodies, forcing us to become the demons that lurk underneath, while this beautiful exterior you see remains."

"Thank you for telling me."

He nodded, rising from his chair. "Starting tomorrow, we will begin construction. In between gate creation, you will educate yourself on each of my brother's territories and the demons you will encounter."

I nodded. "Thank you Gor ... really," I said.

"You're welcome, little goddess.

Chapter Twenty

Gor wasn't exaggerating when he said it would take a lot out me of to create this gate. The first week was spent trying to harness my magic into a physical entity, which was harder than it sounded. Once I mastered that, I had to build the damn door piece by piece. I willed my magic into a solid object that I could summon at any moment. The process was slow and grueling. Each night, I opened the door in my mind, just enough to tell Deus I was still alive, and then slammed it shut before he could strum up a conversation. I needed to focus, and he was my greatest distraction.

Gor insisted I take weekends off. During this time, we traveled across Egypt, sightseeing and studying the amazing history the land held. He was a vat of information, as if born to be a professor. He took me inside pyramids, sharing stories about the pharaohs who had been buried deep within. He had spent most of his life in this part of the world, after his initial travels and studies. He was kind and caring, something I truly admired about him. He was also patient, which came in handy when I had to meld the gate.

I had completed about two-thirds of the damn gate in a five-week time span. My power seemed to be weakening with each passing day. I was channeling my darkness towards the gate, forcing it into a solid state when I collapsed to the ground. Gor was there instantly, holding me on the floor. I was sweating and felt dizzy. I had exerted too much.

Gor brought some tea up to my lips. "Take it easy," he whispered. I took small sips, able to sit up on my own a few moments later. I wiped my brow, shaking. I felt Gor's eyes assess me.

"I'm just tired," I said, resting my head on my arms, still laying on the ground.

"I can see that." He looked me over slowly. I recognized his thinking face at this point. "Is the horned god's vessel not your mate?" he finally asked.

"No, unfortunately."

He laughed. "Why do you say that?"

"Because Orion is perfect in every possible sense of the word, but somehow I'm defective."

"You're not defective, Seren."

"Aren't I? He loved me, was willing to sacrifice everything for me, and yet, my stupid heart couldn't love him ... wouldn't. And I tried, believe me."

He laid down next to me, resting his head on his propped elbow. "Let me ask you this. Have you ever been in love before?"

"Yes."

"And what would you have done to protect that love?"

"Anything. I almost destroyed myself trying to hold onto it."

"Exactly. Now, imagine a love ten times more powerful than that experience. A love that you would move hell and earth to protect ... to save. That is what a mating bond is. It's two parts coming back together to form one whole."

"What do you mean two parts?" I asked.

He looked at me with confusion. "Has no one ever told you what a mating bond is? How it started?"

"No. Just that it is destined, and mine should have been Orion."

He shook his head. "Honestly, I don't understand how humanity is going to survive with how lazy they are ... I guess that's good for me in the long run, Sloth and all."

"So, what is it?"

"In the supernatural world, a mating bond between two souls was created in order to balance the power. When our powers were bestowed upon us, the creator realized that the power given was too much for one entity to handle—too dangerous. So, he split each single source of power, placing it into two separate vessels. If the two vessels find each other in their lifetimes, that bond clicks into place. If the bond is nurtured and cared for, meaning the two people are together physical, emotionally, and mentally, the two parts can access each other's power fully. Thus, two parts becoming one."

"Why did the mating bond never click into place for Orion and I?"

"Because ... though the mating bond was designed to balance

the scales of power, it is also tied directly to the souls who carry the magic. I don't know, maybe it was another tactic Father used to control how powerful we became. Just because you found your mate doesn't mean the bond will activate. The two must first come to terms with the love that has grown and then, profess it to each other, accepting one another as they are ... completely."

"I don't understand. I wanted to love Orion. I tried to love him, and I know he loved me. Why didn't it work?"

Gor placed a hand tenderly on my shoulder, looking me intensely in the eye. "Seren, just because you have Aradia's power inside of you does not make you Aradia. Your soul is your own. Your power is your own. Yes, it is mixed with hers, but you are something new. Something powerful. Something ... different."

My mouth fell. "So, you're telling me ... Orion isn't my mate?"

He leaned back and shrugged. "I honestly can't say."

My mind was blown. "Why is this the first I'm hearing of this?"

He chuckled. "It's truly astonishing the amount of knowledge that this generation has at its fingertips, yet how ill-informed they are all."

"I guess that's what I have you for," I said, sticking out my tongue.

Gor pinch the bridge of my nose. "Yes, yes, I am so helpful ... I know. And let's be honest: I am the best-looking brother out of the seven of us."

I laughed. "You all share the arrogant gene; I'll give you that."

"Do you deny it?"

"I'm not falling for this trap."

He looked at me with suspicion. "Ah," he said, arching a single eyebrow. "I see."

"What do you *think* you see?"

He sat up, brushing some imaginary sand off his shirt. "At the Consort ... the way you stared at Asmodeus."

I scoffed. "Don't even go there," I said, pushing myself from the floor.

He smirked. "That's what I thought."

I turned back around to face him as he stood. "Don't do that. Please ... just ... leave it."

He raised his hands. "As you wish, Seren."

The next three days I worked harder, pushing myself to the brink of burnout. Gor had to force me to stop a few times, but the gate was almost complete. That was all that mattered. Sunday morning, I woke early, heading down to the kitchen for breakfast.

For being the demon of Sloth, Gor was a stickler about his schedule. He was already in the kitchen, cooking. I joined in, which had become our norm. I enjoyed cooking with someone else. He cranked the rock music, and we moved around the kitchen in unison, singing and dancing as we prepared fabulous meals. It quickly became one of my favorite parts of the day.

We sat down for breakfast out in the courtyard, as we did each morning. Neither of us said a word. We didn't have to. Gor provided a sense of inner peace my life had desperately been missing. It was refreshing.

"You should be done in a week, at the rate your melding," said Gor, sipping on his coffee. "Then, I'll take you to Hell."

I laughed. "Don't you mean home?"

"I suppose. Though, I haven't visited my territory there in centuries."

"And it shows," said Lucifer, strolling through the door. I went rigid. I felt the magic rippling off Gor as he stood from his chair.

"What in the fuck are you doing here?" growled Gor. "You were not invited."

"Is that anyway to treat your brother?" Lucifer said sarcastically.

"Leave," Gor demanded.

"I will," he replied, sliding his eyes to me. "After I get what I've come for."

"That won't be happening," Gor replied.

Lucifer laughed. "We'll see," he said, snapping his fingers. The ground around us began to rumble and the walls shook. Hordes of demons scrambled through the doorways of the palace. More crawled from the roof into the courtyard, slithering down the walls like spiders.

"Go," yelled Gor, drawing his power out of his palms.

"I'm not leaving you!" I yelled, calling my power to me.

Gor turned, taking me by the arms. "Seren, look at me," he said, his face twisted with worry. "If he gets his hands on you, it's all over. Do you hear me? You know where you need to go. Now, leave!" he growled.

I looked at the beautiful face of a demon who had become one of my closest friends in such a short amount of time. I stretched up, kissing him on the cheek.

"I'm coming back for you," I whispered.

At that moment, a demon charged us. Gor pushed me out of the way, slamming his demonic power into it, blasting the thing to pieces.

"Go now!" he demanded.

I called my shadows forth, engulfing me in darkness as I went plummeting through time and space. I hit the wooden floor with force. I lay on the ground as tears filled my eyes in fear for my friend.

"Seren," I heard his voice before I saw him. It had been almost two months and yet, I remembered every detail, without even laying eyes on him. His hands were on me in an instant, pulling me up from the ground. Icy blue eyes searched my face with concern. "Are you alright?" he asked.

"Save him," I pleaded. "Please, he needs your help."

"Who? What happened?"

"Lucifer knew I was with Gor. He showed up this morning and tried to take me with a legion of demons. Gor saved me, but he's all alone. Please, Deus. Please help him."

Deus looked at me for a moment before nodding. In another breath, he was gone. I ran through the halls in search of my family. I rounded the corner, finding Aunt Thora in one of the libraries. My heart erupted with joy.

"Aunt Thora," I said softly.

She stood, looking more radiant than ever. "Sweetheart, you're back," she said, embracing me. "How was it? Did you find the answers you were looking for?"

"I did. And surprisingly, so much more. Where is Nonna?"

"Here, bambina." Her voice answered from behind me, as she descended one of the staircases in the library. I rushed to her, needing to feel her embrace.

"I've missed you."

She laughed. "And I you, my darling." I pulled away, my heart still heavy with the weight of Gor's situation. "What, honey? What has happened?"

"I was with Gor ... Sloth, when Lucifer found me. He brought a legion of demons with him. Deus has gone to help him, but I am worried about him. I feel like this is all my fault."

"Nonsense. Those demons have enough issues of their own to keep them busy," replied Nonna.

"I'm sure Deus will handle it," added Aunt Thora.

Frankie came rushing into the library in a full sprint. "What is going on. Levi ju—" she stopped, screeching as she spotted me. She took off into a full sprint, barreling into me. "Thank Aradia! I've missed the shit out of you."

I laughed. "I've miss you too, cuz."

"I expect the reason Levi just shifted someplace without a word has something to do with you?" she asked, pulling back.

"Gor was in trouble and needed help," I replied. "Lucifer."

She dropped her hands from me, her face full of worry. "Shit."

"I'm sure everyone will be fine," Aunt Thora assured. "Now, let's all sit down so you can tell us what you've learned."

For the next hour, we exchanged what had happened in the weeks I had been gone. I shared about the gate melding. Nonna informed me that our coven had begun to fight back against the others who opposed us. Just this morning, they had run the other elders out of Castle Salvo and it was safe to return home. Nonna and Aunt Thora planned to leave this evening.

Nonna looked at me with heavy eyes, taking my hand in hers as Thora and Frankie laughed about something on the other side of the table. "Bambina," she said. She diverted her eyes from mine. The lines of her mouth relaxed. Whatever she was going to say was hurting her. "Will you be staying, or will you choose to return home?"

"I'm coming with you, of course," I said. "You're my family.

You're where I belong."

She smiled. "I'm just worried about your safety."

"We're stronger together ... right?"

"Of course," she said, kissing the back of my hand.

I felt a soothing caress against the mental barrier in my mind. I cracked open the door, my magic reaching for his instantly to make sure he was okay. I could feel his strength. I exhaled with relief. *"Come to my room,"* he said in my mind.

I smiled. "They're back," I said, standing from my chair. "I'll meet up with you guys later, when it's time to leave."

Without another word, I rushed down the hall to his room. I threw open the door and was greeted by the sight of Deus and Gor sitting at a table, discussing something that looked private. I didn't care that I was interrupting. I took darted towards them, falling into Gor's lap, wrapping my arms around him.

"Thank God you're alright," I said, pulling back to check him over.

He smiled, bopping me on the nose with a single finger. "Did you really think I wouldn't survive?" he asked.

"I'm so sorry I've brought this upon you," I said, dropping my head. "This is all my fault."

"No, Seren," Gor replied softly. "This is just Lucy being dramatic. He would have found a way to destroy my momentary happiness, whether you were staying with me or not. This is just what he does."

I pulled him back into an embrace. "I'm just so glad you're okay," I whispered. His arms tightened around me.

I heard Deus clear his voice. "Are we done with the greetings, or would you like to borrow *my* room?" he asked.

Gor looked up at Deus, arching a single brow. "Your color is a bit dull, brother. When was the last time you unleashed your power?"

"*That* is none of your concern, Belphegor," he replied. "Now, are we done here?"

I pulled away, looking back at him. "Demon baby," I said, sticking my tongue at him. Gor laughed.

"Yes, well, this demon baby is not happy about his peaceful home becoming a bed and breakfast," Deus answered, drinking a dark liquor.

"What are you talking about?" I asked.

"It seems," answered Gor, "that I'm not the only one who will be staying here for the time being."

I looked back to Deus as he finished off the glass.

"Mammon showed up about two weeks ago, and then Belz last week," answered Deus.

"Five demon princes all under one roof," Gor laughed. "Sounds like we're in for some fun times." Gor and I both started laughing. I felt Deus eyes on us.

"How did he find all of you?" I asked.

"We aren't as powerful as he is," explained Gor. "Deus and Satan can match his ability to cloak themselves with little effort, but if

Lucifer wants to find the rest of us ... he will."

"Why now?" I asked.

Gor shrugged. "He probably always knew where we resided. He just never had reason to seek us out until we had something he wanted ... you."

Gallo appeared. "The room for Sloth has been prepared, master," screeched Gallo.

"Excellent," said Deus. "Gallo will show you to your room."

"It appears my brother already wishes to be rid of me," Gor said, smiling at me.

"Yes. He can be moody like that," I whispered.

"Still here," added Deus.

I smiled. "I'll come see you before I leave," I said.

"Leave?" asked Gor.

"I'll explain later." I slid off his lap, and he followed Gallo to his room, leaving Deus and me alone.

I sat in the chair Gor had occupied. "Thank you for helping him," I said.

"He's a brother I don't loath. Of course I was going to help him," he replied, pouring himself another glass. He leaned back, tapping his finger on the rim. "You two seem cozy."

"I've come to like him very much," I admitted. "Honestly, he's amazing."

Deus laughed. "Only you would find the prince of Sloth *amazing*. Though, I suppose you could do worse. Mammon, for instance."

I chuckled. "It's not like that," I added.

"No? Could have fooled me."

"Deus, come on. He's ... he's, my friend."

"We demon princes don't have friends, love." He shot back another glass.

"Then what are we?" I asked.

"Mutually benefited parties with shared interests."

I shook my head, allowing the words to hit my heart. "I see," I said, standing to leave. He shifted in front of me before I could reach the door.

His head cocked to the side as he stood with his hands in his pockets. "You're leaving tonight?" he asked.

"My coven has regained Castle Salvo. I'm going home," I replied. I tried to move around him, but he stepped back in front of me. "What do you want?"

His eyes blazed red at the question. "Do you want me to answer that honestly, or would you rather I dress it up with a bow?"

I took a step back. "Excuse me?"

He stepped forward, closing the space in between us. His hand slid slowly around my side to my back, pulling me into him while he dragged his thumb against my bottom lip. "Can I tell you a secret?" he whispered. "I like the way you taste, and I've been wondering if there are other parts I would like the taste of as well."

My eyes widened in surprise. I let out a nervous laugh, turning my head away from his hand. "Deus, stop playing."

He tilted my face back up to his forcefully. "I'm not," he said in a deep voice that dripped with lust. His eyes softened as he leaned his head into mine. "You've been away for a long while and during that time, I've come to realize I've missed you. I want you, Seren. Give me your consent," he whispered, brushing his lips against mine teasingly.

His hand slid from my face down my neck, caressing over my breast before heading to my pant line. He began walking forwards, forcing me to his bed. When the back of my calves hit the mattress, I stopped.

His fingers released the button of my pants. He slid the zipper down ever so slowly, while his eyes locked onto mine. I felt the heat beginning to build inside of me at the smell of him, the warmth. I had dreamt about this moment for so long: what it would be like to taste him, to touch him, to feel him inside of me.

My head was spinning. What had changed? Why now? It didn't matter. This ... 'exploration' could benefit both of us. I could sate the need to know what he felt like, to have him, while he fed off our lust. It could be a physical relationship only. No emotions involved. I could do this. I had to do this.

He pushed his hand down inside my pants. I closed my eyes allowing my body to press against him. I could feel the callouses on his hands, but they slid against my abdomen so perfectly. His middle finger reached the seam of me first and I gasped.

I heard him laugh softly. I opened my eyes to his beautiful smile. "You're already wet for me, love. That didn't take much."

Feeling foolish and a bit embarrassed, I pulled his hand from my pants and went to step away from him, but before I could, he grabbed ahold of me, forcefully pressing his lips to mine. He held my body against his while his hands consumed me. His kiss was laced with lust and passion. His tongue slid across mine while his teeth bit on my lip, needy ... hot ... devouring.

I ripped at his shirt until I felt his warm, toned body underneath my hands. I forced the fabric to the floor, focusing on removing his pants. He tore my shirt over my head and then pushed me on the bed before yanking my pants down, leaving me in my underwear and bra. He froze, his deep red eyes scanning every inch of my body. His pants were unzipped, teasing me with the part of him I had fantasized about so many times.

"Consent," he demanded.

"What?" I asked.

He leaned down on the edge of the mattress, placing a hand on either side of my knees. His fingers tightened as he spread my legs open. Without breaking our eye contact, he placed lips on the skin of my inner thigh, kissing and licking. I arched my head back, feeling my body beginning to unravel. My sensitive skin lit up from the feeling of him. I could feel my clit begin to swell between my legs. My underwear was drenched.

His tongue made a path up my thigh, spending equal time on

each leg. Finally, he slid his tongue along the seam of my underwear, only an inch from where I needed ... where I wanted him to taste. I let out a groan. My breasts felt heavy and ached to be touched. My nipples hardened against the fabric of my bra.

"Say it," he said, taking a finger and playing with the edge of the fabric. "Say I can have you."

I closed my eyes, biting on the bottom of my lip. "You can have me," I whispered. In the next breath, he pulled my underwear, ripping it apart. His hands gripped my ass cheeks, forcing me higher until his mouth began to consume me. I screamed as his lips kissed and grazed across the sensitive skin, as if he knew ever part of me intimately. His tongue teased my entrance before focusing its attention back to my bundle of nerves. His sucked and stroked until I was a wet mess.

My legs began to quiver. I was unable to control myself. The heat and tightness inside of me swelled with each pass of his tongue. He held my lips open with his thumbs as he sucked on the nerves until I couldn't restrain the screams that erupted from deep inside of me. With one more pass of his tongue I exploded in the most intense orgasm I had ever had. He held his mouth over me, allowing me to finish until my body fell softly to the mattress. I was completely out of breath. My body felt extraordinary.

He reached down to the floor, pulling my phone from my pants pocket.

"What do you want me to do with this?" I asked, confused.

"Text your family and tell them you'll join them tomorrow," he said, his voice still deep and haunting.

"Deus," I said.

"Do as I say, now," he growled. I typed the message to Nonna. As soon as I pressed send, Deus ripped the phone from my hands, tossing it to the ground. "Good. Now, take off your bra."

I obeyed. His eyes blazed with heat. He rose to his knees in between my legs, taking in the site of me. I looked up at his perfectly constructed body, finally glimpsing the rest of his tattoo. The masculine etchings of the wings, so intricate and detailed, continued to his collarbones and wrapped around his shoulders, extending to his back in the sexiest pattern. His tan body glistened.

He reached his hand down in between my legs again, sliding a finger over my slit. I whimpered as my body screamed for more. A deep and sensual laugh left his lips as he brought his finger to his mouth, tasting me. He moaned. "Just as I thought ... delicious." He hooked his thumbs in the side of his pants, removing them from his body. My eyes widened at the sight: at the sheer size of him. "Don't worry," he said with a hint of humor. "I'll take you slow ... at first."

I could feel my heat seeping from inside of me at his words. He took his cock in his hands, sliding the tip up and down my slickness. I laid back, waiting for him to enter. The weight of his body pressed against mine, his lips moving to my nipples, taking each of them one at a time in his mouth while his hands kneaded my full breasts gently. He grazed his teeth against the skin while his hands explored every curve of my body.

He sat himself back up on his knees, trapping my eyes with his. He looked down at himself, placing the tip right at my entrance. His eyes slowly rose as the demon inside of him smiled. With a slow and controlled motion, he entered me, just a little. My entire body lit up from the contact. I gripped the sheets on either side, feeling myself coming undone. With another push he entered further. My insides gripped around him, demanding more. His thumb circled my bundle of nerves as his eyes watched my every movement.

He continued this careful, restrained action until his thick and hard cock was settled at the very top off me. He pressed his body against mine, bringing his lips to my ear as he slowly thrusted inside of me. He bit my earlobe, wrapping his arms around my body. “Good girl,” he whispered, picking up his pace while he held my body tightly.

I wrapped my arms around him, holding onto his beautiful form while he destroyed me. I cried out in pleasure, allowing his sensual motions to take me to heights I never knew possible. His mouth was on mine, consuming my screams as if it was the very thing that kept him alive.

His hands knew every place I wanted him to touch. His lips knew just where to kiss and his tongue ... God, that devilish tongue sent me over the edge. He buried his teeth into my neck as his thrusts became more forceful and needy. I tangled my fingers through his thick, black hair, holding his mouth there, arching my hips so he could go deeper ... harder.

"Deus," I screamed as my orgasm finally came, tearing through my body, erupted every nerve inside of me. I cried out, trembling while he held me, pinned to the bed as he continued to pound into me.

Finally, he let out a roar, slowing his pace while he came to a finish. His grip on me softened, before he rolled to the side, panting for breath. My body felt heavy and numb. I laid there, looking up at the glass-windowed ceiling, unsure of what happened next.

He got up from the bed, and walked over to the table, still naked. His body was forged from the purest, most perfectly constructed mold. His legs were muscular and toned. His back had more muscles on it than I knew a body contained. And his ass ... dear God save me.

I pulled the sheets over me, watching him intently. He poured a glass of brown liquor and knocked it back before pouring a separate glass of water. He walked over to the bed, extending it to me. I took it, looking up at him. "Drink up," he demanded. "We're going again."

That night, we fucked half a dozen times before my body demanded sleep. Around five in the morning I was woken by his sinful fingers tracing the sides of my breasts. Before I knew it, he was inside of me from the back, kissing and biting on the crook of my neck while he clutched my breasts, holding me close to him so he could go deeper.

After, I finally peeled myself from the bed, barely able to walk. I went to the shower, welcoming the warm, soothing water. Just as I washed the conditioner from my hair, Deus joined me. His eyes were again ravenous with hunger. My body was sore and throbbing from our night of exploration, but something inside of me still yearned for him. He slowly walked into the shower, pinning my arms above my head against the cold tile. With one hand, he lifted me by the ass and took me as the warm water streamed down our bodies. He nipped at my breast and chest, leaving his mark wherever his lips had tasted. My insides cried out from his powerful thrusts. Every muscle in my body tensed. My nerves where on fire in the most satisfying way, sending me over the edge into another orgasm.

After I got dressed, I headed down to the kitchen where, to my surprise, Gor had already begun cooking. He smiled as I entered. "Well, good morning," he spoke first. "I can tell you've had a very rough night." He winked.

I couldn't help but smile as I hit him in the arm. "I don't want to talk about it," I said, pulling the flour and sugar towards me.

"Sure ... but tell me again how you don't have a *thing* for Deus," he said, moving my hair from my neck. "Now, was he fucking you or trying to eat you? I can't really tell by these markings." We started laughing as I swatted his hand away.

"Okay, so I fucked him," I answered, "big deal. He fucks everyone. It's not like I'm special." The realization of how true those words were hit me like a ton of bricks. My heart constricted and my breath felt heavy.

Gor leaned down close to my face. His eyes full of compassion. "But you are special, Seren," he whispered. "Never forget that."

I smiled at him. Mammon and Belz walked around the corner.

"Well, well, well," said Belz. "What do we have here?"

"Good morning, demons," I greeted, making cinnamon dough.

"It is a good morning now that I know you're here," said Mammon, sitting on the edge of the island next to Belz.

"Leave her the fuck alone, fucktard," growled Gor.

Mammon and Belz started laughing, looking at each other. "Oh, little brother," Belz taunted, "has someone grown a soft spot for the little goddess?"

"Oh, fuck off," replied Gor.

"Alright, alright," I said, intervening. "Enough bickering, more dancing." I turned up the volume on the rock music, moving as the tune blared. Gor smiled down at me, beginning to mouth the words alongside me. Mammon and Belz filled their plates with food. I smiled, twirling the pastries onto a baking sheet.

Gor took me into his arms, dancing me across the kitchen without a care in the world. He twirled me around, flour and sugar spreading through the air. I laughed, feeling complete. I turned back to island, catching Deus leaning against the doorway. He had his arms crossed and was smiling ... watching. I smiled back shyly, returning my attention to the pastries.

After breakfast, I said my goodbyes to Gor and the others. I didn't know when I was going to see them next, but with Lucifer out for blood, I was sure it would be sooner rather than later. Deus appeared in my doorway as I shoved some things into a bag. We hadn't talked about what had occurred between us, and I honestly didn't know if I wanted to. Frankie was right about one thing, though. After being with one of them, I didn't know how anything else was ever going to compare.

"You're actually leaving then?" he asked, walking towards me.

"I have to. My coven needs me."

"Back to Orion and Antonio it is." He stopped inches from me with his hands in his pockets.

"I suppose so," I replied, looking up at him. "I ... I took a few things. I hope you don't mind."

"Anything here is yours to take," he said softly.

I grinned, dropping my eyes from him. If only that were true. "Right. Well, I will keep you updated if anything else happens on our end, and I'm hoping you will do the same."

"Of course," he said softly with a smile. I waited ... waited for him to tell me not to go, to stay, to admit that last night wasn't just him needing to release his power ... anything.

"Okay then. Off I go."

"Goodbye, love."

And with that, I shifted back to my room at Castle Salvo. My heart was wrecked. I slumped to my bed, thinking about the last twenty-four hours. It was a mistake to sleep with him. I knew that, but I couldn't resist. I had been doing nothing but fighting the need to have him for months. And when the opportunity finally presented itself, I couldn't say no.

"Shit," I said to myself, my heart longing for him. I took a moment to center myself, before getting back to business.

Chapter Twenty-One

The coven debriefed us on what we had missed during our time away. There were no signs of Obsidian and the attacks on our kind had stopped, at least for now. Covens Soleil and Vento stood with us, backing my family's claim. Orion and Delphine were on an assignment but should be returning this evening. With the covens divided, we were vulnerable to an attack. We needed to find common ground, and fast.

The Simonelli family still resided in our walls. It seemed like their own coven didn't want to risk bringing them home. After the meeting, I went to Giana's room to check on her. Antonio sat by her bedside, holding her hand. I knocked. His eyes turned to me with an emptiness I had never seen.

"Hi. Can I come in?" I asked. He nodded. I took a seat next to him. She was asleep, hooked up to machines. "How is she?"

"Not good. She's dying," he whispered. My heart felt for him.

"The healers are unable to stop it?"

"No. They gave her a few weeks at most."

"Tony, I am so sorry."

"This just isn't fair," he replied. "After everything I did, everything I sacrificed: she is still going to die."

"I'll speak with Orion and see if there's anything else we can do." I went to stand, but his hand stopped me. His hazel eyes were full of so much pain.

"She can't die," he whispered. "After everything ... she can't." He fell into my arms, and I held him while he cried. I knew the love he had for his sister, and the lengths he would go to protect her. I admired him for it, even. We sat there like that for a long while. Even after everything, my heart still hurt for him.

That night, Orion returned. I waited by his room once I got word he had arrived. As soon as he turned the corner, I barreled into him. He picked me up, smiling and twirling me around as I took in his familiar warmth. He pulled me into his room, still holding onto me.

"Gods, I've miss you, little dove," he whispered.

"I've missed you too. Where's Delphine?" I asked.

"With her coven, trying to sort out the mess Torrian has made."

"Yes, well ... thank you for standing by us."

"Of course. I trust you Salvos. You've always done what's best for the covens. Even when it was maybe not what was best for your family. And your Nonna was right. We need every advantage we can get in this fight." We took a seat at the table. "So ... where did you run off to?"

"Well, my family stayed with Deus," I said.

"Lust?"

"The one and only. But I stayed with Gor ... Sloth." His eyebrows rose in question. I laughed. "No, it's not like that. He knew Cecilia back in the day. He is very intelligent and helped me hone a new power."

"Gor," Orion said, thinking. "So that's where she was all those years she and Amon were apart."

"Yes. He was helping her to gate weld."

"Are you going to make me ask?" He smiled.

"I was building suspense. Anyways, it appears I can create a gate to walk between realms. Meaning, I can go to hell and back. I can also commune with spirits. I haven't started practicing that one yet, but it's on my to do list."

"Really? I thought the horned god had those abilities."

"Apparently not. You have the power over life, but when it comes to death, that's all me. Thus, your healing power and such. I also found out about the mating bond. Gor told me that when all supernatural beings were created, a power source was split in two, placed inside separate vessels because one could not handle the immense force. When the two come back together, the source is reunited, allowing them to feed off one another's power. But the two must be united mentally, physically, and emotionally."

He said nothing, but something changed in his expression.

"Orion ... what is it?"

He smiled, shaking his head softly. "Delphine and I ... we've mated."

My mouth dropped in shock. "What?" I asked.

He laughed. "I know. It completely took me off guard—the feeling, the action—but it's happened."

"When?"

"About a month ago. I think I finally made peace with the fact that you and I didn't have a future. When I let go of that hope, my heart felt like it exploded in my chest, as did hers. It was a pulling force. I thought I was having a heart attack but then, I felt her in a way I've never experienced. Not even with you. We discovered a few days later that we had access to each other's power." He paused, smiling from ear to ear. "She's my mate, Seren. It's always been her."

I began laughing, throwing my arms around him in an embrace. "I am so happy for you, Orion."

"Gods, so am I," he said.

I pulled away, wiping the tears from my eyes. "Have your other powers developed?"

He nodded. "But I haven't figured out how to heal someone yet." My face fell, thinking of Giana. He took my hand. "As soon as I do, she will be the first I will save."

"Thank you," I whispered.

"Now, about these demon princes," he looked at me with suspicion.

"They're moody, unhinged, annoying, complicated, and temperamental," I answered.

"Yet, powerful, ancient, and sinfully beautiful," he replied.

"There's that," I said. An image of Deus's perfect body positioned over me flashed through my memory. My body instantly warmed in response. I was still sore from him and God did I love the feeling.

"Little dove, where did your mind just trail off to?"

I jolted myself back into reality. I bit the side of my lip. "I've gone and done something stupid again."

He smiled softly. "You've fallen for one ... haven't you?" I nodded. "Which one?"

"Asmodeus."

"The one who almost tore Torrian's head off? I like him."

I laughed. "Yes, well ... it's pointless. He was involved with Victoria Prather and still holds a torch for her. Leave it to me to fall in love with an ancient demon who's in love with a dead woman."

"Yes, that does complicated things a bit. Have you two ..." he paused.

"Yes, but he's the demon of Lust; so I don't think it meant anything to him."

"Have you asked?"

"I don't know if I want to know the answer," I admitted honestly.

Orion took my hands in his, leaning towards me. "If he can't see how extraordinary you are, he doesn't deserve a single part of you."

I smiled, forcing my emotions back into the little box I had hid them away in. "Enough about me," I said. "Tell me all the drama I've missed."

We spent the next few hours talking about everything and nothing. When I finally left for my room, it was after one in the morning. I opened my door and slid inside. I was exhausted. I took off my shoes, heading for the bathroom when I glimpsed a shadow in the corner. White flames erupted from my hands in defense. The figure stood, casually walking towards me. As he entered the moonlight peering through my window, I could see it was Deus. He looked stressed and tense. I relaxed, allowing my flames to extinguish.

"What in the hell are you doing lurking in the dark?" I said, calming myself.

"It's one in the morning. Where in the fuck were you?" he said in a firm tone.

"Um, excuse me, last time I checked, I didn't have to make you aware of my movements."

"If you took that damn wall down in your mind, I'd be able to sense you, but instead, I have to waste my time tracking your ass down."

"I'm fine, as you can see. You're free to go," I said, moving around him.

He grabbed my arm. "Where. Were. You?" he asked. His eyes were dark.

I pulled away. "I was with Orion," I replied.

Shadows began to seep from him. Static red sparks zapping around the clouds. He closed his eyes, tightening his jaw. "You were with the horned god?" he growled, gritting his teeth.

"Is that a problem?"

Before I could say another word, he slammed me into the wall, pinning my arms as he leaned his body into mine. "Did I not satisfy you enough this morning?" he snarled.

"Deus, it wasn't like that," I said, surprised by his response. "He's mated to Delphine. The bond clicked into place a few weeks ago. We were just catching up."

His face softened as did his grip. Before I could process what was happening, his lips were on mine. He pulled me into him, tearing my shirt down the middle before unlatching my bra, desperate to get his hands on me. I tore at his shirt, ripping it over his head before fumbling with the button of his pants. He lifted me in the air, bringing me to the bed, never removing his lips from mine. He pressed me against the mattress, sliding my pants off my legs. His fingers automatically slid in between my legs. The sensation was too much. I gasped, digging my nails into his arms.

His mouth moved to my neck, sucking and biting wherever his lips touched. He reared up, kneeling in between my legs, looking down at me with insatiable desire. He ripped his belt from his pant loops, placed it around my wrists, secured my arms above my head to the headboard.

He slid his pants off, taking my hips in his hands as he lifted me to him. Without hesitation, he slammed into me, sending me spiraling into darkness. Night surrounded us, galaxies and constellations pouring from the sky. My night was filled with red streams of light as our powers swirled together as one.

He took me hard and desperately until he was panting above me. His hands trailed over every inch of my body, leaving no part of me untouched. His lips kissed and sucked the sensitive parts of my skin until I was screaming his name, not caring who heard. I wanted to touch him, to explore him, but my hands remained restrained to the bed as he slammed himself deep inside. He arched his beautiful head back, presenting me with the sexiest view of his perfectly toned body. His fingers dug into my hips while he held me, sliding in and out.

I felt myself building with each stroke. I strained as I began to come. My entire body erupted as heat seeped from between my legs all over him. He smiled, keeping his eyes closed until he let go, filling me with his release. He hovered over me for a moment, catching his breath. He unlatched his belt from the bed, sliding to the edge as he pulled his pants back on.

I sat up. "Deus," I whispered. He paused, looking back at me from the side. "What was that?"

He stood, bending down to pick up his shirt. I covered myself with my hands. "That, my love, is called fucking," he replied arrogantly.

In that moment, I felt it. For the first time, I felt what it was like to be used in a physical way. I was foolish to think this could ever mean more to him than just that ... fucking. I pulled a blanket over myself, moving toward the bathroom. "I want you to leave," I said, forcing my emotions down.

He twirled me around to face him. "Now, now. Based on the water show you just gave me, I presume it wasn't that bad," he joked, still with that smug smile on his face.

"Go find someone else to release your power with, Deus. I'm done," I said, trying to pull away, but he held me firmly in place.

"Seren," he said more seriously. "What is going on? What is this about?"

"Is that how you talked to Victoria when you had gotten what you needed?" I screamed, the feeling the pain rise inside of me. "Did you just use her for fucking?"

His eyes glassed over. "I'm not talking—"

"Yeah, yeah, I know. You don't want to talk about your precious Victoria. And I don't want to be used like this. So please ... leave."

"I don't understand what is happening," he admitted. "Yesterday and just now was good for the both of us. I felt it. I felt you."

Tears began to fall from my eyes. "Deus, if you don't know by now, I'm not a woman that just wants to be fucked. Especially by you."

"What are you saying, Seren?"

I took a few breaths, gathering myself. "I'm trying to say I can't be with you like this because ... because I have feelings for you." My heart felt relieved and smothered all at the same time. "I fought against them. I really did, but I ... I can't lie to myself any longer. And I know you've already had the love of your life ... your mate. And nothing can ever compare to that. So, for both of our sakes, I need you to stay away."

"Seren," he whispered, taking a step towards me.

"No!" I cried. "I am not doing this. Please do as I've asked. Please," I said, moving to the bathroom. I closed the door, allowing myself to feel. I needed to get it out.

Once I had finished with my shower, I reentered my room. He was gone.

The next few weeks went by slowly. Nothing exciting happened around the castle. Frankie was in and out, spending half of her time here and the other half with Levi at Deus's castle. She knew I was off, but I told her I didn't want to talk about it. I focused on melding my gate and training. Then, I received the news.

I rushed to his room as quickly as I could, not thinking about what I would say or do when I reached him. I threw open the door. Antonio sat in a chair, looking out of his window. I knelt in front of him, taking his hand in mine, tears already in my eyes. His focus remained on the window.

"Antonio," I whispered. "I am so sorry."

His bottom lip quivered before his body slouched. He held onto me while he broke. I wrapped my arms tightly around his body.

His sister was dead; the one he had risked, and lost, everything for. I brushed his hair softly with my hands, holding him as tightly as I could.

That night, I didn't leave his side. In the first time in almost a year, I slept beside him. There was nothing sexual about our intimacy. I was there for him in a way he needed. I didn't want him to be alone.

The next morning, I sat with him for breakfast. Though he didn't eat, he began to open up, sharing stories of their childhood and how close they were. I listened, laughing along with him as he relived those precious moments.

Over the next few days, I helped Tony and his family prepare for her funeral. It was late September at this point. The air was beginning to change, and darkness was a welcoming comfort. For her funeral, we prepared her body with oils and herbs as ritual customs called for. We held a service and then lit her remains on fire, send them off to the afterlife. Tony had gone numb. No matter my efforts, he no longer interacted with anyone, and he seemed to be a shell of himself.

I buried myself in research and training. The gate was finally complete, but I didn't dare pass through the doors alone. Once I had imbued the gate with my last blast of power, it began to radiate with a dark magic that was foreign to me. I had to talk with Gor, but that would mean returning to Deus's castle. According to Frankie, they were all still shaking up together.

I had a plan. Get in. Find Gor. Get answers. Get out. This way, I would avoid Deus at all costs. I clasped the key around my neck and thought of him. I imagined the throne in the ballroom and shifted. I landed on the pedestal smoothly where I had intended. It was quiet, which I was thankful for. I headed out in search of Gor. I knocked on his door.

"I swear to Father, Mammon," came his voice. "If you bring me one more dead—" he swung the door open, his eyes wide with surprise.

"What dead creature is Mammon torturing you with?" I asked with a smile on my face.

He laughed, wrapping me in his arms and twirling me around. "Seren, darling. How I've missed you," he said, pulling me inside. "Father, it is good to see your beautiful face."

"I've missed you too, Gor."

"I'm surrounded by idiots here," he said, running his hands through his hair. "I can't get a moment of peace."

"Family reunion not going as expected?"

"It's going exactly as I expected. That's why I stay the fuck away from these twats. Now, why have you returned? Is everything okay?"

I smiled. "I finished the gate," I said softly.

His face lit. "You did, did you? How wonderful, Seren."

"Yes, but now, I'm scared to death to open it."

"You should be," came a female voice from behind me. "It's

scary as fuck in Hell."

I swung around, searching for the voice. "Who's here?" I asked Gor.

He laughed. "What are you talking about? It's just me and you."

"No. There was a girl. I heard her," I replied.

"Over here, Salvo," said the voice again. I turned to the edge of the bed where Giana sat, staring at Gor. "Who is he? He's cute."

"Giana," I said with astonishment.

Gor looked to the bed and then back to me. He smiled and nodded. "Ah, you're seeing a spirit, aren't you?"

"How?" I asked, not daring to take my eyes off her.

"Now that the gate is complete, spirits have a direct link to you," he answered.

"And thank the gods," she said. "I wasn't about to cross over into that hellhole. All the crying and screaming. Not my vibe."

"How do I move her on?" I asked.

"Uh, you're not," she said with a bit of attitude. "I refuse to remain in Hell for eternity."

"What is she saying?" he asked.

"She's refusing to move on," I answered.

"Ah, one of those," he smiled.

"Who is he?" she demanded.

"His name is Gor. He's the demon Prince of Sloth."

She circled, assessing him from head to toe. "A demon prince, huh."

He stood as if he knew she was close. "If you learn how to detach from Seren," he instructed, "I can see you too, little spirit."

"You can see them too?" I asked, astonished.

"All seven of us can. She is tied directly to you right now, so as soon as she figures out how to pull herself fully from you, we will all be able to see her."

She smiled, looking from me to him. "I'll figure this out," she said with excitement. "It's not like I have anything else to do." She wafted into a smooth fog.

"Dear Lord, help me," I said, feeling overwhelmed.

He laughed. "Now, what have you come to ask?"

"I'm ready to venture into the depths of Hell."

His face fell. "We can't, Seren. Not right now at least."

"What? Why?"

"None of us have been able to return since Lucifer found you at my estate and figured out we're all working against his plans to capture you. The five of us can't use our powers to reenter Hell. He's put a lock on them. I can only image what he would do if we tried. It's a risk none of us are willing to take."

"Dammit. All that work for nothing," I said, feeling disappointed.

"Not for nothing. Look at all you've learned. And now, you have your very own friendly ghost."

"Ha, ha. Not my idea of a good time, being haunted by my ex-fiancé's sister."

He laughed. "Could always be worse." His eyes shifted to the door. "We're going to have company." Before I could ask who, the door swung open, and Deus stood on the other side. His eyes locked onto me. He looked to his brother and then smiled.

"Gor, can we have a moment, please?" Deus asked.

"Sure, in your own room," he replied. "I'd like to keep my bed ... clean."

Deus nodded, stepping to the side, gesturing to the hall. I rolled my eyes and followed, not wanting to give Gor a front row seat to our drama. We walked a few feet in silence. This awkwardness was exactly what I had been trying to avoid.

"Entering my lands without even coming to say hello?" he asked.

"Sorry. It was about business," I replied.

"Oh? Care to share?"

"Not really."

He laughed. "Love, don't make me beat your secrets out of poor little Gor."

"You wouldn't," I snapped.

"Don't test me."

I sighed in annoyance. "I've finished melding the gate in between worlds and wanted to take a stroll through Hell."

Deus stopped, turning towards me. "You will not enter Hell by any means. Am I clear?" he said aggressively.

"Yes, I know. Gor has already informed me about Lucifer."

"Seren, I am serious. He will trap you there."

"Okay, okay. No Hell visiting. I get it." I finally allowed myself to look at him. He appeared paler than usual. His eyes weren't as bright, and his hair seemed disheveled. As if I couldn't control my own body, I stepped towards him. "Deus, are you okay?"

Something I couldn't place flickered behind his eyes. A small smile appeared at the corner of his mouth. "I'm fine. Never better." He went to turn away, but I reached for him. At that single point of contact he lost control. He wrapped me in his arms, taking my mouth with his own. He pressed me up against the wall, kissing me with desperation. His hands roamed across my body, searching for any amount of skin he could find.

I lost hold on my own leash, allowing him to kiss me, to touch me, even after I had promised myself never again. I slid my hands through his hair, enjoying the feeling of his warm and toned body. My heart screamed with pleasure and despair. He lifted my ass, propping me against the window ledge. He fought with the button of my pants, trying to get to me. I took a breath, pressing my hands against his shoulders.

"Deus, stop," I said. He continued to try and kiss me again, but I stood firm. "Deus, I said stop!"

He took a deep breath, placing a hand on either side of me. He slammed his fist into the wall with rage. "Fuck!" he screamed. The entire building shook from his power. He ran his hands through his hair.

I slid off the ledge, walking towards him. "What is going on with you?" I asked.

He put his arms out, preventing me from coming closer. "Stay away from me," he demanded.

"Deus."

"No. I need you to stay away," he growled, storming down the hall in the opposite direction.

What in the hell was going on? I quickly rushed to Levi's room, knocking impatiently until he answered. He finally opened the door as I stormed in, not waiting for an invitation. Frankie was sprawled across the bed, reading. She sat up with a smile on her face. "Seren, I didn't know you were coming," she said with surprise.

"What is wrong with Deus?" I asked bluntly. Frankie's eyes snapped to Levi. I turned to him, but he refused to answer. "Someone better start talking, now," I demanded.

"He's weakening," answered Frankie.

"Francesca," growled Levi.

"Why? What is happening?" I asked.

"He hasn't taken anyone in weeks. He refuses," she answered. She slid off the bed, making her way in front of me. "This wouldn't have to do with why you've been so ... off, would it?" My mind was spinning. What in the hell was happening? "Seren?"

Without answering her, I shifted to his room. He was sitting on the couch with a bottle of whisky in his hand, staring into the fireplace. He turned around and his face paled. "Dammit, Seren," he said, standing to his feet.

"What are you playing at?" I asked, needing answers.

"I don't play games," he snapped, moving past me to his wet bar to fetch another bottle.

"Then why are you allowing yourself to become weak? Especially with your brother on the hunt? Frankie told me—"

"Your cousin and my brother need to mind their own damn business."

"Deus, talk to me," I said. "Why are you doing this to yourself?" His entire body was tense. I knew he wasn't going to tell me, so I resorted to our minds. I swung open the door I had built to keep him out, and slammed my shadows forward with a force I didn't know I possessed. As soon as I made contact with his magic, I could feel his pain, his conflict, and weakness.

He pulled away instantly, only me allowing a glimpse of what he was feeling. "Stay out of my head," he growled.

"Oh, doesn't feel so good, does it?"

"I need you to leave," he said, turning the top off the bottle. I stood firm, thinking over my choices. He brought his eyes back to mine. "Seren—"

Pushing all sense and rationalization aside, I lunged for him, slamming my lips into his, pulling his body into mine. Unable to control himself, his hands were on me instantly. I unfastened his belt buckle, forcing his pants down. He pulled down my pants, lifting me up against his body as he walked us over to the bed. He placed me down, looking at me for a moment. He slid my shirt over my head, skimming the sides of my arms slowly with his fingers. He seemed to be ... studying me.

I followed his pace, pulling his shirt over his head. I grazed my hands against his firm torso up to his neck, taking his face in my hands. He leaned into my touch, seeming to relish in the feeling. I pulled his lips into mine, kissing him softly, like the night of the ball, when we had made our second bargain. I felt my magic well inside of me as I allowed it to escape. He wrapped me in his arms, caressing my skin ever so softly.

He laid me onto the mattress, never removing his lips from mine. Before, when we had been together it had always been hard and forceful; yet this time, he was tender and soft. He placed himself at my entrance, looking down at my face while trailing his fingers along my jaw and lips. A small smile appeared as he pushed himself inside of me. I gasped, exhilarated by the feeling of this man. I took a deep breath in as he began to move softly inside of me.

He continued kissing and caressing, holding me firmly underneath him as he cared for my body in the most extraordinary way. My body lit from the contact. I could feel every groove of him inside of me, as if we had become one. I ran my hands along his smooth back, enjoying his beautiful skin. I arched my hips, begging him to push further inside. He hissed, picking up his pace.

The idea of him, the feeling of him ... it was all too much. My orgasm came without even trying. Having him like this, in this intimate and all-consuming way, was what I had craved. He held onto me, until he found his.

A massive wave of power released from him. He collapsed on top of me, panting. I remained under him, more confused than ever. A moment later, he pulled back and looked at me. His sun-kissed color had return. The bruises under his eyes vanished. He kissed me tenderly, moving a strand of hair from my face. I felt the emotions welling inside of me. I loved him. I truly loved him. This wasn't like Antonio, or even Orion. It was something more; something profound that I couldn't fight. I felt a tear fall from my eye.

He furrowed his brow, wiping it away. "Are you alright?" he asked.

I moved to sit up. "Yes, of course." I slid to the edge of the bed, reaching for my clothes. "Are you feeling better?" I asked, pulling my shirt over my head. I felt his hands on my shoulders and froze. I had to get myself out of here. I turned to him, noting the glow that had returned to his complexion. "Afraid I only have time for one go around?" I stood, forcing my foot back into my boots.

"And what is so pressing?" he asked.

"Well, since I've finished the gate, I've recently had a few unexpected visitors that I need to handle."

He stood from the bed, pulling his pants up over my favorite part. "I see."

Not knowing what else to say, I called my shadows to me, preparing to return home. He pulled me out of the shift, slamming his lips against mine. I couldn't breathe. I focused on the feeling of him, on how much I wanted to stay wrapped in his arms, but he wasn't that type. At least, not with me.

He finally pulled away, kissing me gently on the head. "Thank you," he whispered.

I nodded, stepping back before blasting my shadows around me. I landed in my room. I picked up the phone and called Frankie. She arrived within minutes. We sat in front of the fire as I told her everything, while my heart completely shattered.

Chapter Twenty-Two

October was here and thus approached another birthday. Giana had become a nuisance. She had figured out how to detach herself from me as an anchor, which meant she could go haunt someone else for a change. I didn't tell Tony or his parents about it. I didn't know if it would make it worse or better. Tony was still a shell of himself. He spoke with me a few times, but about nothing of importance. I could tell he was suffering, but I didn't know how to help him.

Lucifer and Obsidian remained silent, and I didn't hear from Deus after our last encounter. A part of me was relieved, while another part craved him.

"Come on, come on, come," whined Frankie. "It's your birthday ... we must celebrate."

"Frankie, there is nothing to celebrate," I replied.

"I beg to differ," added Orion. "Plus, I've always wanted to know what it was like to hit the town with the two of you. All the rumors I've heard ... " Frankie and I chuckled.

"Just rumors, Horned God," said Frankie.

"Still a hard pass for me," I replied.

"What's a hard pass?" asked Antonio, taking a seat next to me.

"These two want to go out for my birthday. I'm not a fan of the idea."

"Why not?" he asked. "You should go do something for yourself. You're always taking care of everyone around you. Time to celebrate you for a change."

"Traitor," I said.

He laughed. "I think I could use a night out myself," he said. "Care if I tag along?"

"Hey," said Frankie, "if it gets her to agree, then the more the merrier."

"I hate you all," I said. They laughed as we sat around the table and ate lunch in peace.

That night, I prepared for going out with my friends. I wasn't excited about it, but I was happy Tony was willing to get out of the house. Nonna had agreed to release him from the confines of the castle for my birthday. I met them all downstairs as we piled into Orion's truck.

We arrived at the rave Frankie had insisted we attend. It was underground in some kind of old tavern. The lights were strobing, and the glow sticks came in droves. The techno music was so loud, I could barely hear myself think. Orion and Tony grabbed us drinks at the bar while Frankie took me by the hand, leading us to the dance floor. We knocked back two rounds of hard liquor and then danced.

I forced my mind to go silent, not wanting to think about anything or anyone. I just wanted to feel. Orion and Tony joined us, bringing more alcohol with them. I had never seen Orion this uninhibited. Now that he was mated, he had changed in the best way possible. He was happy and truly free. Antonio pulled me into him as we moved across the dance floor, allowing our bodies to sway however they pleased. He smiled, for the first time in weeks. I felt my heart warm.

After an hour of dancing and hard liquor, the effects were taking hold, yet something in the air had changed. A warm feeling spread through the room like a virus, affecting everyone around us. I closed my eyes, basking in the familiar tingling sensation. My body heated in response, my hands slowly drawing up and down my skin, yearning to be touched. Around me, couples and strangers began making out: touching, groping, and kissing whoever was in arms reach.

Frankie and Orion were clearly trying to fight the effects. Tony appeared in front of me, desire burning behind his eyes. He reached for me, caressing his hand down the side of my face to my neck.

"Tony," I whispered, stepping out of his touch. I fought the urge to let him take me right there on the dance floor. I looked around, trying to get ahold of myself, when I saw him.

Deus was sitting in a red velvet chair. Three women flanked each side, touching and kissing him, yet his eyes were focused on me. The sight of him snapped me out of the trance. I marched over towards the platform he had perched himself on like a king, avoiding the people who had already undressed. He smiled, arching one of his eyebrows.

"Stop," I demanded, finally standing before him.

"Why?" he replied. "Seems to me like everyone is enjoy themselves. Including little Simonelli back there." His eyes leveled on me.

"Reel yourself in, or I'm going to open the doorway to Hell and kick your ass through it," I threatened.

He laughed, opening his arms as a blast of red fog swept into him. The crowd exhaled, looking around at one another in confusion and embarrassment. The music continued as the humans tried to play off the near-orgy they had been participating in. The three females still fussed over Deus, unable to stop themselves.

"Get off him," I snapped. Their eyes turned towards me.

"Why?" asked a brunette.

"He isn't yours," said another.

"He's meant to be shared," added a blonde. And with that comment, I lost my mind.

I grabbed the blonde by her hair, launching her off the podium. The other two took a step back, fear overriding their need for sex. "Get the fuck out of here," I demanded. Orion, Frankie, and Tony came up behind me while Deus laughed.

"Jealous, are we?" Deus asked.

"What in the hell are you doing here?" asked Tony.

Deus tilted his head towards him and smiled. "I could ask you the same thing. Yet, by the looks of things out on the dance floor, I can guess what you're after, little warlock." Deus's eyes returned to me. "Happy birthday, my love." He extended a small black box towards me. I stared at it. He stood, walking slowly towards me. He took my hand, placing the box in my palm. He leaned into my ear. "Usually, when someone offers you a present, you take it and say thank you," he whispered. I pushed the box back into his hand, not wanting anything he had to offer.

"Deus," said Frankie, moving to a chair on the landing. "Stop being so dramatic."

"Would you have me any other way?" he asked, reaching for Frankie and kissing her on the head. "Nice to see you out of Levi's room, Francesca." Deus's eyes turned to Orion. "Horned God," he said with a nod.

"Prince of Lust," replied Orion, taking a seat in a chair next to Frankie.

"We're sitting now?" asked Tony. "Fan-fucking-tastic," he said, moving to a couch. I stared Deus down, moving to join Tony.

Deus took his seat, looking around at us. "Well, isn't this quite the interesting ensemble. Orion was engaged to Frankie, yet he married her cousin, who was engaged to Tony, who is the bastard that betrayed her, sending her into my bed. In a way, we're all connected," he said, grinning from ear to ear.

Tony stood, heat blazing from him. "You're lying," he snapped.

I pulled him back to the couch. "Don't let him get to you," I whispered.

"I'm sorry if speaking the truth offends you," continued Deus. "I could teach you a few things she likes, if you ask nicely."

Tony stood, ripping his arm out of my touch. "I'm leaving," he spat.

I turned back to Deus. "Really?" I said, before chasing after Tony.

I caught up with him, dodging through the crowds of people. "Tony, wait."

He turned around as soon as he reached the street, anger rolling off him like steam. "I can't believe you would actually sleep with that thing. Frankie, I can understand, but you? What are you thinking, Seren?" he yelled.

"It ... it's complicated," I replied. "I didn't mean for this to happen."

He took a step towards me, placing his hands on either side of my arms. "Seren, you are good and pure, yet you allowed that thing to use you. I know you. Even after everything, I still know you. I know what your heart desires, yet you've chosen to give yourself to the demon of Lust? A creature that is incapable of committing itself to one person; who will use you to suit its own desires and needs; who will never be able to give you the life that you want.

Make me understand ... after everything we've been through, why you would allow yourself to be used in such a disgusting and vulgar way?" His eyes were full of pain.

Tears fell from my eyes as I thought over his words. "You're right," I whispered, dropping my head in shame. I had never felt so disgusting in my life. "Everything you're saying is the truth. You don't think I feel like an idiot for allowing myself to be used like this? To be discarded, like I mean nothing?" Emotions welled inside of me.

"Then why, Seren? Why even allow him near you?"

I stood in front of Antonio, unable to allow the words to escape my mouth. I loved Deus. That was the cruel, sick joke of it all; that I had allowed myself to feel this again, but for a demon. One who was everything Antonio described, and so much more.

"You're better than this," he whispered, before turning away from me.

I stood on the street, unsure of myself. My heart had led me astray so many times before. I thought back to when Giana had once told me to trust my heart. I had ... and where had that gotten me?

"Well, that was a bit dramatic, don't you think?" said Deus, strolling beside me out of the shadows.

I turned on him, the humiliation of Antonio's words sinking in. "How long have you been there?" I asked.

"Since you stormed after your ex-fiancé downstairs. I was worried he might hand you over to your mother again."

"He's changed," I whispered.

He took a few more steps towards me, closing the space between us. "Maybe, but I wasn't going to take that risk." He stood above me, silently watching. I couldn't manage to bring my eyes to his. "Why don't we head back to my place? I'll have Gallo cook us up something special and we can—" he went to touch my face, but I recoiled, repulsed by the thought of him.

"No, Deus," I said softly.

"Love, come now. You don't actually believe anything that came out of that jealous prick's mouth, do you?"

I brought my eyes up to his, my heart crumbling in my chest. "He's right ... about all of it. I'm a fool." I went to walk away, but he stopped me.

"There is nothing foolish about you. Let's shift back to my place, and once you open—"

"I said no, Deus. I can't do this anymore. I'm done being your fuck toy, and I'm done with all this complicated shit that comes with knowing you."

"Seren—"

"No, I mean it. Being with you ... it hurts. I don't want to hurt anymore, Deus. I just want to be happy and make sure the people I love get to live." He didn't try to speak anymore, just stared at me, impassive. "Thank you, for everything," I said softly, "I really do appreciate all you've done for me and my family."

He smiled softly with a nod. “Of course.”

“Goodbye, Deus,” I whispered.

“Goodbye, my love.”

I shifted back to my room, leaving my demon prince behind. I crashed into my bed, feeling every emotion at once. I wished there was some way to just turn it all off, to not feel at all. That would make my life so much simpler. I went to take off my jacket, feeling a weight in the right pocket. I slid my hand inside, my fingers curling around a cube. I pulled it out, realizing Deus must have slipped the box into my jacket when I wasn’t looking. I opened my nightstand drawer and tossed it inside, shutting it, willing myself to forget it existed.

The next week, I focused on finding Lucifer. I didn’t know what I would do when I did, but at least we’d have a chance at finding out what he was planning ... what he was hiding. It was a good distraction. I had thought of a million ways to lure him out, but the best possibility was using me as bait. Nonna and Aunt Thora were completely against the idea, but it wasn’t up to them. There had to be a way to find where Obsidian was hiding. I was done waiting for them to come and kill me. I wanted this battle over.

"You know, I rather liked our impromptu wedding," said Orion, lounging across my bed. "There was no color schemes or cake sampling. Everything was just done for us. Why can't this one be like that?"

I laughed, poring through a book at my table. "Because this wedding has time and love put into it. You're preparing for a future with your mate."

"Gods, I can't wait until it's over."

"Oh, stop being such a baby. It's going to be beautiful."

"I'm so glad I'm going on a mission tonight. I need to kill something," he said, pulling himself to a sitting position.

"Yes, I'm rather looking forward to it as well. It will be nice to get out of Triora, even if it's just to transfer a few demon witches."

"Can I come?" asked Giana from behind me.

I jumped. "Dammit," I yelled.

Orion laughed. "Hi Giana ... wherever you are," he greeted, looking around me.

"Tell him I said hello," she replied. "Gor misses you. He says it's not fair you can't come visit just because of his stupid brother."

"Well, tell him we can arrange a meetup once I get back from the transfer," I replied. "I miss him as well."

"Oh, goodie," she replied. "He'll be so happy."

"What are you doing haunting him anyways?" I asked.

She shrugged. "Just keeping myself busy. He's not bad to look at, either."

"You realize you're dead, right?" I asked.

"Stop reminding me," she said, crossing her arms. "It's so not fair. I finally meet a real man and I've gone and died already."

"He's a demon, Giana. It's better this way," I replied.

"Whatever. Don't project your demon prince problems onto my demon prince. They are nothing alike."

I laughed. "Keep telling yourself that."

"Okay, I am still here," said Orion.

"Right," I said, looking towards him. "Sorry."

Giana rolled her eyes and flashed out of my room.

"Is she stalking one of the princes?" Orion asked.

"She's become obsessed with Gor."

"Ah, I wonder how that relationship is going to pan out."

"Stop being a smart-ass. She never got to explore this part of her life. I feel bad for her."

"Well, at least we don't have to see him all the time, like the other one."

I laughed. "You mean Levi?"

"Yes. He's begun sparing with Roric and me. He makes us look like children."

"That's what being literally created for war and alive for thousands of years will do to you, I suppose."

"Still, I can't say I'm unhappy about what I've learned, but I'm glad there's only one of them."

"Right," I replied, my mind trailing to Deus. "Speaking of sparring, care to go a few rounds before we head out?"

"I would love nothing more."

We headed downstairs, warming up and practicing before we were scheduled to meet the witches from the Soleil coven for the demon transfer. These were the first ones we had gotten our hands on in months. Nonna was fired up to begin interrogation, in hopes of finding what Obsidian had been up to.

Orion and I shifted to Madrid, Spain, where we had been told to meet the other coven members. When we got there, the courtyard was barren. No witches, no humans, no birds. Nothing. The silence was unsettling.

"You thinking what I'm thinking?" Orion asked.

"Yup," I replied. "Now I'm regretting telling Loriana and the others to stay home."

"This was supposed to be a quick hand off. We should be on our way home by now."

"Well, looks like there was a change in plans."

Orion got his phone out and called the witch we were supposed to be meeting. I heard a ringer off in the distance. I walked over, picking up the cellphone that was lying under a stone bench. It was covered in blood.

"Orion," I whispered, holding the phone towards him.

"Shift, now!" Orion yelled. *Buzz.* Our powers slammed into the cage. "Fuck!"

"Nice try, gods," said a voice I recognized. *Wrath.*

"Satan, let us go," I demanded.

"Not a part of the grander scheme, but your objection to the plan is duly noted," he replied. "And here I thought we were going to have to fight. I am very disappointed."

Orion grabbed my hand, pulling me close. "What do you want from us?" asked Orion.

"Your powers," he answered. "If you're nice, I may convince Lucifer to drug you during the process, so you won't feel the pain that will surely ensue."

"You'll start a war between your brothers and the two of you," I pointed out.

"Do you see me complaining?" he said, stepping into the cage with us. "Enough of the side chatter. Time to get this show on the road." He reached out to grab us when Orion released the fire of the sun. I released my shadows, trying to restrain the demon. Satan blocked the attack, his eyes flaring into a mix of blue and red fury. His mouth turned up into a wicked grin.

"I don't think so, little gods," he said, slamming his fist into the cobblestone pavement. Cracks spread out all around us, splitting the stones apart. From underneath, demons swarmed, crawling out of the depths of Hell. I quickly dropped my shields around my mind, reaching for anyone who was listening. A familiar dark haze met mine, off in the distance. Deus.

The demons attacked; Orion released another wave of power, incinerating them to ash. I flared my white flame, throwing wave after wave into the hordes. Wrath took out his sword, slicing through the air towards us. I dodged the blow, pulling my gun from my belt, sending bullets zipping towards him. He dodged every one. Orion continued to fight off the legions of demons. Cold fingers wrapped around my ankle, pulling me to the ground. I had stepped too close to a crack the demons were crawling through.

I turned my gun back, nailing the thing in the head, but two more appeared, grasping my legs, and pulling me towards them. I gripped the ground around me, trying to shift, but the shield was still up.

"Orion," I yelled, but he was swarming with demons, unable to reach me.

"Seren," I heard Deus in my head. I fought to keep myself above the ground, but more demons appeared, pulling me into the opening. *"Seren, where are you!"* I heard him yelling in my head. *"Tell me now!"*

"Madrid, Spain," I thought, but before I could hear his response, the tips of my fingers gave way, sending me plummeting into a portal of pure, white light. The demons clawed and grabbed at me, tearing my skin into ribbons. As soon as I hit the other side, my head bounced on something hard, knocking me unconscious.

Chapter Twenty-Three

My head was throbbing and the room around me spun. My mouth was dry, and my eyesight blurred. I heard the sound of a machine pumping. My arms and legs felt numb. I turned my head, realizing I was strapped onto a cross-shaped table. Orion laid across from me, restrained on a cross of his own. He was hooked up to a bunch of cords and a machine next to him pumped, pulling his blood through the tubes.

"Orion," I cried, trying to wake him. "Orion!"

His eyes opened slightly. The color was leeched from his skin. His dark brown hair was full of sweat and he looked weak. "Seren," he whispered, trying to keep his head up. "You need ... you need to get out of here."

"What have they done to you?" I asked.

"They're ... they're siphoning Cyrus's power from me."

"No," I cried. I tried to pull my arms free of the straps, but I was too weak.

"They've used the poison on us. There's no use."

"Don't stop fighting, Orion. Think of Delphine. Think of your future."

I reached out into my mind, searching for Deus. I sent out my tendrils of magic through the small doorway. Our bond was created with his power, not my own, so the poison might not affect it. *"Seren,"* I heard him say in my mind.

"Thank God," I thought; tears fell from my eyes.

"Where are you?"

"I don't know. Orion and I are strapped to a table, and they're using some machine to separate him from Cyrus's powers."

"Do you recognize anything? Anything at all that can tell us where they're holding you?" I looked around, but we were in a windowless room, surrounded by medical equipment and torture devices.

"I'm in a dungeon. There's a lot of medical supplies and weapons." I pulled at my arms again, trying to free myself.

"Look at the labels on the equipment. Look for any writing."

"There's none, Deus." Orion cried out in pain. *"Deus, they're hurting Orion. Please."*

"I'll find you baby, I promise. Just hold on and keep this door open. Whatever you do, don't give up on me, you hear me? You keep fighting."

"Okay," I whispered out loud, my head swarming with pain, sending me back into a deep sleep.

I woke up to a bucket of water being thrown in my face. I gasped for air, opening my eyes to see Lucifer and Satan standing before me. "Well, good morning, little goddess," said Lucifer. "You've been sleeping a long while. I was starting to get worried." I looked back to Orion. His body hung there, unresponsive. "Pull it out and give the poor warlock a rest."

Satan made his way over to Orion, reaching behind him, pulling a long needle from his spine. Orion yelled in pain, gritting his teeth as the needle slide free from underneath his skin. Satan unstrapped him, tossing his large body over his shoulder before hauled him out of the room.

"Where are you taking him?" I demanded.

"To a cell," answered Lucifer. "I wanted some alone time with you. After all, it's been months since we've seen each other. Time to catch up. Now, have your little powers locked into place yet?"

"Fuck you," I said, spitting in his face.

"Right," he said, pulling a handkerchief from his pocket and dabbing his cheek. "I was sure by now they would have after ... Ah, never mind. Onto plan C."

"What are you talking about?"

"Well, since your powers seem to be as stubborn as you are, we're going to have to experiment a little, to see if we can get them to come out and play." He reached around me to a table, grabbing a hammer and two large iron nails. "Just don't die on me, sweet Seren."

Before I could reply, he hovered the nail over my shoulder and with one powerful swing, slammed the nail into my flesh, pinning me to the surface. I shrieked in pain, my entire body erupting.

"Love," I heard Deus in my mind. I opened my eyes, unable to speak. Lucifer hammered the nail deeper. With every swing and vibration, I cried out.

"Deus," I cried in my mind, feeling the blood pour from my shoulder.

"I'm here, baby. I'm coming for you. Just hold on."

Lucifer hovered the second nail over my other shoulder, then sent it deep into my flesh. A gut-wrenching yell bellowed from deep inside of me. The pain was excruciating. I felt sick. The room was spinning and my skin was heating with fever.

"It's just pain. Remember what Mal taught you. Pain is only physical."

"It hurts," I cried.

"Now, time for the fun part," said Lucifer. He took two clamps, fastening them to each of the iron needles buried into my shoulders. He placed a mouth guard in between my teeth. "Clamp down now. Wouldn't want to ruin that pretty smile of yours."

"Seren, focus on a memory," said Deus. *"Focus on something that makes you happy. That you love."*

I closed my eyes, trying to think, but everything was hazy. I was fighting not to throw up. I heard a click and suddenly, electrical shocks spread throughout my body, needles of fire stabbing at my muscles. I shook, biting down on the mouth guard with all my might as my muscles seized and spasmed from the horrendous pain.

The machine clicked and my body fell against the restraints, hanging there unresponsive. Black shoes appeared in front of me. "Feeling any new powers yet?" Lucifer asked. He bent down, looking up into my face. "No? Well, that's a shame. Let's turn this baby up a bit and see if that jogs anything into place." The machine beeped.

"Deus," I cried silently.

"I know, baby. Please, just hold on. Don't give up on me, okay." The machine clicked and my body arched as the electrical pulse rattled through my bones, setting every nerve ending on fire.

The torture continued for what felt like hours. Eventually, I was so tired even Deus's voice no longer made sense in my head. I was too exhausted to even think. Satan hauled away my body once Lucifer had enough of me. I was thrown onto cold ground, but welcomed the change in temperature. My flesh still felt like it was on fire.

A hand caressed the side of my face. I opened my eyes to see

Orion looking back at me. I began crying. He struggled to pull me up against him. We laid there in one another's embrace until the next morning.

For days, I was tortured. They continued to slowly siphon Orion's power from him. He wasn't healing anymore, and the toll on his body was becoming evident. Lucifer continued to experiment on me, carving me up like a turkey, using other methods of torture while trying to force my full power to surface. My mental state was slowly but surely shattering.

For what felt like weeks, he locked me inside of a box. There was no light, no food, no water. I was alone in the darkness. I lost track of time, trying to talk myself through it until I reached the end. Deus whispered softly to me, but even the connection to him was beginning to fade.

After the box, he threw me into an ice bath, sending electrical currents through the water. I swore at one point my heart stopped. I was relieved at the thought, but then my lungs inhaled, reminding me that I was still alive, stuck in this never-ending cycle of hell.

Soaking wet, I was thrown into the cell with Orion. He was unconscious. I crawled next to him, still able to hear his heart beating faintly. I curled my knees into my chest and cried.

"Love." Deus's thoughts broke through the pain and fog.

"I'm here," I thought.

"Do you know what I was thinking about today?"

"What?"

"That night you showed up in my room, ready to burn the place down. I remember thinking how amazed I was at your strength and power. And then, when your flames finally faded away, how beautiful and perfect you were, just lying there on my bedroom floor."

"I was surprised you let me stay."

"I was happy to have you. I enjoyed our banter, and it was nice to no longer be alone. Have I told you how cold my bed has been since you've left?"

"Where is your revolving door of female companions?"

"There's only you, Seren. The only person I want in my bed ... in my life, is you."

"Stop being so nice. I like you better when you're an asshole." I heard him laugh and I swore I felt a smile stretch across my exhausted face. *"Deus?"*

"Yes, love."

"I'm afraid for Orion. I don't think he's going to make it."

"We're doing everything we can to find you."

"I know. I'm ... I'm scared," I said, the fear threatening to consume me.

"I am going to murder every person who laid a finger on you. I swear."

"I don't know if I can take much more."

"Yes, you can. And you will. You hear me? You are stronger than him. You are stronger than any of us. You need to be strong for yourself and for Orion."

"Little dove," I heard Orion rasp.

"I'm here," I said, lifting my eyes to him.

"Are you alright? Why are you wet?"

"Newest attempt to get my powers to surface. Water and electricity."

"Oh, Seren," he whispered, coughing.

"How are you?"

"I feel weak, but I'm still here."

"I bet Delphine is moving hell and high water to find you. I wouldn't want to see that one mad."

He laughed. "She is quite the sight." He ran his hand through my hair, wrapping his arms around me. "We're going to get through this. You deserve to live."

"So do you, Orion." I pulled away, looking at him. "Did I ever tell you how handsome a groom you were?"

He smiled. "Is that so?"

"I felt so lucky in that moment. You look good in a suit, Mr. Camerino."

He laughed. "And you looked stunning yourself. I couldn't keep my eyes off you." His chest rattled. His grip was weak and his face so pale ... too pale.

"I love you, Orion," I whispered.

"I love you, little dove. So much." He pressed his lips to my head before we fell asleep, wrapped in each other's embrace.

The next morning, we were woken by demons ripping us from

one another and pulling us from the cell. "Good morning, vessels," said Lucifer, standing prim and proper on the other side of the cell.

"Let her go," roared Orion.

"Not just yet," replied Lucifer, turning to me. "Today, we're going to try a new approach. Off we go," he said, leading the way.

We were dragged down the hall to a room I had never seen before. When the demons opened the doors, we stood high above a platform in the center of the room. A table with straps was placed in the middle of the round platform. Artifacts I had never seen before were staged in a circle with a large light hovered high above.

The demons dragged us down the stairs. Orion attempted to fight his way to freedom but was too weak. Once we reached the bottom, I was handed off to Satan, who restrained me. They hauled Orion up to the table and strapped him down, cranking the metal surface into an upright position. Lucifer appeared from the back, carrying my mother in shackles. Her face was busted open, and she was bruised and weak. Black poison shown through her veins underneath her skin.

"History time, little goddess," said Lucifer, brushing my mother's hair from her face. "Would you like to know how your mother became the evil, wicked witch you know her to be?"

"I don't care," I growled, focusing on Orion. The demons were hooking him up to some type of machine.

"Oh," said Lucifer, "but I think you will. It involves you. She became this to save you." He smiled.

Annalise looked as if she could murder him on sight.

"See," he continued, "a little over twenty-three years ago, your mother got into an awful car accident, with you nestled inside of her tummy. Thankful, an angel appeared to her just in time." His eyes turned to me. "She made a deal. In exchange for saving you, she sold her soul to that angel, and agreed to do his bidding until released." He smiled. "I'll give you one guess who that angel was."

My heart fell into my stomach. I looked at Annalise, trying to rationalize the words he had just spoken. "You're lying," I said.

"Am I?" He held out his hand. A white, murky substance twirled and formed above his palm. "Do you want to know how I fixed you? Simple, really .... I placed some of my demonic power inside of you, which healed all your little broken parts, creating the first supernatural tribrid. Part witch, part goddess, part demon. The perfect mixture of what I need, in order to become a god. That's why your magic calls to me."

"No," I whispered, devastation settling in. I thought back to Aradia during the rite; the dark power she had touched inside of me. It was his. All along ... I had been his.

"Yes, my little creation." He tilted his head up to the ceiling. "See, Father?" he yelled. "You're not the only one who can create something magnificent. My creation is the strongest in all your worlds. Thee of little faith!" He grinned at me. "You are the perfect vessel to hold the power I am owed. The power I deserve."

He picked up my mother by the back of her neck and slammed

the white substance into her chest. She cried out in pain. Her skin glowed an unearthly hue as her eyes lit and her veins burned yellow. He dropped her to the floor while she squirmed and scratched at her own skin. I unconsciously lunged for her, but Satan held me against him. She continued to yell and thrash on the floor, her body morphing into different unnatural positions and angles.

"What is happening?" I screamed. "What have you done to her?"

"I've rejoined her soul to her body," he said, walking onto the platform. "She's no longer of use to me."

My mother calmed, beginning to breath steadily. She slowly pushed herself up on her arms, looking straight at me. Her face was different: softer. She reminded me of Aunt Thora. She sat back on her knees, looking at her hands while shaking. Her eyes filled with tears.

"Oh, my gods," she cried. "What have I done?" Her eyes flashed back to me. She covered her mouth as tears fell down her cheeks. "Seren. My baby," she jolted forward, trying to reach me, but two demons restrained her. She fought like a wild animal, slashing and kicking the her captures.

One of the demons bent down too close to her face. In a second, she lunged at him, latching her teeth onto the side of his neck, ripping out his jugular. Two more demons came from the side, restraining her to the ground. She tore at their skin, kicking and punching. She fought until one of them punched her so hard she passed out.

"Feisty one," commented Lucifer, "isn't she? Now ... on to the horned god."

My gaze snapped to Orion, my anger blazing. "Don't you fucking touch him," I snarled.

"I'll make you a deal. You activate those powers of yours, and I'll leave the horned god alive."

"I don't know how to activate them, you son of a bitch!" I yelled. "If I knew, I would have already given you what you wanted, just to have this shit show of yours end."

"Well, let's see if your desperation is key then ... shall we?" Lucifer smiled, picking up the long needle and inserting it into Orion's spine. Orion yelled, his entire body flexing.

"Orion," I screamed. "Look at me, Orion. Stay focused on me. We're going to make it out of this, remember? You and me." His eyes were already heavy. *"Deus,"* I said in my mind, searching for him. *"Deus!"*

"I'm here, my love." I felt him reach for me.

"Lucifer is going to kill Orion," I cried. *"Please Deus. Please!"*

"I'm trying, love. I'm trying to get to you. I promise. What do you see?"

"We were brought to a new room. It looks like maybe a college observatory, or a classroom. There's stadium seating. Ten large windows above us. Lucifer has six ancient artifacts. Orion is attached to table in the center. Deus, please."

"We're searching colleges now. Please hold on, baby. I'll find you."

"Little goddess," Lucifer said. "You might want to say your goodbyes. Won't be long now."

"Orion," I cried. "Hold on Orion. They're coming."

"Little dove," he said softly. "Please ... please tell Delphine how much I love her. Please tell her I fought to get back to her."

I sobbed hysterically, trying to free myself from Satan's grasp. "You will tell her yourself. Come on, Orion don't give up. You're the strongest man I know. Please, Orion. Please don't leave me!"

His eyes lifted to mine. I saw the tears fall down his face. "Seren, I never stopped hoping," he said, coughing in between words. "A part of me never stopped hoping we'd find our way to one another. Regardless of Cyrus and Aradia, I would have loved you." I was losing my mind. everything inside of me panicking. He couldn't die. He wasn't going to die. I had to get to him. I had to save him, just like he had saved me so many times before.

Lucifer appeared in front of me with a smile. He looked from Orion to me. "Anything?" he asked.

"I am going to kill you!" I screamed. "I'm going to make you suffer, you psychotic fucker! You piece of shit!"

He laughed. "Are you ready for another little tidbit of information?" he asked. The demons working on Orion left the platform. A large electrical dome activated around Orion and the artifacts. "Cyrus's power is nothing compared to Aradia's. He contained maybe a fraction of what she possessed. She was the one that began the rite that imbued the covens with power. I've been after her power for a long time now, but could never access it, thanks to the genetic difference. Yet, here you are, alive, thanks to my plan. I orchestrated the series of events perfectly. I knew your mother carried the next vessel. From setting the car accident in motion to this very moment, I placed the people who loved and betrayed you directly in your path. Your entire life has been written ... by me."

He reached out to touch my face. I snapped my teeth at him, begging him to get close enough. He laughed. "It was the perfect plan. I wouldn't have gone after your sweet little horned god, but you left me no choice. Think of him as my insurance policy."

Lucifer snapped his fingers. The machine attached to Orion began to pump. Witches surrounded the circle barrier and began chanting. Orion screamed in pain, his neck extended towards the ceiling, every vein in his body raised. The six artifacts began to glow. shooting yellow beams of light towards him.

"No!" I screamed, flailing and fighting to get free. I was able to kick Satan's legs. He let go for a moment. I scrambled towards the barrier, banging my fists against the shield. "No! Orion! I'm here. I'm not going anywhere. I love you, Orion. Stay with me!" Satan confined my arms, hauling me against him. I cried uncontrollably as I was forced to watch the best man I had ever known suffer.

The light glowing from the artifacts grew as Orion's body began to shake. He was dying, and there was nothing I could do to stop it. Orion managed to pull his head down, locking eyes with me.

The whites of his eyes were bloodshot. I tried to think of any way to stop this. "Please," I cried. "I'll do anything. Just stop. Save him. Please."

"You know what I want," said Lucifer.

"If I knew how, I would give them to you. Please." My heart felt like it was going to burst from my chest.

"Dove," I heard Orion's voice call from inside the barrier. I raised my eyes back to him. "I will find you," he said, gritting his teeth together. "If not in this life, then the next." With those words, the ground below us shook. The light from the artifacts slammed back into their vessels and the barrier faded into nothing. The witches stopped chanting, moving away.

I was in shock. I was sobbing but I couldn't hear myself. I couldn't hear anything. All I could focus on was Orion's lifeless body on the upright table in front of me. Satan finally released me. I pulled myself from the floor, running to him. I picked his face up, trying to wake him, but he was so cold. I already missed his warmth. He no longer smelt of summer.

"Orion," I whispered, rubbing the side of his cheek. "Orion, it's over. Time to wake up." I reached around, holding onto him as I sobbed. "Please wake up, Orion. Please don't leave me."

"I'll never leave you, little dove," I heard from behind me. "Not fully." I turned around to see his spirit.

I fell to my knees, unable to breath. I shook my head and screamed. "No! No! You're not dead. You can't be."

He knelt beside me, reaching out to my face, but I felt nothing "My time has come, Seren. I'm no longer in pain. I'm okay."

I collapsed to the floor, feeling like a piece of me had died along with him. Three demons approached me, trying to take me away from his body. I attacked, only seeing red. I slammed my fists into their faces, clawing and kicking until there was blood. So much blood. More demons surrounded me, just begging to return to Hell. I granted their wishes. A burning rage inside of my body erupted. Even though I didn't have access to my powers, I was still a killing machine. Mal had made sure of that.

After destroying a dozen of them, Lucifer approached the platform. I backed towards Orion's body, ready to defend it with my life. His face was twisted with frustration and rage. "You stupid bitch!" he yelled. "What is it going to take for you to release those powers of yours? Ah!" he screamed, slamming his hand into one of the demons that stood too close to him, ripping its heart out of its chest. He squeezed, exploding it in his hand. "Take her back to her cell," he ordered.

Satan came from behind me, injecting me with the poison. I continued to fight, not wanting to leave Orion's body, but a few moments after, my light faded, and the poison took me under. I focused on Orion's beautiful face.

"I'm here with you," I heard him say. "I won't leave you. Not until you're safe. I promise."

"I'm sorry," I whispered.

"You have nothing to be sorry about, little dove," he said, softly walking next to me. "Now … it's time to survive."

Chapter Twenty-Four

I was thrown into the cell … alone. Depression overcame me. I lost track of time. I mourned the loss of a love I had never fully explored. It made a hole that was now carved out inside of me. I mourned for the man I should have saved. My sorrow turned into rage. As time passed, I fought to call my magic forth, to burn this building to ash. I slammed myself against the cell door, trying to get free, but it was pointless. I screamed and yelled like a wild animal trapped in a cage, but no one came.

Orion's ghost sat with me, never leaving my side. I spoke to him, needing to hear his voice, to feel his presence. He was calm and patient, like always. He distracted me by sharing stories from his youth: how he, Tyler, and Roric would terrorize Castle Salvo. He shared the moment he found out he was the vessel. I learned more about Delphine and through him, I found that I shared his love for her. My heart ached for his widowed fiancé. Did she already know? Could she feel the moment he died?

Time passed slowly. The darkness of the prison consumed me. I slept, silencing all around me as I traveled to the balcony of Deus's room. I would imagine him waiting for me; it had become my one saving grace. To survive, I desperately clung to my mind's ability to create a fictional reality. As I slept, we danced, laughed, and made love. We fell asleep next to each other every night, buried deep in his bed. His beautiful face was the last thing I saw as my mind slept. When I woke, I was alone, in Lucifer's prison.

I wasn't sure how much time had passed when the demons finally came for me. With Orion dead, and the chance of Deus and the others finding me withering away by the second, my motivation to live was deteriorating. They dragged me to the torture room, where they once again tried to bleed the power out of me. Lucifer was fed up and began to use the machine that had killed Orion on me. The large needle was inserted at the base of my spine, extending the length of my back until it reached my shoulder blade.

Orion stayed with me through it all. He coached me through, remaining in front of me so I had something to focus on. My power was ripped from me. With each compression of the machine, I became weaker. Deus's voice became softer. I cried, praying to anyone who was listening to save me.

One evening, after their experimental session, I was thrown back into my cell, bleeding from cuts and needle holes. I heard a rustling in the cell next to mine. My mother's hands wrapped around the bars, her face appearing in the dim light of the torch. "Seren," she whispered. "Are you alright?"

"I'm still alive, unfortunately," I replied, barely able to talk because of the swelling in my lip. I heard her begin to cry.

"I am so sorry." She wept. "I didn't know this was going to happen when I made that deal. Please, you have to know, I was desperate to save you. I already loved you so much."

"What happened after?" I asked. "After your soul was taken?"

"It's all a bit fuzzy. I remember Lucifer keeping me in a room until you were born. I was able to hold you, only for a moment, before he took me away. He took my soul and ordered me to bring you to Montecassino Abbey. I remember looking at you, thinking I should feel for you ... love you, but everything was numb. I felt like a puppet. After I dropped you off, he forced me into a deep sleep, until ten years ago. When I woke, I didn't think of you, or Mamma, or Thora. All I could do was serve him." She began to cry.

"Gods, Seren. The things I've done. The innocent people I've killed. How I've been towards you and ... Francesca." Her sobs grew. "I deserve to die."

I reached through the bar, taking her hand for the first time. "You didn't have a soul," I whispered. "You were controlled by a demon. You weren't responsible for your actions."

"I made the deal. I knew what he was. This is my fault."

"Annalise," I said softly. Her eyes turned to me. "I forgive you," I whispered.

She looked at me blankly for a few moments and then smiled softly. "You are truly the best thing I ever did. Regardless of all the terror my decision caused, I do not, for a second, regret choosing to save you, little bean." I thought of Orion. Tears began to well in my eyes. "Talk to me, honey."

"I ... I couldn't save him. All this power, and I couldn't save him. How am I supposed to live without him? How am I supposed to tell his fiancé I let him die? That he died because of me?"

"Oh, Seren. None of this is your fault. He didn't die because of you. Lucifer is the reason for all of this, and we will find a way to kill him. Orion seemed like a wonderful man who loved you. He would want you to fight. He would want you to live. Plus, you're forgetting one very important thing."

"What's that?" I asked, wiping my face.

"Lucia De Salvo is your Nonna. I can promise you, she is moving Heaven and Hell right now to find you. That woman has never failed at a damn thing in her life, and she isn't going to start now." We both laughed.

"I almost forgot." I smiled at her.

She reached through the bars and touched the side of my face. "I am so sorry for all the time I've missed. I have so many regrets," she whispered.

I touched her hand on my face. "Let's not focus on the past. Let's focus on the future. Our future," I said, smiling at her. She nodded, holding my hand as we fell asleep side by side, with only the bars of our prisons separating us.

"Wakey, wakey, Salvo witches," came Lucifer's voice.

My eyes snapped open. I was still holding my mother's hand through the bars. Orion was beside me, smiling softly.

"Remember," Orion said, "it is only flesh. You will heal. You are strong."

I nodded, smiling at him.

"Today is the day, little goddess," Lucifer said, smiling. "I can feel it."

"Will you shut up," I spat. "God, I pray you kill me just so I don't have to listen to you talk anymore." *Bam.* He hit me across the face, busting my lip open. I licked at the blood, happy to know I got under his skin.

"Keep your hands off my daughter, you wretched creature," yelled my mother, on her knees on the other side of the bars.

"Don't worry, Annie," he said, smiling at me. "You will have a front row seat while your daughter takes her last breath." The demons pulled me up.

I continued to fight and thrash. I wasn't going out without a fight. Lucifer brought me to the room Orion had died in. We hadn't been back here since that day, but this time, I was the one that was strapped to the table.

They inserted the needle up my spine. Though I tried to resist, I screamed from the pain. The machine began to pump, siphoning my power.

Lucifer appeared in front of me with a smile on his face. “I’m curious,” he said, “did you actually believe my brother would love you as much as Victoria?” I bore my eyes into him, not giving him the satisfaction of a response. He laughed. “Very well, I’ll do all the talking then. I had the privilege of watching him suffer for the past three hundred years over her. He gave up everything to save sweet little Vicky. And here you thought a year of you loving him would change his heart to favor yours? I almost feel bad for you.”

“I don’t want nor need your pity, you prideful prick,” I growled through my teeth.

He leaned into my face. “You had a man who was willing to give you the world, who loved you entirely and completely with his whole soul, yet you chose a demon who had given his heart away centuries ago—resulting in Orion’s death. How will you ever live with yourself, dear Seren? Oh, wait. I almost forgot; you won’t be living at all.”

“It doesn’t matter if I live or die. They will stop at nothing until you’re dead,” I said.

“Once I have your powers seeping through my veins, I will be unstoppable.”

“Leave her alone, Lucifer,” yelled my mother, shackled to the side of the platform.

He looked at her and laughed. “Ever the protective mother, isn’t she,” he said mockingly.

I looked at him, feeling the love of Orion next to me. “And to think,” I began, “this is all because Daddy chose the poor helpless humans over you. After getting to know you, I can see why. With your endless talking and boasting, I would have wanted to be rid of you as well. Time to face the truth, Lucy. Regardless if you succeed in siphoning my power or not, you will never be as powerful as your Father.

“He has created worlds, universes, all at the snap of his fingers. And then he created you ... flawed and pathetic. You think the humans are so weak and frail, yet they are the ones he created after you. He saw where he fucked up with you, and made a better model. Something not so ... needy. This is all just a big temper tantrum, because you have Daddy issues.” I started laughing. “Awe, you’re a psychopathic demon, who didn’t get enough love from dada.”

He struck me across the face, but I didn’t feel it. I continued to laugh. He hit me again, but I felt nothing. “You will be dead soon,” he said through his teeth. “Then we’ll see who’s laughing.”

A massive force slammed into the room. As the fog faded, Nonna, Levi, and the elder leaders stepped out. Another power surged, and Gor, Belz, and Mammon appeared, along with dozens of coven members. A final black fog erupted in front of me, laced with red lightning. My heart leapt. Deus appeared, slamming a sword right through Lucifer's chest, sending him stumbling back.

"Deus," I cried with a rush of overwhelming relief. I smiled, looking at his beautiful face.

He took my face in his hands, kissing my lips softly. "I told you I'd come for you, my love," he said, softly. "I'm just sorry it took me so long." He began to fumble with the straps, but was blasted backwards as Lucifer approached us, pulling the sword from his chest.

"Took you long enough, *brother*," Lucifer said.

Around us, a battle erupted. Demons swarmed as the covens unleashed their powers. Magic, bullets, and fists slammed through the air. Yelling and screaming surrounded us. The smell of copper from the bloodshed filled the air. Lucifer snapped his fingers and a dome shield erupted, locking him, Deus, and me inside. Nonna blasted the shield, but the magical barrier only absorbed her power.

"Save Annalise!" I yelled towards her. She looked at me with confusion. "Get her out!" Without hesitation, Nonna went to her daughter and began to free her from her shackles.

"Let her go, Lucifer," Deus growled.

"Not going to happen," he replied. "But I do have something for you ... a present, if you will."

"I want nothing from you," answered Deus. "Either you free her, or you will die. Even with Satan at your side, the two of you don't stand a chance against the five of us plus the covens."

Lucifer laughed. "Are you really willing to make that sacrifice for her?" he asked, nodding towards me.

"Try me," Deus growled, stepping into his brother's face.

Lucifer looked at him for a long moment and then laughed again. "Oh Asmodeus, you always were a wild card. I loved that about you." He paused, assessing his brother. "I'll make you a deal."

"I'm not interested in anything you have to offer," Deus snapped.

"Oh, once you see your present, I guarantee you'll be singing a different tune. The deal is this; you get to keep your present, and you and our brothers walk free, if you leave Seren De Salvo to me."

"Never going to happen," Deus replied."

Lucifer smiled. "Time to see your gift." Lucifer snapped his fingers.

A white puff of smoke appeared next to Deus. As the fog dissipated, a figured appeared. A beautiful woman with bronze skin, deep chocolate eyes, and thick, long white hair: Victoria Prather. Deus froze. His eyes locked onto her as his mouth fell open. I dropped my head, knowing it was over ... I was dead.

Victoria's face lit at the sight of him. Her eyes welled with tears as she rushed towards him, throwing her arms around his neck. "Deus," she cried softly. "I've dreamt of this moment so many times." She pulled back, looking at him while she ran her hands through his hair and over his face.

"How?" he whispered.

"She never died," explained Lucifer. "That was an illusion I constructed. I knew Victoria was your weakness, and I wanted an insurance policy against you just in case. I've kept her alive all these years, just for you." Lucifer smiled. "You're welcome."

Deus looked down at Victoria. "Are you alright? Has he hurt you?" he asked.

"No," she answered. "He's kept me prisoner for the past three centuries, but he never hurt me. I was alone most of the time, praying to Hecate that we would be reunited. And here, we finally are." She smiled. "Oh, Asmodeus. We can finally have the life we always planned, free from the rite or the covens. It will be just you and me. Like it should have been all those years ago." She reached up, taking his face in her hands and kissed him.

Lucifer turned his eyes to me and made a pouty face. "Alright, you two love birds," he said, approaching Deus and Victoria. "Off you go. I have business to conduct."

Victoria took Deus by the hand, leading him towards the edge of the platform when he stopped, taking one last look at me.

I smiled at him, tears running down my face. "It's okay," I whispered. "I'll be okay." He took a step towards me, but Victoria held firmly onto him. I laughed. "You get a second chance with the one you love, Deus. I want you to be happy. That's all I've ever wanted. Truly."

Deus looked at Victoria and then back to me. He kissed the top of her hand softly and then smiled at her. He let go of her grip and walked over slowly to me.

Lucifer rolled his eyes. "Make the goodbyes fast, brother," instructed Lucifer. "I have a timeline I'd like to stick to."

Deus's eyes search my face. His demeanor was calm and soft. He smiled at me, taking my face in his hands. His thumbs wiped away my tears. "My love," he whispered. "After everything we've been through, do you really think I would just walk away from you so easily?"

My breath caught. My eyes flashed wide as I registered what he had just said. "What?" I asked in shock.

"Deus," Victoria called. "What are you doing?"

Deus never took his eyes off me. "You never opened your birthday present, did you, you beautiful, stubborn, witch?" he asked.

I shook my head.

He laughed. "Well, if you had, you would know that there is absolutely no one, alive or dead, that could keep me from you." My bottom lip began to quiver. "It's always been you, Seren. From the first day I met you out in those woods, I was unable to escape you. No matter how hard I tried, you captivated me, drawing me back into your orbit and I was happy to be there.

"You are the light of my life. The very thing I was meant to love … to protect. I would give anything for you, including my life, if it came down to it. I loved Victoria in a way I never had experienced before. But then you came along and shattered those expectations with one smile, and one sassy comment after another. Seren … I want to spend the rest of our lives together. I want to hear you call me an asshole and berate me about how overprotective I am. I want to wake up to you every morning and fall asleep inside your body every night.

“I can’t get enough of you, and I never will. You are the only person in all the realms that has challenged me to become the best version of myself. You make me a better person in every way possible … I was wrong, Seren. Victoria wasn’t the love of my life … she was a steppingstone that led me to you.

“I love you for everything you are and everything you will be. You amaze me each and every day. Your resilience, your love for those around you, your power and strength … you are incredible. Nothing you could do would ever change that. I accept you for exactly who you are. My future. My purpose. My destiny. It’s always been you, my love. You’re my other half. I love you, baby, and nothing will ever change that.”

My heart slammed forward in my chest, pulling towards him. His eyes widened, looking down at his own chest. A burning sensation rushed through my veins as an invigorating force overpowered my system, causing both Deus and me to glow. I felt like my lungs were being constricted. But then, in the next instant, I inhaled, and felt him in my mind, more intimately than ever before: his power, his consciousness, his strength.

He looked at me and smiled, kissing my lips softly. He pulled away, nuzzling my nose with his. "My mate," he whispered. We both laughed. "Now, let's get the fuck out of here."

"Deus," I heard Victoria cry.

"Now!" yelled Lucifer. The machine that still held me began to funnel my powers more rapidly. Demon witches surrounded the platform and began to chant. The relics glowed with a bright white light as they shot into me. I felt my body extend and seize as the power began to drain, taking my life along with it.

"No!" yelled, Deus, turning to Lucifer. His power ignited and the two brothers began to battle each other inside of the dome. My body was overheating. I could feel my strength and my will to hold on fading.

"No," I heard Orion next to me. "Seren, you finally have it all. You found your mate. He is strong, and so are you. Tap into that power. Hold on. For him, for your future, for a life worth living: hold on, little dove. You can overcome this; I know you can. Don't give the demon what he wants. Hold on!" Orion roared.

My mind was strong, but my body was beginning to fail. The light from the relics seemed to suck the power from inside of me. I couldn't breathe, I couldn't focus, I couldn't think. I opened my mouth and screamed as the pain became too much. I was trying to hold on for the future I finally could see, but everything around me was tunneling. The cold slither of death was fast approaching.

As my last act, I reached through the door into Deus's mind. I felt his magic meet me while he continued to battle Lucifer.

"I love you, Deus. No matter how hard I fought it, I always loved you. You made me feel safe and you saved me from myself. You gave me a reason to live. A love worth fighting for. You are worthy of love. And I am so honored that you chose to love me. No matter how short our time was, it was worth it. Being loved by you has been the greatest honor of my life. One I would choose over everything else. You are my angel. My soulmate. My home. I love you, Asmodeus Râșnov. Forever, I will love you."

"No!" I heard Deus scream across the platform. His eyes locked onto me as he blocked Lucifer's attack. "Seren, no! Hold on!"

I focused on him, wanting him to be the last thing I saw before I closed my eyes. I felt the coldness creeping across my skin, the need to succumb to it: the silent, paralyzing chill of death. I relaxed my body, giving in to the peace that loomed on the other side. A burst of wind blew past me as I took my last breath, the heat finally giving way to the cold darkness.

Chapter Twenty-Five

I floated somewhere between life and death, in a dark room surrounding by nothing but fog and small beams of light. A figure appeared in the distance, slowly approaching. I could make out her white hair and tall figure. Aradia.

"Seren De Salvo," she said softly. "We meet again."

"Did you know?" I asked. "Did you know all of this was going to happen?"

"I am not omniscient. I did not know you were mated to the Prince of Lust: not until the rite. When his power unleashed, whether he was aware of it or not, it was searching for you, needing to reunite with its other half."

"Then why not tell me? Why allow me to go down this path?"

"It was your destiny. I tried to change that destiny, when I attempted to end you ... it seems that fate had other plans. I told you the last time we met; you would always have a choice. And so, you did."

"But ... Orion."

"He will find peace. He is honorable." She paused, smiling at me.

"And ... the enlightenment?" I asked in a panic.

"It has taken place, thanks to Asmodeus's love for you."

"I don't understand."

"The enlightenment period has nothing to do with the bond between the vessels. It has everything to do with you, Seren. You needed to accept your power ... yourself, for who you are. Once a vessel truly becomes one with their power, the magic is restored to our people.

"For me, it was finding Cyrus. Before him, even being what I was, I felt lost and unfulfilled. He made me whole in so many ways. He showed me what love was and because of him, I fell in love with myself and everything I represented. Asmodeus did the same for you. He gave you what you needed to find yourself. To accept who you are and your calling.

I took a moment, thinking back to our last seconds together. "When he told me he accepted me for who I was," I whispered. "I felt the pressures of my station melt away. I felt safe. Whole. Complete. Hearing him admit he loved me, for me, allowed me to accept myself. I had a purpose. A mate. A home." I brought my eyes to her. "That's what triggered it? Me accepting myself ... my calling."

"Correct. The covens are safe."

"But, if I am the moon goddess's vessel, how is Victoria still alive?" The sound of her name leaving my lips made me ill.

Aradia arched an eyebrow, her lips going taut. "Two goddesses existing in the same generation was never supposed to happen, but it's not impossible. Even after death, they still possess the power that I blessed them with. That power, the power of a god, is endless, but it is also unique to each vessel. It is just as much yours as mine. It seems like the Morningstar has found a way to work around nature's course."

A familiar cold darkness rolled over my skin. It slithered inside of me, searching, calming. I shuddered. "But what about Lucifer? If he gets ahold of my power, they're all dead."

Aradia smiled. "Don't worry. I'm confident that part will work itself out ... thanks to your mate."

The darkness wrapped around my heart. It sent a zapping sensation throughout my entire body. "What do you mean? What are you talking about? Stop with the riddles and just tell me!"

Her deep laugh rumbled. "Goodbye, Seren. I hope we don't meet again anytime soon."

"Wha—" before I could say another word, I felt my spirit being ripped from this plane. I was pulled down an endless tunnel of darkness at such speed it was hard to breath. I went to scream, but nothing came out. With an overpowering force, I slammed into something hard, electricity searing through my body.

"I love you," Deus said in my head. *"Make them pay ... make them burn."*

I inhaled, my lungs expanding as the air burned. My heart was racing. My eyes flew open in a panic. I was on the ground, looking up at the ceiling. My hearing returned with the sounds of fighting and screams saturating the air. I was alive ... and then, something inside of me snapped, as if it had broken in two.

I sat up, looking around me. My mother, Nonna, and Aunt Thora fought side-by-side, slaughtering any demon that came near. Frankie and Levi were on the other side, covering each other's blind spots. Gor and his brothers battled Satan. Vibrant colors of power stretched through the air. Fire erupted, causing the walls to rumble in response.

On the floor next to me, Deus lay unconscious. I reached out with a smile, stroking my hands across his face. I froze. His skin was like ice. I flipped him on his back, checking for a pulse, but there was none. I pressed my ear against his chest, in search of a heartbeat. I was met with silence.

"No," I cried, piecing it together. "No, you stupid demon. Don't leave me, please." I gathered his head in my lap, kissing his face, brushing the hair from his forehead. "Wake up, Deus. Please. Wake up, my love. I can't live without you. I won't."

I heard Lucifer laugh. "You stupid prick," he growled, looking down at Deus. His laughter morphed to a growl laced with a promise of revenge. "You just had to go fuck everything up. Gifting your life force to save her, all for the sake of *love.*"

I gently placed his beautiful head on the floor and stood to my feet. The power inside me welled like never before. There was something else there: something dark and uneasy. I looked down at my arms as black ink spiraled up my veins. I let it consume me, traveling throughout my body, up my neck and to my face. It pulsed, begging to be released.

Everything began to make sense. The path I had to follow to become who I was. A witch. A god. A demon. Gor was right. I was something unique. Something new. I wasn't broken or damaged. I wasn't defective at all ... I was power.

White flames laced with red and black specks appeared in the palms of my hands. I breathed heavily, fighting to control myself. Lucifer's eyes went wide. I smiled. "You are going to pay," I growled in an unfamiliar voice. "For Orion, for Deus, for everyone you've hurt."

I flung my arms wide, unleashing my full potential. I screamed as the powers from my witch blood, the goddess, and my demon poured out of me. A loud hum vibrated the room before a massive explosion unleashed, sending Lucifer, Satan, and their demons hurtling towards the perimeter. The cement walls exploded, revealing a snowy mountain outside. The white flame enveloped everything in its path.

I let go, allowing my shadows to slash and slice, whipping them around me, killing any demon that had the audacity to stand. The coven witches fought by my side. I calmed myself, still allowing the darkness to stretch through my veins. I walked over to Lucifer. He stood slowly, moving like he was in pain.

He smiled. "You are extraordinary. Just as I planned."

I lit my flame in one hand and my shadows in the other. "Your reign is over."

He laughed. "You can't kill me, little goddess. No power, goddess or witch, is capable of truly killing me. Since your little mate ruined my plans, I will be leaving to regroup, but I shall return to claim what's rightfully mine. Anything you'd like me to tell Asmodeus?" He winked.

I unleashed. Fire, ice, and shadows consumed him entirely. As the elements faded, Lucifer reappeared, laughing. "Nice try. I'll take that as a no. Bye, bye for now. I can't wait 'til we meet again." He shifted out of sight, Satan along with him.

I screamed, unleashing another wave of power. With Lucifer gone, the demons stopped appearing. I incinerated the last of them, only leaving my allies standing.

I let go of the magic, rushing back to Deus's body. I gathered him in my arms. "Please, come back," I whispered, kissing his face tenderly. Our family, friends, and covens gathered around us. I rocked his body slowly. "Deus, he's gone," I said. I reached into my mind, searching for his power, but I was alone. I cried harder, trying to make sense of it all. "I can't live without you. Please, Deus. I won't live without you." I sobbed, pulling him against me, willing my lifeforce inside of him, but nothing happened.

"Bambina," I heard Nonna say over my shoulder. She caressed my arms, her face soft and caring. "Let's get you both out of here.

Let's go home."

"I won't leave him," I cried.

"Orion," I heard Delphine's voice ask, as she made her way towards me. "Where is Orion?"

His spirit appeared next to her, looking at her with love and tenderness.

I sobbed harder. "He ... he didn't make it. I'm sorry."

Delphine fell to the floor, completely losing herself. He knelt beside her, going to touch her face, but unable to make contact. "Can you tell her something for me?" he asked.

"Anything," I whispered.

Delphine's eyes looked up at me. "Who are you talking to?" she asked.

"Orion," I answered. "His spirit is here with us. It's another power from the goddess. He wants to talk to you."

She looked around for him, her face agonized with despair. "Orion," she whimpered.

"Tell her," he said. I began to relay his message. "That her love was everything I could ever ask for. That loving her made my life worth living. No matter what the universe threw at us, we were always going to find our way back to one another, because our hearts were one. I regret that I will never be able to call her my wife, or see her walk down the aisle, or grow old with her, traveling the world like we had planned. But most of all, tell her I'm going to miss her smile. Her laugh. Her strength. She was the best decision

I ever made." He paused and laughed. "And lastly, tell her I liked the lemon cake the best." Delphine laughed, wiping away her tears. "I love you, Delphine Mystic. You are my ... Orion Camerino's soulmate. Forever."

"Thank you," she whispered, holding my hand. I nodded. I looked back at Orion. He was smiling.

"Take care of her for me, will you?" he asked.

"Of course," I replied.

He looked up at a white light that appeared over him. He returned his eyes to me. "Knowing you has been an honor, Seren Lucia De Salvo."

"I am the one who is honored," I whispered, my heart being ripped in two. "I love you Orion."

"And I love you, little dove," he whispered, before misting into the light.

I looked back at Delphine. "He's gone," I said softly.

She collapsed to the floor. Her mother came up next to her, gathering her daughter in her arms. I turned my focus back to Deus. I kissed his cold lips again.

Levi knelt next to me. He smiled softly, shifting Deus's body into his arms. "May I carry him back?" he asked.

I nodded.

Frankie stepped forward, her face full of tears. We didn't need to speak. She wrapped her arms around me and held me close. "I love you," she whispered.

"I love you too," I replied.

"Let's go home," Nonna said, looking back to Annelise. "All of us." My mother stepped forward, taking Nonna's hand. The five of us stood in a circle, hand in hand, as I shifted us back to our castle.

I locked myself in my room, not wanting to speak with anyone. My family brought me food and water, making sure I was still alive, but nothing mattered anymore. I had finally found my mate: the person who I was created for, created from ... and he was gone.

I closed my eyes, reliving our memories in my mind. I revisited the last time we slept together, how soft and tender he was. Why didn't I see it then?

My mind shifted to my birthday. How harsh and unforgiving I had been towards him. He wanted to take me home, to our room. He wanted to celebrate with me, but I wouldn't have it. I sat up quickly, remembering his gift. I dug through my nightstand drawer in search of that small black box. I pulled it from the clutter and held it tightly.

I cracked open the top of the wooden case. Inside, a beautiful red ruby lay on a black pillow. The lid was engraved: *Hold me close and think of me.*

I did as he instructed, thinking of the demon I loved ... my angel. The stone warmed in my hands. I pulled back and looked at it, just as a projection of Deus sprouted from the center. I fell back onto the bed and smiled, allowing tears to fall from my eyes.

He was smiling, and laughed a little, looking a bit nervous. He finally raised his eyes up to me. It was a recording. "Happy birthday, my love," he said softly. The sound of his voice destroyed my heart. "It's hard for me to fathom sometimes how young you are. How such a beautiful and naïve woman has utterly and completely destroyed me. But you've done just that, Seren. You've stolen my heart, and I can't seem to find it, nor do I wish to." He paused, licking his lips. "I know I haven't always made things between us easy, and for that I am sorry. If I'm being honest, the thought of you loving me scares the shit out of me.

"I can't understand how someone as pure and good as you could love something like me, but you do. Your goodness and kindness have awakened me. Before you, I lived in the darkness. With you, I bask in the sunlight." He laughed at himself. "I guess what I'm trying to say is that ... if you'll have it ... for your birthday, I want to give you, my heart. My whole being. I've come to realize that life without you is pointless. Now that I've had you, I never want to breath a single breath unless you're by my side.

"Your love is all-consuming, in every way. And Father only

knows how desperately I want to consume you, Seren." He laughed and so did I. "I don't want another. I only want you ... forever. I love you, Seren Lucia De Salvo, and I can't wait to spend my life with you, starting tonight on my favorite day of the year. The day that you entered this world, and my life began." He smiled, looking down nervously before he ended the projection.

I held the stone to my heart, trying not to hate myself for refusing to open his gift. If I would have, none of this would have happened. Orion would still be alive. Deus and I would have been together for a month and we all would have been happy. I held the stone tightly in my hand as I gripped the key around my neck.

I shifted to Deus's castle. His room was a mess. There were maps, books, and papers scattered everywhere. His bed was unmade, but I didn't care. I curled myself underneath the covers, smelling his pillow. The faint scent of lilac remained. I thought of him again as the recording played. I fell asleep to his face and scent, wishing he was there, wrapped around me.

Chapter Twenty-Six

A month had passed before I was able to free myself from confinement. I spent half my time at Deus's castle with his brothers, and the other half at Castle Salvo. My mother was recovering from living the past twenty-two years without a soul. The memories of what she had done under Lucifer's control tormented her. Aunt Thora barely left her side. Even though my mother was fighting to regain some sense of normalcy, I could tell Aunt Thora was elated to have her sister back.

Delphine and Orion's mother had packed up his room and returned to their covens. The castle felt lonely without his presence. Roric, Tyler, and the girls seemed to lose all interest in sparring and fighting. I insisted they return home to spend time with their families. They were hesitant to leave, but eventually gave in. Everyone needed time. With Lucifer forced underground to lick his wounds, we needed to do the same.

I sat on a terrace off the main library, taking in the last of the sunlight. Winter was on the horizon ... my favorite season. Antonio appeared, taking a seat next to me. Giana popped out of nowhere, looking at him with concern. I furrowed my brow, trying to silently communicate to her.

"He's depressed," she said. "He needs to let me go and stop acting like such a blubbering baby."

I laughed at her.

"What is it?" he asked.

I looked at him, no longer wanting to keep this secret. "Your sister is here," I said softly.

His eyes went wide. "What?"

"After she died, she refused to move on. She's been haunting me ever since."

"Okay, let's not be so dramatic," she said sarcastically. "I've been leaving you alone of late."

"Correction," I clarified. "She's been haunting me and a prince of hell."

"For fucks sake, Giana," he said. "You're dead and you're still going to give me a heart attack." He smiled, his spirit seeming to lighten.

She laughed. "Oh, brother, how I've missed that smile."

"She says she misses your smile," I repeated.

"And I miss your beautiful face, little sis," he replied.

"I'm sorry I didn't tell you sooner," I admitted. "I didn't know if it would help or hurt matters."

He reached out, taking my hand in his. "How are you with ... everything."

I bit back the tears. “It still doesn’t feel real,” I admitted.

He huffed. “Leave it to you to be mated to a demon.”

“I was just as surprised as you.”

“I wasn’t,” added Giana. “The heat between you two ... Wow!”

I laughed. “I like your sister,” I said to Tony.

“She’s entertaining alright,” he added. “It’s amazing how much has changed in a year. I never thought this was how it all would turn out.”

“Neither did I.” I paused, thinking of the ones we had lost. “I still can’t believe Orion is gone.”

“I wasn’t his biggest fan, but he was a good person. He was a better man.”

“I don’t know where to go from here,” I admitted.

“I don’t think any of us do. For now, let’s just leave that to the elders. I think we all have sacrificed enough for one lifetime.” We sat there together, staring out into the mountains in silence.

That night, I returned to Deus’s room. I had slept in his bed every night since I had found the red ruby. It was my only way of feeling close to him. I went through his paperwork and book collections, trying to keep myself busy. I came across a book labeled *Pride*. I pulled it from his shelf and began to read.

Deus had documented every inch of Lucifer’s territory in Hell. He had blueprints of his castle and all his holdings. Documentation of the demons he kept on his lands, where their weaknesses were, and how to kill them. Everything one needed to know if you were going to—

I stopped in mid thought. My heart leapt and my mind began racing. I looked back to the book, scouring through the pages, absorbing the information like a sponge. I slammed the book, rushing out of my room to Gor's. I flung the door open without even knocking. He was sitting by the fire in mid conversation with Giana. He sprang to his feet.

"What is it?" he asked. "What's wrong?"

"I found a way to get him back," I yelled in excitement. "I know how to bring Deus back."

"Seren, darling, I know you're hurting right now, but there is no way to bring him back, unless—" His eyes widened. "Absolutely not. No way."

"I'm going, Gor," I said adamantly. "There's no discussion to be had." He grabbed me by the arm, shifting us to the kitchen where Belz, Levi, and Mammon were eating. I pulled away, pissed. "Let go of me," I yelled.

"Go on," Gor said. "Tell the rest of the class your crazy-ass plan. Let's see how they react."

"What's going on?" asked Belz.

"Must have been something good to get Mr. Drunk on Love pissed," mocked Mammon.

"Oh, shut the hell up," Gor growled. Mammon laughed.

"What is going on, Seren?" asked Frankie, coming up behind Levi.

"I've found a way to get Deus back," I said without shame. They all looked at each other in question.

Belz's eyes flickered. His smile followed. "You're going to Hell," he said softly before he began laughing.

"You've got to be kidding me," said Mammon. "That's your plan? Seren, sweetheart, that's a suicide mission."

"I don't care," I said calmly. "I'm going, with or without your help."

"And how do you expect to get around down there?" asked Belz. "You don't even know where Lucifer's territory is, let alone what traps he has set and the demon creations his tormented mind has concocted."

I smiled, handing him Deus's book. Mammon and Gor leaned over his shoulder as Belz flipped through it.

"Little prick," Mammon whispered.

"Does he have one of these on all of us?" asked Belz.

I shrugged. "I don't know, but this will help me find him."

"He's not in Lucifer's castle, Seren," said Levi. "He'll be in the tormentor's pit."

"What's that?" asked Frankie.

"Where the worst souls end up once they die," answered Mammon.

"To be tormented for eternity," added Belz.

There was a moment of silence between them. Their eyes were heavy with thoughts of their brother. "I don't care where he is," I said. “I’m getting him back. If I have to go into the darkest parts of Hell, I will. He would do the same for me.”

“If Lucifer finds out you’ve entered his realm,” said Mammon, “you won’t be coming back.”

“Then at least Deus and I will be together,” I said. “If not in this realm, then in Hell.”

“Once you find him,” said Levi, “how do you plan on getting him back topside? He’ll be tormented and broken beyond repair.”

“He’s my mate,” I whispered. “I’ll figure it out.” They went silent.

Gor looked to his brothers. “You’re going to talk her out of this, right?” he asked. “This is crazy. Especially now. No one has ever been brought back from Hell, except for Father’s bouncing baby brat.”

Levi grumbled. “I mean, no one’s ever really tried.”

“Who am I to stand in the way of a mated pair?” asked Mammon.

“If she thinks she can do it, let her try,” added Belz.

Gor ran his hands through his hair in frustration. “You’ve got to be kidding me,” he rasped.

I went to Gor, placing my hands on his arm. He turned around and looked at me with worry. “I have to do this, Gor,” I said softly. “My life means nothing without him.”

“That’s not true,” he replied.

I smiled. “I’m resourceful, remember? I’ll figure it out.”

"I'm going with you," Frankie said out of nowhere.

"Absolutely not," said Levi.

"I am, and there is nothing you can do to stop me," she said with sass.

"Don't test me, Francesca," Levi growled.

"Well, if our soon-to-be sisters-in-laws are going," intervened Belz, "you all will need a tour guide. I suppose I have a few free days to spare."

"I have nothing better to do," shrugged Mammon. "Nothing compares to Hell in the winter."

Frankie turned to Levi. "You can either stay or come, but I'm going, you stubborn baby," she spat.

"Fine," he growled.

Our attention turned towards Gor.

He flung his arms out. "I guess we're all going home ... dammit!" he yelled, before stomping back down the hall.

"We leave tomorrow," I instructed. "I'm not leaving him there a minute longer."

"Agreed," said Belz. "I'll call Akira. We're going to need all the support we can get."

"Do what you have to," I said, turning to leave.

Frankie grabbed my arm. "Should we tell our family?" she asked.

"We'll write them letters tomorrow before we leave, but no," I replied. "They will only try and stop us. Plus, they're needed here with the enlightenment and rebuilding of the covens." She nodded with a small smile.

I walked back to Deus's room. Once I got there, I called Mal and Hashen. They appeared in a matter of seconds. I poured us all a glass of scotch as we sat at the table.

"What is the meaning of this?" asked Hashen. Always to the point, that one.

"I'm going to Hell," I answered. "I'm going to bring Deus back."

Mal sat straight up. "You're going to get yourself killed," she pointed out.

"I don't care," I replied. "If there is a chance I can bring him back, I'm going to take it, but I need a favor from the two of you. An insurance policy, if you will."

"Anything," Hashen said.

"I need you to rally Asmodeus's legions," I explained. "I need them to be ready to attack Lucifer's territory, if and when I give the order."

"Are you expecting to go to war with the Morning Star?" asked Mal.

"Eventually, it will happen. My main plan is to get into Hell undetected and get out. But I want back up in place, if things go south ... well, further south. I'm either leaving there with Deus, or not leaving at all. Returning without him isn't an option."

"You're brave, for how young you are," Hashen said.

"Well, you know what they say: love will make you do crazy things," I replied.

"We'll handle his legions," Mal confirmed. "You have our word."

"Thank you both," I said. They stood and left, leaving me to my own thoughts.

That night I constructed letters to each of my family members, including Antonio. After, I called for Giana. She appeared a few moments later.

"I was in the middle of watching Gor shower," she snapped. "This better be good."

I laughed. "What if I told you it was possible you could be showering with him in a few days?"

She stilled, her eyes going wide. "I'm listening."

"We're going to Hell to save Deus, as I am sure Gor has told you. You're coming home with us." A grin grew across her face. "But first, I need you to do something for me."

"Anything," she said too eagerly.

"I need you to find exactly where Deus is being kept. Time moves slower there, so you should have a large enough window to find him and report back by once we enter through the gate in the morning."

"Seren, that place scares me," she admitted. "I still have my powers. I can feel the souls mentally and emotionally. It's horrible."

"I know. And I'm sorry to have to ask this of you, but the faster we find him, the faster we can all come home."

She thought for a few moments to herself. "Okay, I'll do it."

"Thank you, Giana. Please, be careful."

She smiled. "I'll see you tomorrow," she said before disappearing.

That night, I studied through Deus's books and Gor's notes about Hell, refreshing my memory, trying to absorb every little detail. I didn't sleep much. I was too anxious. This plan could work. I finally shut off the light, curling up underneath his sheets. I held the ruby and replayed his birthday message. I smiled. "I'm coming for you, my love," I whispered.

Chapter Twenty-Seven

"Ah!" Lucifer screamed, blowing up anything that he was near. He began to throw chairs at walls, breaking anything glass or fragile. His temper was flaring. "You stupid little fuck!" he screamed at me.

I laughed. "Seeing you like this," I replied. "Worth it."

"You just had to go and sacrifice yourself for that little bitch!" he screamed. He took a breath in, calming himself. "Doesn't matter. Your sacrifice is pointless. She will die soon enough."

"She's stronger than you think, Luc. She'll find out how to kill you. I have no doubt."

He smiled, walking over to where he had me shackled to the ground. He bent down, looking into my eyes. "Want to know what I've discovered?" he whispered. I didn't respond. "She's coming for you, sweet brother. Your witch is coming to Hell ... to try and save you."

My heart dropped. "No. The others wouldn't let her," I said softly.

"Oh, they're all coming too. This is going to be quite a production."

I pulled at my chains, desperate to wrap my hands around his neck and pull his head from his shoulders. "They will destroy you," I yelled.

He laughed again. "They will try, but doubtful." He smiled, tracing his fingers over my chest. "Hmm, the most brilliant of plans just formed in my magnificent mind."

"You're diabolical."

"Maybe," he shrugged. "I wonder how the little goddess would like you without your soul." I froze, realizing what he now had planned. "I do miss my old brother dearly. This new one ... with all his *feelings*, has been a pain in my ass. I think it's time a bring the old you back out to play."

"Lucifer, don't," I said, gritting my teeth in a panic.

"We were inseparable once," he said in a soft and almost wistful tone. "You have always been my favorite, Deus. I want you by my side when I take the power I am owed. We can finally finish what we began all those centuries ago ... together. As it always should have been. Don't worry; without a soul, you won't care if she dies or lives. We'll rule together, just like we always planned."

Without another word, he slammed his hand into my chest. His cold fingers wrapped around the part of myself I cherished most. I couldn't breathe. I held Seren's face in my mind. *Remember her. Remember how much you love her. Don't forget.*

In a quick yank, Lucifer removed his hands from my chest ...

my skin knitting quickly back together. I looked at the murky white substance he held in the palm of his hand. In an instant, it disappeared.

Lucy snapped his fingers, my shackles releasing around my wrists. I stood, looking down at myself. "Dear Father, what am I wearing?" I asked.

Lucy laughed. "You're a bit dirty from our little squabble earlier today," he answered, "but that can be remedied."

I looked at him and smiled. "I would have beat you if I was at full strength. You and I both know it."

"Now, now, little brother. Don't get overzealous," Lucy said. Satan walked into the room, his eyes going wide as he stared at me.

"What in the fuck is going on?" Satan grumbled.

"Our brother is home," Lucy said, putting his arm around my shoulder.

"Sorry, Satan," I said with a wicked smile. "Time to get in the back seat where you belong."

"The fuck I will," Satan said, taking a step towards me. I snapped my fingers, and he went flying across the room, slamming into a table and then onto his ass.

Lucy began to laugh, turning to face me. "Oh, how I've missed you," he said.

"Frankly, I've missed myself," I replied. "Thank you for freeing me from that nuisance. I haven't felt this alive in centuries."

"I should have done it three hundred years ago," he replied.

"Think of all the fun we could have had."

"My evil older brother," I said, placing my hands on his shoulders. "Where would I be without you? Now, what is on the agenda? I'm ready to wreak havoc."

"Your little mate should be heading down to our humble abode shortly," he paused, assessing me silently. "Seren De Salvo. How do you feel about that?"

I paused, thinking back to the little witch with white hair. I remembered her face, her smile, and laugh. I recalled the way her body felt underneath me, and my dick pulsed in response. "She was a fun fuck, but not the most adventurous I've had," I answered. "Why? Was she important?"

Lucy began to laugh. "Not really. She's just the vessel I need to extract my power from. She won't survive the transfer."

I shrugged. "But you'll have your power," I replied. "A means to an end."

Lucy laughed, slapping me on the shoulder. "Exactly. Now, what do you say you spend some time amping up those powers of yours, and then I'll agree to a rematch."

"Oh, you're going to play fair for once?"

"I didn't say that." Lucy snapped his fingers and the doors opened. A dozen beautiful women stood on the other side. They came in different, colors, sizes, and shapes.

"I think I've died and gone home," I said with a smile on my face.

"You are home, brother. Finally," Lucy replied happily.

I walked towards the women, filling with excitement at the anticipation of burying myself into each one of them.

"Hello, Prince of Lust," one said, running her hand up my thigh.

"Hello, love," I whispered, following them out of the throne room.

ACKNOWLEDGMENTS

This story has taken me on a rollercoaster of emotions that ultimately led me down a rabbit hole of historical research; both worldly and biblical.

First, I want to thank my editor Kara. You make this process seamless. I appreciate your support and comical comments that lead to constructive criticism. I wouldn't want to work with anyone else on my projects.

Thank you to my wonderful and supportive husband. I appreciate you putting up with my crazy rants on religion and history during this writing process. I love you so.

Thank you to my friends and family for loving me through this process. For supporting me as I've grown as a writer and a woman. Like, many, I've struggled with loving myself and finding my calling in life. Writing has been my salvation and I am so thankful I get to share my stories with each of you.

ABOUT THE AUTHOR

Jessica Ann Disciacca, an Italian American from Kansas City, Missouri, holds a Master's in Educational Leadership from Northwest Missouri State University (2023). Graduating in 2015 from Park University with a diverse Bachelor's degree, she now pursues a career in educational administration while teaching.

Beyond her professional life, Jessica is an avid artist and writer, finding solace in family moments. Her lifelong passion for literature and storytelling led her to debut as an author with "Awakening the Dark Throne."